THREADING THE NEEDLE

BAEN BOOKS by
MONALISA FOSTER

Threading the Needle

THREADING THE NEEDLE

MONALISA FOSTER

THREADING THE NEEDLE

This is a work of fiction. All the characters and events portrayed in this book are fictional, and any resemblance to real people or incidents is purely coincidental.

A Baen Books Original

Baen Publishing Enterprises
P.O. Box 1403
Riverdale, NY 10471
www.baen.com

ISBN: 978-1-9821-9308-9

Cover art by Dominic Harman

First printing, December 2023

Distributed by Simon & Schuster
1230 Avenue of the Americas
New York, NY 10020

Library of Congress Cataloging-in-Publication Data

Names: Foster, Monalisa, author.
Title: Threading the needle / Monalisa Foster.
Description: Riverdale : Baen Publishing Enterprises, 2023.
Identifiers: LCCN 2023035153 (print) | LCCN 2023035154 (ebook) | ISBN 9781982193089 (trade paperback) | ISBN 9781625799425 (ebook)
Subjects: LCGFT: Science fiction. | Novels.
Classification: LCC PS3606.O76565 T4485 2023 (print) | LCC PS3606.O76565 (ebook) | DDC 813/.6—dc23/eng/20230915pcc
LC record available at https://lccn.loc.gov/2023035153
LC ebook record available at https://lccn.loc.gov/2023035154

Printed in the United States of America
10 9 8 7 6 5 4 3 2 1

For Chiune-Sempo and Yukiko Sugihara

ACKNOWLEDGEMENT

Leigh Brackett.

Where to start?

We could start with the fact that she was known as the Queen of Space Opera. And that initially the term "space opera" was coined as a derogatory reference to a "horse opera" (i.e., a western) in space. We should start there because *Threading the Needle* is a space opera with horses and space cows and a fiery old bitch named Dame Leigh Stark inspired by Her Ladyship herself. We could start there because the main inspiration for *Threading the Needle* was the 1966 John Wayne western, *El Dorado*, whose script was written by Leigh Brackett.

I've lost count of the number of times I've seen *El Dorado*, just like I've lost count of the number of times I've seen *The Empire Strikes Back*, another story written (in part) by Leigh Brackett. Although the final version of *ESB* was substantially different than the one initially penned by Her Ladyship, you can see her fingerprints all over it, especially in the princess and the pirate dynamic between Han Solo and Princess Leia. As a newly arrived immigrant who was still learning English, the story of the "jet-eye" wasn't nearly as interesting to me as that of the princess and her scoundrel.

Know then that *Threading the Needle* is a space opera packed with romantic elements like adventure and camaraderie and love of one's brothers- and sisters-in-arms. Something incredible happens when your life is saved, when someone sacrifices flesh and blood on your behalf. When you bleed for others and they bleed for you. That is the essence of this, that willingness to put it all on the line for someone who is a brother- or sister-of-choice.

So, why westerns? Why westerns in space?

I like space operas because they are so versatile. You want adventure, romance, military stuff, genetic engineering, an Old West, Victorian era, and Meiji-restoration aesthetic, trains alongside spaceships and cyborgs, swords and guns, where do you go? Space opera of course. The future and the past mingle ever so perfectly.

I grew up with westerns, yes even me, with little bits of highly censored and chopped up material watched over a grainy TV because Ceaușescu's communist regime was evil. Dubbed in Hungarian or Romanian, I grew up watching "bocoi" (my childish mispronunciation of "cowboy" that sounds like bo-koi) movies and pirate movies, so John Wayne and Errol Flynn were swashbuckling archetypes I knew even though at the time I didn't know the actors' names.

For a real-world feel, I mixed in some stories I grew up with as we huddled in the cellar with our illegal radio, listening to Radio Free Europe, wishing America would come and liberate us. Stories told by men who had fought in both world wars. Men who were dead by the time communism fell, who never got to breathe free air like I did. Like I am.

And since I'm talking about gratitude for freedom and life, this book is dedicated to Chiune-Sempo and Yukiko Sugihara, who saved thousands of Jews by granting them visas to flee the Nazis. Hundreds of thousands of people are alive today because of their efforts. Because *that* is how you count lives saved.

Moving on from thanking those who are no longer with us, to those who are…

I couldn't have written this story without Toni Weisskopf who encouraged me to give it a try and who told me to go ahead and make it about space cows. And to indeed, call them exactly that. Sometimes you need "permission" to do certain things.

Nor could I have told it without the help of my tribe, the gang known as the "Itty Bitty Calm Your Titties Committee," who got pinged out of the blue with stupid questions about how to get a man with a broken leg onto a horse, what do you call the weird finger thingies on the old syringes, and how reliable are radios really. True friends answer the call of, "Guys, I need a name for a drug that makes people prone to suggestion," and, "I want SONS as an acronym for robots but how? Help!" without asking why.

When I decided to make Talia a cyborg it raised inevitable questions like: How does it feel to have a missing limb? How much does it hurt? How do you feel about it? My thanks to Michael Nedrow for putting up with my probing questions.

The Hampson-effect power source is named in honor of Dr. Robert Hampson who happens to work with prosthetics and brain implants and also happens to write sci-fi. He helped me with some of the fiddly technical details pertaining to Talia's prosthesis and implant.

One of the reasons I prefer space opera to just about any other genre is because it is, first and foremost, fantastical and puts the story first. Nevertheless, I take responsibility for any errors, inaccuracies, or badly welded rivets. Some are intentional and were needed to make the story work. After all, I'm filing for copyrights, not patents.

I must also thank Justin Watson (who writes great mil-sf) and Scott Bell (who writes great thrillers), both of whom did a beta read for me and have been encouraging, supporting, and putting up with me for years. I couldn't have done it without you gentlemen. Thank you.

And speaking of encouragement and support, I can't leave out my husband, Rick, and my daughter, Olivia (who finally gave in and read one of mom's novels). She did it for the dogs and the fact that she liked it gave me the greatest hope for this particular work.

I must also admit to shamelessly stealing the pen names of Daddy Heinlein, because if it hadn't been for him, I would definitely not be who I am, much less a writer, and I wanted to pay tribute. The names of Lyle Monroe, John Riverside, Caleb Saunders, and Simon York were all pen names used by Heinlein. Why all four? Because if it's worth doing, it's worth overdoing, that's why.

My two dogs figure prominently in this work. They are the only characters based on real, living beings. DespairBear and CorgiSan are both real and their behaviors are based on my real-life dogs. Also know that in keeping with my personal philosophy on writing that no dogs (real or otherwise) were harmed or suffered in this story.

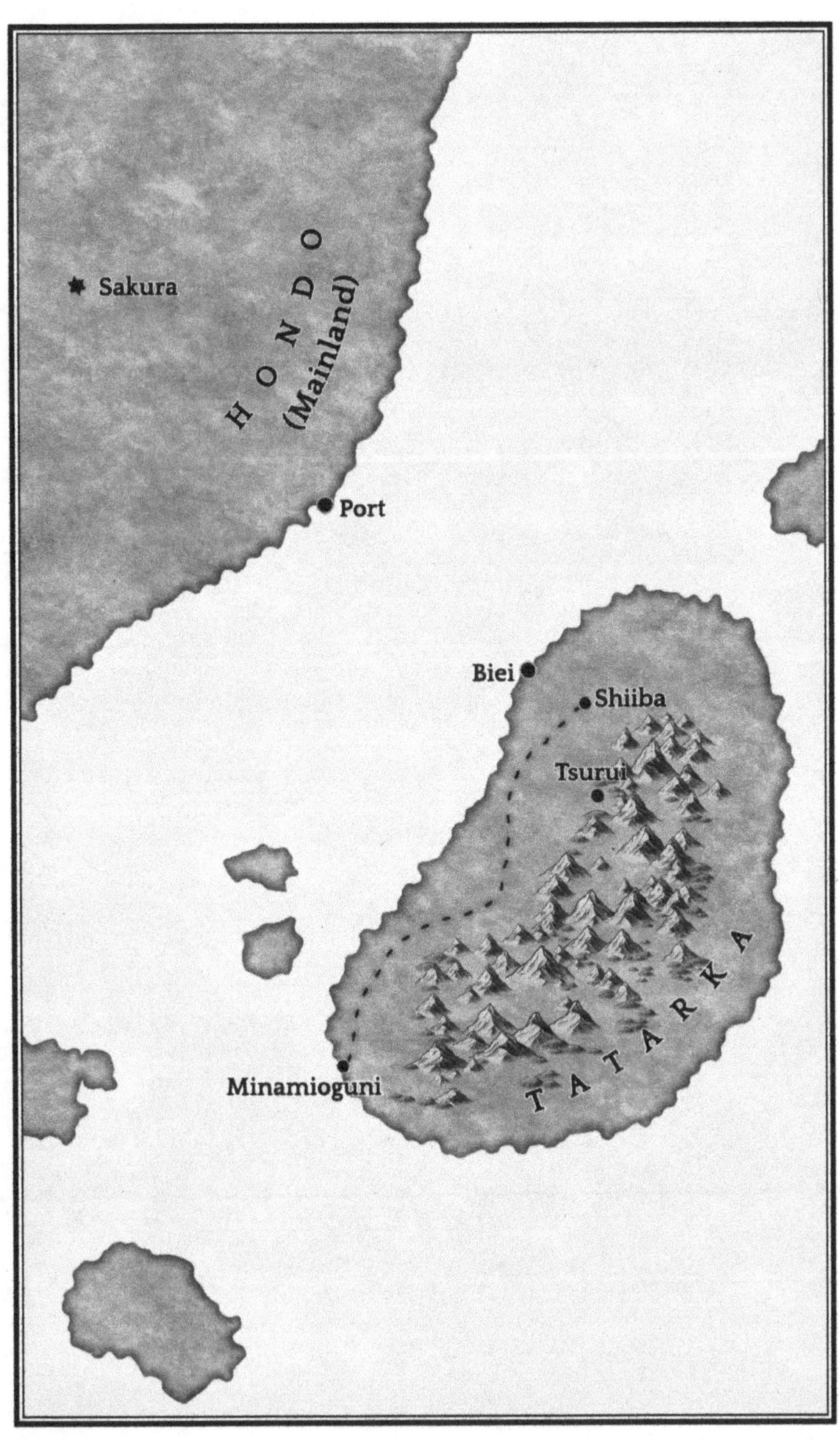
Sakura
HONDO
(Mainland)
Port
Biei
Shiiba
Tsurui
Minamioguni
TATARKA

PART ONE

CHAPTER ONE

A NEW MOON WAS A SNIPER'S BEST FRIEND, OR MAYBE HER LOVER or her talisman. There was beauty in that all-absorbing darkness, that new beginning, that promise of renewal. Delicate as a soap bubble, that edging sliver of a new moon's shimmering light would quiver in the air like something struggling to be born.

Trembling. Fragile. Defiant. Standing its ground, defiant of all that light.

By the same token, a full moon like tonight's was the enemy. Talia wasn't going to read anything into it. After all, she wasn't a sniper anymore, and hadn't been one in over a decade.

It had taken her only seven Earth-years to pay off her indenture. Seven years of playing bodyguard to Gōruden's rich and paranoid. Seven years of endless meetings, functions, and parties, where her resting bitch face was her main weapon. Seven years where she'd never had to draw her gun in anger, but had to live as if that moment—the one where she had to act, where she would have to take a life or risk her own—could happen at any time.

She'd thought it would be easy work. After all, she'd been a soldier. She hadn't thought it would be all that different, but it was. Putting her life on the line for her friends, her unit, her country was one thing. Putting it on the line for people because they paid for her services was another.

But what was an out-of-work sniper to do?

Work off her indenture, and then start fresh once again by

taking her sorry ass away from the city, to the frontier, where she could at least pick her own clients. And enjoy what she had actually come to Gōruden for—a simpler, freer, unencumbered-by-government way of life.

The best way she could think of starting that life—and a new day—was with a hot bath. The Full Moon bath house, or more appropriately given this was Gōruden, the Full Moon onsen, had been built around a hot spring, its wood-paneled walls wrapping around the natural pools. Plants poked through, reaching eager branches through the trellis roof above the steaming water.

Talia sank deeper into the heat, inhaling the rich mineral scents, allowing the warmth to soothe abused muscles. Water falling nearby made a whispering, lulling sound that wrapped her in a calming embrace.

She let her head fall back against the ledge, careful not to let her hair—freshly washed and rinsed and contained into a bun—get into the water. Her Japanese grandmother—her *sobo*—would turn over in her grave if she did, she was sure.

It had taken Talia twenty-three days—Gōruden's day was only twelve minutes shorter than Earth's so everyone just pretended they were the same—to get from the planetary capital of Sakura to the little frontier town of Tsurui. Time travel was impossible, but traveling from Sakura with its late twenty-first-century technology to Tsurui had been like taking a trip into the past. The farther one got from Sakura, the less technological it was. She may have started her trip from just outside Gōruden's only spaceport, but she had ended it on a stagecoach. One pulled by horses, hay being easier to grow than gasoline or diesel was to manufacture. At least for the time being.

She'd been wanting to come to Tsurui ever since she'd learned that some of her fellow rebels had settled on the island of Tatarka. With the slow, sporadic communication outside Sakura, Tsurui was the kind of place where people could truly get lost, escape their past, and start anew. Hopefully without being haunted by foregone deeds, mistakes, and regrets.

A fresh start. Impossible on Earth or any of the "civilized" worlds, where privacy was something only the rich and powerful could afford.

Talia rubbed the stump of her right forearm, careful to avoid cutting herself on the ceramic-composite spike protruding from the little bit of forearm the surgeons had left in place, just below the elbow. Her cybernetic prosthesis was sitting in a basket in the onsen's changing room, atop a fresh change of clothing and her gun. The old-fashioned kind of gun, Saint Browning's hack-proof, no-power-signature, God's-very-own, the 1911.

She had inherited it from her grandfather. Besides the prosthetic and too many bad memories, the old gun was the only thing she had left of her past. Of a lost war, of her family. Of Earth.

Sinking deeper into the water, she closed her eyes and let her head fall against the fluffy towel rolled up on the ledge.

Today her new life would begin. She'd never fancied herself as much of an instructor, but after paying off the indenture, she was broke. One Signore Ferran Contesti had been willing to forward a respectable advance and pick up her traveling expenses just to interview her. Undoubtedly, he wanted to verify her skillset. And perhaps hear about her "kills." The former she was willing to demonstrate. The latter—

"Well, well, well, if it isn't Talia Merritt."

Heart racing, she pulled her head off the ledge and opened her eyes. A twitch of her bicep betrayed her as she went for a gun that wasn't behind her hip with a hand that was no longer part of her, even though she recognized the voice and the man that it belonged to.

Reflexes. It was fair to say they had a mind of their own.

"And in her full glory nonetheless," he continued.

"Damn it, Lyle." Left hand on her sternum, she settled back against the ledge and looked him in the eyes.

Still imposing, even if a bit thicker in the middle, her old friend, the other half of their sniper pair, one Lyle Monroe, had collected a few crow's feet at the edges of his brown eyes. They went well with the silver at his temples and the sun-darkened skin.

The look on his face, however, wasn't that of a friend, much less that of a brother-in-arms.

He had *his* hand on his gun. A large-caliber revolver if she was to guess. Something that fit his large hands but not slow his draw. It was holstered at his side, retention flap undone. Jeans, dusty and splattered with mud; boots, well-worn and functional rather than decorative. Hat—brown with a plain band. Duster coat, a black fading to gray. Badge—a copper star with six points. He looked like something out of a history book. Smelled like something out of one too—horse and human sweat vied for supremacy, souring the onsen's cleaner mineral smells.

Slowly, she raised her hands—well, one hand and what was left of the other arm. The stump remained under the water line, along with her other vulnerable bits.

She hadn't intended to embarrass him, but a wash of red darkened his face. She knew the source of that shame, recognized it whenever it crept into his face, his eyes, right along with the guilt that went with it all because Talia would've been whole if she hadn't saved his life.

His hand, however, was unashamed. It remained where it was, resting lightly on the holster's leather.

Like he didn't trust her. Like he thought she was a threat.

Had it not been for *Sobo's* rules she might have brought her gun with her, if she'd been that paranoid. Which she wasn't.

Maybe you should be.

Maybe the rumors she'd heard in Sakura were true, and this was a lawless place where violence reigned, and people were shot for looking at each other wrong. Thinking them ludicrous, she'd dismissed those stories for big-city attitudes and prejudices.

"Rumor is that Signore Contesti hired an assassin to take me out," Lyle said.

"I am not an assassin." The slow, deliberate cadence of her words belied the rush of adrenaline in her veins. "And I certainly wouldn't take a job that required me to go up against you. Not that I couldn't."

That last bit was not all bravado, but time and experience had cured her of any need or desire to participate in pissing contests. It had taken her years—almost a decade—to bury the killer inside her, to finally lay her to rest as Talia carved out a new life for herself. She wasn't going to be goaded into waking her.

"Then why are you here?" he asked, leveling assessing eyes at her.

"Freedom. Liberty. That sort of stuff. Same as you." She flicked water off one finger. "It is true that Signore Contesti asked me to come here. He wants to interview me for a job."

"What kind of job?"

"Not as assassin," she said, no longer bothering to hide her annoyance. "What an ineffective assassin I would make. Caught naked and unarmed in a bath, not an hour after arriving in town."

Lyle seemed to relax, his shoulders dropping slightly, his right hand drifting down to just hang at his side beside the revolver.

"Then as what?" he asked.

"Marksmanship instructor. He said his people need training. Lots of threats out here. Human and otherwise."

She needed to move or the adrenaline accumulating in her blood was going to make her tremble, despite the hot water, and the last thing she needed was for him to see how much he'd unnerved her.

"I'm feeling a bit waterlogged," she said matter-of-factly. "Do you mind?"

He pulled a towel off the low table by his knee and tossed it to her.

She caught it, flashing a bit of breast despite her best efforts. Rising, Talia held the towel to her torso and let it drag into the water as she waded toward the steps.

"Do you mind if we continue this as I get dressed?"

He reached behind his back and pulled out her 1911.

"Not at all."

If he was sorry in any way for having her at a disadvantage, it didn't show on his face.

She didn't blame him. City work had made her soft, taken her edge.

Talia gave him her bare back.

CHAPTER TWO

TALIA COULD FEEL LYLE'S GAZE BORING INTO HER BACK, BUT HE must have taken her at her word, at least somewhat, because he merely followed. The women's changing room was empty. Baskets sat atop the row of neatly arrayed shelves filling the center of the room. The teak wood floor creaked as she walked across it. Only the wall paralleling the hall had a shoji door—a sliding divider made up of a translucent sheet on a lattice frame. It was typical of the architecture here on Gōruden's frontier, where the first wave of colonists had settled specifically with a charter to preserve Japanese culture and aesthetics.

The heat on her skin faded as the water evaporated. Surely that was the source of the prickling, crawling sensation. It had to be because he made no objection to her stepping behind a screen so she could get dressed.

Talia dropped the wet towel and plucked the gray and black prosthetic from the basket. Made of magnesium-based ceramic doped with nanopores, electrostatic polymer membranes, neodymium magnets, inductive pickups and powered by Hampson-effect forces, it had been engineered to function just like a real limb. It even weighed exactly as much as her own lost parts had, down to a fraction of an ounce.

She grasped the cybernetic limb by the wrist and pushed it onto the spike protruding from her stump. There was a prickling sensation like ants crawling when the contact points in the prosthetic and the spike came together. A sense of presence manifested, like her phantom limb coming to life, something outside the cybernetics themselves, something unquantifiable and indescribable to anyone who hadn't lost a literal pound—or more—of flesh.

Except that this presence, this phantom, was as much a part of her as anything else. When it merged with the prosthetic they worked together to achieve that real-limb functionality. She knew when it was cold or warm, when the sensitive fingertips came into contact with vibrations, when the pore-analogues experienced contact with acids and bases, when the sensors registered the variability of internal friction. She could experience the sensation of something being thick or smooth, viscous or grainy, wet or dry.

Talia flexed her phantom's fingers. Even now, after so many years, it sometimes still surprised her to see it manifest as motion in the prosthesis. It wasn't perfect, but it was close enough. Close enough for most things, anyway.

"I almost didn't recognize you with the long hair," Lyle said.

"Sakura Executive Protection sometimes put us in formalwear," she said. "My boss thought I needed to look more feminine."

She finger-combed the dark lengths into a semblance of order and pushed them behind her shoulders.

Sobo had gifted her with that blue-black, stick-straight mane that, paired with a slight lilt to her eyes, made her look exotic. Or so an old lover had told her, although she'd never thought of herself as anything more than average looking.

Nothing memorable.

Nothing memorable was good in her line of work. She slipped into her panties, shrugged into a bra and snapped the front closure together.

"Didn't figure you for bodyguard work," Lyle said.

"It pays the bills."

She stepped into a pair of loose, flowing trousers—something that had once been called a split skirt—the current style in the city. One of the advantages of working for Sakura Executive Protection had been that, like the military, she had been issued everything she needed. The money she'd earned by working extra details had gone toward paying down her contract early. But she owned nothing outside of a change of clothes, her heirloom gun, and a bag to put them in.

"But Contesti wants you as a trainer?" Lyle sounded doubtful.

"That's what he said."

Furrowing her brow in concentration, she buttoned the high-collared white blouse. It took more focus to work the fine motor controls of her phantom fingers and have them manifest properly in the cybernetics. The upside was that the deliberation eliminated unintentional muscle twitches. Especially under duress.

She wiggled her toes into the pull-on oxfords.

"Contesti lied," Lyle said. "Or at least, he didn't tell you the whole truth. And I guess you'd have no way of knowing better. I doubt that people living in Sakura actually understand what goes on out here."

Talia stepped around the screen and faced Lyle. Her still-wet hair dripped down her back, making the fine fabric of the blouse cling to her skin.

"So tell me."

"Contesti came out here just a year or two ago. Rolled right in with a lot of money—a lot of off-world money—to set up his own little fiefdom. Doesn't seem to understand that those who came before him—in some cases, decades before him—really did come here to get away from those whose mission in life is to tell them what to do."

"So," she said, crossing her arms in front of her, "Contesti is a 'rules for thee' kind. I know the sort. Plenty of them in Sakura."

"Oh, there's more to it than that. When money doesn't work, he uses other means to intimidate people into doing what he wants."

"Intimidate how?" She could guess, given the look on Lyle's face.

"Kidnapping and extortion, for certain. Other, worse things, I suspect."

"But that you can't prove."

"That I can't prove." He shifted his weight. "But the reason I wear this badge now is because Contesti's behavior pushed the people around here into forming a sort of government. One he's also tried to take over in various ways. And he's all but declared war on the oldest settlers in the area—the Haricots.

"They've been working on a terraforming problem for a couple of generations now. And they're on the verge of something big. Probably why Contesti moved in here in the first place. This is not, by far, the place people like Contesti would come to unless things were about to change. There's nothing here worth that much intimidation and pressure. Much easier, safer places for someone like Contesti to peddle his mantra of benevolent despotism."

What sounded like pure rage had snuck into that last. She couldn't say she blamed him.

"The people running Sakura may not know much about what goes on here," she said, "but I think I understand. These last seven years I got to see and hear all kinds of stuff. Far too many SEP clients who come to Gōruden for all the wrong reasons. They confuse minarchy with anarchy and think that they can do whatever they want. Likewise, they assume that others will do whatever they want and that's why they're convinced they need bodyguards to protect them."

"And in some places, that's true. But not here. Not in my town." He said it with no small amount of pride and determination.

Jealousy took a quick stab at her, its razor-sharp edge scraping up against her insides. Years ago, they'd talked about the future, what they wanted out of life. Not just the two of them, but everyone in their unit. It was part of who they were and why they fought, suffered, and, in some cases, died. He'd always said he wanted to find a quiet place to settle down, to find a community to which he could truly belong. He'd even talked of marrying and raising a family. She had too. It looked like he'd found it. And she wasn't going to ruin it for him.

She waited for him to ask her to come in on his side, to join him. Had she come to Tsurui on her own, shown up on his doorstep destitute and in need of help or a job, she had no doubt he would have. But as it was... Maybe he didn't need the help. Maybe she was nothing but bad memories and bad dreams and a fresh start didn't include baggage or a past or a history.

"Very well," she said. "I'll tell Contesti that I'm not interested after all and be on my way. I have another offer that's still open. Good enough?"

SEP would take her back. Once they'd realized she was about to pay off her indenture early, they'd even made her a generous offer. For what it was, the work in Sakura was relatively safe. Most bullet wounds were not fatal there, not with so much advanced medicine from Earth readily available, even if it was expensive. They'd even offered to upgrade her prosthetic. Dangled their connections in front of her, certain she'd be tempted by the possibility of military upgrades. If all went well, in a few years she could save enough money to strike out on her own. Step off the path she'd been on, the path of protector, and take up something she'd forfeited—the chance for family. For making life instead of merely protecting it.

"Good enough," he said.

"Can I have my gun back, or is this one of those places where the sheriff gets to keep it?"

He pulled her gun from his waistband and handed it over carefully, finger off the trigger, barrel pointed down.

She took it, checked it. It was still loaded. She cocked and locked it, slipped it behind her right hip, right into her waistband's built-in holster. It had been specially designed to sit at just the right angle for someone with her curvature and reinforced with leather. Her wardrobe—what there was of it—had been built around her gun. Concealment was key where people wanted protection but didn't feel "safe" if they could actually see the unsightly tools with which it was provided.

"We can try calling him up on the radio—"

"I'd rather do it face-to-face," she said. "I took his money, spent it to get all the way here. I owe him a face-to-face."

"You'll have to ride out to Contesti's place," Lyle said. "Do you want me to come with you?"

"No, I think it's best if I do this alone, don't you?"

"As you wish." His tone said he'd rather do anything than comply with her wishes. "You should probably change though."

She frowned. "Into what? My other set of clothes looks just like this one. What's wrong with them?"

The shoji door between the changing room and lobby slid open making the bell attached to it ring softly.

Lyle turned.

A woman with long red hair came through and slid the shoji shut. Other than being barefoot, she was dressed much like Lyle but with a shorter, knee-length duster that had a feminine flare. Clothes reminiscent of America's Old West, mixed in with late Victorian-era and Meiji-era styles seemed to be the standard around here. The onsen's hostess, an elderly lady of Japanese descent who reminded Talia of *Sobo*, had been dressed in a *yukata*, a floor-length robe, held together by an obi.

"Lyle," the redhead said, setting her hands on her hips. "What are you doing in the women's changing room? If Yui finds you in here, and with the boots on, she's going to come after you with that *ko-naginata* she keeps up front."

Lyle took a deep breath and gave her a look that was half annoyance, half amusement.

"Maeve, meet my good friend, Talia. She's going out to Contesti's place and is going to need a set of clothes, a map, and a horse."

He turned back to Talia. "You do know how to ride one, don't you?"

"Yes. SEP made sure. Had several clients who liked to ride." It had been one of the few perks of the job. She liked the animals well enough. Gentle giants, most of them. Smart too. Smarter than the people who sometimes rode them.

Talia put out her hand. "Talia Merritt. It's nice to meet you, Maeve."

Without hesitation, Maeve took the cybernetic hand and shook it. She may have held onto it a second longer that she would have otherwise, but her smile reached her eyes and betrayed no morbid curiosity or judgement. The extra contact let Talia feel the slight callouses at the top of Maeve's palm.

Maeve shook her hand as if—despite appearances—it was one of flesh and bone.

"Nice to meet you too. He's told me about you, you know." Mischief floated in Maeve's blue eyes.

Maeve looked Talia up and down. "I hate to admit it, but Lyle is right. If you're going to go to Contesti's, you'll need a horse and a few other things. I'm sure I have something to fit you. Jeans might be a tad long, but maybe we can find you some boots to tuck them into and then it won't matter."

She sidled up to Talia and used herself as a measuring stick.

"I don't want to be—"

"Trouble?" Maeve said. "My dear, you're already that and clothing won't change what you are. I can tell. Oh, don't frown. Own it. It's the right kind of trouble, if I'm guessing right."

Maeve shot Lyle a questioning glance.

He shook his head.

Talia wasn't sure what passed between them.

"She'll be leaving just as soon as she's done with Signore Contesti," Lyle reassured Maeve.

"Oh. All right. I think I understand." Her tone, however said that she didn't.

For as long as Talia had known him, Lyle had had a thing for redheads, especially ones with lots of freckles. He was never odd or awkward around them. Never hesitant. Up until that moment when Maeve had walked in, he'd been confident, fulfilled, a man who had found his place in this world and wanted for nothing. A man who was sure of himself and what he was doing, who had everything he wanted.

And then the reason for the change in him flashed in front of her eyes. Maeve was wearing a wedding ring. And it wasn't his.

Oh, Lyle.

CHAPTER THREE

YUI, THE ONSEN HOSTESS, MADE A STRANGLED SOUND AS SHE slid the door open and saw Lyle.

"It's all right, Yui," he said, raising his hands defensively. "I was just leaving."

Yui's face had turned red, and she was sputtering off in what to Talia's ear sounded like some mix of Japanese and perhaps Korean. She definitely understood the word for "horse's ass" and something about inserting a pole arm into it as Yui shooed Lyle out of the changing room. Her scolding voice receded as Talia squeezed water out of her hair.

Talia followed Maeve through the lobby with its neatly stacked shelves full of baskets filled with soap cakes and jars. Folded robes sporting a full moon logo had been stacked, waiting for the day's patrons.

Maeve shrieked as she stepped out of the onsen and into the muted light of sunrise.

Talia looked down at the source of Maeve's distress. A gray robot that looked like a desperate teddy bear with its long body and stubby legs stared up at her with a pair of mismatched cybernetic eyes. It must have tangled itself up in some netting because it looked like it was wearing a ghillie suit. Branches and odd bits of junk, flowers, and grasses clung to the netting, in cartoonish parody of a sniper's camouflage.

A second robot, covered in brown plates that looked like they'd been salvaged from a dump, bumped into Maeve's other leg and nuzzled into her just like a real dog would. The aperture of one of its cybernetic eyes seemed to be stuck, making it look like it was perpetually judging whatever it looked at. Just as long and short as the gray one, this one was wider in the body thanks to a set of what looked like compressed gas cartridges—a luxury this far out from Sakura and probably empty—tucked atop the panniers welded onto the shell.

Talia did a double take—were those maneuvering nozzles of some kind, riding where the tail would have been?

On Earth and in big cities like Sakura, Talia had seen something less doglike being used for police work. She'd even worked with models used to help carry supplies on the battlefield. But those robots had been long legged and donkey sized. Unlike the headless military models which looked more like spiders, this pair had swiveling heads with segmented plates that made them look like they had muzzles and gave them terribly expressive faces.

Maeve reached down and petted the brown one. The gray one pushed its counterpart aside, vying for equal treatment.

"Might as well pet them," Maeve said. "Or they'll tangle up in your legs until you do."

"What are they?"

"These are my sons," a male voice said. "Trial and Error."

Talia looked up. A man in his late fifties or early sixties, with a mostly white beard and a bald head, was coming up the steps leading into the onsen. Worn cowboy boots with peeling decorative trim encased long legs covered in jeans. Instead of a duster he wore a leather jacket that rode high above his waist. The blue-and-white checkered shirt looked like it had been made of thick, padded material. He wore a sheathed bowie knife at his belt, but no gun. At least not one that she could see.

"Excuse me?" she said.

"SONS—Sustained Operation Neural Suites," he said.

"You're kidding."

"Nope. That's what they are," he said proudly.

"John, this is Talia. Old friend of Lyle's. Talia, this is John Riverside, resident scout, cartographer, and curmudgeon."

John took Talia's hand but instead of shaking it, he turned it over, bending down to examine it as he plucked at the tips of her cybernetic fingers and bent her wrist one way and then the other.

He looked like he wanted to take her prosthesis apart.

"Runs on Hampson-effect, doesn't it? Just like my SONS' brains."

"Yes, I—"

"This is remarkable, truly remarkable."

"Thank you. May I have it back?"

"My apologies," he said, letting her prosthetic go. "I meant no offense. Truly. Just don't see this kind of thing out here much. Robotics fascinate me. Cybernetics even more."

"So which one's Trial and which one's Error?" Talia asked to change the subject.

"Depends on the time of day," he said, a grin on his tanned face.

"Actually, their names are CorgiSan and DespairBear," Maeve explained as she scratched their heads. "The one with the netting is DespairBear, because, well, he looks like a much-loved teddy bear who's been patched up too often. John here uses them for field work."

"They go out, scout the terrain, explore the caves," John said. "Much safer for them than for people. They're practically indestructible."

Talia gave them a second look. Their legs were very short, undoubtedly for ease of movement over rocks. She'd once seen a Skye Terrier—who, come to think of it, did look like a teddy bear—practically flow over rocky terrain that would have made a long-legged dog or the military robot version of them wobble and topple. While they could right themselves, the long-legged, top-heavy models really didn't do that well moving over rocks. Their center of mass was just too high for that kind of terrain.

Underneath the metal plates both CorgiSan and DespairBear seemed to have some sort of silicone or silicone-like center that covered the deeper components like a protective layer. The frames of their legs and paws were covered by the same under the segmented, almost laminar arrangement of metal plates.

"I didn't realize people out here were reprogramming robots as pets," Talia said.

John looked sheepish and cleared his throat. "They were hacked."

"Hacked?" Talia asked.

Maeve stood up. "Someone loaded VR software—"

"Dog-simulation VR subroutines," John corrected.

"—onto them and John here doesn't have the heart to reboot them."

"It's got nothing to do with heart," he said defensively. "I don't have the time to go back to the mainland for that kind of thing. It's not enough to reboot them. They'd have to be reprogrammed. It's in the firmware, the operating system, everything. And I came to Gōruden to escape the software tyrants and their bloody licensing agreements. Besides, the VR behavior only manifests when they're around people. It's not interfering with their scouting work."

"Uh-huh," Maeve said with a doubtful tone.

John gave her an annoyed look and turned to Talia. "Nice meeting you, ma'am. If you'll excuse me, I need to get my bath in before it gets too crowded around here."

He pushed the onsen door in and waved the SONS through. The brown one lingered just a moment, until it was prompted again.

"Rumor is he hacked the SONS himself," Maeve said as she led Talia up the cobblestoned street.

Neat little houses with curved, elongated eaves designed to protect the windows from rain stood behind the walls separating them from the street. Trees with long, languid branches hung over the walls, sprinkling tiny leaves between the cobblestone's grooves.

"Why would he hack his own robots?" Talia asked as they passed a roofed gate braced by boulders as tall as she was. Sturdy replicas of paper lanterns hung from the arch of the gate.

"Won't talk about it. Gets rather prickly, as you saw. So just go along with it. Everyone else does."

A crazy array of streams and brooks carved up the little town of Tsurui. Maeve led her over one of the many bridges and through a hinged gate about halfway up a gently sloping hill. Slate steps led up to a raised, covered walkway, which led to another, and another.

"I'm taking you up the back way," Maeve said. "Good chance Contesti already knows you're here, but this way his people won't know where to start looking for you."

"They're that dangerous?" Talia asked.

"I know that you and Lyle, being who you are, may not see it that way, but the rest of us, those that have been here the longest, have learned to be careful. And there are some here who aren't that welcoming to newcomers, whether or not they see them as additions to Contesti's . . . forces."

Maeve led her into a large room filled with long, sturdy benches. They were covered with racks of test tubes and jars. Other things that looked like they belonged in a university chemistry lab lined some of the walls. The air was heavy with a heady mix of bitterness, sweetness, and ripeness.

"You're a pharmacist?" Talia asked.

"I dabble," she said, amusement clear on her face. "The storefront says apothecary though."

A sliding door revealed a living space that was small by comparison with the previous workroom.

Folding screens depicting images of old-Earth mountains and oceans bracketed a wood stove and a small low table meant to be used while sitting on the floor. Morning light spilled through decorative slats carved to look like a giant lotus flower.

"Care for some jasmine tea?" she asked, checking the kettle atop the stove.

Maeve didn't wait for an answer, but scooped some tea leaves into cups and lit the stove.

A curtain had been pulled back from a trio of steps leading up to a platform with heavy blankets and oversized pillows that probably also served as a bed. Vases were tucked into corners, each one filled with dried flowers. Bouquets of dried herbs hung from the rafters.

"Have a seat," Maeve said, indicating the pillows by the low table.

Talia inhaled the delicate scent and sat, tucking her legs underneath her, fighting with the split skirt before settling in.

Maeve moved one of the screens, revealing a quintet of wood trunks with metal latches that had been stacked like a pyramid, three on the bottom, two on top.

"Are you and Lyle just friends?" she asked as she opened the lid and reached inside. She pulled out a stack of neatly folded clothes and sorted through them, using some mysterious system to determine what got pushed Talia's way and what didn't. Some of the items looked well worn and mended. Others seemed newer.

"Yes," Talia said, "just friends."

Maeve pulled down the second trunk, set it next to the first one.

"Here, try these on." She handed Talia a pair of men's jeans. "It won't be a great fit, but the legs are long enough. And I have suspenders. Somewhere."

As Maeve dove back in to dig through the packed clothing, Talia picked a man's work shirt off the top of the pile. The blue fabric was soft with age and wear, but not threadbare, although it was heading that way.

"Whose are these?" The clothing didn't look like it would fit Maeve's curves.

"Are you superstitious?" Maeve asked as she looked around the room. She dropped into a squat and opened another trunk.

Hinges squeaked to reveal a pair of boots, a display box full of medals and what could only be a sword. It was wearing a black silk sheath and gold braid. Maeve handed her the sword and returned to digging deeper.

The tactile smoothness of real silk—old silk—transmitted by the phantom's fingertips made goosebumps rise on Talia's skin as soon as the sword was in her hands. She slid the silk down the length of the curved scabbard of the katana.

"May I?" Talia asked, voice trembling, as her phantom's fingers drifted over the scabbard's—the *saya's*, as her grandmother would have insisted—polished wood.

"Go ahead," Maeve said without looking up. "Everyone wants to see it. And before you ask, yes, it's real. As in real sharp. Now where did that other pair of boots go?"

A gentle pull and the sword clicked out of the mouth of the scabbard, its mirrorlike blade reflecting Talia's black-in-black eyes and heart-shaped face. *Sobo* had owned a *daishō*—a set made up of both katana and wakizashi—that she'd inherited from her parents. Talia had been taught how to use them. She still had the scar between her thumb and forefinger where she'd cut herself resheathing her great-grandfather's too-long katana.

She could still remember the scent of clove oil and chalk as she'd cleaned it after test cutting. She could almost hear it slicing the air as she worked with it, using the calming motions of katas to work through a teenager's anxiety, through the grief at her parents' death when she was fifteen, through the anger at her boyfriend's betrayal.

Maeve resurfaced from her excavations.

"It was my husband's sword," she said, sitting back on her heels.

Just then the kettle whistled. Maeve rose and poured water into the waiting cups.

Slowly, Talia slid the sword back into the scabbard and pushed it back at Maeve.

"You handle it like someone who knows how," Maeve said and offered Talia the other cup.

Carefully she took it and blew on the tea. Jasmine was her favorite. She'd grown up drinking it unsweetened, although she enjoyed it sweet as well.

"Not much use in modern militaries for them, but *Sobo*—my Japanese grandmother—trained me to use them."

"You should keep it then."

"No, I can't possibly." Talia offered the katana again.

"He's dead," Maeve said. "A few months now."

"I'm so sorry."

"For weeks I've been thinking that I needed to go through his things." Maeve held up the boots as if they confirmed her intent. "Make sure they were put to use. And then you showed up, and I just had a feeling that you were meant to take possession. The pants are just the right length. I bet the boots are just the right size too. He was not a big man."

As if it had a will of its own, Talia's cybernetic hand wrapped itself tighter around the sword. Sometimes it did that, manifesting subconscious things just like a flesh-and-bone hand would. And if she didn't hand the sword back now, she never would. Not much use for a sword back in Sakura either. And that's where she was going just as soon as she was done with Contesti.

"I am honored by your offer, but I must, respectfully, decline."

Holding the sword across both hands, Talia offered it again and bowed over it. Maeve took it from her hands, set it atop the trunk.

"Should you change your mind, it will be waiting for you."

"Thank you, but I won't change my mind."

If—no, when—she got back to Sakura, signed that lucrative new contract, if she still wanted to indulge a sense of nostalgia, she would buy her own *daishō*. She might even join a dojo. Pick up the art again. Honor the memory of her ancestors, as it were.

Maeve gave her a skeptical look and handed Talia the boots. "Unless you plan on waiting for Signore Contesti's carriage to take you to him, you're going to need better shoes than those fancy, shiny things."

Talia had never thought of her working shoes as fancy. Merely functional. They looked and felt a lot like her old uniform shoes.

"How did your husband die?" she asked.

"Superstitious about wearing a dead man's clothes?"

"Not really, just curious."

"You mean why am I not more broken up about it, since it hasn't been that long?"

"That's not—"

She held up a restraining palm. "It's fine. Everyone is probably wondering the same thing, just too afraid to ask. They probably think I'm just being brave, that I will break down eventually, or that I'm just mourning in my own way. I loved Simon. I do miss him."

Intent on changing into the offered clothes, Talia undid the top buttons of her white blouse.

"But I'm second generation," Maeve said. "I was born here. Perhaps because we don't expect to live to be a hundred and twenty like the people on Earth, we are just more accepting of death. Every day Simon went out to scout, I knew there was a chance that he would not come back."

Talia's hair was still a little damp as she shrugged out of the blouse and put on the blue shirt. Its buttons, wider and sturdier than the ones on the blouse, were much easier to work.

"Sometimes he'd be days overdue," Maeve continued. "Other times, weeks. Once, he was two months late. And then, finally, one day, someone brought what was left of him wrapped up in a sack. He was too far gone for the doctor to tell us much. I cried. I mourned. I will continue mourning. But he's gone and I'm still here and he would have wanted me to go on living."

Talia stood and pulled her pants down, holding on to the gun and then folding the fabric neatly underneath the built-in holster. Simon's jeans were wide enough that she was going to need those suspenders and a gun belt, but the length was fine.

"That's very . . . practical." Talia took the boots, pulled them on.

"How are they?"

"A little wide in the toes, but otherwise fine."

"A second layer of socks. Here you go." Maeve dug around and produced another pair.

Talia took those too, pulled her feet out of the boots, and plunged them into the socks.

"I even have an orphaned glove you're welcome to," Maeve said. "You'll need spurs and a hat too. You can give them back when we return."

Talia was wiggling her toes, determining if the extra socks made for a too-tight fit. "We?"

Maeve's hands were back on her hips. "Lyle may be fine with letting you ride up to Contesti's ranch on your own, but I'm not. You may be the best city rider on Gōruden, but you don't know where you're going."

"I can read a map," Talia said, as she tucked Simon's pants back into the boots. "Or follow directions. I'm very good at following directions."

"I have no doubt of that, but I'm still coming with. Now, if you want, I can ride behind you and we can pretend that you know where you're going, or I can guide you. Your choice. Either way, I'm coming with."

CHAPTER FOUR

THE NIGHT BEFORE, TSURUI ITSELF HAD BEEN JUST OVER THE horizon from Biei, the island of Tatarka's smaller port town. Talia's boat—a sailing ship that made a semiweekly run from the mainland—had pulled into the dock during the night. The only passenger, she'd boarded the waiting stagecoach and slept propped up against the corner. Exhausted from the weeks of travel, Talia couldn't remember if she'd even bothered to look out the window. Bad form, really, for someone in her position, but city living really had blunted her edges.

At Talia's insistence, Maeve had shown her a map before they set out. If one was generous, one might charitably call the path to Contesti's ranch a road. It looked like someone had thrown tangled spaghetti at a piece of paper, smoothed out certain sections, but left others a jumbled mess. It was a volcanic island after all, young geographically speaking, as one of her protectees—a scientist from Earth—had delighted in telling her.

Talia sat atop one of Maeve's horses—a reddish-brown mare that answered to Rosie—as the hills closed in around them. The green of the vegetation was so intense it was blinding, even with her sunglasses. It wasn't the sun so much as the way the color assaulted her eyes and made her want to just stare at the lushness of it all.

Talia adjusted her seat in the saddle. The too-big jeans were chafing in all the wrong spots, and while the glove may have spared her blisters, the jeans didn't seem to be doing as good of a job protecting her thighs.

"So who are these Haricot people? What have they got that's making off-worlders like Contesti take such a keen interest in things?"

"The Haricots were one of the first groups to come out to Tatarka after the Neo Bravo colonization effort failed. Caleb Saunders Haricot, the patriarch—now dead—was some sort of genius. Married to Dame Leigh Stark, matriarch and self-proclaimed domestic goddess, a fiery old bitch."

"You say that like you like her."

"I respect her," Maeve admitted. "She's held the whole thing together through drought, famine, hostile takeover attempts, frivolous lawsuits, and a few outright assassination attempts. The extended family she leads is made up of specialists—ranchers, veterinarians, biologists, geneticists, and many others with esoteric knowledge."

"That sounds like, shall we say, a strange mix."

Maeve shrugged. "Given what they're doing, not really."

"And what requires that kind of a set up?"

"Space cows."

Talia gave her an incredulous blink.

"Don't look at me," Maeve said. "That's what they're called. Seems that old man Haricot worked some supersecret statistical magic to figure out what genetic modifications had the best chance of yielding a cow that could be inserted into the environment to modify the biome—the soil bacteria to be specific—so as to complete the terraforming."

"How do cows modify anything?"

"By making the right kind of fertilizer."

"This is about cow poop?" Talia asked.

"Yup, highly specialized, genetically modified space-cow poop."

"Gōruden is already so Earthlike. I didn't realize further terraforming was needed."

"The mainland doesn't need terraforming," Maeve said. "Something about the latitude. But here, on these islands, on the other continents, it's a different story. There's something in the soil that wiped out the original colonists. Earth thinks it was some freak one-time kind of thing. But the Haricots think it may be due to a periodic organism of some kind—Gōruden has several—and they are determined not to let it happen again."

"So, why not just steal the cows? Clone them."

"Oh, Contesti, and others like him, have tried. Thing is, that all the gen-engineering tweaks were done back on Earth by Haricot. He brought a few thousand specialized cow embryos here with him. But those were just the start. It's taken generations of breeding for the right genetics to finally yield the right cows. No way for anyone but the Haricots to know which cows are the ones with the right genetics for the next iteration.

"Rumor is the Haricots are close to a breakthrough. Like within a few generations, which means cow generations, so just a few years."

Maeve took a drink from her flask. The day had warmed and she'd shed her duster, stuffed it into her saddlebags.

"Stealing the cows is no good without the key to the specific genetic modifications," she continued. "As I understand it, Contesti would have to figure out which cow was producing the right kind of waste. And I must say, the thought of Contesti, with his fine clothes, and fine manners, standing over manure, trying to figure out if it's got the right things in it is very amusing."

She put her flask away, dragged the back of her hand over her smile.

"And even though he's been caught sending stolen genetic samples back to Sakura to be analyzed, no one there has been able to figure it out. When the Haricots get the final iteration, they will file for a patent. If they can show that it will complete the terraforming, it'll not only open up the rest of Gōruden for colonization, but we could declare our independence from Earth. That's a dream we didn't think would come true for hundreds of years."

"Unless Contesti stops them."

"Contesti doesn't necessarily want to stop them. He wants to control them, steal their secrets, adapt their methods not just for this, but for other applications.

"Dame Leigh is not the kind to turn the needed data over without a fight. I was there when she looked Contesti in the eye and threatened to burn it all down. Seems she's a fan of salting *and* scorching the earth."

They emerged from one of the many hairpin turns. Below, an expanse of gently rolling land stretched in front of them. A small lake sparkled like a sunlit sapphire amid a field of emerald.

"Breathtaking, isn't it?" Maeve asked.

"Yes," Talia said. Rosie had come to a stop as if she, too, were admiring the view.

"Contesti's estate," Maeve said.

The main house was in the same Japanese style as the smaller homes in Tsurui. Multilevel, it had three wings and was laid out in a U shape. Several other buildings—what looked like barracks and barns—bracketed the sprawling house. Two layers of fencing surrounded them. Small specks milled about.

Talia raised her right hand to shield her eyes. Her left hand sweated inside the glove, and the prickly way her brain was "filling in" the missing sensation for her right hand kept making her want to pull off the glove. But sweating was better than getting blisters.

"Goats and sheep, mostly," Maeve said, answering an unspoken question. "Japanese serow, technically. Or close enough."

"What do you mean?" Talia asked.

"Contesti's own little rival operation. The Haricots have most of the flat land ideal for cows. This land is steeper, better suited for sheep. They, too, have been genetically modified for Gōruden. The scientists can tell the difference, although no one else can. Not even the animals themselves."

"Sounds like there's a story there," Talia said.

Maeve chuckled and spurred her horse, a gray gelding. As they got closer, the grandeur of Contesti's ranch spoke of the wealth backing him—a parabolic dish perched atop the roof of the smallest barn and a strip of land had been flattened. Talia was no expert, but it looked long enough to allow a small plane to take off and land.

A pair of riders came out to greet them.

"Oh, look, they're pulling out all the stops to greet us," Maeve said, her voice dripping with sarcasm.

The men were dressed in paramilitary uniforms—a nonadaptive flecktarn camouflage, the shades of green not quite right for Tatarka.

"Good day, Mrs. York," one of the men said as he and his companion stopped in front of the women.

"Francesco, Lorenzo, we're here to see the boss," Maeve said.

"Who's your friend?" the taller one asked, eyeing Talia.

She'd contained her hair in a tight bun at the nape of her neck, and wearing Simon's too-big clothes and gear, she must've looked like someone in disguise—suspicious, if not exactly threatening.

Harmless. I'm harmless.

The 1911 at her hip said different, but that shouldn't have roused their suspicions—she had yet to see a single unarmed person on Tatarka. Even the hostess at the onsen had had a gun tucked into her obi.

"Lorenzo, this is Talia Merritt," Maeve said. "She has business with your boss."

Lorenzo's eyebrows rose. The other rider, the shorter one, touched his throat mic and asked if Talia was expected. Then he repeated himself twice, the volume of his voice rising as if that was the problem. Francesco must have gotten confirmation because he gave Lorenzo a confirming nod.

"You know the way, Maeve," Lorenzo said.

Talia and Maeve made their way up to the house. A colonnade wrapped around an interior courtyard. Rosie neighed and horses from the stable in the distance answered her. She tossed her head.

Talia considered the lines of fire as they passed under the gate leading into the courtyard and didn't like what she saw. It would be like shooting fish in a barrel with her as the fish. The tickle at the base of her neck became an itch, one that she hadn't felt since she'd stepped on Gōruden.

She counted five men. Two were just standing about in the shade, looking bored and wary. Three were sitting at a table under a canopy, one of them cleaning a rifle. The scent of solvents tainted the air. They were dressed not in jeans but in cargo pants and combat boots. Caps kept their faces in shadows. They looked like men who were working very hard to look unconcerned and at ease.

The hairs on the back of Talia's neck felt like they wanted to reach out and tap her on the shoulder or bitch-slap her. It wasn't what the men were doing so much as the way they looked, like out-of-work mercenaries. Ironic, given that she was, technically, also one.

What did you think you'd be training? The local version of the boy scouts?

Talia spurred Rosie forward, taking the lead.

A saber of a man came out the front door, wearing a pristine white shirt, a tailored suit—not the latest fashion in Sakura, but last season's short-waisted, double-breasted style with a silk cravat at the throat—and shoes so shiny she had no doubt she could use them as mirrors. Contesti, no doubt.

His dark eyes assessed her from the shade of the porch. Unlike the others who looked like they'd spent plenty of time in the open, his skin was pale, a contrast to the pitch-black hair of his goatee and mustache, his long hair. His hands, so long-fingered they had a skeletal look to them, looked like they should be playing a piano or performing surgery.

"I'm Talia Merritt."

"So you are," Contesti said, his cultured accent coming through. "Please come in, Ms. Merritt. We can talk in comfort."

He did not have the look of a man who'd been sweating, not even in Gōruden's midday sun. Talia hadn't felt the comfort of climate control since she'd left Sakura. It was amazing what comforts one could get used to in seven years.

But she had a feeling that while he might have invited her in to keep their conversation private, he wasn't all that happy about her appearance. Mud had splashed up on her boots, and she no doubt smelled more like Rosie than not. Talia could feel the stickiness of her clothes, the way that sweat had collected under the band of her bra, pooled at the small of her back as Rosie shifted her weight underneath her.

The man who'd been cleaning the rifle lined up the barrel, buttstock, and upper receiver. She kept him in her peripheral vision.

"I just came to tell you that I'm sorry," Talia said, "but I'm no longer interested in the job offer. Sorry about your expense money, but—"

"I take it you spoke to that so-called sheriff."

Talia leaned forward in the saddle. The man at the porch table had finished assembling the rifle. He reached down into a box under the table, brought his hand up, and palmed a round into the chamber.

He was about to close the action on a live round. She was sure of it.

"I wouldn't do that if I were you," Talia said looking straight at him.

The man's fingers froze midmotion and he gave her the most innocent of looks. Amusement danced in his eyes though, and the quirk of his lips made her want to smash in his toilet-bowl-white smile.

Her silence and her gaze promised retribution.

His hand hovered by the action as if frozen.

"Don't be an idiot," Contesti said. He could have meant either of them, but his man dropped his hands to the table, laid them flat. The smile was gone. So was the innocent look. The other men, the ones who'd looked ever-so-bored, had perked up. Everyone was paying attention now.

"Tell your men to back off," she said.

"Please, gentlemen, excuse us," Contesti said. "You're making our guests nervous. Go grab some food or go lift something. Surely you can find something to do."

Slowly, with the smug grin back on his face, the man at the table stood up. Reluctantly, all of Contesti's men obeyed, walking down the colonnade and disappearing around the corner.

A quick look at Maeve confirmed that she was on alert too. Her shotgun was very conveniently placed, practically across her lap.

"Please, Ms. Merritt," Contesti said. "Come inside. You too, Maeve. At least allow me to tell you my side of the story."

"Doesn't matter what your side is, Signore," Talia said. "It's the wrong side."

"Because Monroe said so."

"Because I won't go up against Monroe."

"I didn't ask you to, Ms. Merritt. I brought you here to train my men, that's all. Who do you think told me about you? Monroe said you were the best, and I buy the best."

He made a careless wave to indicate his surroundings.

He bought the best. Not hired, but bought. That's all she really needed to know. She was done being bought and sold.

"Tell me, Signore Contesti, did Lyle tell you that I was the best before or after he decided to stand against you?"

His face answered for him.

"So, you're going to take sides without even giving me the chance t—"

"Not taking sides. Just not getting involved. Leaving as a matter of fact."

"He scared you off."

She offered him her arm-candy smile, the one she'd learned for when the job had called for pretending that she was an escort, not a bodyguard. "If you'd like."

"What about you?" Contesti asked, looking pointedly first

at Maeve and then her shotgun. "I thought you weren't taking sides either."

"I'm not," Maeve said.

"Backing her play isn't taking sides?" Contesti's tone had lost its smooth calm.

"No. Just making sure a stranger finds her way back. Can't have the busybodies in Sakura worrying about newcomers becoming lost out here in the wild. Raises the wrong kind of concern. The wrong kind of governmental attention."

"Sounds very much like taking sides to me," Contesti insisted.

"Refusing to sell to you and your men is taking sides. And if you push me, that's exactly what's going to happen."

His face flowed from raw anger to congeniality in the blink of an eye.

He flashed the most insincere smile Talia had ever seen, and she'd seen plenty of those as the elites pretended to be honest with themselves and each other.

"Very well, then. I hope you have a safe trip back, Ms. Merritt."

She'd seen people glare daggers at her before.

But never like that.

CHAPTER FIVE

THE NEXT DAY, TALIA EMERGED FROM THE HOTEL, STILL WEARING Simon's old clothes. Maeve had refused to take them back, insisting that they made for better travel clothes than Talia's city attire. They'd parted ways after getting back, Maeve pleading the need to get back to her store. Talia had taken dinner alone in the hotel. At first she'd thought the veiled contempt with which she was treated was due to being a stranger. Then she'd caught snatches of conversation, murmurs wondering why she'd come to serve Contesti. Not work for, but serve.

It was obvious that Lyle was well liked and Contesti was not. That she was seen as a threat to one and a servant to the other. It made her eager to get back to Sakura, put this whole thing behind her.

After a quick breakfast and a quicker cup of tea, Talia headed for the stagecoach/post office.

She made it a few feet from the hotel door before the dog robots came trotting down the street. They seemed to be making a race of it, their little legs kicking up leaves as they took turns taking the lead, racing a golden retriever.

A horse tied up in front of the hotel gave a nervous nicker and tossed its head. A whistle from down the street made the golden retriever stop, look behind, and then head the other way.

She didn't expect the two robots to veer her way. CorgiSan took the lead and ran a circle around her, barking loudly. The horse shifted its weight from one hoof to another, eyes tracking the not-dog with nervous intensity.

DespairBear nuzzled up to her, butting his head against her leg. She reached down to pet him.

John had to be nearby. Surely he didn't just let them roam.

A coach passed through, pursued by a barking CorgiSan who lost interest in it after a few seconds and trotted back up to her to demand his share of her attention.

"I have to go, boys. I really do."

They weren't having it though. She'd make it a step or two and they would nudge her calves or circle her, keeping her from moving forward.

By the time she made it across the street, she was scolding them with firm noes.

"I'm going to step on you," she told DespairBear.

He sat and tilted his head.

"At least let me get out of the street."

They followed her into the office and posted themselves at the door like sentries.

The young man behind the desk was reading a book with torn and curling edges as he nursed a cup of coffee. He looked up, bleary eyed, like he hadn't slept in ages.

At the edge of the counter, an insulated coffee pot and extra cups beckoned to her. Better not. The fewer pit stops the better.

"Here for the stagecoach?" The clerk looked her over like he was seeing her for the first time, although unless he had a twin brother, he'd been on duty when she arrived as well.

"Yes. Am I late?" She set her bag down atop the bench along the wall.

"Nope. Early. Thing is, it's not going anywhere. Broken axle."

"Oh." She said it quietly, like a whisper, despite wanting to scream.

With her limited funds she didn't have the luxury of staying another night, and if the boat sailed, she'd be stuck in port for who knew how long. Visions of sleeping on the street like a vagrant danced in her head.

And she didn't want to call on Maeve, or Lyle, for any more favors. All she wanted to do was put distance between herself and Contesti, lest he decide she warranted further persuasion. The kind that could not be refused.

She'd tossed and turned last night, worried about what he might do to Maeve. Or Lyle. Worried that she wanted to stay and help and didn't have a single reason to. If Lyle had wanted her help, he would have asked for it.

Had he, would she have said yes? She looked down at her cybernetic hand, saw the flesh and bone one she'd lost instead. Saw it as it had been, pinned and crushed under a beam too heavy to lift. Saw the blade come down—a flash of sharp steel—to sever it, a last, desperate measure that saved her life.

Once, long ago, she'd been able to thread the needle. Not just the kind used for sewing. But for killing. But no more. Not really. Oh, she was still very good, but not as good as she'd been. Nothing man-made was as good as the original or people would be running out and getting cybernetic replacements for all sorts of things. Good thing that she didn't need that kind of precision anymore.

She made a fist, placing the phantom palm under the phantom fingertips. Now that was a unique sensation, a doubling of the awareness of just how much that part of her wasn't flesh, wasn't bone. A shudder boiled up inside her, spending itself as it climbed out of her gut.

Lyle came in before she got a chance to ask about alternate transport. He'd taken off his hat and looked very much at ease, his duster flapping behind him, a fresh salmon-colored shirt underneath. He looked happier to see her than he'd been at the onsen. She still couldn't believe that he'd thought her an assassin—a mercenary for hire. That part still hurt.

"There you are. Thought I'd find you here."

"Where else would I be?"

"Coach won't be ready to go until tomorrow. Maybe the day after."

She sank onto the bench, suddenly in need of coffee.

As if he'd read her mind, Lyle poured two coffees and sat down next to her.

"What did you think of Contesti?"

"I think he has at least five men itching for a fight," she said and took the offered cup. It was unadulterated coffee, her least favorite kind because you could actually taste the bitterness of the beans. "I think you're going to have your hands full when he decides to make a move."

He made a thoughtful nod toward his drink. "It won't be for a while, not with just five men, but yes."

"Do you have a plan?" she asked.

"Always do."

It was her turn to nod. Yes, that was Lyle.

The old Lyle—the one who'd been her partner, the one who'd come to get her, the one whom she'd saved, the one who'd bound her forearm tight just before he'd severed it with one swift stoke—would have shared his plan with her, asked her input.

But the new Lyle, the one who'd traded being a soldier for becoming a cop, the one who'd never forgiven her for saving him, that Lyle, did not.

She understood. She didn't like it, but she understood.

"There's another coach leaving out of Shiiba later today. It's a straight shot north. Maeve radioed ahead, let them know you might be coming. Rosie's saddled up at the stable for you. Maeve would ride with you but can't. Something about timing a large batch of antibiotics, I think. I'd take you, but I also have something that can't wait. Or you could stay here until this coach is repaired. Maeve says she could use some help in the shop."

He was studying her, eyes intent, like he wasn't sure what else to say. Like it had cost him a lot to say the little he had.

"I'll take the Shiiba coach." She hadn't meant to sound defensive, like she wanted to be talked out of leaving, or into staying. She didn't.

Simple. She wanted simple. Simple was back in Sakura and now that she was a free agent, the money would be good. At least as long as she didn't take that fork in the road, the one that led to vulnerabilities like kids and family. She'd find ways to entertain herself, take advantage of the amenities of the city, do all the things she'd denied herself when her only goal was to buy out early. Maybe find a dojo and reconnect with her roots.

Lyle would be fine. Maeve would be fine. They had done well for themselves without her help. It was arrogance to think otherwise.

He reached inside his coat and took out a map. "Just stay on the road running along the stream."

CHAPTER SIX

TALIA KNEW WHEN SHE WAS BEING FOLLOWED.

Even in this unfamiliar place, she knew.

The valley in which Tsurui was located had narrowed into a ravine as she'd followed Lyle's map. Whenever the walls narrowed, they echoed the sounds of another horse. According to the map there was a waterfall up ahead. Sometimes she even caught the sound of its rushing waters as it bounced off rocks.

Moisture beaded on her face and ran down her cheek as she prodded Rosie to pick up the pace. The mare seemed eager to go, her nostrils flaring, undoubtedly at the promise of a drink. When she had a chance, Talia would have redo her bun. It had loosened. She needed to find a better way to keep it off her sweaty neck. The strands plastered to her face and neck itched, making for a distraction she didn't need.

She made a turn and then another, keeping along the stream, taking advantage of the shade on the western side. The sounds of falling water became more than a whisper as a tiered cascade came into view. The top of the ridge from which it fell was hidden by trees in bloom, their canopies speckled with red, purple, and orange flowers.

It was the kind of thing one saw on posters and advertisements for Gōruden, like the vast expanses of pink and purples that she'd seen when she'd first landed. She still remembered that affirming moment that said that Gōruden was everything it was promised to be, that it would make the coming years of servitude worth it.

She looked about, confirmed that whoever was following her would have no choice but to come around that last corner blind. There was always the possibility that they could have access to something like a drone with a camera, but in that case, she couldn't do much about it anyway.

Still stiff and sore from yesterday's ride, Talia dismounted and let Rosie loose so she could drink and graze to her heart's content. Chances were, no one was after Rosie. As tempting as it was to cool off in the stream, Talia limited herself to a quick dousing from her hat, redid the bun, and went to one knee behind a large, moss-covered boulder. The ground was soft and squishy, and moisture seeped right into the denim covering her knee.

Talia was beginning to think that she'd been wrong, that she wasn't being followed after all, when Rosie picked up her head and greeted the black gelding as it came around the bend.

A boy—he couldn't have been more than fifteen—with a pistol on his hip and a shotgun in a saddle holster brought the gelding to a stop. He didn't seem to have any malicious intent or expectations as he looked around, undoubtedly wondering what happened to Rosie's rider.

The gelding raised his head and snorted, grayish-black nostrils flaring and questing. He tapped his hooves in place like he was eager to get to the stream or perhaps to give Rosie a closer inspection.

For a second, Talia thought that boy and horse were simply going to do just that.

"Anyone th—"

A sound like an explosion made the gelding rear up, hoofs clawing desperately at the air. His enormous chest made a startled, whooshing sound that cut the boy's words short.

A startled Rosie jumped into the stream, putting distance between herself and the rearing horse.

Another explosion.

It was so loud that Talia could barely hear the boy shouting. He shifted in the saddle and pulled on the reins for control, his words lost in the cacophony of horse screams and pop-pop sounds emanating from the trees.

Talia drew her gun and rose from her hiding place just as the gelding reared up again. This time it lost its footing on the soggy, slimy soil beneath. Out of control, the horse twisted its torso and toppled in a mess of thrashing legs, tossing head and twisting neck, ending up atop his screaming rider.

The horse rolled, scrambled up and backed away, still snorting, its huge eyes wide with panic, its hooves seeking purchase on the patch of ground made even more slippery by its landing.

The popping sounds had been wrong for gunfire, and now that they'd stopped, Talia holstered her gun.

Hands out in a placating motion, Talia moved slowly toward the gelding. He was bleeding from at least a dozen wounds, most imbedded with tiny little spikes. No wonder he'd reared. His eyes were wild with pain, his lips foaming, and for an instant she thought he was going to come at her.

"Easy, easy, now."

Slowly she extended her left hand toward the reins. His hot breath came at her in desperate, uneven spurts.

"The seeds," the boy said. "You need to get the seeds out of his hide."

Talia shot a glance his way. He was down on his side, torso curled toward his legs. Blood darkened a spot on his chin, and another on his chest where one of the vicious little spikes, or seeds as he'd called them, had landed.

"You okay?" she asked, training her gaze back on his horse.

The gelding's nostrils flared as his hooves moved back and forth, almost like a human would hop nervously from foot to foot.

"Broken leg. I'll live." The boy pulled at the spikes, freeing them from his face and chest and tossed them aside.

She got her hand on the gelding's reins but kept the tension slack. No sense in jerking the horse needlessly. Or more likely, being jerked around by it.

"Try not to get any of the toxin on your skin," the boy said as he dabbed at the swelling and purpling spot on his chin.

"All right." Not a problem with cybernetic fingers. She tugged one of the seeds loose. It was curved like a claw, and wicked sharp. It had embedded itself about a half inch deep. The pores in her prosthesis reported a burning, stinging sensation. She let it fall in the water.

With each one she removed, the horse seemed to relax. The oozing wounds remained puffy along the edges, looking like angry welts that cried blood.

"Wash them if Nero will let you."

She pulled her hat off, used it to scoop up some water and poured it over the wounds until they ran clear. Rosie came up to nuzzle the gelding and let out a nicker.

Talia turned toward the boy.

He'd drawn his pistol, a revolver with a huge barrel that looked like a black tunnel as those things tended to be when they were pointed at her. His hand was unnaturally steady like he was used to handling a gun even when hurt or in shock. Or maybe it just hadn't hit him yet.

"I'm just trying to help," she said, keeping her hands level with her shoulders.

"You working for Contesti?" It came out a little strained. Sweat was pooling on his lip.

"No."

"He didn't hire you to carry samples back to Sakura?"

"No. Now put that gun down and let me help you."

She could see the debate going on behind his eyes. Like he knew that he was going to pass out and once he did, she could do as she liked. Time was on her side. Everything about the pain in his eyes said that he knew it too.

He lowered the revolver, whether out of fatigue or good sense, she wasn't sure. She reached for the snaps by his heel and pulled the chaps open. There was a bulge under the denim, just above his boot.

"See. Just a broken leg."

If the bone had broken through the skin, the denim would be soaked in blood.

"I don't suppose you have a radio?"

He shook his head.

"I need to set this." This she knew. However, her first-aid classes hadn't covered setting a broken leg. There was usually a medic around, or a call away.

The horses seemed content for the moment, even though Nero's wounds still oozed and the foam around his mouth continued to drip. His head twitched and so did the muscles all along his enormous neck.

The boy. Worry about the boy.

Talia picked up several sturdy branches. The boy had put the gun away at least and propped himself up so his leg was straight out. He'd also gotten the black leather chaps off, used a knife to cut through the seams, and made smaller strips out of the longer pieces. They laid under his leg, waiting. The knife he'd embedded into the soft dirt and damp leaves was within easy reach.

"I'm Talia." She set the branches alongside his broken leg.

"Elias. Elias Haricot."

"You ever done this before, Elias?"

"Made a splint? Yeah."

"Set a leg." She brought a strip of leather together around his boot like she was going to tie the ends.

"Mom's a vet. Seen it done."

"So you know it's gonna hurt."

"Like a sonofabit—"

In one quick motion, she set the leg. He was still cursing as she tied the splint tight.

She looked up. There was blood seeping from his mouth, dripping onto a faded tan shirt. He wiped it away.

"Bit my cheek."

"How do I get you home, Elias?"

"Bring Nero over."

She did and by the time she led him over, Elias had put the knife back in its sheath and was balancing precariously on one leg.

He made cooing noises at Nero, patting him on the cheek, careful to avoid the sores on the horse's face and neck. Elias lined himself up even with the saddle.

"Over on the other side, please. I'm going to need you to pull me over so I can get my good leg into the stirrup."

She clasped him by the forearms and pulled. She was pulled forward the moment he was no longer supporting himself and just dead weight. Digging her heels in the soft soil she put her back into it. He was heavier than she'd expected, but his chest and torso slid over the saddle, going over the hump.

Elias got his hands under his chest and balanced, keeping himself from sliding off.

"Can you help bring my leg over?"

She went around, took hold of the splint, helping him keep the leg steady as he pivoted in the stirrup and shifted his body. He was shaking by the time he got the leg over but sat up and scooted forward.

"Are you sure you can do this?" she asked, eyeing the way his broken leg dangled by the stirrup.

"Don't have much of a choice."

"Here," she said, passing the blanket up.

He wrapped the quilted fabric around his shoulders as she mounted Rosie and brought her to his side.

"Thank you for saving me. I didn't think one of Contesti's people would've bothered." He pulled on the reins and Nero headed for the road.

"I'm not one of Contesti's people," Talia said as she followed. "Now which way?"

"West at the first fork. Then twenty miles down the mountain. There's a bridge that we'll have to cross. It's made of three wooden arches. Leads right onto Haricot land."

He seemed steady, at least enough for her not to have to take the reins.

"We need to hurry," he said, voice betraying pain as he set Nero to a canter.

At his age he shouldn't have been able to hide pain so well.

She rode behind him, splitting her attention between watching him and their surroundings. She didn't want to get lost, not the way these mountain roads were. Lyle had said a straight shot north, just stay on the road, but that was no longer an option. Not if she took Elias home, and she already knew she was not going to leave him.

When Elias slowed Nero to a trot, she matched his pace.

"I need a moment," he said with a shuddering breath and took out his canteen. His Adam's apple slid up and down under a rivulet of water tracing over dry skin.

"Tell me about the spikes, the seeds, or whatever you call them."

He gave her a look that said that he knew what she was doing—distracting him from the pain. It was only half true.

"Dynamite tree. Gōruden's version of the sandbox tree."

"Heard about it. Thought it was a myth. One of those stories to scare newcomers."

He shook his head.

"Why did it go off?"

Elias adjusted himself in the seat, rubbing the thigh of his broken leg, making himself wince.

"Why did it go off, Elias?" she asked again as he took a too-long blink.

"It's how it propagates. Launches its seeds at lethal speeds."

The ravine walls bracketed the stream tightly, showing no indication of widening up ahead.

"What triggered it?"

"Nothing. Bad luck. If you'd have passed within a hundred or so feet at the same time it'd have gotten you too."

She glanced back. He was falling behind, shoulders rounding. His grip on the pommel was tight, but the reins were slack.

"How far to the turn, Elias?"

Elias slumped and toppled, landing facedown in the stream.

She pulled Rosie to a stop, spun her around, and sprinted toward him.

Get up, damn it. Get up.

Nero backed away, hooves making splashes in the water as Talia dismounted. She almost lost her balance on the slippery rocks. They slid under her heels as she took the three steps to reach him.

She turned Elias over, slapped him on the cheek. He couldn't have drowned or suffocated. It hadn't been long enough.

Blood threaded its way down his wet face, penciling its way from his slack lips and into the water before it disappeared.

"Elias? Damn it!"

Her fingers searched for a pulse, found none.

Talia centered her hands on his chest, locked her elbows, and shifted so her shoulders were directly above and counted.

Thirty compressions.

Two breaths.

Her phantom hand pushed in concert with her living one, pushed the heel of the palm into his sternum, felt the elasticity of his chest as it caved in and bounced back. Should she press harder? Would it help?

Thirty compressions. Two breaths.

She had a vague memory of being in Elias's place, looking up at a smoke-filled sky, having Lyle come into view, his face covered in dirt and blood.

One, two, three . . . Two breaths.

Her ribs bending underneath Lyle's hands. Her wishing he'd stop. The scowl on his face. It coming closer in a parody of a kiss to push breath into her lungs. Tears escaping from the corner of her eyes.

Twenty-eight, twenty-nine, thirty... Two breaths.

Lyle pulling away, letting go of her nose. Her heart seizing up in her chest. Blood in her mouth. A tunnel closing in. The sting of a slap.

Compress. Breathe.

Over and over again.

Lyle hadn't stopped. He hadn't given in, hadn't let her go. He'd insisted that she live.

Sweat had dripped from Lyle's face as he'd worked her chest, kept her heart pumping. Pushed air into her lungs. Breathed for her.

Even when she'd lost the will to live, he hadn't.

Talia blinked her eyes to clear them.

The fusion of her phantom mirroring the fatigue tearing through her living hand while the cybernetic components continued without cramps, without pain, pulled her out of the memory. Out of the count, the rhythm of it.

She lifted her left hand. Bruises were forming atop it from where the unyielding ceramics had pressed into it. Sensitive, the top of the hand. Thin skin. No protective layer of fat.

Her phantom shared the bruised sensation, the tenderness of abused flesh, fragile bones, a ghost occupying the same mindspace as the feel of her cybernetics.

Something soft and warm nuzzled at her ear. Warm breath huffed at her neck. She reached up to pet Rosie's muzzle. So soft. Like petals. Like a rose.

Elias's eyes were looking up at the cloudless sky, at the ravine's forest-covered walls, the branches of intensely green trees. Light played across his face, cast by the swaying canopy.

The horses' tack made small noises against the background of bubbling stream.

Talia took a deep breath and closed Elias's eyes.

Water sluicing around her, she rocked back on her heels... and wept.

CHAPTER SEVEN

BY THE TIME TALIA REACHED THE BRIDGE THAT MARKED ENTRY to Haricot lands, anger hadn't replaced guilt, merely kept it company. A flagging Nero carried Elias's body, trailing behind Rosie like a dark shadow in the fading light.

Wings fluttered overhead, streaking past her and the horses, betraying a cauldron of small, brownish bats.

The land on the other side of the bridge was mostly flat. Cows grazed in fields separated by a meandering road. They didn't look any different than the cows Talia had seen on Earth. Most were brown or black, or some combination thereof. They certainly smelled the same.

What did you expect? Three horns? Six legs?

The Haricot compound looked like a village in its own right, with a dozen smaller homes built around a grander one. Farther out, several hangar-sized livestock buildings backed to the mountain.

Talia passed under a bright red gate and headed for the center of what might be called the village square. Pumpkin-shaped paper lanterns hung from eaves and poles as if they were waiting for the sun to surrender. It was low in the sky, almost, but not quite, touching the tops of the surrounding mountains.

A young woman hanging laundry on a line looked Talia's way and stopped what she was doing. A little boy who looked much too old to be hers clung to her, his wide-eyed face smudged with dirt. Her knowing gaze came to rest on Nero's cargo. Her shuttered gaze met Talia's for an instant. She shooed the clinging boy toward the house.

Shouting preceded Talia as she approached. The main house sported three stories. Balconies ran around the upper level and the reaching branches of a giant tree betrayed the courtyard at its center. Green tiles reflected the sunlight like polished jewels. She calculated sight lines, angles, distances as she straightened in the saddle.

A woman with white hair pulled into a high bun and held in place with a fan-shaped comb stepped out onto the veranda to stand between columns of cherrywood stained to a darker, deeper wine red. She wore a simple gray bolero jacket over a lavender blouse with a high collar and a sturdier version of the split skirt currently in fashion in Sakura, also gray. The polished cane under her hand looked purely decorative as she tapped it to a stop. Its dark, black sheen reminded Talia of a sword's scabbard.

Another woman about Talia's age with blonde hair razored brutally close to her skull followed close behind. A dark-skinned man with shoulders so wide he barely fit through the door came out after them. Another man, light of skin and less imposing, exited last wearing sunglasses that looked like goggles. Their faces were grim, their hands holding shotguns at low-ready. Hats hung down their backs, held in place by stringy chin straps. Dirt clung to their boots and they looked and smelled like they had been working out in the fields, the dirt on their faces carved by rivulets of sweat.

From the corner of her left eye, Talia caught sight of a shotgun pointing her way.

"Dame Leigh?"

"That would be me," the white-haired woman said, her voice strong despite her age. She held herself rod straight, her blue eyes sharp, piercing, a weapon themselves.

"I'm Talia Merritt."

"We know who you are." Goggles was standing at Dame Leigh's side, just slightly forward of her as if he was ready to step in front of her and take a bullet. The lines in his weathered face were filled with dirt and sweat and he needed a shave.

"I didn't kill Elias," Talia said, leaning on the pommel. "I tried to save him."

"Why should we believe you?" The voice came from the side,

probably from behind that shotgun, the one aimed so that it would get her but not risk shooting Dame Leigh and her companions.

Motion on the roof above caught Talia's eye. A double-barrel, its line of fire similarly designed to be a threat only to her, slid out from the shadows cast by the peaks of the upper roof.

Talia met Dame Leigh's gaze. No one would make a move without her signal, without her order, of that she was certain.

"Dame Leigh, you wouldn't have let me come this far if you were certain that I killed him, so would you please ask your people to lower their guns. I don't want to be shot by accident."

"How did he die then?" This from the woman with the crew cut.

"I don't know. He had a broken leg. I set it. He fell off Nero on the way here. I gave him CPR, but . . . it . . . it was too late."

"Lower your weapons," Dame Leigh said. "Otto, get Çaspar out here." The dark giant hovering at her shoulder backed into the house.

Talia waited for the shooter on the left to lower the shotgun, then flicked her gaze to the one up above. The double barrels lowered. It would have to do.

Talia tugged Nero's reins forward and the horse moved up between her and the veranda.

Crew Cut and Goggles set their shotguns down and hurried down the steps, spurs and holsters clicking lightly as they went. Nero tossed his head as they cut Elias off and lowered him to the ground. Goggles soothed Nero by patting his neck and running his fingers carefully around the wounds left by the dynamite tree seeds. He shot Dame Leigh a questioning look.

Dame Leigh leaned on the cane, her jaw set tight, and shook her head.

A man with a braid of long, brown hair trailing down his back came running out from a side building, a leather doctor's bag at his side. He set it down beside Elias's body and examined him, fingers probing, his face becoming grimmer with each passing minute.

"Who set this splint?" Caspar, the doctor, asked as he popped it off.

"I did," Talia said.

Caspar made a face as he cut Elias's pant leg open. His calf was a swollen mass of dark red and purple.

"Well?" Dame Leigh asked.

Caspar stood up, a resigned look on his hawk-nosed face. "I'll have to do an autopsy to be sure, but I'm guessing the broken bone cut the popliteal artery as he rode."

"Any other injuries?" Dame Leigh asked.

"No bullet wounds if that's what you're asking. Looks like a dynamite tree got him though."

"Is that what happened?" Crew Cut asked.

"I heard two explosions," Talia said. "Didn't know what they were at the time. They made Nero rear. Elias fell. Nero slipped and fell atop him."

"Sounds like you were nearby," Caspar said as he helped Goggles load Elias's body onto the quilted blanket.

"Close enough to see it, yes."

"But not close enough to get hurt," Crew Cut said, her voice edged with suspicion.

"I was hiding behind a boulder. He was following me."

"How do you know that?" Dame Leigh asked.

"Because he told me so. Thought I was working for Contesti. Accused me of being a courier."

"I told you that Elias was going to—"

Dame Leigh raised her hand, cutting off whatever Goggles was about to say.

"Get him inside," Dame Leigh said. "Get word to his parents."

Goggles and Caspar folded Elias's body into the quilt, hefted him on their shoulders, and took him inside, past Dame Leigh. She passed a wrinkled hand along the shrouding blanket, a long caress that betrayed the emotions her face would not.

Talia opened her mouth to speak, but a force from above knocked her off Rosie, sent her sprawling face first in the dirt. She landed with a thud that knocked the breath out of her, made her see sparks. Something hit the back of her head, right at the base of her skull.

Once... Dirt and grass filled her nostrils—

Twice... Her mouth filled with the tang of blood.

Her neck lit up with sparks of pain.

She aimed her elbow at whomever had jumped atop her, connecting with solid flesh. She rolled on her side, raising her arms, crossing them in front of her. It took a third blink to clear her spotting vision. A fist impacted with her cybernetic forearm. A yowl and a screech followed as her vision came into focus.

Eyes full of rage. Gritted teeth. A face contorted, tear streaked and dirty, full of pain, of impotence. She'd seen death in people's eyes before, ones who'd wanted to kill her. But this was different. This was a child's face. It shouldn't know that much grieving fury, that much pain, that much determination.

A curse crumbled to dust on her tongue.

Otto pulled the child up by the scruff of the neck. He was twisting, kicking, and howling to be let go, to be put down. He looked about twelve, if that.

Talia spit the blood and dirt from her mouth, dragged the top of her hand across her lip. She needed a moment. She was still dizzy, the base of her skull smarting. She reached up. The skin atop and around the implant was tender, throbbing, but there was no blood.

The child continued kicking and screaming Elias's name as Otto hauled him up over his shoulder as if he were nothing but a sack of misbehaving potatoes. They disappeared into a side door that slammed shut behind them.

"Sorry about that," Dame Leigh said, although she didn't look or sound the least bit sorry.

"I guess I deserved that. Let myself get distracted." She propped her elbows on her knees. Her 1911 was still in its holster by the feel of it. At least the child hadn't had the presence of mind to pull it out and use it to kill her.

Adrenaline became a fist in her stomach.

Dead. You should be dead.

"Hmm," Dame Leigh said, contemplating. "You did come here at Contesti's behest, didn't you?"

"I came to Tsurui on his behest, yes," Talia said, rising and dusting off her jeans. "Didn't realize what I was really getting into. Lyle set me straight. I refused Contesti's offer. Was on my way to catch the stagecoach in Shiiba."

"Are you couriering for Contesti? Taking back something? Anything? Perhaps something as innocuous as a message. Or a data chip."

"No." Talia picked up and reseated her hat.

Dame Leigh narrowed her eyes. Studied her like one studies a specimen under a microscope before deciding whether or not to take it apart.

Sweat trickled down behind Talia's ear, slipping behind it to trace a path down her neck.

"Thank you for bringing Elias back to us," Dame Leigh said.

"I don't think a murderer would have done that. So I'm going to have Otto take you into Shiiba, make sure you get on that coach."

"Thank you." Talia made more of a show of brushing the dust from her clothes.

"Don't come back."

Talia straightened and let her hands fall to her sides. Kept them relaxed, straight, rather than allow them to form fists like they wanted.

"Dame Leigh, I'm sorry for your loss. I truly am, but I don't take orders from you. And I'm tired of being bossed around."

Dame Leigh raised her chin. "On your way out, Otto will take you by the graveyard so you can see how many of my family have died. So you can see where Elias will be buried instead of going on with a full life, instead of taking care of his little brother Sam, instead of marrying his sweetheart and having children with her, all the things that are still an option for you."

That last hit Talia so hard she felt it in her soul.

"And I want you to remember all those gravestones and what they represent," Dame Leigh continued, "and what we have sacrificed. I want you to remember that in case Contesti's offer were to ever tempt you again."

"You don't have to worry about me coming back here, Dame Leigh. Truly. You don't."

"Otto, get her out of here."

Otto towered over Talia, a dark shadow with mahogany skin and a stark, white grin. He looked like the kind of man that could either eat or bench-press an entire cow. He probably outweighed her twice over and most of it was muscle. Bandoliers stuffed with shotgun shells crisscrossed his chest.

"This way, ma'am." His deep voice resonated as he made the gentlest of gestures toward the road. "If you please."

"Have a safe trip, Ms. Merritt," Dame Leigh said, the look on her face denying the words coming from her mouth, the look in her eyes like that of a judge passing a sentence of death.

Talia had no doubt that Otto would get her safely off Haricot lands. Likewise she had no doubt that if she ever came back, Dame Leigh would have no qualms about making it known that she wouldn't mind if Talia met with some sort of unfortunate accident.

What had Henry II said? Oh yes.

Won't someone rid me of this troublesome priest?

CHAPTER EIGHT

OTTO'S MOUNT WAS ONE OF THOSE TREMENDOUS HORSES USED to pull things. She couldn't remember exactly. A Percheron maybe. Beautiful animal. He was as sturdy as his rider.

Otto was a man of few words. Every one of them polite and spoken with a tone she'd have expected from a butler or perhaps a poet.

Her head and neck throbbed, and she couldn't get the taste of blood and dirt out of her mouth. Some semblance of propriety kept her from swishing water around in her mouth and spitting it out.

Her old self wouldn't have been so proper. Damn Sakura. Damn this whole thing.

She needed a drink. And a tumble with a tall, dark, and handsome stranger who had no expectations beyond a mutual and brief good time. If she'd been in Sakura, she could have dialed one up, given him a made-up name, and never worried about emotional entanglements, and then spent the next week or month feeling shitty about it before she moved on.

"How long to Shiiba?" she asked.

"Another hour or so, ma'am, but I think you may have missed the coach at this point. May I suggest we ride back into Tsurui? Catch a coach there."

His horse made a noise that sounded like agreement, one echoed by Rosie.

She wished he wasn't so polite. That his voice wasn't so deep. That her emotions weren't so dark and determined to rise to the surface. She could feel them pushing at her tear ducts, tangling up in her throat, threatening to take her voice like they sometimes did in moments of extreme anger.

"I don't think so."

"Very well, ma'am."

"Call me Talia."

"Very well, Miss Talia."

She had been looking straight ahead but something about the way he'd said her name, made her turn her aching head. It had come out like he was in a tunnel or the bottom of a well. He even looked like he was inside a tunnel, one that swirled around him like a whirlpool.

"Are you all right, Miss Taaaallllliiiiaaaa?"

She blinked.

The tunnel around Otto swirled forward like a giant mouth and closed around her, swallowing her whole.

The darkness still had her. Had her in its grip, refusing to let her go, refusing to let her join the others.

Their voices echoed in the distance like they were chasing each other in caves, distorted, sometimes loud, sometimes distant.

"There's nothing I can do." A man. Familiar but not.

"The doctor already tried everything." Maeve. Maybe.

"She'll be fine. She's tough."

Thanks, Lyle.

"The doc said to give her until tomorrow."

"I'll sit with her."

"Don't you have something brewing or percolating or something?"

"Shush. Go."

"Fine. I'll come back at midnight."

"You need to sleep."

"So do you."

Barking. Neighing.

Dreams.

Sobo showing her how to make bread. The rich silkiness of flour atop a kneading board, flowing from her fingers in a steady stream to settle into a mound. The plop of the egg yolk, successfully separated from its white by her own young hands. The stickiness of the dough, unrelenting between her fingers while *Sobo* laughed and planted a kiss on her cheek. The rolling pin sliding under their palms as *Sobo* taught her that there was a rhythm to the stretching of dough.

Their motions cast shadows on the kneading board and with shadows, the dream dissolved despite her best efforts to hold on to it. Her mind yielded to nightmares.

The woman in Talia's sights was already dead. The man hiding behind his daughter, using her as a shield, wasn't. Not yet.

Those two times her emotions had almost gotten the best of her. The woman had put on a bomb vest. Talia had seen her do it. She'd walked out among the crowd, making her way to where children were. No matter what Talia did or didn't do, she was dead. It was just a matter of how many more went with her.

The man—no, the coward—hiding behind his own child. That one had been easy. She told the therapist so. She shouldn't have. The therapist hadn't understood. It had cost Talia, telling her the truth, being judged for it. People often said they didn't judge. They were liars.

Talia flinched awake, or nearly so, consciousness tracing upward from her trigger finger.

Her phantom hurting. Jolts of pain traveling up her arm, consuming her. The doctors telling her that they would have to take more of her forearm in order to make a prosthetic work. Her refusing. Them doing it anyway.

Non compos mentis.

CHAPTER NINE

TALIA WAS JOLTED AWAKE BY THE SCENT OF COFFEE. IT PLUCKED her out of the depths, made her eyes pop open.

Things dangled above her, their shapes coming into focus as she woke. Actuators and springs. Force sensors. Hip and knee motors. Ankle joints. Rims and vents. Housing cases and ring gears. They hung like wind chimes above her bed, a macabre collection of robotic body parts.

She was not at Maeve's. Nor the hotel either.

The room was hardly bigger than a closet. Water in a glass sat atop the tiny nightstand to her right. The mattress felt very much like a feather mattress and the bed frame underneath it creaked as she shifted her weight. Someone had put her in an oversized, overlong night shirt. She swung her legs down. Her calves brushed up against a knot of rope—oh, a rope bed.

She pushed her hair out of her face.

Her own secondhand clothes were neatly folded atop a footlocker, next to her bag. Everything still smelled of Rosie, of dirt and her own sweat, of river water and horse blood. Her 1911 sat atop the pile, action open and pointing toward the wall. A loaded magazine sidled up next to it.

Friends. She was definitely among friends.

As she changed, her hand bumped up against the bandage at the base of her skull. Carefully, she felt around it. Someone had shaved the right side along the bottom of her skull. It was still tender to the touch, like it had been bruised.

The boy. Sam. Elias's little brother.

She hadn't thought that he'd hit her that hard.

But she didn't remember being knocked out. She remembered Otto. She remembered riding toward Shiiba. But not the stagecoach. They hadn't made it. Not even as far as the graveyard.

Damn.

She finished dressing, loaded her gun, and pushed the door open. The room was at the top of a long, narrow staircase. She was in someone's attic. A spare room, probably.

Voices drifted up the staircase.

Voices and the scent of coffee, of eggs, and of bacon. Her stomach made a feed-me noise.

She followed her nose and emerged into a tiny kitchen. Wood burning stove, icebox, a sink with a lever pump. John at the stove, flipping pancakes on an iron griddle. Steam rose from what was presumably the lifesaving pot of coffee.

CorgiSan and DespairBear were in a down-stay, atop what looked like charging mats. They looked up in unison, heads tilting—CorgiSan's to the right, DespairBear's to the left. The articulating segments of their muzzles and eyebrows moved to give them both happy-dog expressions. The apertures of their cybernetic eyes expanded and contracted over the lenses and CorgiSan made barking noises—obviously recorded ones coming from a diaphragm that was part of a speaker in his chest. They didn't sound as loud as the ones he'd made in town. Maybe he had a volume control.

John, looking very casual in a too-big shirt and too-loose trousers held up by suspenders, tossed a look over his shoulder.

"Oh, good, you're up."

DespairBear pushed up to a standing position and came up to her, nuzzled her leg. He'd traded the old odds-and-ends tangled in his netting for a fresh batch and Talia imagined him rolling around in piles of dirt and leaves just to refresh the contents of his ghillie suit.

"You," John said. "Back on the charger. You're not done yet."

DespairBear swung his head in John's direction and then promptly ignored him, pressing into Talia's leg and stepping on her toes with one of his robotic paws.

She reached down to pet him, and he eased off on the pressure.

"You not going to come say hello?" she asked CorgiSan who was very happily wagging his tail nozzle on his mat.

"Coffee is almost done," John said. "Yeah, that one is fully charged, but good luck getting him off his mat. That one loves his charger. Would sit on it all day if you let him."

"How come?" she asked as she scratched DespairBear's "chin" with her cybernetic fingers. They made an odd but satisfying scraping sound.

She wished someone was around to take a picture for the irony of it. DespairBear flopped on his back, "stretching" underneath her hand until it was in the right place, which was apparently a spot on his "belly" that looked like it might be some sort of sensor array.

"Corgis are gluttons," John said. "The simulation program is merely mimicking that."

"And the scratching too?" she asked, rubbing the "belly" harder and finally being rewarded with a "tail" wag. DespairBear didn't have a nozzle like CorgiSan did, but that didn't keep him from wiggling his hindquarters like a dog with a tail. It made the netting overhanging his rear "wag" in poor imitation of a tail.

"Yup, the scratching too. And the whining."

CorgiSan made a low, whining sound as if to prove a point.

"It's . . . adorable."

The kettle whistled and John took it off the burner.

"How are you charging them?" Talia asked as she got a robotic leg to thump. She could see now why John was reluctant to undo the programming. The soft and pliable silicone parts under her hand gave off subtle vibrations that felt "soothing." She was willing to bet that it was part of the simulation algorithm, something designed to make the robots elicit the same emotions that dogs evoked.

"I have a kerosene-powered generator outside. It's hooked up to my workshop."

Talia looked around the little kitchen. There were kerosene lamps in sconces, but nothing else that seemed to run on electricity.

"I have a charger for the boys here," John said as if guessing her thoughts, "for their companionship."

She smiled and bent to pet CorgiSan. He might not have been willing to leave his charger to get petted, but he was making subtle—almost subsonic—sounds. The low, electronic "whine" came to a stop as soon as she touched him.

Maeve and Lyle came in through the door on the opposite side of the kitchen.

"See, I told you she was tough," Lyle said. His eyes couldn't hide the relief though. He *had* been worried.

Maeve wrapped Talia into a hug as soon as she reached her.

"Are you hungry?" John asked while she and Maeve still had their arms around each other. She rarely made friends this fast, but she had the feeling that Maeve was one of those people who made friends easily and fiercely.

"Very hungry," Talia said when Maeve let her breathe. She let herself be guided to the table. Lyle had already taken a seat and bent down to pet DespairBear, who was bumping up against his legs.

"How do you take your coffee?" Maeve asked.

"Sugar, milk. If you have them."

"How much milk?"

"About a quarter of the cup. Thank you." Talia lowered herself into the chair. "Anyone going to tell me what happened?"

She felt the shaved spot at the base of her skull, phantom fingers probing, probing, probing some more. It was almost like when her tongue had to inspect a new filling a thousand times before it decided to accept a change.

"Don't you remember?" John asked as he brought her a plate stacked high with pancakes, bacon, and eggs.

Talia shook her head as she picked up a mismatched knife and fork. "Otto was escorting me to Shiiba. That's the last thing I remember."

"Otto said you passed out and fell off Rosie," Lyle said as an even bigger plate of food landed in front of him. "He took you back to the Haricot estate. Caspar Yagrich, their doctor, treated you. They sent one of the kids into town to let us know. We rode out to get you, brought you back in a wagon."

Talia chewed. Washed her food down with some coffee. She didn't remember any of that. Not a smidge of it.

"Did I hit my head when I fell off Rosie too?"

"Both Otto and Caspar said no." Maeve waved away John's offer of food. John made a face and put the plate down in front of her anyway.

"How long have I been out?"

"A couple of days," John said as he leaned up against the wall and swirled coffee—what was presumably coffee—in a mug.

No wonder she was so hungry. "Who shaved my head?"

"Doc did."

"The Haricots' doctor? The one with the long hair? Oh, these are really good," Talia said pointing at her plate. The eggs had dark yolks, the bacon was perfectly crisp, and the pancakes were just sweet enough. "Coffee too. Really good. Thank you."

"Told you she'd be fine," Lyle said and folded his arms across his chest.

"Caspar is the Haricots' only medical doctor. Trained as a surgeon. He was trying to figure out if Sam might have damaged your neural implant," Maeve said.

She reached down and picked up DespairBear, who settled in her lap like a forty-five-pound dog instead of a heavier robotic version.

"There was a lot of swelling," Maeve continued. "Concussion he said."

Talia's ambitious chewing came to a full stop. She set the fork down. She rotated her cybernetic wrist, touched her thumb to each of her fingers in sequence, relief growing with each successful motion. The one thing she could not get fixed on Gōruden was a malfunctioning implant. She'd have to go back to Earth for that.

She picked up a slice of the crisped bacon. The cybernetic fingers moved in sync with her phantom. She could feel the texture of the bacon, the slickness of it. Yet... Her phantom and the cybernetics had become one the longer she'd had the prosthetic, but now she was quite aware of them as separate again, despite the mirroring of function.

"I guess I owe the Haricots again," Talia said. She wouldn't be sure that her implant was fine until she did something more challenging like buttoning her blouse, or threading a needle, but—

"Owe them?" John asked as he picked DespairBear off Talia's lap. The robot wiggled as John maneuvered him to the charging mat and ordered him to stay.

"They told you about Elias, didn't they?"

"They don't blame you for Elias's death," Maeve said, placing a placating hand on Talia's cybernetic forearm.

"Dame Leigh does. I saw it in her eyes. My incompetence killed him as surely as if I'd shot him in the gut."

"There's not a single person in this room who wouldn't have done exactly what you did," Lyle said. "Probably with the same result."

"There was no way for you to know," Maeve said. "Caspar's assessment, not mine. And he's the best doctor on this island."

"You didn't see the look in that little boy's eyes," Talia said.

She'd barely gotten a glimpse of Sam's face, but she'd never forget the rage in it, the pain.

"Sam is young," Maeve said. "Eventually, he too will understand that you tried to save his brother."

"Had I left Elias by the waterfall, gone to get help—known enough to know how to get help—he would still be alive."

"You don't know that," John insisted. "None of us know that."

The food she'd eaten was no longer sitting well. She pushed away from the table, throat tight.

"I need to get back to Sakura," she said.

"Still intent on leaving?" Lyle asked.

"Yes." She pinned him with a glare.

She and Otto had never gotten as far as the Haricot graveyard. But she didn't need to see gravestones to know that Dame Leigh was right—Elias would never get to do any of the things that were still a possibility for her. A possibility, not a certainty. She'd certainly had more time to do those things, and hadn't. That fork in the road seemed to loom ahead of her once more.

"There you go again," Lyle said, "taking blame for things that aren't your fault, bearing burdens that aren't yours, punishing yourself for things beyond your control!"

"Lyle," Maeve said, flabbergasted.

"What is it that you get out of guilt?" Lyle was leaning forward aggressively now. "Is it some sort of martyr complex? Do you still think that you can save everyone, that it's your job, that it's in your power? Or is it something else? Is it survivor's guilt? Is that it?"

He got up, knocked the chair over in doing so, and stood with his fists at his sides.

There was a low growling sound coming from the robots, one that John quelled by opening the door and saying, "Patrol mode." They slipped out the door and the look on John's face said that he wanted to go with them. Instead he let the door fall closed and took a renewed interest in the dishes in the little sink next to the stove.

Lyle, however, remained standing, fists clenched, the muscle in his jaw twitching, pulsing, his gaze blazing. It was an old argument. She'd lost track of how many times they'd had it.

And it had always ended with rage wrapped in silence. With tears, although they did not come today. Oh they were there, behind her eyes, in her throat, choking her, making it so that she couldn't speak.

Adrenaline was tightening every muscle in her body, making her stomach clench, forcing it to twist upon itself. The back of her skull throbbed as if it was being pounded upon again. Her phantom throbbed too, in time with it.

They stared each other down again. Just like last time. Just like every other time before.

You should have let me die.

His words, not hers. His words for when she'd come after him, lost three men in the process. Lost her hand.

She'd thought she'd worked through the survivor's guilt, the martyr complex. But if she had, she would be able to speak past the lump in her throat, the rage that had stolen her voice.

She knew that if she were to speak, she would cry, and she was not going to cry. Not in front of him. Not again. Never again.

Lyle turned, slammed the door behind him, making the rafters shake.

Maeve's gaze met Talia's—apologetic, confused, hesitant—for an instant, and she rushed after him.

Long, awkward moments hung in the room, interrupted by the clatter of dishes. She was grateful for that, for the normalcy of it as her adrenaline dissipated.

She gathered the silverware, set it atop the remains of her meal. Her stomach was far too knotted for her to tax it any further.

"John, I'm sorry about the wasted food. I don't suppose your robots like scraps." Of course now her voice was back. Just in time to make a pathetic attempt at a joke.

John made a sound halfway between a scoff and a harrumph. "No, but DespairBear has been known to dig up the compost heap. Stupid terrier."

It was enough to make her laugh.

He took the plate from her, set it in the sink.

"Can I still make the stage?" she asked.

"If that's what you plan on doing."

"It is."

"I know that the people around here haven't been very welcoming," he said as he washed the dishes with a cloth. "Contesti and his people represent the elites of Earth. So naturally, the good people of Tsurui are suspicious, particularly of anyone that might be a mercenary or just Earthers with an agenda. They still remember the depopulation brought on by the Fertilizer Wars on Earth. By those who insisted that things like cows were killing the planet."

"I am not a mercenary. Nor an . . . Earther."

He turned the water off, wiped his hands dry on a towel.

"I know, but they, well, they're going to need a little convincing. Anyway, once you get to Sakura, I'd find a specialist if I were you. I'm no doctor, but Caspar isn't a roboticist. And as a roboticist much better suited to fixing the external components of your prosthesis, I'm telling you to find a cyberneticist. Find one as soon as you get back. Have yourself checked out.

"Don't wait for something to go wrong. By then it might be too late."

CHAPTER TEN

ON EARTH NO ONE WOULD HAVE CALLED A BUILDING WITH TWENTY floors a high-rise. But on Gōruden, offices in that building, one of the tallest in Sakura, were a sign of prestige. They were also expensive.

It had taken Talia six months to save up enough money to afford to have the one and only cyberneticist on Gōruden take a look at the implant. She'd been brutally frugal with everything. She never did get to buy a sword much less practice with it. Or do any of the things she'd thought she might finally get to once she got back to Sakura. Priorities. They were a bitch.

Priorities meant moving back into the same tiny studio that she'd lived in as an indenture. It meant pulling extra shifts, extra details, as many as Sakura Executive Protection would allow. Being busy also kept her from thinking about it too much. It wasn't the first time that work had kept her sane.

Talia tapped her foot as she looked out the high-rise window at the glimmering city below. To the west, the vast expanse of the spaceport sprawled. There were two other high-rises completed now, with more in the works. A highway cut through the center of the city, its ends melting seamlessly into a narrower beltway that circled the land that had been set aside by city planners. On Earth, Sakura would have never been called a teeming metropolis, but it was definitely planning to be one. Someday.

She'd worn a skirt and heels for the occasion, something businesslike that said, "I'm not a bodyguard." The skirt was magenta, the blouse that color known as salmon—not quite pink, but closer to a faded brick red that hinted at peach. It was her favorite. Yet it hadn't really seemed to change her reflection nearly enough. The problem with being very good at something horrible had always been about not letting it be all she was.

She heard the door open and turned. Dr. Valentin Frowst looked like he belonged on a billboard, wearing nothing but a thong. He had cheekbones and eyelashes that most women would kill for and he wore everything, including his designer clothes and expensive jewelry, without the barest hint of arrogance.

The cut of his jacket hinted at something with oriental roots, the lines simple and bold like they had been drawn with flair and somehow that flair had been rendered in cloth. Silk by the look of it. A pale, milky green like chrysoprase or a granny smith apple mixed into cream. The matching shirt underneath had a texture to it, one rendered by sewing seams like bold slashes into the fabric with artistic flair.

"Sorry to keep you waiting," he said as he closed the door behind him. "Please have a seat."

As she sank into the indicated chair, she crossed her legs one way, and then the other.

Nervous? Not me. Snipers don't get nervous.

He was looking intently down at the smart-glass of his desktop. From her angle she couldn't make out whatever he was looking at—a diagram maybe.

"You know we have full patient confidentiality, don't you, Ms. Smith?"

"I know."

"And that your implant has a trackable serial number, as do the components of your prosthetic."

"Yes. But I didn't think your front office staff had access to *that* information."

He looked up. "I take it that you're keeping secrets from your employer, Ms. Merritt. Is that so?"

"A bodyguard with a cybernetic arm that might be damaged doesn't exactly inspire confidence, Dr. Frowst."

"*Has* it been malfunctioning?" He pinned her with those intense, dark eyes, the irises not quite as dark as his pupils, showed a hint of green, probably a reflection off his clothes.

"No. There's nothing wrong with the prosthesis itself." Of this she was certain. Almost a hundred percent certain. Almost.

"But you do know that there's something wrong." He sat back, steepled his fingers. They were long, elegant. He wore a single ring—a signet with some kind of logo on it—of white gold. It sparkled against the olive skin. She hadn't been able to get a good glimpse of it, even when she'd shaken his hand.

"I can't thread the needle," she said.

He raised an inquisitive brow.

"When I shoot, there's a slight disparity between what I think I'm doing and what I—or rather—my cybernetic index finger is actually doing. It's enough to ruin the shot."

"But you don't shoot for a living anymore, Ms. Merritt. Do you?"

"I made my last round of qualification shots," she admitted. "But it was one of my worst performances. I told everyone I was having a bad day, which, I guess, is true enough."

"So your job is not in danger."

"Not for the time being no."

"But you're worried that it might be. And you would be right."

She braced herself.

"There is some signal degradation from your neural implant to your prosthetic. I can't say for certain if it's ongoing, since I only have one data set. You shouldn't have waited so long."

She let go of the breath she'd been holding.

"It wasn't by choice. I came in as soon as I could afford it."

"I would have seen you." He played with the signet ring, twisting it around his finger like a fidget toy. "We could have worked something out."

"I don't want charity, Dr. Frowst. I will not be in anyone's debt again. The cost is too high."

He dropped his hands in his lap, furrowed his brow. "A laudable attitude, with some value here on Gōruden. I won't argue it with you. You do realize that I can't fix the problem. You'd need a new implant and all that entails. Retraining, reprogramming, debugging. All of it, from the start."

Having her fears confirmed didn't lighten them as she'd expected.

"You can't reboot it?"

"I could. It would be like starting over again, so you wouldn't be fully functional until you retrained your implant. But the problem isn't with the firmware. It's with the component itself. Physical degradation. Due to damage. How did it get damaged?"

"I took a few blows to the head."

"Job related?" he asked.

"No. It had nothing to do with my job."

I fucked up. I let my guard down.

"I take it that you're the kind of woman who would insist on resigning from a job she couldn't do."

"How long do you think I have?" she asked.

"When did you take these blows to the head?"

"Six months ago."

"And did you notice the degraded superposition between your phantom and the prosthesis right away?"

She had to think about it. Had she?

"No, at first it was just that my phantom no longer fit the prosthesis as well. They were no longer merged, no longer one. My phantom used to fit like a glove. It and the prosthetic were one. Now it feels like the glove is either too big or too small, or just slightly twisted like it no longer fits."

"Have they drifted further apart? Do they ever feel like they're further offset from each other?"

"Not really. After the swelling went down, they functioned as one well enough for most tasks, but not for threading the needle."

"I would need you to come back on a weekly basis, so I can track the degradation in order to give you an idea about how long before you lose significant superposition. It may be months or years. Hard to say. But an implant would have to be ordered from Earth and it will take at least two years for it to get here."

Two years. She'd known it would be that long, yet... yet having it confirmed, having it made real—her stomach sank.

CHAPTER ELEVEN

THERE WAS ONLY ONE KIND OF JOB THAT WAS GOING TO EARN Talia the kind of money that she would need to be able to afford the new implant—actual murder for hire.

Gōruden was the kind of place where most people did their own killing. That's why the rich and paranoid liked to hire people like her. They thought that someone might not only attack them, but issue a challenge to a duel. They thought that belligerents and their seconds met at dawn the next morning.

It wasn't quite the way it worked.

Dueling was rare. So rare that when it happened, it became a major source of news and gossip. And it wasn't exactly legal. Meaning that the marshal's office, the only polity equipped to deal with things like murder or attempted murder—which is what dueling was—took a dim view of it and actively worked to stop it.

With how spread out the population was on Gōruden, that usually meant that the marshals showed up to take a report. Sometimes they would pick up someone whom a local citizen or sheriff arrested for murder.

Sakura itself had had one duel in its entire history. It was such a big deal that it had acquired a cult status, with reenactments celebrating it every year.

Even the places run by warlords, egotistical maniacs, and religious fanatics didn't have duels—no, duels were too formal, too ritualistic. In those places, people just killed each other as they had for thousands of years. No ritual involved.

Truth was, most people outside of Sakura and some of the larger towns were too busy surviving and making a living to worry about something as frivolous as dueling.

Nevertheless, the man with the trio of parallel scars crossing his face looked just like the kind that might have come to Gōruden with a duel in mind.

He stepped out of the spaceport elevator carrying a fencing bag slung over his shoulder. His dark hair was short, not a military cut, but a very neat style that had probably been rendered by a hairstylist rather than a barber. The scars distorted a handsome face just enough to give it a lot of character and pulled part of his lip into a perpetual near-sneer. He towered over one Karolina Bates, a petite woman wrapped in a yellow sheath dress with a split that started high on the right side. She was clutching a large shoulder bag to her side. Platinum blonde hair. Gray eyes. So thin that the ribs below her clavicles showed.

The woman, Talia knew. Or knew of. She was the protectee, the woman she'd been assigned to pick up from the spaceport. Sakura Executive Protection had sent a car and a chauffeur as well, but only someone like Talia herself with her bodyguard's license could venture this deep inside the spaceport's security perimeter without a boarding pass. Today she was the only person on the concourse reserved for disembarking VIP passengers.

"Miss Bates," Talia said, stepping forward and flashing her identification badge. "I'm with Sakura Executive Protection. Talia Merritt, at your service."

Even in Sakura, even for the elites coming here from Earth, a cybernetic hand evoked at least being noted. Not for Bates though.

"Oh lovely," Bates said, her voice lilting upward. "Where were you five minutes ago?"

"Pardon?"

"Five minutes ago, when that thug almost knocked me over."

"What thug?" Talia asked.

"The one that was in such a hurry to get off the ship. He stomped on my foot, almost knocked me over. If it hadn't been for Mr. Rhodes here, he would have too." She looked adoringly at the scarred man who was still hovering at her side, a smile on his face.

"Miss Bates exaggerates," Rhodes said with attentive politeness. He was looking Talia over, studying her, as if trying to place her.

His gaze lingered in the right place—her right hip—long enough to know that she was armed. Nothing about the swing of her plain, black split skirt or the cut of her even plainer jacket fooled him. That much was clear.

"It was nothing," Rhodes continued. "The gentleman was merely inattentive. Nothing to worry about."

He didn't look familiar at all, even though he had not just an athletic build, but presence. The kind of presence one saw at state dinners or on a balcony watching troops pass in review. It was the high collar of his double-breasted suit, the way it and the trousers suggested a uniform without being one. You could slap some epaulets on his shoulders, add a name tag or a row of ribbons, perhaps an armband, and it would complete the look. The only thing that worked against him was the shirt. The string tie, a blood-red ribbon of silk, was out of place, almost like he put it there to spoil the look.

Talia gave him an appreciative nod as Bates tilted her foot and gave her a better glimpse at the scuff on her yellow shoe's polished surface. It was about half an inch long with the thickness of a pencil line.

"The driver is waiting, Miss Bates," Talia said, gesturing with her prosthesis. "Your luggage is being transferred to the car. We'll take you to the hotel, see you settled prior to tonight's event."

"Jerod, you simply must come," Bates said, placing a manicured hand on Rhodes's shoulder and placing herself between him and Talia. "I won't take no for an answer."

Bates was mistaking Talia's bodyguard scrutiny of Rhodes for something else. And she probably didn't like the way that Rhodes's attention had latched onto Talia either. More than likely, it was her prosthesis that caught his interest, but that wouldn't matter to someone like Bates.

Talia was used to her kind. Rich and spoiled, the type of woman who thought the world revolved around her because she had married well or been born lucky. Prone to exaggeration. The scuff on her shoe notwithstanding, Talia would bet a week's wages that she'd been the one to run into the "thug" and not the other way around.

"Well, if you insist, Miss Bates." Rhodes sounded like he'd wanted to be convinced. And that smile of his, bright and full, like a shield. It didn't reach the golden green of his eyes. Not at all.

"Karolina," Bates said and there was a little purr on the edges of it, as she batted—actually batted—her eyelashes at him. "I insist you call me Karolina."

"Miss Bates," Talia said, "I'm sorry, but I'm not cleared to allow anyone else t—"

"Cleared?" Her eyebrows rose and those batting eyelashes with them. Her entire demeanor changed. She no longer looked soft and flighty, and the coquettish smile had been replaced by a grimace. "Mr. Rhodes is my guest. I'm clearing him."

Bates threaded her arm through Rhodes's and forged ahead as if Talia didn't exist, and neither did her objections. Rhodes himself gave Talia an apologetic look when Bates couldn't see him do it. The eyelid underneath the scars might even have tried to produce a wink.

They exited the VIP section and emerged onto the public concourse. New arrivals milled about, looking lost. A handful of children were running around the display kiosks playing hide-and-seek as their parents waited for luggage.

One of the kiosks was blaring a reminder that Gōruden was not a party to the Corporate Accords and that while there was no legal penalty for repairing one's own property, doing so was still dangerous, possibly life-threatening. That last was delivered on a dire note by a stern-looking safety-first type in a lab coat. That particular actor, or bureaucrat assuming it wasn't an actor, had always reminded her of a murdering megalomaniac, the type who'd conduct surgery without anesthetic or declare himself the embodiment of science.

In direct opposition, the next kiosk was an advertisement for workshops of all kinds—"Learn to mend your own clothes, prepare your own food, program your own machines. Embrace a life free of government and corporate meddling."

A young woman wearing poorly fitting clothes that looked like pajamas or perhaps a prison uniform, was standing in front of that kiosk, mesmerized. She reached out and snatched a passing man wearing the same type of clothing by the wrist, pulled him to a stop.

"Look, dear. Can you believe it?"

His face fell, and he went white as a sheet at the rolling footage of a dead duck being dressed for cooking.

The next video in the queue was the one about Gōruden's

infamous cyanide "bugs." Well, not bugs exactly, nor worms. Whatever they were, she had yet to run across them.

Talia followed her chattering client and her client's willing victim down the concourse, into the elevator, and out to the curb. A few thousand cars weren't a lot for an entire planet, but ninety-eight percent of them were in Sakura. It was the only place where the roads were built for them, where the right fuel was manufactured in large enough quantities to make them practical.

It was also the only place on Gōruden that had the benefit of cellphone towers. A satellite in geostationary orbit serviced the needs of the entire planet. No wonder Sakura's denizens considered themselves the center of the world—in essence they were.

Bates and Rhodes chatted, making idle conversation as they waited by the curb. Bates didn't seem to mind the delay at all, and if she was happy, well, it made Talia's job easier. Talia pulled out her cellphone and let Elliott, her boss, know that the client had insisted on an addition. He texted back a few minutes later as Rhodes opened the car door for Bates. It was a brief message: Rhodes was cleared to ride to the hotel.

Talia sat up front with the driver, keeping a close eye on the rearview mirror. The privacy barrier was up, a smoky pane of glass that still allowed her to see what was happening in the passenger seats. Bates hadn't activated the opacity filter. Maybe she wasn't as flighty as Talia had thought.

While Bob the driver negotiated the roads to the hotel—traffic was light compared to Earth—Talia requested additional information on Jerod Rhodes. She split her attention between the cellphone and rearview mirror, just in case.

The data said that Rhodes was an Olympic fencing champion. He was cleared to travel with his foils, all of which had been certified as safe. Talia snorted.

"What's so funny?" Bob asked, his gaze still on the road.

"The lies we tell each other."

Bob gave her a sideways look before turning his attention back to the road.

It didn't matter on Gōruden, at least not once one got away from Sakura, but it wouldn't take much to turn any blunted foil into a sharp one. Simon York's katana had probably made it here the same way, in an unsharpened state that was soon remedied.

She wondered what Maeve had done with it. If it was still

under her bed or if she'd found someone to sell it to. And Lyle. Had he worked up the nerve to tell Maeve how he felt about her? How much closer were the Haricots to their breakthrough? Was Contesti still trying to steal their secrets?

She shook away the intruding memories. Turned back to the cellphone. Looked up Tsurui. Found the same data as before—location, estimated population, and not much else. A search for the Haricots yielded some sparse data on their corporate filings, the date of Caleb Haricot's death, and an old picture of Dame Leigh.

No mention of Elias's death.

Damn. She hadn't thought of him in days.

CHAPTER TWELVE

TALIA TOOK HER POST OUTSIDE OF BATES'S SUITE THAT EVENING. At least Elliott hadn't made her wear a dress this time, just a better version of a black pantsuit.

There'd been no compromise on the gun though. Her heirloom 1911 was in a safe. SEP had recently decided to issue them lightweight Earth imports chambered in ten millimeter with integrated laser sights. She'd breathed a sigh of relief that they weren't those idiotic "smart guns" that read fingerprints before firing. Obviously no one had ever had to fire one under duress when the skin sweated, distorting the fingerprints. Although in her case, there were no prints to read. It wasn't a bad gun, except for the double stack. She didn't care for how it compromised her grip. But she hadn't had to use her gun once in the last seven-plus years, so she didn't make a fuss about it.

Bates emerged from her hotel room in a cream-colored silk dress. The bodice clung to her hourglass figure while the mermaid skirt hugged her legs in a way that Talia would have found hobbling. Bates's hair was in an updo held together by jeweled pins. She swept past Talia as if she wasn't even there, stuck her nose up in the air, and sashayed her way down the hall.

Elliott had refused Bates's request to replace Talia. He'd probably told her that he had no one else, although it was his unspoken policy not to replace people who'd done their jobs just because of a client's whim. Not unless that client was one he didn't want to lose under any circumstances. Apparently, Bates didn't warrant that status.

Instead, Talia had gotten a discreet message to keep her distance. Another guard had been assigned and would stay closer. She recognized him as soon as she walked into the foyer. Charles was dressed in a tuxedo and fit right in with the guests. He would, no doubt, charm Bates and she would think nothing of how close he hovered and assume he was like her, one of the rich and powerful, not a peon assigned to keep her safe.

It wouldn't be the first or last time that Talia and Charles had had to play good guard, bad guard.

The night's event was a get-together, an opportunity for the higher-ups of some investment conglomerate to socialize. A dinner was also planned, but by then Talia would be gone. Another guard, a new woman named Phillipa, was supposed to relieve her at the end of her shift.

About a dozen tables had been set up within the ballroom, each one featuring a scale model for the conglomerate's plan for Gōruden. Mostly they consisted of cities, of their vision for the future—bridges, roads, resorts. A hospital and university were also part of the improvements, as well as satellites and shipyards.

Talia adjusted her ear-mic. The damned thing always itched, no matter what she did.

"Having a good time?" She recognized the voice on the other side. The new woman, Phillipa.

"Charles certainly is," Talia subvocalized.

Talia listened to the guests congratulating each other on their vision, of bringing Gōruden out of the Dark Ages. She swallowed a laugh.

"Do these people have any notion of what the actual Dark Ages were like?" That voice she didn't recognize. One of the other guards, male.

"Not a clue," Talia said as she skirted the edges of the ballroom, her gaze sweeping the crowd, occasionally meeting those of her counterparts.

Waiters threaded their way through the crowd, bearing trays of sparkling champagne and layered finger foods made into the shape of company logos—shields and stars and banners of all kinds. Some even had flags or had been sprinkled with edible gold.

Rhodes walked into the ballroom, wearing a tuxedo with

embroidery flowing down the shoulders. Bates let out a shriek that ended in his name. The shrillness of her voice drew all heads as he bowed over her hand and kissed it.

"Well, I'm deaf," someone said over the earpiece. Suppressed chuckles followed.

"Cut the chatter." Elliott.

"Sorry, sir," echoed over the network, and it went quiet and stayed that way.

The guests had been taking turns introducing themselves by stepping up on a small stage and taking the mic, a handheld model that most of them seemed to think required tapping to activate.

A whale of a man—with a mop of red, greasy, slicked-back hair and a shawl draping his shoulders—stepped up on the stage, making it creak. Like the others, he did the obligatory tap, causing the speakers to make that grating feedback noise that set everyone's teeth on edge.

His voice boomed as he went through a rather extended introduction in Russian. At first, everyone seemed to ignore him, but as we went on, self-aggrandizing tone rising, he brought the room to a hush.

"Cut the shit, Yuri Khvastinov," a man with an ambassador's sash said. "No one here speaks Russian. You speak English just like the rest of us. Absolutely no one is impressed."

Laughter followed. Khvastinov turned beet red and sputtered as the mic was taken away from him.

"Good God, just how small do you suppose it is in order to need that level of constant validation?" the woman standing in front of Talia asked. She'd introduced herself as the head of some think tank just ten minutes before.

Talia pressed her lips together so that she wouldn't make a quip.

"I doubt he's seen it in ages," another woman whispered. "Truly, think about it."

Talia did not want to think about it.

"Arrogant ass," a man behind her grumbled just loud enough to be overheard but not necessarily draw attention to himself.

Moments later, Rhodes had somehow escaped Bates's attentions and was making his way toward Talia, champagne flute in hand. The fake smile he'd been wearing for Bates was gone. Instead it had been replaced by one meant to impress.

He was going to be so disappointed when he found out that she was not impressed, not by lean height and dark hair, not by lofty ambition nor devouring dreams.

"Good evening, Ms. Merritt," he said. "I'd offer you a drink, but I know you're on duty."

"I appreciate that, Mr. Rhodes." She kept her gaze on the crowd as they went through additional introductions.

"I would like a few moments of your time this evening. Perhaps after you're off duty."

"We're not allowed to freelance, Mr. Rhodes. It's in the contract. I'm sorry."

Rhodes smile hardened, faded. "Understood."

It wasn't just his tone that was anything but understanding. It was his eyes, the way he stood. A man who didn't hear the word "no" very much; a man who, even when he heard it, didn't have to listen to it; a man who was used to getting what he wanted.

He drifted off, back into the crowd. The light caught the subtle pattern of spidery flowers woven into his jacket's fabric. Spider lilies maybe. An odd choice, it tickled at her mind as he lingered in her peripheral vision for a few moments before he went back to socializing.

"Talia." Elliott's voice was tight over the ear-mic. "I've switched you to a private channel. I need you on the northeast balcony on the third floor. Now."

"On my way." She ducked out of the reception hall and kept to the just-a-guard-walking-the-perimeter pace until she hit the northeast stairwell.

From there she ran up to the third floor, swung the door open and looked down the hallway, expecting to see Elliott in his tux. He wasn't there.

"What's going on, boss?" She crossed the hall to the balcony.

"One of our younger guests went missing," he said.

"Who?"

"Little girl. Birgitta. Mr. Muhonen's grandchild. Found her nanny dead in her room about ten minutes ago."

Nanny. Shit. Nanny meant young. Very young. Damn. *Next time lead with that, Elliott.*

"Shouldn't we call for help?"

"Police have been called. But we have to take care of this ourselves. We can't wait for them."

"What do you need me to do?" Talia asked.

"I'm going to go out in the garden. Security cameras have the kidnapper by the fountain. Little girl seems okay. Mr. Muhonen says he got a death threat but didn't take it seriously. I'm not taking any chances though. I want you to take out the kidnapper."

Out in the center of the garden, a multitiered fountain stood. Backlit curtains of water fell into a pool ringed by a curved metal lip like that of a bowl.

"I have the fountain in view." She drew her gun from behind her right hip. "Don't see anyone."

"I'm going to draw him out. Bring him to you."

"Elliott, what are you doing?" She had a sinking feeling. Elliott was far too level-headed to play the hero in any scenario. Or so she'd thought.

"I'm going to distract him. Offer myself in exchange. As soon as you have a shot, take it."

"Take it, as in kill him?" Really, there was no other choice. Either he was enough of a threat to warrant being made dead, or he wasn't. It was a binary answer. There was no middle ground, no shooting to wound, no absurd idea that such a thing was even plausible.

"You're my best shooter. You're the only one who can do it."

Oh, I doubt that.

She really did.

Before she could object, Elliott stepped out from the shelter of the trees, a big man in a tux cut loose on his large frame so that he could carry without scaring the clients. He shrugged out of the jacket and shoulder holster, placed them both on a stone bench. Looked up at her.

She nodded.

He loosened his tie, ran his hands through his thinning hair. She heard the trickle of the fountain and the soft voice of a child giggling.

"You have my back, right?" He didn't wait for her to answer, but stepped forward, arms raised.

"Don't shoot. I'm unarmed," Elliott said, loud this time, no longer subvocalizing.

"I need a target, Elliott. Still not seeing one."

Birgitta—who looked about six, with long, blonde hair down to her waist—came around the curve of the fountain. She was wearing a nightgown and was barefoot, stopping every two or three steps to dip a toe into the water.

"I see the little girl. Where's the kidnapper?"

Elliott continued moving slowly to his right, away from her, keeping the fountain between himself and what?

And then *he* came into view.

The kidnapper—a teenager by the look of him—was dressed like a waiter. He was holding the gun at his side like it was something he had picked up and forgot to put back down. He was looking right at Elliott.

Talia raised her gun, thumbed the safety, and brought it to bear. Compared to a rifle, a pistol was so unforgiving. The tiniest movement could throw it off, even an easy shot—a close shot—like this one. She'd much prefer the accuracy and precision of a long bore—as long as possible. The ballistics were better too.

Hands raised, Elliott was making his way around the fountain, holding the kidnapper's attention. Birgitta pivoted on one foot, nightgown swirling, and tiptoed back toward the kidnapper. She seemed oblivious to any danger, still giving out a giggle on occasion as she dipped her toe in the water.

"Fishies like my toes," she said. Another dip. Another giggle.

"I didn't kill that woman," the kidnapper said. His voice had a slur to it, like someone who might be drunk. He stood like one too, not quite right.

"No one said you did," Elliott said. "We just need you to let the girl go. Birgitta, honey, your grandpa is asking for you."

Birgitta looked up. "But I wanna play with the fishies."

She craned her neck around to look at the kidnapper. "Are we still going swimming?"

Elliott cleared his throat.

It was a prompt. It was an order.

Talia's sights were on the kidnapper's center of mass, but he was presenting his side to her. The bullet would have to go through his arm to hit his heart. She centered the sights on his head, kept her fingertip atop the trigger, but didn't actually touch it. Once she did, the laser sight would come on, give her away. Perhaps catch his peripheral vision, make him move.

The details of his head—how dark his hair was, how smooth his skin was—blurred in her vision, along with everything else. Birgitta faded. Elliott faded. The garden melted away. It was just her and her target, a silhouette of a head. Her and the sights. Her and the finger resting ever so gently on the trigger.

Her phantom and her prosthesis were as one, fused, perfectly aligned.

Elliott was offering himself in exchange. Being refused. The kidnapper's voice no longer calm, but rising with anger. Birgitta's soft voice turning into a scream.

The phantom spasmed, recentered, realigned.

The sights followed the target.

Talia's breath stilled in her lungs, not an inhale nor an exhale, but simply a ceasing of movement.

There was a part of her that knew only the sights, only the gun. There was another part that seemed to watch from outside of those two things. It saw the moment when the kidnapper decided to move, the intent betrayed by a slight shift in posture, a shift of his center of mass, a twitch of the hand as it moved ever so slightly upward.

Bang.

The bullet leapt from the barrel—a surprise.

The push of recoil, traveling up her prosthesis and into her phantom at the same time, an odd duality. The slide moving. The scent of gunpowder. The sights, the gun, her arm, her phantom, they all followed the target. It exploded in a bloom of crimson, as momentum from the bullet pushed the silhouette away from her.

A scream.

A curse.

A ringing in her ears.

She was running down the balcony steps, gun thrust out in front of her. Birgitta was in Elliott's arms, her head tucked into his chest.

Elliott's eyes were wide with shock.

Talia pointed her gun at the corpse. It had dropped the gun.

Within her, something long dormant stirred, woke, assessed.

Nice. Very nice. See, we had nothing to worry about.

CHAPTER THIRTEEN

TALIA SAT BESIDE THE FOUNTAIN, SIPPING A HOT CUP OF CHAMOMILE tea. Someone had brought her the tea, put it in her hand.

As she set down the white china cup with its tasteful swirls etched into it, there was a slight tremor. Hard to tell if it was the damage to the implant or not. She'd not shot anyone since getting her prosthesis. Almost a decade now. A record.

Talia wrapped the fingers of her left hand around the prosthesis, using the thumb to massage the inside of the palm, the rest to massage the top. She'd always had tremors after it was all over. After was good. She'd always been like this—calm during, trembling after. *That* had not changed.

Yet, somehow, it felt . . . different.

Slowly, the tremors worked themselves out of her phantom. She picked up and turned the spent ten-millimeter cartridge over and over. Old habits die hard, and a sniper picked up her brass. No longer warm, it still smelled of powder, defeating the softer scent of tea, defeating even the stronger scent of blood.

Elliott had ordered everyone out of the garden. Someone had thrown a sheet over the corpse. The dark spot atop it gave it away though. Dark center, the fibers soaked, fringed by rings of lesser red, surrounded by splatters. There was a sick sort of symmetry to it.

She flexed her hands. The phantom seemed off once again, yet she'd made the shot. Maybe Frowst was wrong. Or the degradation wasn't going to matter. It was so tempting, wanting to believe that.

She rolled the cartridge back and forth between thumb and forefinger, like it was a fidget toy. Back and forth. Over and over again.

Up on the balcony, Rhodes and Elliott were talking, their unintelligible words drifting on the thick, blood-scented air. Rhodes must have said something to convince Elliott to let him through. Charmer that one, no doubt about it. He made his way down the steps and came to sit beside her.

"Your reputation precedes you, Ms. Merritt."

She took a sip of the tea.

"I'd like to hire you for a job," he continued.

"Elliott doesn't allow us to freelance," she said. Back and forth the cooling metal went. "Surely he told you that. It's in our contracts. Conflict of interest."

He smiled. "Yes, but I'm not talking about a side job. I'm talking about something outside of Sakura. Not a conflict of interest."

"Not much call for a bodyguard outside Sakura," she said. "And you don't look like the kind of man who wants or needs one."

"Territorial dispute on the islands. Could use someone like you. Someone with experience."

"Someone who can kill." That's what he really meant. The indentation made by the firing pin was a little imperfection in the primer, like a pimple on a teenager's face. A face like the kidnapper's.

Don't. It does no good. Old or young, it doesn't matter.

"Rumor is you have three hundred verified kills."

"Three hundred and one as of tonight." Back and forth the cartridge went, sparkling in the light. She downed the rest of the tea, wishing it was something stronger.

"I just watched the security cam's recording. Excellent shot, by the way. He was going to kill that little girl."

"Was he?"

"That's the way I saw it. The way the police are going to see it too, assuming they ever get here. You saved a little girl's life today. I can tell that's important to you. Saw it in your face. How would you like to be part of something that's going to make life better for everyone on Gōruden? Make it better for all the children here? And for their children too. You could be part of that."

Do it for the children. What a familiar crock of shit that was.

"Sounds too good to be true," she deadpanned.

"Not this time."

"People like me aren't usually called on to build things. What exactly are you offering me, Mr. Rhodes?" The tip of her little finger could fit right inside that empty cartridge.

"Jerod. Please call me Jerod. I have a contract to bring armed security forces to one of the southern islands. My client is in dispute with a rival over the best way to move the territory forward. If he wins, it'll make it possible for us to bring all sorts of things to Gōruden. Technology. Medicine. Education. It's the lack of such things that's keeping young families from settling out there. Young families with young children just like that little girl."

"That little girl doesn't have to worry about any of those things, Jerod." She gave him a smile full of irony. The bastard was using pretty words and empty promises to tug on her emotions. She slipped the cartridge into her pocket.

He smiled. "Very true, Talia. May I call you Talia? But one of my employer's goals is to turn a wasteland into, well, a nice, safe place like Sakura. He wants to turn a frontier into a paradise."

Rhodes made a gesture, his sleeve exposing his wrist as he did so, flashing a patch of red, like tattooed blood drops. Undoubtedly, the gesture was meant to convey that their current surroundings constituted that very paradise, ignoring that it wasn't safe or they wouldn't have been having this conversation at all.

She scoffed.

A wasteland? Had he not seen the beauty and splendor she had when the ship had broken atmosphere? Who had he been talking to? Or did he really buy into what he was selling?

"The contract is for five years. A million credits. Enough to make you rich."

A million credits. That was enough to buy her ten implants. Maybe she should do just that. Buy them in bulk.

"That's a lot of money, Jerod. Not usually the kind of thing that comes with purely noble intentions. What's the catch?"

"No catch."

She pushed up from the stone bench.

He put his hand on her wrist, like it didn't matter that it wasn't flesh and bone. It was a light touch, nothing she couldn't shake off. Instead she held his gaze.

"No catch, Talia. Just an obstacle. Local law. Someone who fancies himself a sheriff. Pinned a badge on himself and everything.

But it shouldn't be too hard to deal with him. He's a drunk. Unfortunately, the local people can't see him for what he is. They're backing him up. I just need a few good people, like yourself, to deal with him. Show the locals what he's keeping from them."

"Where?" Her gut knew the answer. Knew it and still needed to hear it.

"Island of Tatarka. Town's name is, I believe, Tsurui."

She winced.

"Sheriff's name Monroe by any chance?" There was always a chance that someone else was sheriff now. Or that he was lying, enticing her into an easy job. She knew Lyle. Knew him well enough to know that he would never take to drinking.

"Yes." A frown. "How did you know?"

"Because your boss—a Signore Contesti, isn't it?—he tried to hire me a few months back. He gave me a different story though. Thing is he didn't quite tell me everything. His price has gone up quite a bit too, and apparently he didn't tell you everything either."

Rhodes made a face like he didn't quite believe her but let go of her arm.

"And what would that be?"

"That Contesti has moved in with a lot of off-world money. That he's used, shall we say, questionable tactics, to intimidate the locals, that he's tried to steal terraforming secrets."

He gave her a bland look.

"You don't seem too surprised, Jerod. Or perhaps you don't care. Mercenaries—true mercenaries—usually don't. I think you've mistaken me for one of your kind."

"Semantics. No one threads a needle like you do without feeling some bit of satisfaction, of pleasu—"

With her left hand, she belted him in the mouth. He landed with a thud and rolled over, his lip split. For a moment she thought he was going to get up and fight. He wiped at the blood with the back of his hand, looked at it as if it surprised him and laughed.

Elliott came running down the steps.

"Something wrong here, Talia?"

Rhodes pushed up from the dirt, dusted himself off.

"Nothing to worry about, Mr. Elliott. Death's Handmaiden was just showing me some"—he worked his jaw from side to side—"professional courtesy."

CHAPTER FOURTEEN

"Are you insane?" Elliott asked as he shut the door to his office behind them.

No one had called her Death's Handmaiden in . . . well, in a very long time.

"No, not insane. Just a little mad."

Elliott's hotel office consisted of a desk and two chairs shoved into a tiny, windowless room that had probably been meant to be a closet. It was the place he took people when he needed to talk to them in private.

"I always knew you had a temper," he said, tugging the already loosened bowtie off. He'd redonned his shoulder holster but not his jacket. "Could see it in your eyes. But you never acted on it before. Why now?"

Why indeed?

It wasn't like she'd never shot someone that young before. It wasn't that she had doubts about the need for it. The kidnapper had been holding a gun. He'd already used it to kill the nanny.

Talia sank into the chair that Elliott pulled out for her. He reached down and tugged on a drawer. It made a squeaking sound. He brought up a bottle of scotch, took a swig, passed it to her.

The amber liquid burned its way down her throat, almost made her cough. It'd been a long time since she'd had anything like it.

So, this is where he keeps the good stuff.

"The little girl," Talia said. "Something is bothering me about Birgitta. She didn't seem afraid."

Elliott settled back in his chair. His big shoulders rubbed up against the worn fabric, reminding her of a bear scratching an itch.

"She's not all there," Elliott said. "Never was. Not something that her grandfather makes widely known."

"Is that why you didn't call the cops?" It was a guess. She wasn't sure that he'd lied to her about that. But not even Sakura's cops took this long to answer a call from this kind of hotel.

He had the grace to look sheepish. "I did call them, I just did it after. They just entered the grounds. I'm sure they'll want to talk to you after they've looked at the surveillance footage. It's just a formality. Dotting I's and crossing T—"

"Why? Why did you wait?"

"Because I knew that you'd take care of it before they got here. Because I don't like it when they get involved. They're sloppy."

"And you're stroking my ego." Or trying to. He probably thought he had her figured out. Poor man.

Even I don't have me figured out.

"Careful, Talia," he said. "You're wearing your heart on your sleeve again."

He told her that at least once a month. Apparently, her resting bitch face wasn't as good as she believed it to be. Hard to tell without constantly looking into a mirror.

The bottle passed between them. She gave it an idle turn, admiring the way the amber liquid lazed around the interior.

A nice warm buzz was forming from the burn at the back of her throat. It spread out, reaching all the way to her fingertips. Even the phantom joined in, and she made a very unladylike snort.

Elliott raised his brow at it.

There was a knock at the door. It opened without invitation.

Rhodes stepped through, a grin on his face. The fresh cut on his lip seemed to balance out the older scar, the one pulling his mouth into a perpetual near-sneer. He looked immaculate, from the top of his coiffed head to the tips of his mirror-shine shoes. The cleft in his chin gave him just the right amount of roguishness that women tended to find appealing.

Other women. Not me.

Elliott was halfway up in his seat. "Mr. Rhodes, I'm sorry, but could you come back later?"

Rhodes shut the door behind him.

"I'm not here for you, Elliott. I'm here to talk to her."

Elliott gave her a sideways glance. She shrugged. Now or later, Rhodes was going to insist on talking to her again. Might as well do it now while she had a witness. That way her temper was less likely to flare. It was bound to.

Men like Rhodes tended to bring out her... color.

Rhodes wouldn't be the first one to make the mistake of stroking her ego to find out how she really felt about mercenaries. So many automatically assumed that her willingness to do the honest work that Elliott offered her somehow translated to a willingness to do anything if enough money was involved. And it was tempting, sometimes.

Reluctantly, Elliott lowered himself back into the seat, a slow smile pulling at the edges of his mouth. Maybe he did know her a little bit. Seven years she'd worked for him. Yeah, he knew her a bit.

"May I?" Rhodes indicated the bottle.

"Be my guest," Elliott said.

Rhodes winced as his busted lip touched the rim.

He offered her the bottle back. She shook her head. Her throat was still burning from the last shot.

"I'm still very much interested in acquiring your contract, Ms. Merritt. And I'm willing to negotiate a release of her indenture with you, Mr. Elliott. I'm prepared to pay it off and add a bonus to it as well. A finder's fee as it were."

"She cleared her indenture more than seven months ago, Mr. Rhodes. Who told you otherwise?"

"Oh?" He looked like a man who hadn't even considered that possibility.

"It hardly matters then does it." Rhodes rubbed at his brow. "Ms. Merritt, what would convince you to come work for me?"

"An act of God," she said. It wasn't the liquor. She hadn't had enough for that kind of courage.

"I apologize for my inconsiderate words earlier," he continued, smooth as silk. "I didn't mean to imply that you enjoyed killing people."

"Sure you did. You're just sorry that I don't."

He placed both hands on the edge of Elliott's desk and leaned forward. Somehow he managed to make it look casual rather than aggressive.

"That's precisely the kind of attitude I need. Someone with integrity. You seem to have it in spades. Everyone says so."

She reached for the bottle. She was going to need fortifications for this kind of "charm." Rhodes was clearly a manipulator. The kind that enjoyed a challenge. And her refusal was making her an irresistible mark.

Great.

Maybe Death's Handmaiden sounded too cuddly after all, 'cause he sure seemed to think he could appeal to her soft side. First with the "it's for the children" argument. Now with "integrity." What was next? Honor? Maybe she could play up her Japanese ancestry. See if he'd go all bushido on her.

Perhaps being punched hadn't been enough to convince him that she had not inherited her Japanese ancestors' dislike for direct confrontation.

Elliott pushed the bottle her way, a smirk on his face. *Don't smile too much. I'm not quite done with you, boss.* She still wanted to know why he'd lied to her about calling the police. She wasn't buying his "you're the best" routine either. Not even close.

"Well, Ms. Merritt," Rhodes said, straightening. The way he looked down at her. He liked it. Liked it a lot, that looking down.

She had another drink, set the bottle down.

"Mr. Rhodes, information being what it is out here"—she imitated the careless wave he'd used earlier in the garden—"I can forgive your outdated information. I am not interested, nor is there any amount of money that will make me interested, because I won't go up against Lyle. I told Signore Contesti the same exact thing."

"You're afraid of him." He said it like he didn't quite believe it.

She frowned. Looked over at Elliott. "Why is it that men always assume I'm afraid?"

Elliott made an exaggerated shrug and helped himself to more scotch. "Better than thinking you're screwing him, I guess."

She rolled her eyes.

"Are you?" Rhodes asked, his curiosity clearly piqued.

She counted backward from five.

"No. Never have. Never will."

"Well, if it's not fear and it's not sex, then what is it? For my own satisfaction, Ms. Merritt. I promise, if you give me an honest answer, I will not bring the matter up again."

"We served together. He saved my life. And I know him well enough to know that whomever told you that you were going up against a drunk, lied."

Understanding. A hint of envy. Then nothing. He really did have an expressive face when he let it show.

"I understand, Ms. Merritt. Thank you for being so candid. I will take my leave now, as promised."

He opened the door, hesitated in the threshold, and leaned back in, almost like he'd had an afterthought.

"I am going to go up against him, Ms. Merritt. Drunk or no, I'm going to take him down. Shall I give him your regards?"

There was light in his eyes, the kind that she would delight in putting out. *He* was very much a needle in need of threading.

In her dreams, she always had both her hands, even the ones that took place in the present.

At some point, one of the shrinks had told Talia that she wouldn't have full acceptance of what had happened to her until she dreamt of herself as an amputee, until her prosthesis was part of her dreams. The same shrink had less to say when Talia had told her that she had dreams where her entire body had been replaced, one piece at a time.

That's how Talia knew that she was dreaming. She still had both of her hands. There was enough dirt under her fingernails that it would take weeks of baths to get it all out, to get them to the point where she might consider something as frivolous as going in for a manicure. At least one that didn't send the manicurist into sputtering fits.

Time flowed differently in dreams too, even when she was conscious of it twisting in on itself, like it was doing now as the familiar dream flickered behind her eyelids, trapping her in its depths like she was a genie in a bottle.

She and Lyle had been doing what snipers usually did—protecting friendly troops. And they'd been doing it using Barretts because they had access to a large stash of the right ammunition.

Talia liked the M82's ten-round magazines and its low recoil. A fall had damaged Bunny's—her rifle's—scope, forcing Talia to use the flip-up iron sight.

"There, there," she told Bunny, "we'll get you all fixed up soon."

"Girls," Lyle said, dismissing the comment with a laugh, like he didn't talk to his M95. He may not have named it, but she'd heard him whisper to it when he was about to take a shot, especially a long-distance one. He'd whisper encouragingly to it.

Things like "If we make this shot, we can go home," and "Don't fail me now, girl. Don't let that full-figured gal show you up."

The full-figured gal being Bunny of course. She was heavier, and that was one of the reasons Talia liked her. Even if it wasn't always the most pleasant rifle to lug around, it was the shot that counted. And her scores were better with the full-figured girls. Marginally better, but still.

Better was better.

They were in a no-man's-land between lines that shifted far too often. Lines that the people on the ground ignored because rules were written by people behind desks who didn't understand how things really worked and never would. Both of them had failed to claim kills because they would have prompted too many questions about coordinates and positions. All that mattered was the knowledge that that shot, the one they were not supposed to take because of some idiot's concept of engagement, saved the right lives. And the lives they saved knew it too.

That's how the thing about needles had started. Someone had brought her a needle threaded with a bit of string and stuck into a piece of cloth that turned out to be a name strip off an enemy uniform. It had even had blood stains on it. An unofficial kill.

There had been a note with it, torn and dirty, also splattered with blood. It had said, "You saved my life today. Thank you."

She'd saved the note, folded it over the needle and thread and carried it as a memento in her pocket for months, until she'd lost the jacket. Sometimes, when she doubted herself and what she was doing, she'd think of that note, of what it meant, feel it in her hands and know that she had to keep saving lives. Saved lives should have been the count everyone was keeping, but that number wasn't as clear, as solid, as well defined.

Her dream-self reached into that pocket now, found the note and the needle. It pricked her, drawing blood from her forefinger, her trigger finger.

Note forgotten, she looked down at her finger, at the welling bead of blood on it, and smiled. She used the edge of her thumb to push up against the inner surface so that the blood bead would swell and shimmer and she could feel it, really feel the throb, the ache that told her that she was whole.

Time flickered once again, thrusting her forward. Lyle was gone. He'd crawled off to his position. They were waiting for the light to shift so that the sun would reflect off Lyle's scope. A deliberate move designed to give him away, to make him an irresistible target.

She'd objected. Even though it was his turn to play decoy.

"We need to draw him out," Lyle said, his determined face both smudged yet far too clean against the dreamscape of broken girders and piles of rubble and bodies. "Then you can pick him off when he exposes himself. It's the only way."

"We'll figure something else out." Her own voice echoing.

"We don't have time."

"What if I miss?"

CHAPTER FIFTEEN

DESPITE THE NIGHTMARE, TALIA WOKE LATE AND WITH A SOLID hangover as company. She remembered finishing off the bottle. Elliott escorting her to her room. Helping her onto the bed.

"You did good," he'd said just before he closed the door.

As hangovers went, it wasn't that bad. She'd take both a hangover and a nightmare over darker things.

She took a shower, turning the water as hot as she could bear it. As she toweled her hair dry, she leaned into the mirror and wiped at the condensation.

Talia took a long look at herself. The dark eyes with a hint of Asia in them, the high cheekbones. Same as the day before and the day before that. No haunted look, no ghosts on her shoulders.

Her reflection stared back, broken only by tiny beads of water streaming together to drift down.

"We count lives saved."

How many would that boy have taken? Birgitta, Elliott, himself.

You.

If he'd gotten past her, he could have killed more. Many more. Maybe.

Damn Rhodes.

She'd come here to get away from her past, from her reputation. *Sobo* used to say that you can never escape your own shadow. But it had sure looked like she'd had. At least for a while.

How had Rhodes recognized her anyway?

Your reputation precedes you, Ms. Merritt.

Elliott knew the details of her past, but the rest, her being a sniper, that was information that no one else at SEP knew. Yes, they knew her as a good shot, but not as Death's Handmaiden, not as a woman with three hundred confirmed kills.

Drunk or no, I'm going to take him down. Shall I give him your regards?

"Like hell you are, Rhodes. Whoever you are."

She downed two cups of coffee as she dressed for the day, opting for the salmon shirt, a set of navy pull-on pants, and a matching jacket. She pulled up the duty roster on her cellphone. Vaguely, she remembered Elliott telling her to take the day off as he'd helped her to her room. Indeed, he hadn't scheduled her. She brushed out her still-damp hair. She missed being able to braid it and swirl it into a bun. But no matter what she did, strands of it caught in her prosthesis.

Well, it wasn't a duty day. She left it loose and took the stairs down to the sublevel where the hotel's mail room was hidden. She greeted a housekeeper rolling a cleaning cart past her and dodged around another cart full of fresh, clean laundry.

There was a sign on the mail-room door that said, "Back in 10 minutes."

She just needed to make sure that Lyle was all right. To warn him about Rhodes. It was probably a good thing that she couldn't just outright call him. She could hear that conversation right now:

Hey, I called to make sure you didn't all of a sudden take up drinking for no reason. Rumors you know. I have a tendency to believe them even when I know I shouldn't because I know you, and you'd never, but I need to hear it, okay. It's because I had a bad dream. One I haven't had in a while. I'm sure it's actually tied to me killing a kid.

Yes, he needed killing. I saved a little girl, but you know...

Anyway, you're not a drunk. And hey, while we're at it, there's this Rhodes character that took the job that Contesti offered me, and he is most definitely coming after you. It sounds kinda personal, which, to be honest, is freaking me out.

No, I have no idea who he is. Some fancy pants with an épée or a foil, you know the kind, the ones with fencing medals. I don't know if he's the real thing or one of those who thinks combat is like a movie or a video game where people level up by taking the powers of those they defeat in battle.

So maybe this is a warning, and not because I don't think you can take care of yourself, because I know you can, but anyway, how is Maeve? You tell her you love her yet?

Anyway, if you need me, I'm here.

I can be there in God knows how many weeks, even though I can't possibly afford to come to Tsurui, and by the way, have I mentioned that I need a new neural implant, mine may fail at any time, like when I'm there to watch your back, so I may just end up getting in the way.

It'll be just like old times.

She groaned. Oh yes, that was going to be a lovely conversation. She sounded like an idiot.

The ten minutes ticked by. Whomever was on duty must've decided to take an early lunch or gotten called away. She was about to grab another cup of coffee when she finally heard squeaks and footsteps coming down the hall.

An empty mail cart was making its way toward her, pushed by a young woman with short, black hair cut into a bob. A brass nameplate on a black blouse named her "Sara." She tucked her skirt against her knees as she slipped by the cart and shoved a keycard in the wall receptacle.

Twice it beeped red. She took it out, flipped it around, wiggled it. Red again.

"Come on, you stupid thing."

She repeated the procedure and it turned green. The latch clicked open and lights came on. Shelves lined the mail room walls, crowding in all around them. The musty smell begged for ventilation.

"Let me hold it open for you." Talia kept the door propped open while Sara pushed the cart in.

"Thank you. Can I help you?"

"Talia Merritt. Sakura Executive Protection. We contract out for the hote—"

"Bodyguard. Gotcha." Sara ducked behind the counter.

The space behind her was crowded with all sorts of machines—a computer, printers of all kinds, fax machines, and a landline.

"How can I help you?"

"How does one send a message to the islands?" Talia asked. "Or better yet, make a call?"

"That depends. Which island? Which city or town?"

"Tsurui," Talia said.

"Is that a city or an island?"

"A town, actually. Technically, more like a village. On the island of Tatarka."

Sara's left eyebrow shot up. "No, no calls. That's carrier-pigeon territory."

"Surely not."

A smile. "Not quite. Are you looking to send a physical message, like a letter, or something like a telegraph."

"That's it? Those are my choices?"

"Afraid so."

"It's important," Talia said.

"Telegraph then. We'll send it out as far as the island via radio, then it'll be relayed by wire."

"How long before I can expect an answer?"

"The message itself should be there by nightfall. To the post office in Tsurui that is. How often does the recipient come into town."

"Probably daily."

"Then it's possible to have an answer by tomorrow. Unless the lines are down or it's someone who doesn't want to be found. Do you want notice of delivery?"

"Yes. How much?"

Sara quoted a fee that made Talia wince.

She wrote out the message five times before settling on "Credible threat named Rhodes hired by Contesti to take you out. The price has gone up. Be careful." Yes, short, and specific.

The landline rang. Sara picked it up.

"Yes, she's here."

Talia looked up.

"It's for you." Sara handed her the receiver.

"I know that you're not on duty," Elliott said, "but Muhonen wants to thank you personally."

"No need," Talia said. She reached into her pocket, pulled out the cellphone. It flashed a "no reception" warning at her. But there were security cameras. She tended to forget about them, even though she shouldn't have.

"It's not the kind of invitation one refuses," Elliott said.

"Fine. Where?"

He gave her a room number.

"When?"

"Half an hour. Don't be late."

Tall and thin, with a head full of stark white hair and a trim beard to match, Matthias Muhonen was the epitome of graceful aging, the kind bought with a lot of money.

Lunch was being served in a private dining room, atop a tablecloth, accompanied by real silver cutlery and a waiter with starched gloves.

She sat uncomfortably in the padded chair the waiter pulled out for her. For a moment she saw the teenager she'd shot.

Do you still think that you can save everyone, that it's your job, that it's in your power?

No, Lyle, I can't save everyone.

Teen or six-year-old. Boy or girl. Disturbed young man or not-quite-all-there child. Life or death. Not her choice. Not really.

Death's Handmaiden wouldn't have cared. She was an instrument. A tool. Just like the prosthesis. Just like the gun.

Except when she wasn't, like when she haunted Talia.

The waiter set a napkin in Talia's lap, poured water into a crystal glass. It started to sweat right away, the beads of moisture pooling and hanging on like little jewels.

He set out a salad in front of each of them. Richer, warmer scents snuck through from a serving cart that held three domed serving dishes and a bucket of ice cradling a bottle that was probably wine.

Muhonen watched her through a pair of rimless glasses. He wore a silk suit that probably cost an entire month's wages, a cravat with a jeweled pin, and a matching pocket square. His cane reminded him of Dame Leigh's. It was a registered weapon, a sword stick, something only the bodyguards supposedly knew about. Not many of their clients carried a weapon.

She felt entirely underdressed for the "audience." She should have gone back to her room to change.

"How is your granddaughter?" she asked. It seemed the right thing to say.

"Fine, thanks to you." He waved the waiter away.

When the door closed behind him, Muhonen cleared his throat.

"I thought you'd want to know a few things about that unfortunate young man," Muhonen said. "Giuseppe Priser. Indentured, along with his family. Survived by a twin brother and his parents. It seems that he's been showing symptoms for weeks, but everyone wrote it off. Apparently, he mistook my Bri for his long-dead sister at least once before, but no one had thought much of it, not even the nanny."

"Symptoms? Symptoms of what?" Talia asked. The salads sat untouched in front of them both.

"Hypnolin addiction. It's a nasty drug. Leads to poor decision making, lack of coordination, slurred speech, loss of memory, confusion. With extended use, also a propensity for compliance with suggestion.

"If he'd been an employee, he'd have been fired," Muhonen continued, shifting to official cadences. "An indenture is not as simple. Technically, it was the contract holder's duty to provide treatment. In this case that means the third party that contracted his services with the hotel. The treatment paperwork has been winding its way through the system."

He took a stab at his salad then, spearing a cherry tomato. He chewed it while watching her.

"The intricacies of Sakura's workings elude me," Talia said. It was the kind of neutral nonsense that people told each other when they didn't really want to discuss things. Not that it was untrue.

"I'm afraid that everyone, from the hotel management to the police, are eager to just sweep it all under the rug. It's bad for business. They want to move on." He took a drink of water.

"How do you do it, Ms. Merritt? How do you move on?"

Ah, there it was.

Probably the most interesting question that people didn't ask her. Kills, yes. How do you feel about it? Do you have nightmares? Guilt? Are you some cold, unfeeling bitch, some inhuman being we should all hide our children from? How do you stand yourself? How do others stand being around you? How do you deal so readily in death?

"I compartmentalize. I'm very good at it. Most of the time."

He blinked. "A very blunt answer. Thank you."

"How *is* your granddaughter?" she asked again. She tipped her fork with a cucumber and swirled it around in the creamy white dressing.

"Thankfully, she doesn't remember it. She thinks it was a bad dream. I intend to encourage that belief."

"Does she ask about the nanny?" The cucumber was a burst of freshness and creamy buttermilk on her tongue.

"Yes. I told her that she had to go away. Can't very well tell her the truth there, and still encourage the belief that it was a bad dream."

"I understand."

She chewed on her salad, unsure of what else to say. She wanted to ask inappropriate questions, like how an indenture had gotten hold of what was still supposedly an off-world drug.

Muhonen finished his salad and reached into his jacket. He pulled out a credit chip. Wafer thin, it was about an inch on each side. The embedded circuitry made it look like a finely etched piece of platinum jewelry.

He set it on the table and slid it her way. "Ten thousand credits."

That little piece of metal was the closest thing to what used to be called "cash" because it was untraceable. Gōruden's tax authorities hated cryptochips but couldn't do anything about them. The powers-that-be had too much invested in freely moving their own wealth around to devote anything but lip service to stopping their use.

"Exactly what is this for, Mr. Muhonen?" There was a brittleness to her voice, one she couldn't help.

His eyes shimmered as he tented his fingers in front of his face. "Bri is the apple of my eye, the one thing in this world that brings me joy. She is a special child. A vulnerable child. But also a blessing. One that I very much want to keep safe. I was hoping to entice you to come work for me. I'm offering you a job as Bri's bodyguard, her protector. I'll double whatever SEP is paying you."

She sat there, unbelieving. Had she misheard? If he truly knew who she was, what she was—

"Do you want more? Is that it? Name your price."

"No, sir."

"Your voice says no, but your eyes—forgive me for the phrase—say yes."

"That's very generous, sir, but forgive me, if I . . . I do not know you. I just learned a very harsh lesson about agreeing to work for people I don't know." Her phantom flexed. "And you don't know me. You don't know who I am."

A wry smile. "Then tell me."

She wanted to tell him her moniker, how she'd earned it, but couldn't.

He pushed the chip toward her.

"Take it. Think it over," he said. "You don't have to answer me now. We'll be here for a couple more days. Perhaps your Mr. Elliott can vouch for me and mine."

He undoubtedly could.

She reached a trembling hand for the cryptochip. The prosthesis always had trouble with things like coins and this was flatter still. It was very light for what it represented—a quicker, easier path to getting her implant.

"I'll talk to Elliott."

"Excellent."

Working for someone like Muhonen, someone with connections, would undoubtedly have its perks.

Dare she?

"There was a man at the function last night. Has a very distinctive scar on his face. Goes by Jerod Rhodes. Do you know him?"

"I don't," he said. "But I do remember him. He was Ms. Bates's guest, as I recall."

"Yes, that's him. I want to know who he really is. And I need the information yesterday."

CHAPTER SIXTEEN

AFTER HER LUNCH WITH MUHONEN, TALIA HAD HER POLICE interview. It took all of fifteen minutes to answer the question of whether or not she had seen Giuseppe Priser as a threat. If she'd feared for Birgitta's life. For Elliott's. They had not asked her if she'd feared for her own.

"Do you feel compromised by this event in any way?"

"No."

"Please seek professional help if that changes."

"Thank you, Inspector. I will."

Boxes were checked.

Forms were signed.

The gun she'd used would be returned tomorrow. She half expected it would come back tied with a nice bow. Maybe a side of chocolates or a flower arrangement.

After the police left, she talked to Elliott. Told him about the job offer. Asked him for information about Muhonen. He wasn't happy, but to his credit, he agreed to "do some digging."

She convinced him to let her go back to work the next day. She'd argued that the last thing she needed was to spend a bunch of time alone with Giuseppe Priser's ghost. She needed the distraction of work. About the unanswered messages she'd sent.

She'd been surprised when there hadn't been one. She'd anticipated at least an acknowledgement. Instead, nothing. Not even a confirmation that it had made it to Tsurui.

Talia checked the duty roster in the breakroom. It was done with black marker on a whiteboard. Lockers lined the other wall. A small kitchen and a gun safe with extra weapons and ammo finished out the room.

Someone had pinned a note to the schedule. It said, *Talia, we're stuck on the tiles. Help.*

She grabbed the unsigned note with a smirk. "Come on guys, you can do this."

They meant the mahjong tiles. They were set up on one of the gaming tables. She had played endless hours of it as a child. It had taught her to see little inconsistencies that had made it easier to spot movement. Her coworkers however, were used to the electronic version that could be prompted for hints.

She found a pair of matching tiles—the only pair of unlocked tiles by the look of it—and stuck the note atop one of them as a hint.

Phillipa Cordage, the newest of the female bodyguards, burst through the breakroom doors, her white blouse sporting a sizable reddish-brown stain. On the large side, with brown hair pulled into a bun, she hadn't been here long, but she'd always done her job cheerfully. Today she looked frustrated and pissed.

"What happened?" Talia asked.

"That Bates woman. She's impossible." She crossed to the sink and turned on the water, soaking a towel with trembling hands.

"She did that?"

"After what happened the other night, she doesn't want waiters in the room. 'Too dangerous.'" She imitated Bates's high-pitched whine of a voice. "So Elliott said to play waiter. I was trained as a cop. I've never been a waiter in my entire life. She zigged. I zagged. I swear she did it on purpose. I'm never going to get these wine stains out. This is my best shirt."

Phillipa looked at the soaked towel in her hand, scrunched up her face, and dropped it into the sink. She unbuttoned the blouse, slipped it off, and ran it under the water.

Better wine than blood.

"There's some hydrogen peroxide in the first-aid kit," Talia said instead. She opened up a couple of the nearest cupboards. "I think there's some vinegar in here too."

The shelves by the sink were full of condiments but not vinegar.

Phillipa poured dish soap and rubbed vigorously at the stain.

"Do you suppose you could head to the Plum Blossom room?" she asked. "They're having some kind of presentation and Bates was on fire about making sure there were plenty of refreshments. She was yelling after me to make sure I sent someone who knew what they were doing as soon as she stopped laughing."

"I'll take care of it." Would Elliott fire her if she somehow stumbled and doused Bates in wine? It would certainly be a test of his post-shooting good graces. It wasn't like she needed to worry about getting fired anymore.

"Thank you," Phillipa said. "I knew you'd understand. Kitchen has refreshments waiting. I'll talk to Elliott. Maybe he can finally draw a line with this client."

"Sure. No problem." Talia reached into her pocket.

Static hissed in her ear as she put her ear-mic in. There was no chatter on the common channel, not unusual given the time of day. The police holding on to the company gun had given her the perfect excuse to carry her 1911 again. She slipped into the wide-cut jacket.

"Derrick is on duty inside," Phillipa added.

Glad to have something to do, Talia headed to the kitchen. They had a tray on a trolley waiting for her. She wheeled it onto the elevator, rode it up to the conference-room level.

When she got to the Plum Blossom room the doors were locked from the inside.

"Derrick, I'm at the doors. They're locked."

"Bates insisted," Derrick said over the wire. "Can you bring it through the service corridor?"

With a resigned sigh, she keyed a code into the door and pushed the trolley down the corridor.

If there was a presentation on, she'd be able to slip into the darkened room, transfer the trays from the trolley to the table, and be gone before anyone noticed her. Bates seemed to have less of an issue with male bodyguards. Had Elliott noticed? Maybe she should bring it to his attention.

Sure enough, the service corridor door was slightly ajar, and the conference room flickered with shadows.

She waited for her eyes to adjust.

The looming shape just inside the service door belonged to a broad-shouldered former army guy named Derrick. A glass eye prevented him from shooting well, but she wouldn't want to go up against him in a fight. He was solid muscle piled atop solid muscle, and an all-around good guy. He helped her with the trays.

"Can I get a five minute bio-break?" he whispered in her ear.

She nodded and slipped in as he slipped out, their bodies scraping past each other. Talia made herself a shadow.

The man giving the presentation looked about twenty, with thick glasses that told her that he was probably not inclined toward physical tweaks or couldn't afford them. He stood behind the hologram being projected downward from the ceiling, controller in one hand. It washed out the dress pants and vest, casting them and him in bluish-gray tones. For some reason, he looked like a kid pretending to be a detective in an old movie. All that was missing was a pipe and a matching cap. He even had a bit of an accent, although she couldn't place it.

His audience of ten sat on two large semicircular couches that bracketed his hologram. Bates herself was perched on the arm of one of them, her back to Talia. A glass of wine dangled from her fingers, and she was turning it back and forth. Her pose reminded Talia of a cat flicking its tail.

Some of the others she recognized from the night before, shakers and movers who wanted to develop Gōruden and bring it out of "the Dark Ages." A few were leaning back, arms spread on the couch backs as if they were staking out territories. Others were leaning forward, intent on the holographic representation of the planet. The three-dimensional image of charts and tables dissolved and reassembled itself into a map of Hondo, the mainland, and the southern islands.

"Why was Hondo not affected by these fungal blooms of yours, Dr. Temonen?" one of the men leaning forward asked. He was just a silhouette to Talia, but she recognized him as one of Bates's business partners. They had exchanged air kisses the night before.

"They're not my blooms," Temonen said, pushing his glasses up his nose. They slid right back down. "But we think that it's most likely because of the latitude."

"And this catastrophic event?" the man next to the first one asked. Him, Talia could not see, positioned as he was.

"A peak in fungal activity that will cover the entire biosphere, wiping out both flora and fauna and all that depend on them, including humans. We need to figure out how to keep these fungal blooms from flaring again or everyone on Gōruden will starve."

Talia was inclined to tune these kinds of presentations out. She was supposed to be working, keeping her eyes and ears on sources of potential danger. And looking too interested in what a client might consider a trade secret wasn't exactly career enhancing either. Looking dumb and bored was better. She'd learned that early.

"That's just a theory, Dr. Temonen," the other woman in the room said. She was the opposite of Bates. Short, round, the kind of person you'd expect to be a schoolteacher or librarian rather than a mogul. The bluish-gray light emphasized her age by lengthening the lines on her face.

"The fossil record clearly shows a correlation between massive die-offs and fungal blooms." The hologram fast-forwarded through what a lay person like Talia would have called seasons, the colors shifting, expanding, then retreating again.

"The cycle repeats at somewhat regular intervals. Each time these organisms bloom, they leave behind dormant spores which then cause a stronger bloom, which then leaves more dormant spores."

Back and forth the images went, running through the cycle, showing an encroaching blanket of blacks and grays wiping out the small dots representing Gōruden's towns and settlements.

Did the Haricots know this? Surely they did.

"Correlation is not causation," someone else said.

"Then why isn't everything dead?" came another objection. "Your model shows the devastation shrinking after it reaches its maximum. How do you account for that?"

Good point, whomever you are. Perhaps it was that simple. Models were, what was it called? Oh yes, garbage in, garbage out.

"We're not sure," Temonen said. "There's some other mechanism that seems to be at work, perhaps coinciding with solar minima."

"You're suggesting that cold weather is responsible for the eradication of these fungal blooms."

"That would make sense, yes," Temonen admitted. "But we don't *know*." There was desperate edge to that last, a break in his voice like that of a boy's voice changing. He wiped his upper lip with a handkerchief he'd plucked from his vest pocket.

Young he might be despite the title, but at least he wasn't pretending that his models were infallible. Talia could respect him for that.

"So," Bates's high-pitched voice rose clearly above the others. "It might be reasonable to say that, if one was to wait for the right point in the cycle, one might be able to come in after one of these solar minima, after the fungal blooms have been killed off, and start over. It would be like a clean slate."

Talia choked back a rude noise. Bates wasn't a flighty, spoiled little rich girl after all. No, she was a cast-iron bitch. Well, one perk of working for Muhonen would be not having to protect people like Bates.

"Yes, Miss Bates, but millions would die," Temonen said. "I'm talking about everyone on Gōruden."

"You're exaggerating," she said. "There's not a million people on Gōruden."

Someone else made a choking sound that turned into a cough. Several of Bates's compatriots turned to look at her, some astounded, some concerned.

"How was this missed in the precolonization surveys?" the rotund man asked.

"This is absurd. Your models are pure theory."

"Yes, but—"

The objections blended together. Temonen carefully folded the handkerchief and put it back in his pocket, a long-suffering look on his face. He waited for their objections to die down and then let the silence linger as he used the controller in his hand to change the hologram. It homed in on Sakura and the surrounding environs, showing them awash in the same deadly grays and blacks.

"Surely not Sakura, not the bigger towns," the dowdy woman said.

"Oh yes, the bigger towns," Temonen said. "Sakura, too, an—"

"We've heard enough."

Talia didn't recognize the voice. Loud and booming, it came from the man sitting by Bates. His back was to Talia as well. Bates's hand rested casually on his shoulder.

The hologram flickered off, leaving Temonen standing there, looking shaken and uncertain. His audience was talking among themselves, arguing back and forth.

Talia couldn't shake the sinking feeling that had settled in her gut. She'd watched too many of these kinds of things, pretending not to hear the clients' plans. Most of them were corporate espionage, often things that were beyond her understanding.

But this.

This was the kind of thing that she could understand, and it twisted her gut, made her subconscious screech like an air raid siren.

Temonen looked like a deer caught in headlights or perhaps a fawn cornered by a pack of wolves. He was trying to answer their questions, but as soon as he opened his mouth, he'd be shouted down or he'd be drowned out by a side argument.

She took a step forward.

Got jerked back.

She snapped her head toward the beefy hand that had landed on her shoulder. Derrick was back.

"What's wrong with your ear-mic?"

She pulled it out of her ear. The little status light said it was on, but she hadn't heard anything from it.

"One of the bigwigs has been asking for you." His gaze flickered up to the people behind her. His face twisted with annoyance. "I'll take care of this. Go."

CHAPTER SEVENTEEN

MUHONEN'S ASSISTANT, A MIDDLE-AGED MAN WHO LOOKED AS IF he'd been born a butler, led Talia into the penthouse suite.

Luggage was stacked in the foyer, ready to be loaded. A large room with an enormous desk bracketed by bookcases, all polished wood and leather, waited. Inside, Muhonen was sitting in a wing chair by the window while Birgitta played at his feet. The afternoon sun lit the room, barely muted by sheer white curtains. The little girl's long, blonde hair was in pigtails, and she was wearing one of those baby-doll dresses made with pink eyelet fabric and edged in lace that spread out around her like a bell.

"Ms. Merritt, sir," the assistant said.

Birgitta made no sign that she was aware that anyone had come into the room. She continued combing her doll's hair, humming at it softly, head tilted slightly to the side.

"Bri," Muhonen said. "Go with Dale, please."

Dale approached Birgitta, bent down, stiff-backed. "Miss Bri, your hand please."

She looked up, smiled, and placed her hand in his, allowing him to help her stand like she was a lady being helped out of a car. She folded the doll into her chest and leaned in to peck Muhonen on the cheek.

Dale escorted her and her doll out.

As soon as the door shut, Muhonen's entire demeanor changed. His smile faded. His face and eyes hardened.

"You sent for me, Mr. Muhonen," Talia said, undeterred.

"Your Mr. Rhodes is corporate nobility." He stood and picked up a folder from a nearby table. "Fallen corporate nobility, but nobility nonetheless. Elliott told me that Rhodes tried to hire you. That you turned him down. Are you reconsidering his offer?"

"And if I was?"

She couldn't help herself. She waited, wanting to see his reaction. She hadn't lied to Rhodes when she'd said that it would take an act of God to get her to work for him or Contesti. And it was still true, her concerns about Lyle and the fact that she still hadn't heard back from him notwithstanding.

"You'd work for . . . for a war criminal? I'm truly disappointed in you, Ms. Merritt."

He thrust the folder at her.

She flipped it open. Rhodes was indeed corporate nobility, the scion of one of the major shareholders in what had once been known as the West Coast of the United States. Now, its own country, one of the seventy-or-so corporate-owned nations that had formed after the balkanization of the North American states, China, India, and Brazil.

Like a lot of the elites, the lines between old world nobility and corporations had been blurred by marriages—political and otherwise. Heads of state and their heirs, corporations that had more power than some countries, political families with long lineages of "public service," they had all come together to rule.

Rhodes was from a wealthy family that had ended up on the wrong side of a proxy war.

She flipped past the records about Rhodes's family and stopped at his school record. Olympic fencer yes, but also much more. Competitive shooter as well. He'd joined the military, earned himself a chest full of medals—the kind you get for combat.

Came home a war hero.

She flipped to the next page. It, and the remaining pages, were nothing but military forms and court records filled with one word: redacted.

Her gaze snapped up to Muhonen's. He was sitting on the edge of a large desk across from her, watching her intently.

"His crimes are hidden, even from me."

"Where did you get this?"

"You don't really expect me to answer that, do you?"

She flipped through the folder again. "Lots of people come here to make a new life for themselves. I'm one of them."

"Funny, your record has no redactions."

His fingers perched atop a much thicker file laying on the desk next to him. If he hadn't known her reputation, her moniker before, he certainly knew it now.

"Why defend him, Ms. Merritt?"

"I'm not." She sank her teeth into her lip. "Just playing devil's advocate."

"Yet you turned him down. With prejudice, according to Mr. Elliott. You're not reconsidering, are you?"

"Elliott talks too much."

"What are you going to do?"

She'd been wrong to dismiss Rhodes as just another mercenary. Now, in the sober light of day, with the information Muhonen had just given her, she couldn't dismiss Rhodes's story about Lyle being a drunk as a ploy, part of his recruitment tactic just like "do it for the children." Now... now it was bothering her.

What if it wasn't a ploy?

She had to get to Tsurui.

She set the folder down, flexed her phantom.

Frowst wouldn't be happy either. He had been adamant about weekly check-ins.

She was going to have to disappoint him. Her ability to function and do her job depended on her prosthesis and her phantom working as one. But she was more than her job, more than her skill set, more than Death's Handmaiden who could thread a needle at two miles.

"Do you know where Rhodes is now?" she asked.

"He left yesterday."

She closed her eyes. Took a deep breath. Reached inside her jacket and pulled out the cryptochip.

"Mr. Muhonen, I'm afraid that I can't work for you after all."

She set the cryptochip down on the table.

"Are you going after Rhodes?"

"I'm going to save a friend."

"Then I don't think you're thinking this through, Ms. Merritt."

He picked up the chip, held it between two fingers like a card.

"Everything I've found says you have no assets. Whatever you're about to do, I'm going to assume you're going to need money. Since you earned this"—he wiggled his fingers, making the chip glimmer in the light—"I'm going to insist that you keep it."

He was right. She needed money. She wasn't going to get very far without it. If it turned out that Lyle was a drunk, she was going to kick his ass. And she couldn't do that from Sakura.

"It's a reward for saving Bri," he said. "No strings."

She held his gaze as she plucked the cryptochip from between his manicured fingers.

"Good luck, Ms. Merritt."

"Thank you, sir."

PART TWO

CHAPTER EIGHTEEN

TEN, FIFTEEN YEARS AGO, RUNNING A MARATHON AT SPRINT speeds had just been part of Talia's life. Hell, it had been part of everyone's life. You pushed and pushed and pushed some more. Sometimes you were the one who dragged the others. Sometimes you were the one getting dragged. The important thing was getting the job done. Hopefully without getting yourself and your people killed.

Last time, it had taken Talia twenty-three days to make it from Sakura to Tsurui. This time she was hoping to get there faster. Instead, this trip felt like she was running a sprint at marathon speeds, like nothing was fast enough.

Muhonen's money had allowed her upgraded seating on the train, which meant she'd gotten to sleep in a sleeper car on an actual bed, even if it was the size of a coffin. But nothing, not even money, could make the train go faster or the boat leave early. She'd sent another message to Lyle and a separate one to Maeve. Not knowing what was happening was slowly driving her crazy. It was making her want to sprint. Only sprinting was not allowed.

The train made its last station on the mainland, rolling to a stop by an elevated platform. It spilled out a steady stream of passengers. Most of them headed for the hotel at the end of the street, a five-story building made of brick with a domed roof.

She broke from the crowd, dashing right by the hansom cab

drivers lining the streets. A ship's horn blared in the distance, drowning out the neighing horses, crying children, and the occasional constable's whistle.

Eager for progress, she rushed to get started on the next leg of her journey, the one that would take her from the mainland to the islands.

She had two bags, one tucked under her left arm, the other dangling from her right hand. The 1911 rode her hip, tucked into a dark blue split skirt with decorative trim and covered by her coat. She'd traded her working shoes for ankle boots, the kind that laced up, and tucked her hair under a felt gaucho hat.

The building housing the ticket counter had a large open front, with doors that slid into place on tracks. A bored clerk stood behind the counter, flipping through a book.

She pulled her boarding pass out of her coat and pushed it toward him. He blinked as if he'd just noticed her and adjusted his jacket.

"I'm terribly sorry," he said. "I'm afraid your boat has been delayed by weather."

She pulled the pass back and his gaze traced and lingered on her prosthetic, then darted to her face.

"How long of a delay? I must get to Tsurui. Are there other boats? Any kind of boat. I don't care as long as it gets me there."

He picked up a clipboard and flipped through several sheets of paper, studying each one carefully before looking at his watch. As if he needed to double-check it, he also took a long hard look at the big clock a story above on the opposing wall. To her annoyance, it was almost four o'clock in the afternoon, hours prior to her boarding time, which should have meant that other boats were departing.

"I'm afraid not." He looked up, clearly avoiding any sort of glance at her arm. "The hotel should still have rooms available."

She rubbed at her aching neck. She'd slept wrong and woken up with the worst crick. It had gained momentum, expanding from neck to shoulder and was working its way down her back.

"And how long of a delay do you expect? Exactly."

He shrugged, his palms turning upward in a helpless gesture. "With a weather delay, it's hard to say."

"Guess." It came out a bit harsher than she intended.

"Overnight at least."

He called to a cab driver who was passing by and neatly passed her on to him. She allowed herself to be escorted—dumped really—along with about a dozen other passengers, some of whom were even more annoyed than she was. She could guess how long they had been on Gōruden based on their expectations.

If they expected ice, especially a lot of ice in their drinks, they had been here less than three months. If they wrinkled their noses at their fellow passengers' armpit stains, they hadn't been here a month. And if they looked lost without their cellphones, they'd been here less than a week.

Patiently, she waited her turn, standing in a line leading to the check-in counter. At least the place had electric lights, and fans overhead turned the humid seaside air over.

She'd converted some of Muhonen's money into actual cash, meaning paper as well as gold and silver coins. The port was probably going to be the last place where the chip itself would be acceptable payment. She wore it on a long chain around her neck, tucked safely underneath her blouse.

It was nice not worrying about every penny for a change.

It freed up the energy to worry about other things. Like how much of a head start did Rhodes really have on her. How many men was he going to bring with him to Tsurui. And how long before he got there. There had been something in that departing smirk, that gleam of satisfaction he'd shot her way, that said that the Contesti job had become personal.

She couldn't figure out why. She'd spent hours turning the problem over and over in her head, failing to turn up any reason where Lyle might have done something to make someone like Rhodes take such a personal interest in him.

By the time she was assigned a room, her back was spasming. She passed a sign advertising a spa and decided to send her luggage up to her room with a valet.

On a whim she decided to take advantage of a massage and then, fresh off having her muscles pounded into submission, she decided on one more indulgence—getting her nails painted.

Head thrown back against the cushion, she felt like a queen. It was hard not to, with her left hand being massaged, her toes freshly pampered and nails lacquered in a sparkly slaughter red.

The pain was gone for the first time since she'd left Sakura—fourteen days now, at least. It felt wonderful. Her prosthetic hand was wrapped around the stem of a glass, the fourth—or was it fifth?—mimosa. If she wasn't careful, she was going to float away.

"Miss Merritt?" Annie, the young lady who'd done her nails, said.

"Mmm-hmmm?" The light around her seemed too bright despite the towel resting across her eyes.

"Is there anything else you'd like me to do for you today?"

Talia drew in a deep breath. "No, thank you."

She reached up and pulled the towel off her eyes and blinked against the sharpness of the intruding light. The private room had a small fountain tucked in one corner and a table full of towels in the other. It smelled of jasmine and oil, of powder and heated wax.

Talia spread the fingers of her left hand, admiring the crimson sparkle of her manicure, the sheen of it as she tilted her hand. It felt positively sinful.

"I'll let you dress," Annie said. "Take your time."

She disappeared through the curtain and pulled it tight up against the edges.

Talia sighed. All good things must come to an end. One thing was certain—she was going to have a very good night's sleep. Between the massage and the mimosas, her biggest challenge for the night was going to be making it up to her room awake. Thank goodness for elevators. She was too wobbly to climb stairs.

She stretched, pulling her arms forward and wiggled her toes. Oh yes, she was going to have to do this again. There was nothing quite like sparkly red nail polish to make her feel like a girl.

Talia pushed up from the recliner, got dressed, and slipped her gun into its holster. Her jacket settled around her as she reached for the last of the mimosa. It was maybe a quarter of a glass. No sense in letting it go to waste.

She had her hand around it. What felt like a bolt of lightning went up her arm. It coursed upward from the prosthesis, up through the spike and the bone that connected it to her, along her bicep, her shoulder, her neck, and into the base of her skull.

The pain froze the breath in her chest. Her phantom spasmed and with it the cybernetics closed around the glass stem.

Crushed glass mixed with frothy orange liquid raced to the floor in slow motion, like she was watching someone else's hand squeeze tight around and pulverize the stem.

Release. Release.

The silent command, a residue of long-forgotten integration, something she hadn't had to use since the implant was first put in, was ignored by both her phantom and the prosthesis. They split from each other and spasmed separately, two distinct entities vying for control against a third, against her.

A scream—maybe hers, maybe Annie's—rose around her. The pain in her pounding head, the twisting muscles of her right arm were like a wave moving back and forth, going down to the phantom, into the prosthesis, and then reversing direction.

"A doctor. We need a doctor." Definitely Annie.

Pain had stolen Talia's voice.

Another spasm. Another feedback loop. Phantom and prosthesis as one. Then separate. But worst of all, the pounding in her head like someone had a hold on her skull and was bashing it into a wall, making her see double.

The curtain parted. A man came stumbling through like someone had pushed him in from behind.

"I'm not that kind of doctor."

"Help us!" Annie shouted down the hall.

Talia dropped to her knees. The muscles in her upper arm were determined to tear themselves apart.

The feedback loop was making it buzz inside her skull. It was getting louder, building, building, making it so she couldn't "hear" anything else.

"Off. Get it off."

The man came over, knelt, barely there in her tunneling vision.

She felt pressure above her elbow. He wrapped a hand at her wrist, although she felt it in several places where it definitely wasn't, as though he had six hands and they were all clamped on her forearm. The cybernetic palm was flipping up and down, making it impossible for him to grasp anywhere but her wrist, but the multiplying sensation persisted.

He pulled one way, pushed the other.

For what might have been a moment Talia's phantom curled its fingers together so hard that nonexistent fingernails cut into nonexistent palm. She smelled nonexistent blood, felt her skin being separated by her own nails. Another spasm fired up the tortured muscles like the cycle was going to start up again.

And then it was over. The prosthesis separated from the spike embedded in her flesh, the connection was broken, and Talia doubled over, supported by her left hand as she spewed bile and mimosa all over the floor.

Don't fall.

The last thing she wanted was to plunge face first into her own vomit.

But the man beside her steadied her from behind.

She took a deep breath, braced herself.

Talia looked up. The curtain had been drawn aside and Annie was in the doorway, panic still on her face. An older woman stood behind her, mouth agape, eyes wide, clearly horrified.

Other customers in robes, some with their hair still wet from the sauna, milled behind them. Some looked concerned, but most just had that look of morbid fascination like they were looking at a train wreck and just couldn't look away.

The older woman turned around, shooed the spectators away, raising her voice at some of them when they lingered.

"I thought you were a doctor," Annie said to the man she'd shoved into the room. Now that the crowd had dispersed, she pulled the curtain closed behind her, kept her back against it like she wanted to be close to the exit just in case.

"And I told you I wasn't that kind of doctor," the man insisted.

"You shouldn't be using the title then," Annie scolded. "This isn't a university."

Talia flipped her hair over her shoulder and tilted her head so she could get a better look at him. The young scientist from Sakura was kneeling beside her, his fogged-up glasses perched on the tip of his nose. He looked bewildered and disheveled, like he'd been dragged here against his will. A bowtie hung at his neck, above a rumpled, wrinkled shirt and vest whose checkered pattern really didn't go with his pinstripe pants.

"Miss Merritt," Annie said, "the manager is sending for a doctor. A real doctor."

"I'll be fine." Talia's voice came out a bit hoarse and far too tremulous to be reassuring to anyone, especially herself.

Pulling her hair around and out of the way with her left hand, she got her feet under her and stood. Her prosthesis was still on the rug. It looked like most of the regurgitated mimosa had missed it.

"It's Dr. Temonen, isn't it?" she said.

A concerned frown animated his face. He straightened his tie. "How do you know me?"

"Caught your presentation." She bent down to pick up her prosthesis.

"Can I help you clean that?" Annie asked in a voice that said that she'd rather not.

Talia shook her head. "I have cleaning supplies in my room. I'll take care of it. Sorry about the mess."

Annie gave her a nervous smile and ducked out.

"My presentation?" Temonen's reluctance was clearly threaded with fear. "You're not with the conglomerate, are you?"

"No, not with the conglomerate."

"Then how?" He was edging away, like he might run. "My work isn't exactly . . . public."

"Bodyguard. I just happened to be in the room. You're the mycologist, right? The one that *doesn't* want to let everyone on Gōruden die."

He was no longer edging toward the curtain. His shoulders and hands relaxed too.

Good. She didn't think she was in any shape to chase him. The malfunction had cleared her system of the buzz she'd been enjoying. She no longer felt pleasantly tipsy.

She really needed to get upstairs, clean the prosthesis. Figure out what had gone wrong, although she was certain it wasn't the prosthesis itself, but the implant.

"Exomycologist, but yes," Temonen said. "Are you . . . are you going to be able to use that thing again? Does it do that often?"

"No. Never in fact. First time. And yes, I'm going to use it again. Don't have much choice." She waved the right arm with the spike coming out of it.

His face took on the palest shade of green.

"I might be able to help you, you know, get it back on. Not a cyberneticist or anything, but I had a few engineering-type classes."

She quirked an eyebrow at him. He was trying to be helpful, despite his obvious discomfort. It made her smile.

"Are you squeamish?"

He shook his head despite the lingering green tinge. Great.

From feeling like a goddess with painted nails to making younger men turn green with disgust in a quarter of an hour. Surely, a record of some kind.

"That's all right, Dr. Temonen. I can get it back on. Do it all the time."

"What if the same thing happens again?"

"You do have a point."

CHAPTER NINETEEN

THE STILL-GREEN TEMONEN ESCORTED TALIA THROUGH THE LOBBY, all while trailing a panicked manager who was torn between insisting she wait for the doctor and making sure she didn't walk through his hotel carrying her prosthesis. She was tempted to waggle it in his face just to see if he would faint.

"May I get you something to cover your... your..."

"My spike?" she asked, a tinge of irritation creeping into her voice.

He stiffened up, looking even more like an irritated butler than before.

"Well, yes, ma'am, your, umm, spike."

"What do you suggest she do with it?" Temonen asked, matching her irritation.

"May I offer you a towel, ma'am." He snapped his fingers at Annie who'd been miserably bringing up the rear, looking mortified. She ducked back into the spa and emerged not with one, but with two fresh towels.

She unfurled one and wrapped it around Talia's spike. As soon as she let go, it slid off and landed on the floor.

The manager looked at it as if it was a dead rat that had decided to splatter itself on the rug in front of him.

Talia grabbed the other towel from Annie and draped it off one shoulder, tucking it under her armpit so it wouldn't slide down. It covered the offending sight, made her look like she was wearing a sort of half cape.

"Happy now, garçon?"

At least the manager had the decency to look chastened as he said, "Yes, ma'am, thank you."

Temonen followed Talia through the lobby, into the elevator, and up to the fourth-floor hotel room. He took the key from her and used it to unlock the door.

"There should be a light," he said, feeling inside. "And a fan. Ah, there."

Light flooded the room. The valet had set her bags atop the bed. A wardrobe with a mirrored door fronted one wall. She dropped the prosthesis on the bed and ducked into the tiny bathroom. Some mouthwash made her feel a thousand times better.

Temonen stood by the door, looking around like he was expecting things to jump out of the shadows. His glasses were no longer on the tip of his nose but pushed back, making his eyes look smaller than they really were. She'd bet anything that he didn't need them for close-up work, but couldn't see farther than his hand, if that, without them. Most people with that level of near-sightedness got if fixed before venturing out to a place like Gōruden.

"Were you born here?" she asked. "On Gōruden, I mean."

She opened one of her bags. Back when she'd still thought the issue might be with the prosthesis, she'd bought a small repair kit. She'd never had a chance to use it.

Talia set the repair kit—a small, zippered square like a man's shaving kit—atop the mattress and opened it up. It contained several packets of alcohol-soaked wipes, a variety of tiny brushes and probes, and a small flashlight.

"I can get that for you," he said, taking a step closer.

She passed the sealed packet to him. He handed back the wipe and she used it to clean the contacts inside the prosthesis.

"Here, hold this." She handed him the flashlight.

He clicked it on and held it up helpfully.

She took the prosthesis closer to the source, moved it around, straining to see inside.

"I was born in Sakura actually," Temonen said, holding the light steady.

"Ever been outside of Sakura?" She wrapped the wipe around a probe and used it to get deep inside the prosthesis. The last thing she wanted was to be smelling dried bile.

"No, never. Which is why I'd like to hire you as a bodyguard."

First Muhonen, now this guy. Muhonen she could understand. She'd expect someone like him to want and need a bodyguard, especially after what had happened with his granddaughter.

But this guy?

She eyed him as she set the prosthesis down. He looked a little rumpled, like he'd been traveling too, his shirt wrinkled, the yellow around the collar betraying either inadequate or unavailable laundering. The elbows of his coat were well worn, the cuffs of his pants as well. Despite that, he didn't look like a man on the run. Men on the run tended to want to blend in and his attire stood out.

"After what you just saw, you think I can protect you?"

"Yes. Yes I do."

She made a doubtful sound as she pulled one of the probes from the repair kit.

"There's a small hole on the interior where it lines up with the spike, but I'm having trouble seeing it."

He took the probe and prosthesis, set his glasses down, and looked within.

"What am I doing?"

"Turning on test mode. It'll make it harder for me to move the components, but it'll also prevent it from exerting any potentially damaging pressure or mimicking muscle spasms."

He held the probe like someone who was used to working with fine, delicate instruments or perhaps like an artist with a detail brush.

"There." He handed it back to her.

She shoved the spike inside. It felt like waking up with a numb limb, a dead weight. That crawling-ant sensation wasn't there though, which made it somehow more alien. She made the fingers move. They obeyed, but slowly, like she was having to move them inside a jar of drying cement.

"It's gonna take a few minutes for me to run through all the testing motions. Have a seat."

Reluctantly, he dropped into the only chair and settled back to watch her.

"Why do *you* need a bodyguard?" she asked as she arduously bent each finger.

"I don't know how to shoot. I can't defend myself if someone comes after me."

"Who's coming after you, kid?"

Slowly, her cybernetic wrist rotated counterclockwise. It was like working without her phantom. It made her queasy. She closed her eyes.

"Nobody specific. But you know, you hear stories."

Rotating it clockwise was slow. Very slow. She opened her eyes, looked him over.

"It's really not as bad as the Sakurans want you to think it is," she said. "More importantly, why are you out here?"

"I want to study the exomycelium that's out there on the islands. There's something about the samples that were brought back this year that just doesn't make sense."

"Who's sponsoring your work? Shouldn't they be the ones making sure that you're . . . protected?"

"No one. I'm actually looking for new sponsors, new funding. The conglomerate that initially hired me just wants to bury the information. Those that believe me."

"And those that don't?"

He shrugged. "They just think I'm crazy. It's the ones that are willing to let people die that I'm afraid of."

"You're certain your models are right?"

"No, I'm not certain. That's why I need to go out there, find out what's going on and why. But if I'm correct . . ."

"All right." She pulled the prosthesis off and handed it back to him. "Same switch, if you don't mind."

He inserted the probe. Handed the prosthesis back. "Is that it? That's all it takes to fix it?"

"It's not the prosthesis," she said. "It's something else."

She slipped it on. Her phantom snapped into place over the prosthesis with a jolt. It made the back of her skull throb like a heartbeat. The sound seemed to fill her ears with that strange type of noise that you know is coming from inside, not outside.

She ran through the testing motions once again and the throbbing faded.

"I'll be damned. Now it's working perfectly fine."

"That's good, isn't it?

"I just wish I knew what caused it to glitch like that."

"There's a cyberneticist in Sakura. Maybe you should head back that way. Frowst, I th—"

"I can't go back to Sakura now." She tidied up the repair kit, set it back into her bag. "I have a proposition for you, kid."

"My name is Logan Fitzpatrick Temonen. Not 'kid.' Besides, I'm not that much younger than you."

She sat down on the bed directly across from him. "All right, Logan Fitzpatrick Temonen, doctor of exomycology. I will teach you how to shoot a gun so you can defend yourself"—his eyes went wide and he opened his mouth as if to interrupt—"if, and only if, you will come with me to Tsurui. It sounds like you're already headed to the islands. Tsurui is probably as good as any place for samples. And I'll introduce you to the Haricots. They're like you. Brainy people. I bet they know a thing or two about your mycelium."

He pushed his glasses up his nose and imitated her pose, leaning forward so his elbows were on his knees, so his face was right up in front of hers.

"See these glasses, Miss Merritt? They're on my face because my eyes aren't just bad, they're very bad. I can't shoot for shit."

She smiled. It was strange, hearing those words in his mouth, not because of his youth but because of his professorial tones. There was an innocence about him that, paired up with expertise, made him at once young and old.

"We'll see," she said. "I'm not expecting you to be a sharpshooter. If I can't teach you to shoot well enough to protect yourself, then I'll bring you back here and you can go back to Sakura. Deal?"

She offered him her right hand.

He didn't even look down at it. He just took it in his grasp as if it hadn't been spasming and going crazy less than an hour ago. Well, he might be a fool trusting the safety of his hand to her glitchy one, but he wasn't a coward.

"Deal."

Logan looked a lot like a lost professor as he dragged his trunk aboard the boat—a combination sail and steam liner much bigger than the one she'd taken six months ago. Talia followed him up the ramp, carrying her own much lighter bags.

She didn't like having both hands full, but it couldn't be helped. The muscles on the right side of her body, from neck to elbow, were angry and sore, a constant reminder that she needed to get as proficient with weak-side shooting as she was with strong-side. Muscle memory on the left would take a few thousand rounds to cement. Switching to left-eye dominance, on the other hand, was going to be a bitch.

"What have you got in that trunk anyway, kid?"

"The name is Logan," he said. "And I'm twenty-six."

"Uh-huh," she said. "Sure you are."

He still had so much baby fat in his face that she didn't quite believe him. He forged ahead, giving her his back.

For being wiry, he wasn't struggling with the trunk as much as she'd expected. But then again, he was a young man. Wiry didn't mean weak. It was the glasses, the clothes. The glasses couldn't be helped. The clothes, however. He was going to need something that made him look less professorial, less like a kid playing at being a grown-up. The bowtie would have to go.

"What have you got in that trunk anyway? Logan."

"Equipment. Lab supplies. The tools of my trade as it were."

They presented their tickets, strips of paper with their names filled in by hand. Instead of Temonen, Logan was using Jones. She scoffed but shouldn't have. She was using Smith.

A creative pair we are not.

The ticket taker didn't even seem to notice. "Welcome aboard. Please follow the signs to your cabins."

It was exactly the casual indifference to names and IDs and microchipping and tracing every last move, every single breath, every possible thing that could somehow then be used against you no matter what you did—good or ill—that Talia was here for. Even in Sakura, with its higher tech and "civilization," the attitude was lax compared to Earth. Laissez-faire, that's what it was called. It was why Gōruden was thriving. There were trade-offs but it was nowhere near the lawless place that many on Earth imagined it to be.

The boat only had one deck with passenger cabins. Talia and Logan parted ways, him veering left, her turning right. The announcement that the boat was underway also included a weather report that called for smooth sailing throughout the night with arrival in port early the next morning.

Her cabin was tiny, no more than a closet with a bed shoved into it at one end and a water closet on the other. She had all of five inches of clearance on either side in the shower.

She curled up with a book, with the intent to lose herself in it for a few hours. The lull and white noise of the ship around her intruded, making her eyes heavy. She looked down at her hand as she turned the next page, found it to be flesh-and-bone again. The book faded, and the cabin turned into her old room at her grandparents' house.

Happily, she settled into her dream, running her fingers atop her right hand, over the bumps made by a henna pattern that she had applied in preparation for her friend's—Katia's—party. The dreamscape shifted around her, the henna pattern smudging into brown-black dirt.

She'd taken her gloves off. The familiar weight of Bunny on her back tugged at her shoulder as she and Lyle dragged a body behind them. Lyle was hefting a second sniper rifle, one that looked intact but had a damaged receiver. Up above, the broken ceiling of a warehouse was like a giant maw opening up to the sky. The Moon was slipping quietly over the jagged edges that looked like giant teeth.

"Maybe this isn't such a great idea," Talia said.

"I don't like it either."

They had reached the edge of the walkway. Some of the railing was still intact. It was a great vantage point onto the floor below. It was such a mess down there. Craters the size of cars, fallen beams and pipes, rubble everywhere. The walkway was marginally better, even though segments of it had collapsed.

No corpses though, except for the one they had brought.

So far, Talia had avoided asking who he'd been—friend or foe? It didn't matter. They needed a decoy and he—whoever he was—was beyond caring.

Sorry, buddy.

Talia helped Lyle lay the corpse down. He was heavy, unwieldy in that way that only dead bodies could be, but they got his arms out where they should be, put the damaged rifle in his hands, set his head behind the sight, a helmet with a hole atop his head.

Thank goodness it was cold.

Talia shivered despite herself, despite the effort of climbing up the staircase with such a load. She piled concrete chunks atop the body and covered it in bits of sheet metal and broken glass.

"Not all the way," Lyle said. "He needs to look like the debris covered him after he died."

Numb, Talia nodded, pulled off a couple of the metal sheets. Its edge cut a gash across her palm.

"Shit." She pulled her hand back, curled her fingers against it, and squeezed.

Blood dripped, warm and sticky. Alive.

With a mildly annoyed look on his face, Lyle pulled a rag from his pocket.

"Don't look at me like that," she said. "Your hands are bare too."

"Yes, but I'm not the one who cut himself." He took her hand in his, examined it. "Maybe you won't need stitches."

He wrapped the rag around her palm, tightened it.

"How good are you off-hand?" he asked.

"It's just a scratch. I won't need to go off-hand."

"Be more careful," he scolded and walked away.

She counted back from five. They were both hungry, cold, and tired. She wasn't really mad at him. Nor he at her, she was certain.

She set it aside, following him back down the stairs.

Her hand throbbed against the makeshift bandage. She used it to reach up and adjust Bunny's strap.

Days before, the pounding noise of the bombardment felt like it would never end. Now, the eerie quiet that wrapped around them unnerved her just as much. It was amplified by the stairwell, the stealthy way that Lyle moved.

She put her hand out on the rail, felt its cold, metal smoothness, a slickness as blood seeped from the rag onto the metal. She stopped then, looked down at it, her stomach feeling as if it had taken an elevator down.

The dirt under her fingernails, the oil and dirt smudges atop her hand were gone. Ceramic had replaced them. Cold, pristine, hard. No nail beds for dirt to hide under. No cuticles to be torn. No skin or tendons to slice.

Lyle put his hand atop hers. But he was no longer Lyle. He may have looked and moved like him, but his skin had that gray-blue pallor of death, and his eyes were filmed. He looked more like that corpse.

"Isn't this better?" he asked, taking off the bandage and turning her ceramic palm upward.

"No!"

She tightened the muscles in her bicep, pulled her hand back, but the prosthesis wouldn't move. Corpse-Lyle's grip was too strong as he held on to her wrist.

"Let go!"

Dead eyes stared back at her, unblinking. The skin on his face was like leather, tight and dry, but he would not let go of her wrist.

She struck out with her left hand, palm first, going for his chest. It smacked him just below the notch of his collarbone. Slowly, he fell backward and was swallowed up by the dreamscape that had resettled around her.

When Talia looked down at her hands, they were both made of metal and ceramic and they dripped with blood and if it hadn't been for the ship's horn, she wasn't sure how long she would have been trapped in that nightmare.

She rolled out of the bed, rubbed at the space between her eyes.

Damn it, Lyle. Don't be a drunk. Don't be dead.

When her heart stopped racing, she flexed her prosthesis, curling her phantom's fingers into her palm.

CHAPTER TWENTY

TALIA MADE HER WAY TO THE RESTAURANT AND BAR ON THE TOP deck to seek out dinner and maybe a beer to wash it down with.

She climbed up the tight spiral of the staircase leading directly from the passenger cabins to the restaurant. She didn't get claustrophobic easily, but since landing on Gōruden she'd gotten quite comfortable with the openness of the buildings in Sakura.

The vestibule at the top of the stairs was little more than a booth—a glass and wood enclosure big enough for one or two people to stand in.

She pushed the door inward and stepped into the bar. Right into a brawl.

Four men were exchanging blows, or rather, three were taking turns pounding on the fourth. The bartender, a middle-aged man of girth, was on the sound-powered telephone calling for help.

It really was no surprise that Logan was the fourth man, the one in the role of punching bag.

His hat—the tweed cap—was on the polished floor between them. So were his glasses. They looked like they had spun out of the way and just come to a stop.

Logan followed them, sliding to a stop a foot or so away. He hardly seemed to notice her as he shook his head and pushed himself up, looking pissed and determined. Staggering, he turned around like he was about to go back into the fray, like he didn't know or care that three was more than one.

Talia grabbed him by the shoulder. Arm swinging, he rounded on her. She ducked out of the way. His momentum carried him too far and he almost lost his balance again. His shirt had been torn, as was his jacket, and he had a bloody nose. Other than that, he seemed to be holding his own as he squinted at her.

"Miss Merritt?"

Talia bent to pick up the glasses—he was about to step on them, she was sure—and shoved them into his hands. He centered them on his face.

She gave him her disappointed-mother look, the one she'd perfected once she'd made squad leader. Very handy that look. Worked on privates, corporals, and apparently exomycologists with bloody noses.

The look didn't make him shrivel, but it did seem to take the wind out of his sails. He wiped at his dripping nose and looked around until he found his hat.

Talia faced the three men who'd been beating on Logan. They wore the right attire for the region—boots, jeans, vests over checkered shirts—but everything was new. Even their belts and belt buckles. If they were armed, their weapons were well hidden.

One had shoulder-length black hair pulled into a ponytail. The other sported neck tattoos that wrapped up his neck and onto his bare scalp. The third had short hair in a flaming red that couldn't be natural. They all looked like they hadn't missed leg or arm day in the last decade and were quite used to fighting with their fists or anything else that might be handy—like the broken chair littering the floor, and the broken bottle next to it.

Logan was lucky he wasn't dead. They'd been toying with him by the look of it, cats entertaining themselves by tormenting prey because they weren't quite hungry enough yet. Or perhaps just like bullies everywhere they were merely entertaining themselves, having fun.

"Three against one hardly seems fair," she said. "Care to make it three against two?"

Their gazes were locked onto her cybernetic forearm, held casually at her side. If they had a single brain cell among them, they would know she was armed, even with the gun concealed as it was. But the arm always got the look. Cyborgs were scary. Scarier than guns.

She'd bet anything that they'd been raised on action flicks, that their expectations were still set by them. Cyborgs such as herself were still rare enough that most people hadn't had a chance to interact with them and know that they were unlikely to have enhancements.

If Talia had to draw, she'd get one of them, but which one. That had to be the question running through their feeble little heads. Perhaps along with visions of having their faces bashed in by ceramic knuckles.

Good God, did they think she was going to take them on with her fists? That she wanted to get that close and personal? That she wasn't going to just put a bullet through their heads? That she wasn't capable of killing them in cold blood?

"Our quarrel isn't with you," Ponytail said. He seemed to be in possession of the singular brain cell as he slowly sat back down.

The thud of footsteps told her why: Security had arrived. A man and a woman in uniform, stun-guns on their hips, entered the restaurant through the double doors on the opposite side, the ones that came in from the top deck rather than the cabins below.

"What's the problem here?" the male cop asked.

"No problem," Dye-job said. "Misunderstanding."

"Those three," the bartender said, thick accent coming through. "They start it."

"Gentlemen"—the cop spoke in that tone that said they were anything but—"I suggest you come with us."

The one with the tattoos turned on the boat cops. "Make us."

No, he wasn't afraid of the stun-guns. Wouldn't be. All that muscle and not enough brains. Thug, not soldier, that one.

Talia grabbed Logan's sleeve and pulled him with her toward the stools fronting the bar just as two more boat cops came up the staircase. At least the new arrivals had revolvers. They were drawn, at low-ready.

Ponytail stood and put a placating hand on Tattoo's shoulder. "It's all right. We'll go with the officers. They'll lock us in our cabins for the night, put us off before the other passengers, and pretend nothing happened, won't they?"

The last was aimed at the cops who didn't look amused, but also didn't disagree. Why they were armed only with stun-guns was beyond Talia. This wasn't Sakura. It also wasn't Tatarka. They were literally in a no-man's-land—or rather water—between the civilized city and the frontier island.

Reluctantly, Tattoo let himself be led off, boots pounding loudly as he rolled his beefy shoulders. He had a scowl on his face, one that promised retribution. Dye-job followed him out, a smirk on his face. Only Pony Tail lingered, cast a look Talia's way. The female cop gave him a nudge, encouraging him toward the door.

"You're Talia Merritt, aren't you?" Pony Tail asked.

"What if I am?"

The cops looked confused, like they weren't sure if they should insist that he come with them or know who Talia was.

"Thought it was you. Long hair threw me. Heard you were on Gōruden. I'd like to talk to you, perhaps once we're in port. There's a job th—"

She put her palm out. "I've heard all about this job. Not interested."

"It's a lot of m—"

"The lady said she wasn't interested," the female cop said.

"So she did," Pony Tail admitted. "But she's no lady."

"All right. Come on," the female said, looking like she might be offended on Talia's behalf. "I think you've had enough to drink for the night."

"No, not nearly enough. Not with breathing the same air as Death's Hand."

Well, that was one she hadn't heard before.

The cop gave Talia a wide-eyed look, and then dropped her gaze to her right arm like she could no longer resist staring.

Her partner stepped up. "Let's go."

It spurred Pony Tail to join the others. He made an exit like he was being escorted out, all ego and strut.

Arrogant ass.

"Death's Hand?" Logan asked, his voice thick with mucus. He'd taken a seat on a stool in front of the bar and was leaning on the bar top with his elbows sliding out in front of him like he wanted to lay his head down instead. He kept blinking his eyes like they stung, which they probably did. Broken noses tended to do that.

The bartender handed him a towel with a few ice cubes tucked into the fabric.

"For your nose," he grumbled as he came out from behind the bar with a dustpan and broom.

"What happened?" Talia slid onto the stool next to Logan.

"Nothing."

The bartender made a sound that was more objection than laugh. He scooped up the last of the broken glass littering the floor and dumped it into a bin.

"What kind of nothing?" Talia asked the bartender as he made his way back behind the taps.

"What are you drinking?" he asked.

"Beer. And dinner. I'm hungry. What have you got?"

"Fish, chips, that kind of stuff. Mostly deep fried. This is not luxury cruise."

"Fine. Whatever you have." Talia turned back to Logan. "What kind of nothing?"

"Your friend has smart mouth," the bartender said.

She looked expectantly at Logan who had the ice pressed to his nose. Blood had dripped onto his shirt, and his knuckles looked bloody too. He looked the middle-school bookworm who'd just been beat up despite having done nothing.

"You didn't get bruised knuckles from talking," she said, nudging Logan, who responded with a groan.

"No. He fight. He hold his own. Against one, one and a half."

"Oh good. Tell me you didn't pick a fight with three rent-a-thugs."

He shook his head and snagged the beer the bartender put in front of Talia. He took a sip without a hint of apology.

"I bring another," the bartender said.

"Well, he's not gonna tell me, so it's up to you"—she squinted at the name tag—"Swede."

He slid another beer toward her.

"They make fun of his hands. Too soft, they say. Wanted to know if he is soft everywhere, if he charges extra for being so soft. Instead of walking, having seat at far end, he say he give them 'hand job,' show that he not soft." Swede shrugged. "I don't get joke."

She didn't either.

"You got into a fight because they questioned your sexuality?"

He shrugged. Had some more beer.

"I take it back. You do need a bodyguard."

CHAPTER TWENTY-ONE

THE BRUISES UNDER LOGAN'S EYES DIPPED DOWN TO HIS CHEEKS, making him look like a red and purple raccoon. His glasses sat just forward from where they usually did. Talia winced in sympathy. That had to hurt, having them ride atop all those bruises and the swelling. But he'd made no complaints the entire morning as she'd taken charge of him and his trunk.

Cold, salty air and a slate-gray horizon greeted them as they stepped out onto a deck slick with spray. The distant storm clouds looked like they were dripping into the ocean. Occasionally, a lightning strike would light up the boiling mass.

"I guess that's why we won't be landing at Biei," Talia said.

"No, that's Minamioguni."

Logan wiped his glasses down and then squinted into the distance once again. By the look on his face, cleaning the glasses hadn't helped.

Wind was pulling at Talia's hair, freeing strands from the ponytail she'd gathered it into, and sending it into her face and mouth. She swiped at it, tucked it behind her ears.

"Minamioguni wasn't part of my plans," Talia said, shrugging into her jacket.

"Wait? Minamioguni. Isn't that on the other side of Tatarka?"

"It sure is." Talia wasn't happy about that either. It added unneeded days to their journey, Tsurui being closer to Biei—Tatarka's northern port—than it was to the larger, southern port of Minamioguni.

It was well after noon by the time the port sorted out the unexpected traffic and they were allowed to disembark. Minamioguni's port was conveniently located by the train terminal and a substantial town had grown up around it, taking up all the flat land between the sea and hills. Carriages wound their way down the street, beating out a steady rhythm of clop-clop-clop punctuated by occasional neighs.

A rich honey-vanilla scent from the hydrangeas lining the streets rose up as they pushed Logan's trunk from port to train terminal. The dolly's wheels squeaked and strained as they rolled over the paving stones.

Talia left Logan and his trunk by a decorative fountain inside the terminal and spent far too much time sorting things out with the harried travel desk clerk.

It took the better part of an hour before she rejoined him. Logan closed the notebook he'd been sketching in.

"Looks like we'll have to spend the night," she said. "There's a train that will get us most of the way to Tsurui."

"Only most of the way? And then what?"

"Stagecoach from Shiiba to Tsurui." She opened up the map the desk clerk had given her. On one side, a map of Tatarka. On the other, one of Minamioguni.

Another hour earned them a pair of hotel rooms. Rooms that wouldn't be ready for a few more hours. The bellhop who stowed their things looked about twelve and reminded her far too much of Sam Haricot, all bony angles and innocence ready to give way to fury.

"What's wrong?" Logan asked as he pocketed the claim ticket.

"Nothing," she said, blinking fiercely and somehow keeping the wobble out of her voice.

She took a deep breath and added, "We need a few things before we head out."

"Things? What things?"

"Clothes better suited to riding, for one. Once we get to Tsurui, you'll have to ride—you do know how to ride?"

"Not exactly."

She pinched the bridge of her nose. "What does that mean?"

"I won't fall off the horse is what I mean."

"Terrific."

She needed to get out of here before the bellhop came

back. Logan trailed her as she made her way out of the lobby.

She stopped in front of a directory and compared it with the map the travel desk clerk had given her.

"I need to send a message to Tsurui," she said as she dragged her gaze over the directory. "Here. Four blocks down. Let's go."

Twenty minutes later she was standing at the counter, writing out another message, as Logan flirted with the clerk. She looked about his age and seemed quite undeterred by the bruises swelling his face.

He had opened his notebook and was showing her some of his sketches. "And these good little guys here convert sugar to alcohol," he was saying.

The girl made encouraging sounds. Logan flipped to another page. "I coaxed these lovely ladies into making a yeast that makes bread rise like crazy."

Talia snuck a look. He was showing her mushrooms. Mushrooms of all things. And she looked interested.

"I've never seen these around here," the girl said, drawing the notebook toward her.

Logan obligingly scooted closer. "Wrong latitude, but they could be cultivated indoors."

The girl shot him a "tell me more" smile.

"I hate to intrude," Talia said, placing a coin on the counter along with the message, "but I need this sent right away."

"Sure, no problem." The girl took the coin and the message. She sat down at the radio, donned an earpiece with a boom mic, and worked the dials. After five minutes without success, she returned to the counter.

"Sorry, no answer. The fee covers three attempts. We space them about four hours apart. Do you want me to telegraph it instead?"

"In addition, please."

The store doorbell rang, announcing the entry of an elderly couple. It interrupted Logan's renewed attempts at flirting. The young lady cast him an apologetic look and set about helping the elderly couple wrap a bundle for shipment.

Logan had been sketching the girl's portrait as she'd worked the radio. He was showing it to Talia as they exited.

"Very nice. You do good work," she said.

Motion in the street outside caught her eye as she looked up from the sketch. The man going into the jailhouse across the street was none other than Jerod Rhodes himself. He wore a gaucho hat with a silver band, tailored pants and vest, and two revolvers, one on each hip. Large calibers, by the look of them. Size did have its advantages. And Talia had no doubt that he knew how to use them. And intended to, sooner or later.

"What is it?" Logan asked, following her gaze.

"Nothing," she lied.

"Doesn't look like nothing, unless you wear that face more than you've let on."

"It looks like your friends from last night just made bail."

"What friends—"

She pulled him behind the column of a metal streetlamp with hanging baskets from which flowers spilled. A thick mass, they dangled halfway to the ground.

He followed her gaze.

"Oh, them."

Rhodes was talking to the trio, but they were too far to hear over the street noise. By the look on their faces, he was chastising them. Pony Tail was the only one not talking back. He had shoved his hands in his pockets and was finding the floorboards interesting. Tattoo and Dye-job, on the other hand, were arguing.

"Who's the man with them?"

"Jerod Rhodes." It came out like a curse. She hadn't expected to see him here. She'd hoped their unexpected port call would have resulted in three fewer thugs for Contesti's ranks.

Logan met her gaze. "Should I know who that is?"

"No."

He frowned at the terseness of her answer.

"Say, you never did answer my question. The one about Death's Hand. Is that what you call your . . . your . . ."

"No," she said. "Let's go."

She headed down the street, hoping she'd blend in with the other pedestrians.

"Where we going?" Logan lengthened his stride and caught up with her.

"Clothes. Boots. A hat that protects from the sun."

"I really can't afford all that," he protested.

"I can." She pulled the rolled-up map from her pocket and checked it. It showed a tailor a few streets down.

"You're supposed to be working for me." He bounced off a gentleman heading the other way and apologized.

"Don't remind me." She turned a corner and cast a glance over her shoulder.

Logan was still trotting after her much like a chagrined puppy. It seemed like they'd avoided being noticed, at least for the time being. She needed to keep it that way.

Suddenly, Minamioguni seemed too small a town to avoid running into Rhodes or his thugs. And Logan was still too easy to recognize. For that matter, so was she, with her Sakuran clothes.

Two more turns and she ducked into the small tailor shop. They were greeted by the rat-tat-tat of a foot-powered sewing machine. Behind it sat a man with thin half-glasses.

Talia waited for her eyes to adjust. It was stuffy inside and the heavy smell of machine oil, chalk, and fabric hung almost visibly in the air.

"May I help you?" The tailor looked up at them over the tops of his glasses.

"My friend here needs traveling clothes. Two sets. Something that'll stand up to riding a horse."

"And a gun," Logan added.

"Sure. I have some off-the-rack items over there." His gaze flicked over to the back. "No guns though. You'll have to go down the street for that."

An hour later, she had Logan looking like someone who belonged here. Jeans and cowboy boots, a vest and short coat, went a long way into making him look manlier. He was checking himself out in a mirror as if he couldn't quite believe what he was seeing. He glanced around like he was making sure no one was looking and puffed his chest out as if trying on a new persona.

She picked up a few things for herself—soft cotton shirts the color of new and faded bricks with button-up and string-drawn collars; a couple of corset vests with matching bolero tops and hats; high-waisted pants with decorative trim going down the leg, and a gun belt with an adjustable holster. On a whim, she added a few things for Maeve, Lyle, and John, reasoning that she owed them for their generosity. She passed on a couple of children's toys made of fabric scraps that could have done double-duty as dog toys, reasoning that robotic dogs didn't need to chew.

"What now?" Logan came up to the counter, carrying a bag filled with his spare set and his old clothes and shoes.

"Here, try this on." She handed him a pair of wraparound sunglasses, the kind that could go over the ones he already wore. "You'll thank me later."

She picked up a second pair for herself, paid the tailor and headed to the gun store, the back of her neck prickling the entire way. It was at times like this that she really missed Lyle. He'd watched her back and she his, and now that she knew that people like Rhodes were here to do Contesti's bidding, she desperately wanted a partner again.

Unable to help herself, she looked up at the buildings around them, calculating sight lines all the way to the gun store. The battered metal sign looked like it had been used for target practice. It said "Candy's" and the logo was a cancan girl wearing a geisha wig and hair sticks.

At first Talia thought that they might have come to the wrong place, but the writing on the door said "Gun and Toy Shoppe." Candy apparently had a sense of humor.

The store had a full array of "100% Locally Sourced" items. It carried everything from black-powder guns to centerfire revolvers to semi- and full-automatics designed in the early part of the twentieth century, all neatly arrayed within glass display counters. Rifles and shotguns hung on walls behind the gun seller, a coal-skinned woman who reminded her of Otto. She peered at them over a bodice-ripper novel with a tattered cover featuring a kilted, blue-skinned man. He had his arms around a scantily clad woman with mahogany skin not quite as dark as the woman holding the novel.

"Can I help you?" She lowered the book, revealing that she was sucking on a lollipop. It had turned her lips a bright red. The stem hung out the side, inviting comment.

"Candy, I presume," Talia said as she put a smile on her face.

The woman nodded, her gaze drifting down to Talia's prosthesis. Talia was going to have to stop back in at the tailor and ask for some custom-made gloves—something thin and preferably flesh toned. She'd rejected the idea a half dozen times before, but her prosthesis was going to make her memorable, and the tickle at the back of her neck—a tickle that had nothing to do with the implant and everything to do with being a sniper—was making a convincing argument.

"Love the polish," Candy said as her gaze bounced to Talia's left hand. "Slaughter red, isn't it?"

"Yes, it is. Good eye."

Logan was wandering around the store, looking lost and perplexed. At least he was being quiet as he lurked. It must be a common enough thing, or he had that harmless tourist/newcomer look, because Candy didn't even seem to notice him. And Candy didn't look like the kind of store owner who didn't pay attention or relied on security cameras.

Talia drifted past the handguns and the ammunition crates. Plenty of both in Tsurui and she had brought ammo for her 1911. But now, now she was drawn to the long guns behind Candy. Clones of Beretta shotguns as well as Springfields and Enfields stared back at her. There was an empty space among them, like Candy had sold something and hadn't had time to replace it.

"What's your best long-range gun?"

Something—maybe a flash of annoyance—flickered across Candy's face. "Antimatérial or just antipersonnel?"

"Antimatérial."

In case Candy's annoyance might be at curiosity shoppers looking to ogle a seriously expensive gun, Talia reached for the chain around her neck, drew out the cryptochip and held it up so that the light could hit it.

A dark cloud settled over Candy's face as she furrowed her brow.

"Your boss was already here," Candy said. "I'll tell you the same thing I told him. Special orders take time. Even when you have the money."

Shit. Not good. Not good at all.

"I don't work for Rhodes." It was a guess, but probably a correct one, given Candy's reaction.

What the hell did Rhodes need an antimatérial gun for? *The same thing you need it for. To reach out and really touch someone. Even someone behind cover.*

Candy's gaze drifted over to Logan almost as if seeing him for the first time. She looked him up and down. Frowned.

"My little brother," Talia offered. "He doesn't work for Rhodes either."

"Oh, that I believe," Candy said. "Adopted brother I take it."

Talia smiled. Candy didn't.

"We'll take something you have in stock then. The Model 17 pump-action and the double-barreled Winchester 21. And the M1891 clone you haven't had a chance to restock up there." That last was also a guess. Or maybe a prayer.

"Why that one?" Candy asked.

"It's not fussy," Talia said.

CHAPTER TWENTY-TWO

AFTER AN EXTENDED CONVERSATION ABOUT THE QUALITY OF HER locally made stock and dire warnings about failed adventures that relied on advanced tech, Candy sent them out to test their purchases. She had a place just outside town for her clients to sight in their guns. She also made arrangements for a couple of horses to get them there, and Talia got a chance to assess Logan's riding ability. He could indeed stay atop a horse, as long as it wasn't going very fast.

A few miles short of the range, Logan stopped them, and she thought it might be because he was having trouble with the saddle, but he hopped down and headed for a tree.

"What are you doing?" she asked.

He was down on his knees, poking enthusiastically at something with a stick. At least he seemed to be making an effort to keep his new clothes clean.

"Just checking for mycorrhizal fungi. They tap into the living tree roots for carbohydrates and pay the tree back with minerals."

Her imagination offered the image of a cartoon mushroom paying in gold for a sugar cube.

"Logan."

"Yes?"

"We're wasting sunshine."

He looked up, squinted at the sky. "Oh, sorry." He hesitated, but abandoned the stick and only threw one longing look at the roots before getting back on the horse.

Candy's shooting range turned out to be little more than a bench and a backstop separated by one hundred or so yards of flat land. The strip itself was nestled among the hills overlooking Minamioguni. Everywhere, lilies and hydrangeas crowded everything. It was definitely the most picturesque shooting Talia had ever done.

Liquid-quick calculations slid through her brain as she marked her field of fire. Calculations that she didn't need. Not here. Good to know the skill was all still there though.

She squeezed the trigger on the M1891. The target wasn't nearly far away enough, but hitting the bull's-eye was highly satisfying, doing much to quell the sense of helplessness that had been building ever since she'd realized that a man like Rhodes was here to kill Lyle. Candy's merchandise was as well made as she'd said. It just needed a bit of breaking in.

"That's incredible," Logan said as he lowered the low-tech binoculars he'd found inside the storage locker that doubled as a bench seat.

He'd been hovering at her shoulder, ears plugged with his fingers because apparently the foam inserts weren't enough for him. She didn't blame him, not really, and it did keep his hands off the guns. He was fascinated by them, the same way as someone was fascinated by snakes—afraid to touch but once he did, he was going get hurt.

Talia brought the stock of the M1891 to her left shoulder. It felt as awkward as she remembered it, the motions not quite right, the eyes fighting each other. She lined up the sights, rested her left forefinger on the trigger. The remaining fingers brushed up against the polished wood of the stock.

Slowly, she pushed the breath out of her lungs, paused, squeezed. There was an accompanying twitch in her phantom as it held up the front of the stock. That right index finger wanted to be the one pulling the trigger. Not as much as the right eye wanted to be in charge, but still, palpable enough. Nevertheless, she hit the bull's-eye, but at this distance, she'd have been disappointed if she'd not.

The action locked open and smoke hung in the air as she set the rifle down. Logan reached out to touch it, caressing the wood and tracing a path along the length of it.

"It's warm," he said as if it surprised him and then guiltily pulled his finger away.

Time to end that morbid fascination of his. Talia started Logan off with a safety briefing. She had him load and unload a revolver with spent rounds, until he could do it safely. The 38-special was something she'd added as a last-second purchase. She sat him down for bench shooting.

After determining that he was cross-dominant, he switched hands and shot better. She made encouraging sounds whenever he hit the wood square about seven yards in front of him, which was about half the time.

He beamed up at her as he handed the empty revolver back. His hands were no longer shaking as they'd been when he'd first picked it up.

He was a good student, she had to give him that. Lucky for her, he didn't seem to have much to unlearn.

"Can we put a laser sight on this?" he asked.

"I wouldn't recommend becoming dependent on one. Getting batteries for anything like that out here is going to be a problem."

He looked up at her. "What about your prosthesis? Isn't that powered too?"

"Different technology. The laser sight is too small for a Hampson-effect power source. It would make the gun heavier and bigger, slowing any draw, so it's too much of a trade-off. Hampson-effect is for things like my arm and even for small robots. But too much for guns—unless they're really big guns—and too small for things like radios, appliances, and vehicles. Didn't they cover this in your engineering-type classes?" she teased.

He shot her a glare.

"Now let's try this standing up."

She helped him with his stance, his grip.

He struggled with it just as he'd done before, citing the difficulty in seeing both sights and the target at the same time. Apparently his vision doubled or wavered even once they figured out the eye dominance.

He jerked at the last moment, making his shot go wide. By the third round he was missing the target entirely.

"It's all right, Logan," she said as she took the gun from him. "This kind of thing takes time."

"How much time?"

"It might take a few hundred rounds."

"Let's try the shotgun."

He liked the sound the pump-action made. She showed him how to aim it.

"It has a kick," she said and stepped back to let him take his first shot.

He squinted at the target but closed his eyes at the last moment and the actual shot startled him. No longer as confident, he was slumped over and the muscle in his jaw twitched under the fine layer of stubble.

"Did I actually hit it?"

"Hard to say."

He hadn't. He wasn't ready. She shouldn't have had him try so many guns. She hadn't intended to frustrate him. She just hadn't believed his vision to be as bad as he'd claimed.

"No, it isn't." He set the gun down and looked at his trembling hands like they had betrayed him. "I can hear it in your voice."

"Were you able to ride a bike or swim the first time you tried?" she asked.

"No."

"It's just like that."

"I should tell you that I can't do either of those things."

She let out a sigh. "So you always started out knowing something? Never had to struggle with the learning of it?"

"I didn't waste my time on things I couldn't do."

So, he was one of those. Well, that was good to know, at least, if inconvenient. And it wasn't like he'd be the first student she'd have to shepherd through that process.

"Do you want to turn around? Go back to Sakura?"

"No." Sullen, he wiped at his brow.

"Then I won't make you. And as long as you keep trying"—she pointed at the guns—"I won't pack you back up and send you on your way."

Perhaps she should be relieved that he hadn't done well enough to think about carrying. Given that he *was* into pissing contests, he was likely to do something stupid again.

Something that wasn't going to end just with a broken nose.

The strong, smoky scent of creosote and coal accompanied the occasional "pssssht" of air bleeding off the locomotive's idle engine. The chimney was sending up tendrils of smoke in preparation for departure as Talia and Logan climbed into the passenger car.

They settled into one of the corner booths with padded seats and backs and a table lit by an overhead light. Talia settled her small travel case at the foot of the bench.

Their trunks—she had acquired one too, given her purchases—had been loaded into one of the luggage cars. Even after seven-plus years, it still surprised Talia to just be able to travel without going through a metal detector or showing licenses or permits—or having to pay bribes in order not to be subjected to extensive "enhanced screenings" at the whim of some petty functionary with delusions of grandeur or an axe to grind.

Sitting next to her in the aisle seat, Logan already had his notebook out. He set to flipping through pages and pages of mushroom diagrams. Notes crowded the edges and flowed around the sketches.

Slowly, the train car filled, passengers vying for position, moving their bags for passers-by, or waving to loved ones on the platform. She'd watched vigilantly for Rhodes and his men, but hadn't seen them. She'd even paid a bribe to get a look at the passenger manifest, despite knowing how easy it was to travel under a false name. She was betting that Rhodes was still in the habits of Earthers—used to giving a name to match an official ID, thinking it would be checked and verified.

She'd even given his description to the conductor and ticket examiner. They had both denied seeing anyone like him. Maybe, for a change, luck was on her side. She didn't think that Contesti's money could buy Rhodes or his men faster transport than the next train, which was not due to depart for five days. A five-day start on Rhodes would be a tremendous stroke of luck.

The clackety-clack of the rails and the hum of conversations around Talia made her settle deeper into the seat. Discreetly, she adjusted her gun to keep it from digging into her back as she pushed into the padding.

A little girl with braids sprouting from her head was sitting in a chair, book in her lap, reading to a doll while a boy—probably her brother—who was sitting in the seat behind her, reached up to tug her hair. She'd swat him away and ignore him only to have him redouble his efforts with a swifter tug.

The girl turned around, but he ducked behind the backrest and hid. Undeterred, the girl bent down to look underneath her seat. He shot up, climbed over to the next row of empty benches and lay in wait for her to settle in with her book again. Their tired mother was already snoring next to the girl, her head propped up against a shawl folded into a pillow.

Talia's own blinks lengthened, one after the other as she watched a repeat of the boy's antics. Embraced by the steady motion of turning wheels, the conversations around her swelled and then muffled.

The last time she'd seen Alexei, her brother had been almost-seventeen to her just-fifteen. Her brother who had taught her to shoot. Her brother with the same Eurasian features, the legacies of a people destroyed by a demographic-death spiral they had foreseen but were unable to stop. She and Alexei had been arguing about whose turn it was, just as if they were little kids fighting over a toy or a book or just because it was what siblings did.

Between one syllable and the next, between one blink and the next, a sheet of blood covered his face like someone had poured a bucket of paint over it. He'd touched his forehead. His fingers came away coated in blood.

She'd never forget that puzzled look in his eyes, like he wasn't sure what was happening. The fingers probed at the dent. The side of his head had been cratered in like a boiled egg someone had tapped against a plate.

Slowly, he toppled.

And toppled again.

And again.

Then slid through her arms.

Determined, she strained to keep him from sliding further, but her blood-slick arms couldn't hold him, couldn't keep him from sinking into the mud.

Fear was still pulsing through her when Talia startled awake, Alexei's name caught in her throat.

She'd grabbed onto Logan's arm with her prosthesis, pleating the fabric of his sleeve between her fingers.

"Are you all right?" Crinkled in concern, his eyes searched from behind distorting lenses.

"Yeah." She released his arm, pulled herself up. "Sorry."

"The beverage cart came through here while you were out. It can't be far. Can I get you something?"

She shook her head. "No, thank you. I'm fine. I'll be fine."

He looked like he was going to say something when a pair

of young women wearing matching bib-front pants and swing coats approached. They looked like sisters, with the same brown eyes and full lips.

Logan's face lit up. He straightened his back and ran a hand through his hair.

"Hello, ladies."

"Good afternoon," the shorter of the pair said. "May we offer you this pamphlet?"

She set down a pair of trifolded sheets, all while blazing a bright, eager smile.

Logan didn't even look down at the paper as he said. "Of course. Please. Can I help you pass them out?"

"No, thank you," the taller one said.

They giggled and departed as suddenly as they had arrived and moved on to the next table where they engaged with several young men before moving to the next car.

Logan flipped one of the sheets over. "Huh. Tunnelists."

Talia leaned over. An image of a rectangle folded in half covered the top section of the sheet. The two halves of the rectangle were connected by a tiny funnel, in an early representation of wormholes.

"I've lived on Sakura my whole life," Logan said. "Heard of them, but never seen any. Pretty though. Do you think it matters to them if I'm not one?"

"One what?"

"One of them."

"I don't know," Talia said. "Had some of them come through the spaceport at Sakura, but mostly they just pass through."

"What do you think about... you know?" His gaze lingered on the door like he was considering following them.

Talia smiled. "Their beliefs?"

He nodded.

"Never thought much about it. God creating the hyperspace conduits, the tunnels, so that Man can travel to the many worlds He made just for us seems as plausible as any of the explanations I've heard from the science types."

"Really?"

"Why are you so surprised?"

"I don't know. I just am. I figured someone from Earth would be more likely to credit Elke Mesuvreno for her tunnel drive or Luke Monreeves for financing the AIs needed to make it all work."

Talia turned the pamphlet over.

"Had an astrophysicist come through once," she said. "One of the navigators that works with the AIs that actually pilot the ships. I think I'd been on Gōruden maybe a year. She got drunk. Very drunk. Started to cry for no reason. I got tasked with taking her back to her room. Do you know why she was crying?"

Logan shook his head.

"Because she'd become a physicist in order to make sense of the universe. And the further she got into the physics of the hyperdrive, the less the equations made sense. The more 'magic' was involved. Her words, not mine. She said she had to make a leap of faith every time she turned the hyperdrive controls over to the AI. They're the only ones who actually understand the math. Something about humans not being able to visualize five-dimensional space."

"You still haven't answered my question."

She shrugged. "Logan, I don't know. I don't know how the locomotive works either. Or the implant that makes my prosthesis work. Hell, I'm not even sure how that pencil in your hand is made. Not really. I have a general idea, but I can't build one from scratch."

He put pen to paper, sketching out the Tunnelist's symbol and drew an arrow to the folded piece. He labeled the arrow: n=4, i.e. x, y, z, t. Then he drew another arrow, this time at the funnel representing a tunnel and labeled it: n>4.

"You're going to try to impress those girls with that, aren't you?" Talia asked.

He shot her a smile but didn't deny it.

"Are you an AI?" The words were softly spoken. Talia turned her head and looked down to locate their source.

A little boy with brown curls floating around his head was looking up at her. His hands were clasped behind his back, and he was rocking back on forth on his heels. He had the biggest, brownest eyes Talia had ever seen. And the most utterly adorable dimples in his cheeks.

"Excuse me?" Talia said, not sure she'd heard the boy right.

"Are you an AI?" A little louder. Just as confident. He looked up at her expectantly.

Talia blinked. "No. I'm not." She looked up helplessly. Surely an adult was missing this child.

The boy pointed at her hand. "What is that then?"

A young woman hurried down the aisle, cutting her way around people standing about.

"I'm sorry," she said coming up behind the boy and resting her hands on his shoulders. "He got away from me."

Logan perked up, put his notebook away and rose. "Hello, I'm Logan," he said, extending his hand.

The young woman shook his hand but didn't give him her name.

"Heather, look, an AI."

"Not an AI, sweetie. I'm sorry, ma'am. Sorry to bother you." Heather picked up the boy, propped him up on her hip and pivoted in the direction they'd come from.

"But, Heather—" the boy complained.

"Shush. You're going to miss the tunnel."

"Like the tunnels in the sky?"

"No, not like those."

Logan was looking longingly after Heather. Her errant charge had managed to escape her grip and befriend the girl with the book.

"I think I'm going to go to the observation car too," Logan said. "Get a good seat for the tunnel. Want me to save you a spot?"

Talia smirked. "No, thank you. Have fun though."

"Where you going?" He actually looked mildly interested in her answer.

"Just going to check out the other passengers. See if any of our friends made it aboard."

"Friends? What friends? Oh. Them." He reached up to smooth out his hair again. "All right, I'll catch up with you later."

"Stay out of trouble."

CHAPTER TWENTY-THREE

THE NEXT DAY, TALIA WAS HAVING LUNCH BY HERSELF. SHE'D given up trying to keep track of Logan. He seemed determined to meet every young woman on the train and flirt with her. Fearing provincial attitudes, Talia had, at first, worried that it might lead to trouble. Instead he seemed to be quite welcome, so she left him to it.

Thank goodness he hadn't shown any interest in her. He just wasn't her type.

During the night the train had made a stop and picked up additional passengers, making things far more crowded. She'd spent all morning looking for anyone who might fit the profile of mercenary-for-hire, while reluctantly admitting that just because the three thugs on the boat stood out, that didn't mean that they all would.

The train's horn blew and the cars slowed, making the water in her glass slosh. The waiters swayed in place, hastily compensating for the change in momentum until the train finally rolled to a stop. Strange. They were nowhere near their destination.

"What's going on?"

"Is it bandits?"

"I thought we weren't due to arrive until tomorrow."

"Ladies and gentlemen, please," the head waiter said. "Remain calm. I'm sure it's nothing."

The look on his face, however, didn't match his calming tone.

He leaned toward the bartender and whispered something in his ear. The bartender nodded and set up a tray, filling it with various drinks.

"We'll be bringing complimentary drinks for you, ladies and gentlemen. Just give us a moment."

Some diners settled back. Others twisted to get a better view out the windows. All morning the train had been winding its way through a dense forest where the canopies bowed over the tracks in places. They sent pink and white blossoms in through any open windows. But the train had come to a stop on a relatively clear piece of land. No longer a dense forest, instead copses of trees dotted a mostly prairie-like landscape.

Talia slid out from behind the table, placed a coin on the tablecloth, and wound her way through the waiters delivering the complimentary drinks.

She ducked through the vestibule and pushed forward through several passenger cars. Most everyone had gathered at the windows and some of the passengers had even disembarked.

A uniformed crew member, very official looking in his blue suit and matching tie, made his way down to the track, bullhorn in hand. Talia counted at least a dozen passengers on either side of the train. Some had stayed close to the track. Others had wandered off and were actively stretching their legs.

"Ladies and gentlemen. Ladies and gentlemen. Your attention please. Please stay behind the locomotive. I say again, please stay behind the locomotive. Sir, can I ask you to come back this way."

The young man who'd walked up to the locomotive came to a stop but didn't backtrack.

"Excuse me, ma'am."

Talia turned to face the man trying to get by her. He too was wearing a crewman's uniform but had a revolver strapped to his hip. His cap had a shield on it and so did his vest.

He jumped down to the ground and headed toward the locomotive, grim determination on his face.

Talia followed.

Other crewmen had gone out to persuade the errant passengers to return to the train. They weren't having much luck. A small group made up of young women had gathered about a hundred feet in front of the locomotive. Unsurprisingly, Logan was among them.

"Talia, come see, come see," he said upon spotting her.

The tracks were covered in a thick moving mass of brown-striped, foot-long millipedes. Millions of them by the look of it. The kiosk at the spaceport terminal. The cyanide bugs. Or worms. Or whatever they were.

"Leave them alone, please," the train cop was saying. "They're poisonous. Please, can I have you move back. Please, sir. Ma'am."

Some immediately backtracked, faces hidden behind hats or scarves or tucked into their shirts. Others ignored him entirely.

The train cop moved to another group that had formed and was heading for the swarming mass that seemed to run as far as Talia could see in both directions.

"Why don't we just run over them?" one of the young women in Logan's group asked.

"Because the resulting goo will make the tracks slick and derail the train," another answered. "Don't you pay attention in class?"

"They're gross," a third one said as she gathered up the pleats of her flowing pants. "I'm leaving." She grabbed a younger girl's hand, and they headed back to the train over the younger's rising protests.

"Ladies and gentlemen," the train cop said. "We'll need you to stay back. Please don't touch. There's no need to crowd in. We'll be here for a few hours. Sir, can I have you pull your kids back. Thank you."

About a dozen crew had made it to the front and were working to keep people back. Talia took advantage of the situation to look for Rhodes and his cohorts. She wandered up and down the track, mingling with the crowd.

Several people had brought out blankets and laid them out, and were sitting back, enjoying the sunshine.

A gaggle of little kids was playing soccer well away from the "ooey-gooey's" as one of them had called the millipedes.

That's when Talia caught sight of flowing red hair spilling out from underneath a wide-brimmed hat. The woman—dressed in black overalls—was walking away from Talia, a bag slung over one shoulder, towing a wheeled crate. It bumped along the ground, making the lid rattle.

"Maeve?" Talia said as she closed the distance between them.

The woman turned around.

"Talia!" Maeve rushed forward, closing Talia in a hug.

Maeve pulled back, held Talia by the shoulders. "What in the world are you doing here?" Maeve asked.

"I was on my way back to Tsurui. Didn't you get any of my messages?"

Maeve shook her head. "I've been gone. Three months now. Supply run."

"What's going on?" Talia asked.

Maeve slipped her arm through Talia's, and they headed for the swarm. "I make a supply run every other year. It takes a couple months, but this year, it's just been one thing after another."

"That's not what I mean. Is Lyle all right?"

"Why wouldn't he be? He met and married someone just before I left. I personally didn't care for her, but he's a grown man. Certainly doesn't need my approval."

A bitter look settled on her face as she said this, but it was brief. Perhaps it was nothing. Perhaps Lyle had simply found someone and everything was perfectly fine. Messages were bound to get lost in a system as fragmented as Gōruden's. That certainly made more sense than Lyle falling down on the job.

"Come. Help me. I'm going to collect some train millipedes."

"Whatever for?"

"They make a cyanide-like compound in their sacks. When threatened, they release it as a gas."

"A poison gas?"

Maeve flashed her a smile, reached into the bag slung over her shoulder, and pulled out a gas mask that looked like it had been plucked from a history book. Made mostly out of canvas and glass, it didn't look like something Talia would have trusted.

You're not on Earth anymore.

A conscientious crewman made a brief attempt to stop them but waved them through when Maeve showed him the gas mask and explained that she was an apothecary collecting samples.

"Aren't they going to object to you transporting them on their train?" Talia asked.

"No. The railroad itself would like to know more about them, and since it's hard to predict where they'll show up, I am doing them a favor by helping study them. Besides, only the larger ones—the adults—are actually able to produce a poisonous gas."

They came to a stop about two feet from the teeming brown mass. Talia hadn't thought herself squeamish. More than once she'd knifed an insect or a centipede that had gotten too close. She'd even let snakes slither over her rather than give away her position. But seeing so many of them together—

"They're a periodical organism," Maeve continued as she pulled on a pair of elbow gloves and fished a pair of long, metal tweezers out of the bag. "They swarm every twelve years when they have to find new feeding grounds. I'm going to get myself a few dozen juveniles. Not dangerous today, but maybe dangerous in a year or so. Here, hold this."

Talia gulped as she gathered the empty bag to her chest, holding it up like a shield. Every inch of her skin—real and phantom—was crawling.

"Do they bite?" Talia asked.

"No."

"Why do you need cyanide?"

"Pest control."

Maeve gathered up her hair, secured it into a bun at the base of her neck.

"You going to be all right?" she asked.

"Yeah, just don't mind me," Talia insisted, still holding on to her shield.

Maeve's face disappeared behind the gas mask. Tweezers in hand, she approached the swarm. Using some mysterious selection process, she'd pluck a millipede from the edges of the swarm and drop it through one of the holes in the crate's lid. There must have been some kind of latch mechanism to keep them from crawling back out because none of them seemed to poke back up.

The creatures seemed uninterested in Maeve as they flowed by her booted feet. Some would roll up into a ball only to be pushed along by their brethren before unfurling themselves and slithering away.

The millipedes Maeve was collecting were a paler brown, slightly smaller than most of the ones flowing by them. Still, they were far too long and had far too many legs and segments to endear themselves to Talia. They were too much of a frothing, wiggling mass of antennae, dual-pronged tails, and legs. They looked like living turds as they thrashed about. Bile made its way up Talia's throat.

"There," Maeve declared as she pulled the gas mask down. "I think that should be enough."

She raised a millipede to eye level, holding onto it gently with the tweezers. Antennae probed and waved about.

"There, there, it'll be all right," Maeve said, her voice going soft. "I'll take good care of you."

"Eww . . ." Talia made a sour face and walked away. Her shoulders rose as she tucked her elbows in and shook her palms out in front of her. The skin-crawling sensation manifested in the phantom as well, making her stop and rub at her prosthetic.

"Come on," Maeve said. "We have a lot to catch up on. And it's damned good to see you. I'm so glad you're back. You are back for good this time, right?"

By the time the train got underway again, Maeve had stowed her new acquisitions in a cargo car and changed out of the overalls. She had one of the rare and coveted private compartments. It was cramped, with a bed no bigger than those in the sleeper cars, but had its own bathroom and a small seating area that Talia now occupied. A compact storage compartment above the bed completed the space.

"So, catch me up," Maeve said. "What have you been doing with yourself?"

Talia summarized the last six months, glossing over the whole failing implant thing as Maeve laced the front of her blouse. She brushed out her hair as Talia went into saving Birgitta. The brush strokes paused and then resumed when she mentioned Muhonen's generosity.

"This man Rhodes, the mercenary," Talia continued. "He's convinced that Lyle will be easy to take down. Said he'd turned into a drunk."

Maeve had been leaning into a wall-mounted mirror, sweeping at the curve of her right eyebrow. She stopped midmotion. Turned around and leaned against the shelf occupied by her toiletries.

"It sounds like you believe him."

"No. Yes. I'm not sure how much of it was finding out who Rhodes was"—those pages and pages of redacted dossier flashed before her eyes—"and how much of it was from other things."

"What things?" Maeve's penetrating gaze would not be denied.

"Nightmares. From the time we served. They came back. It probably has more to do with me killing that young man, but it brought it all back. We were a team. He had my back. I had his.

And it just felt wrong. I just can't let him face Rhodes alone."

"Sounds like an attack of loyalty to me."

Talia leaned forward in the chair, rubbed at her eyes. She rested her elbows on her knees for a moment. Then told Maeve about Bates and her conglomerate, about Logan's theories on fungal blooms and the destruction of the biome.

Maeve listened and sank down on the edge of the bed.

"I think you're doing the right thing," Maeve said when Talia's recap came to an end. "Where's this exomycologist now?"

Talia looked up. "On the train somewhere. Now it's your turn. Who's looking after your shop?"

"Cora Haricot. One of Dame Leigh's granddaughters. Very savvy young woman."

"And this woman that Lyle married?"

"Siena Blade." Her tone was acid.

Talia's brow shot up, curious.

"I said that with some venom, didn't I?"

"Yes, some." A lot.

"Shortly after you left, he got tangled up with this woman," Maeve said.

"Let me guess. A redhead."

"Not even a real one, it turns out, but yes. I know that sounds petty, but..." She blinked and looked away.

"Did something happen?"

"I feel so foolish. One night, I was lonely. Earlier that day, I'd given away the bulk of Simon's things and pulled my wedding ring off. I've been working so hard to move on, move past, and have it feel solid, not like an act, not like a brave face. I know that grief comes back, that you find it in unexpected places, that it can ambush you when you least expect it, and I was prepared for that, but I wanted the next step."

She threaded a concho belt through a pair of jeans with decorative seams and pockets.

"Lyle and I," she continued, "we've danced around each other. Flirted. All harmless, all in good fun. And I missed that, because once we knew that Simon was dead, we stopped. It felt too much like desecrating his memory, like cheating. Cheating on a ghost, now that's one I'd never have believed."

There was a pause, a swipe at her eyes.

"That night, Lyle came by as I was closing up shop. I flirted with him. He flirted back then caught himself. And the look on his face, Talia. It was shame and guilt and a thousand other things I wasn't prepared for. His face shuttered and that's when he told me. He'd made Simon a promise. To see me away from Tsurui to some place better, some place safer. Simon had blamed himself for my miscarriage. Thought that it wouldn't have happened if I hadn't followed him to the hinterlands."

Maeve paused and took a deep breath.

"Can you imagine that? Thinking that I wasn't able to judge for myself, that I didn't have my own mind. The two of them, planning the rest of my life for me without so much as a 'Hey, Maeve, what do *you* want?'"

Talia could see it as clearly as if she'd witnessed it.

"So I slapped him. I slapped him hard. And he didn't even flinch. And he let me slap him again. And I raised my hand a third time, and he caught it and told me that he deserved the first two but that was all he was going to allow. And I was so angry, Talia, I've never been so angry, so torn.

"I thought he loved me, or could love me, that he was my friend if nothing else, that he saw me as a person as an individual worthy of respect. Instead... instead he saw me as Simon's wife, Simon's widow, and nothing more."

Talia doubted that last, but left it unspoken. Maeve was probably not ready to hear it.

"I'm sorry, Maeve. I really am."

"The next week this woman shows up. Came out here for all the same reasons he did: to settle down, get married, have children. A perfect match.

"I decided to leave on my supply run a week early. With how things have been going, the way Tsurui had been growing, I was running lower on stock than usual and everything that I could formulate was already formulated."

"And now you're back," Talia said.

"I have enough stock to expand my inventory. I have all these plans." She sprang off the bed and opened up the cabinet above it. It was filled with books. She pulled them down and handed them to Talia.

They were formularies for pharmacists and apothecaries, field guides, reference books. Hundreds of improvised bookmarks crowded the pages, threatening to slip out if given the opportunity. Talia held them all carefully in her lap.

"I'm not leaving Tsurui. I have friends, people who rely on me and what I make for them. I'm respected for what I do. I have a purpose there."

"Yes, you do," Talia said.

"And now you're back too, and I hope you'll stay." Lovingly, she took the books and set them beside her on the mattress. "No matter what Lyle says or thinks."

A matter for another day.

There was still that matter of being seen as an outsider who had first come to Tsurui at Contesti's behest. As the woman who'd brought a dead Elias Haricot home to his people.

"And the Contesti thing," Talia said to change the subject. "Have you heard anything new on that?"

"Shortly after you left, Contesti made Dame Leigh a buyout offer. One she turned down. Everyone expected Contesti to make another move. Bring in more men, turn up the pressure. Instead, nothing. At least not that I've heard. They are fighting this on two fronts. Not just in Tsurui, but in court. Back on Earth. But now, it sounds like he's been waiting for this man, this mercenary. How many men do you think he'll be bringing for whatever they're planning?"

"I don't know," Talia admitted. "That kind of money can buy you a lot of men. A lot of firepower."

CHAPTER TWENTY-FOUR

NOT QUITE AS BIG AS MINAMIOGUNI, BUT BIGGER THAN TSURUI, Shiiba was just as Talia remembered it. A pair of tracks led into the passenger station with its glassed roof. Talia looked up, past the columns supporting the soaring arches. Clouds were gathering in the twilight.

Shouldering her bag, Talia stepped down onto the platform's slate tiles. People milled about, moving hurriedly past the metal and wood benches facing the tracks. The scent of burning coal and oil was thick as Maeve and Logan followed.

She kept seeing Rhodes out of the corner of her eye only to find that it was merely some man who shared a trait with him—height or dark hair or confidence.

Belching a cloud of steam, the train pulled away, leaving Talia, Maeve, and Logan standing by a mountain of trunks and crates—all but two belonging to Maeve.

Logan was waving goodbye to about a dozen young women leaning out the train windows.

"You've been busy," Talia said, amusement twisting her lips.

Red washed up from his neck to the tips of his ears. "You just have to be a good listener."

A line of porters, each leading a hand truck, was making its way toward them.

"You're riding with me of course," Maeve said as she waved at the porters.

The hand-truck wheels made a steady rat-tat-tat sound as they rolled over the tiles, drowning out the idle chatter of the passengers around them.

"Do you think you'll have room?" Talia eyed the crates and trunks.

"The stagecoach seats four, easy. The rest is going to ride in a wagon."

"Mrs. York?" The lead porter tipped his hat at Maeve.

Maeve directed the porters and gave them instructions on which crates she wanted loaded first. They set to work and whisked her cargo through the booking hall and out of the passenger station.

A stagecoach and wagon waited for them at the curb. Eight horses—four for the wagon, two for the coach, and two spares—stomped impatient hooves as the porters handed the baggage to Maeve's men.

She greeted the head man with a hug and a kiss. He was thick with muscle covered in fat, his hands gnarled, skin darkened by the sun to the color of burnt toast.

"Tony. Sorry we're late. It's been one thing after another."

Maeve made introductions all around as Tony's men hoisted Logan's trunk to the coach's roof. On impulse, Talia pulled her newly acquired shotgun out of her travel trunk before handing it over.

Tony yelled at the other men, assigning positions and shifts. He went over to inspect the wagon, tested the ropes that had been used to tie things down, went around the wheels.

"Tony's very thorough," Maeve said.

Satisfied with his men's work, Tony opened the coach door and gestured in invitation.

Maeve gave him her hand, let him assist her up. Talia did the same, imitating the ladylike angle of the wrist. Talia slid into the forward-facing bench and set the shotgun in the corner, barrel pointing up. Maeve took a seat beside her, leaving Logan the rearward-facing seat.

"I sure am glad to see you back, Maeve," Tony said through the window. He wiped sweat off his brow and stuffed the handkerchief back into his pocket.

"How long until we reach Tsurui?" Logan asked.

"Assuming the road isn't washed out again, we should be there by midnight."

"And if it is?" Talia asked.

"Detour. There are a few other ways to get there, longer ways. So morning at the latest. Will you be staying this time, Miss Merritt?"

"That depends," Talia said. "Have a lot of new people come into town? To work for Signore Contesti that is."

"A few."

"Have you seen a man with a scar on his face. Very cultured, soft-spoken. Not a thug."

"No. That I would remember. Why?"

"Just curious," she lied.

They pulled in front of Maeve's shop early the next morning. Tsurui was quiet except for a few scattered pedestrians hurrying through the rain-soaked and mostly empty streets. Tony and his men set about moving Maeve's cargo and supplies into her shop.

Talia made her way to the jailhouse with Logan in tow, ducking under covered walkways whenever possible to avoid the steady rain. She ignored Logan's chatter about his favorite subject—fungi.

They seemed to be growing everywhere, and he would stop and scrape a sample into the test tubes he was carrying with him, then stop to make notes about the time and location in a notebook.

"Do you have to do that right now?" she asked the fifth time he stopped them.

She remained under the covered walkway as he beelined for a small fountain that filled up an intersection. Water spilled from the mouth of a metal *kitsune* statue. It was surrounded by moss, leaves, and apparently mushrooms.

"Yes," he said simply. "These are very delicate."

Water was beading on his hat and running down in little trickles as he wrote in his notebook. The paper had apparently been designed to be usable even when wet.

"Do we have time to go to the temple?" Logan pointed to the torii gate at the other end of the street.

"Not now. Later."

She looked up and around, almost gave in to tapping her foot. Sight lines revealed themselves as always, forming almost like magic out of the air. Fortunately, there was no one behind those lines, just her imagination filling in information as if her mind was like a muscle yearning to be used once again.

Logan skirted the edge of the fountain, bending down far enough to almost touch the moss-covered lip with his nose.

The flesh-toned glove on Talia's prosthetic was getting wet and soggy, sending a different signal than her merely cold and wet left hand. She'd get used to it eventually. At least that's what she told herself. The nearly constant expectation that the prosthesis might malfunction was taking its toll, sending her hyperawareness into overdrive, making her phantom twitchy.

Logan put away his pencil and tucked his waterproof notebook away. For someone with bad distance vision, he seemed quite adept at finding things that caught his eye.

"Oh, look, another—" He headed for a patch of color on a nearby post. At least it was in the right direction.

He leaned close, close enough that for a second Talia thought he might lick it. Instead, he wrinkled up his face.

"What's wrong?" she asked.

"It's just bat guano."

A second later, he headed the wrong way again, and she grabbed him by the collar. "I need to go see Lyle. And I need to do it now. You can go mushroom hunting later."

"They're not mushrooms. Not yet, anyway. Did you know that mushrooms are actually the fruiting bodies of a higher fungus. Their function is to spread spores, in essence to colonize—"

She tuned him out and hurried toward the jailhouse. Like most of Tsurui's buildings, it has been built by the original colonists in late-nineteenth- and early-twentieth-century styles to take advantage of the low-tech base that they expected to maintain. The brick and stone construction, along with the antennae sprouting from the tiled roof, made the jailhouse stand out, but there was nothing else obviously high-tech about the building. Its windows were smaller than those of the storefronts across the street. She'd expected bars but there were none.

"That's far enough," someone said. The voice was familiar, but it wasn't Lyle.

Talia came to a stop. "I'm here to see the sheriff."

The door swung open and CorgiSan and DespairBear came running out, their robotic legs splashing in puddles as they circled her. DespairBear trotted up to Logan. The robot didn't quite give him a sniff, but it did look him up and down.

"John," she said as CorgiSan circled her, a spring in his step like he was happy to see her. "It's Talia. I'd really like to get out of the rain if you don't mind."

DespairBear shook himself, making the netting and all its assorted odds and ends clatter. A bruised hydrangea that had caught in the net flopped into a puddle and swirled around in the muddy water.

Logan was leaning toward the dogs, reaching out as if to pet them, but they were playing keep-away, darting out of reach and then stopping to look at him expectantly.

"Are these guys supposed to be some kind of watch dogs?" Logan asked, amused.

"Not exactly."

She doubted that they had the instincts of dogs, the kind of thing that was supposed to make them tell good guys from bad. They were merely acting in accordance with their programming—pretending to be playful dogs.

A whistle made the robots turn their heads and head for the wraparound porch.

"Who's that with you?" Definitely John.

"Friend. He's harmless."

Logan came up behind her, lingered at her side. Slowly, he raised his hands, as if to confirm that he wasn't a threat.

"A little late for that," she quipped.

The wind shifted, blowing raindrops at his face and settling on his glasses. He blew out a breath, making them steam up.

"I guess you'd better come on in," John said and waved them through.

The door rattled closed behind them.

"What are you doing back in town, Miss Merritt?"

Despite the question he looked glad to see her, a grin on his weathered face. He'd trimmed his beard up as well. It no longer touched his chest, although he did look like it had grayed a bit. The blue-and-green checkered shirt looked freshly pressed underneath a brown leather vest.

She shook off her coat, hung it up on the coatrack next to John's dark gray one, and did the same with her hat. There was a wood-burning stove in the corner and a large desk across from it. Maps of Tatarka decorated the walls, pinned to the boards with crude nails. Benches bracketed the heavy main door.

"Came to see Lyle," she said.

"You heard?"

"Yes."

"Well," John said, "he's in there, but he's passed out. Who's your harmless friend?"

"John, this is Dr. Logan Temonen."

John passed an appraising gaze over Logan like he didn't quite believe someone so young could be a doctor. Maybe she could talk Logan into growing a beard or something. Anything to make him look a little older.

"I doubt a doctor is what he needs," John said. "More like a swift kick in the ass."

"I'm not that kind of doctor," Logan said as he approached the stove and held his hands out over it.

"What kind are you then?" Another skeptical look.

"Exomycologist."

John let out a long whistle like he was impressed. "Well, Tatarka's the place to be then. There's mushrooms everywhere."

He turned to Talia. "He's not going to be happy to see that you're back."

"Oh, I know that. In fact, I'm counting on it."

"He's been doing a lot of talking, when he's not himself. More talking than he's done in all the years I've known him. Now I know why he never talked about you before." John's gaze drifted down to her gloved prosthesis.

So, he must have told John that he'd been the one to cut off her hand. That he'd been the one she'd come to rescue. That she'd lost three men in coming after him. That they'd never really worked out the guilt and blame, that they both felt responsibility for things both beyond and within their control.

She pulled the soaked glove off and set it near the stove on a run of twine that had been obviously strung up as a drying line.

"How long before he wakes up?"

"Not sure. Have no idea how long it's been since he dosed himself."

"Dosed himself?"

"So you *haven't* heard," John said.

The anger she'd been nursing didn't quite evaporate. Instead it seemed to swirl inside her stomach, looking for a place to go.

John settled himself in the desk chair, propped his booted feet up on the desk itself, took out a pipe, and lit it. He blew out the match and with a flick, sent it into a small metal receptacle on the other side of the room.

"Better tell me what you know then, or think you know." He puffed on the pipe.

Talia counted back from five. She wasn't going to strangle him, no sir. That would be foolish. And counterproductive.

"That Lyle is a drunk."

"Is that why you're back?" He narrowed his eyes at her.

"Never mind why I'm back, John. Tell me what happened." Her phantom curled into a fist. One that she had to force open. The prosthetic obeyed, uncurling one knuckle at a time.

"He's not a drunk, Talia. He's an addict. Hypnolin."

Talia blinked. Sank into the other high-backed chair, the one conveniently set up on the other side of the desk.

"From the top please," she said, rubbing at the ache between her eyes.

"Siena—Lyle's new wife—got tangled up with some of Contesti's men. Nobody is sure exactly how she ended up at his estate, but he rode in to 'rescue' her."

"You say that like it wasn't a rescue."

"Picked up on that, did you? Good for you. Contesti's men have stories, but no one knows what to believe. Allegedly, Siena went to the estate willingly. But don't repeat that to him. Not unless you want a taste of his fist."

"That just doesn't sound like Lyle," Talia said. It really didn't. The redhead thing, yes, but not the rest.

"Yeah, well, love does strange things to a man. Clouds his thinking. Hard to say how much of it was infatuation—or love—and how much of it was the hypnolin. He got hurt in the 'rescue' and thought that Siena was just giving him something for the pain. He pushed a deputy badge on me because of it and I took it, figuring he needed the help."

"Did he?"

"Well, he wasn't coming into work as early. Or staying as late. Then he started missing calls. Sometimes didn't come in to work for days. So one morning, Lyle wakes up and finds a note. Siena saying it was all a mistake. That this was not the life she'd been looking for after all. Told him not to bother looking for her. Lyle was the only one surprised. He didn't like our 'we told you so.' Got angry. Went off on the whole town, threatened to resign, disappeared for a few days."

Talia wasn't going to shake her head, no matter how much

she wanted to. She wasn't going to shake it in denial or disbelief. Not a single time.

John blew a smoke ring and then another.

"Caspar and I rode out to his place to check on him. Found him face down at his kitchen table, passed out, gun in hand."

"Did he..." The question died on Talia's lips.

"He might have tried. We found an empty hypnolin bottle. Caspar thinks he was either hallucinating or that...well, hypnolin makes one prone to suggestion and there was no one to 'guide' him, so his own mind took him to places it shouldn't have."

Talia had a pretty good idea of what those places might be. Battlefields, funerals, nightmares.

"How long ago was that?" Talia asked.

"A month or so."

"Where's he been getting the hypnolin from, John?"

"Contesti's new club."

"And why are you allowing it?"

John dropped his feet to the floor, leaned forward so he was up against her face.

"Because he's in pain, Miss Merritt. More pain than he can stand. And I can only watch him endure it for so long. He takes a little and it helps. He functions just fine. His hands are steady as a rock. He's clearheaded, focused, everything you'd want in a sheriff. Until he's not."

"So you just let him have it?" She searched John's eyes and found moisture there.

"No, I don't just let him have it." John pulled away, rested against the back of the chair. "But it's better than the alternative."

"Which is?"

"Finding him with his brains blown out because he can't stand the pain. But now that you're here, maybe you can do what I can't. Now, if you'll excuse me, I have to pretend that the law is still on the job."

He stood up and grabbed a portable radio from its charger by the wall-sized central unit. The slam of the door shook the rafters. The patter of robotic paws followed him off the deck.

"Friendly fellow," Logan said. "Want me to go after him?"

"No," Talia said. "He'll be back."

She was almost certain he would be anyway.

CHAPTER TWENTY-FIVE

TALIA OPENED THE DOOR LEADING INTO THE HOLDING AREA. THE stone walls were even thicker than the front room. A metal grid had been worked into the stone, forming two windowless cages.

What looked like a barrel-fed field shower was tucked into a corner. Lyle was sprawled facedown on the cot inside one of the cages. The door was propped open. There were no electronics here, but the lock looked sturdy enough, at least to her eyes.

Lyle needed a haircut and a bath, as well as a change of clothes. He smelled of vomit and urine, of pain and terror. The pattern of pit and back sweat had rings like a tree, like he'd been wearing the same shirt for far too long.

She covered her nose with her left hand and approached him cautiously, slipping through the open cage door with ease. He was snoring—a loud, droning buzz just like she remembered. He let out a vile fart as she shook his shoulder.

"Are you sure that waking him is a good idea?" Logan asked. He'd stayed back, leaning against the frame of the door leading to the front room.

"No," she admitted.

"Why not just let him sleep it off?"

"Because I'm pissed, that's why. Because I promised myself I'd kick his ass when I got here."

"Think he'd appreciate it more if he was conscious then," Logan said.

"You're right." She put her back into turning Lyle over, but he was all dead weight. Finally, he gave way, ending up with his back against the cell wall, his face slack.

He looked like he hadn't shaved in a few days, and the lines in his face were so deep she'd have thought it had been a decade, not half a year, since she'd seen him. His skin was loose, almost a size too big.

"Oh, Lyle," she whispered. "How could you let her do this to you?"

Lyle let out another fart that filled the little room with the most noxious odor. Logan made a face too, and took a step back.

"What has he been eating?" Logan asked.

"Probably not much by the look of him."

"You know, there's this study that I read about fungi that excrete this enzyme that interferes wi—"

"Not interested in another science lesson, Professor."

Talia took the metal pitcher that had rolled over to the corner of the cell in hand. It was empty but the soaked rug on the floor told her that it had probably once held water. Or at least she hoped that it was water making the rug squishy.

"Fill this up for me, will you?" She held it out until Logan took it from her.

He walked over to the sink and primed the pump. "I doubt that water is going to help unless you get a lot down him. An IV would be better."

"We're not in Sakura anymore," she said. "Have you seen what passes for an IV out here?"

Water flowed as Logan shook his head.

"Big needle, rubber tubing, glass container. The Haricots probably have some on hand. Maeve probably does too."

Logan carried the pitcher over and leaned in to look as he held his nose. "So, what's the water for then?"

"Step back, will you?"

"Why?" He did step back though. All the way to the door leading into the front room.

Talia dipped her hand into the pitcher. It wasn't quite as cold as she would have liked. She stood up. Took a step back herself. And then threw the water right into Lyle's face.

He was up like a shot, fist flying. The first one missed her and hit the bars. He yowled in pain, eyes wide like he didn't see her, or anything.

She sidestepped his second attempt. He slipped, landing in the fresh puddle Talia's pitcher had just created. But he didn't get up.

Blinking, he rubbed at his face.

"What did you do that for?" His speech was slurred and slow. He really did sound drunk. Moved like he was drunk too.

"Hello, Lyle," she said, squatting down so she could look him in the eyes.

"Oh, it's you." He squinted. His face contorted. "When did you get back?"

"Just now."

"And you came to visit your old friend first. How touching." He held out his hand.

Talia stood, offered him her right hand.

He took hold of the prosthesis, looked at it, and let out a little giggle as he got his feet under him.

She held steady, waiting for him to shift his weight.

She didn't expect the punch. He got her right in the eye and cheek, sent her sprawling. She bounced off the cage door's frame, landed on the floor outside the cell. He fell back on the cot, and it made a straining sound like it was considering ejecting him in protest.

"Just give me a minute," he said as his arms and legs worked against each other, reminiscent of a bug on its back. "I'm not done yet."

The orbit of Talia's eye ached and throbbed. Her head did too. The room did a little spin against a backdrop of light flashes and then righted itself, albeit uncertainly.

"I think you are," she said, touching her face with her left hand. It was already swelling by the feel of it. And her eye was watering, making it feel like it was about to shed tears.

Aww, hell. Anything but tears, for fuck's sake.

"You never could take me in a straight-up fight, Talia." He was panting, clutching at his chest as he settled back in the cot, like he'd given up trying to fight against it.

She kicked the cell door shut with her foot. It made the rafters shake but latched shut. She had no clue if that meant it was locked or not.

"I don't intend to give you a straight-up fight, Lyle. I'm not an idiot."

He scoffed. "Get John in here. Tell him I need, I need..." He was wheezing now.

"Need what, Lyle?" she asked as she pushed up. "Hypnolin? Is that what you need?"

"What of it?" He smirked, pulled himself to his feet. He looked surprised, as if he'd not expected to succeed, as if he was working somebody else's body, not his own. He took a step forward and came crashing down, limbs akimbo, right up against the bars, like a marionette with its strings cut.

Drool seeped out of his mouth, dripped down his chin.

"Well, that's inconvenient," Talia said as she made a fist and held it steady.

Lyle slid further down the bars until his chin caught on a lateral piece of metal.

Talia rotated her phantom's wrist and the prosthesis obeyed. She flexed the fingers open. It was working perfectly fine, so well in fact that she'd looked down to check the condition of her manicure. One that wasn't there.

"Damn." She lowered her hands.

"What's wrong?" Logan asked.

"Getting mixed signals from the prosthesis," she said. It was as much detail as she was willing to give him. Telling him that she'd expected to break a nail was going to make her sound crazy.

"Not to go all professorial on you again," he said, "but I have an idea."

Hours later Talia was holding a cold, wet rag atop her eye and cheek, wishing they had ice. Every once in awhile John would bring her a fresh rag from the cold box.

"Well, it could have been worse," John told her as she leaned her elbows on the desk in the front room, contemplating the state of her manicure. The slaughter-red sparkles were still remarkably intact.

She'd been punched before. But that had been years—no, a decade—ago. She'd even been punched by Lyle during sparring bouts and one particularly bad evening after a botched-up mission. She'd always known that Lyle had pulled his punches before, whether he'd done it intentionally or not.

Sometimes it sucked being right. The swelling was moving down to her jaw, making her teeth ache.

John poured her a finger of whiskey. "What did you say your friend was off to do?"

"He said he had something that might help get Lyle off the hypnolin. Just needed to mix it up right. Are you sure your boys understood what was needed?"

"They understand basic speech. They know where Maeve lives. Assuming your buddy is capable of following them, they will lead him to the right place."

John had sent the robots with Logan because he couldn't remember how to get back to Maeve's. Apparently he'd been too distracted by the mushrooms that had sprung up with the rain. She hoped that he was actually capable of just following the robots. She could see him getting similarly distracted and ending up who knows where.

John leaned up against the column in front of the gun racks and radio panel. Muted status lights blinked behind him. Every once in awhile there would be a crack or a hiss. Four handheld units were lined up, charging, the batteries blinking red and amber.

While she understood the reasons for not having a freezer, for saving what electrical power they could generate for important things, Talia still wished they had one. She would much rather have real ice or a gel pack for her face than the soggy rag.

"We need to get this done before Contesti's people find out I'm back," she said, turning the rag over, seeking a cold spot.

"Why is that?"

"Because while Contesti promised that I'd get safely back to Sakura, he made no promises about what would happen if I came back here. Especially if I came back on the wrong side. He might look at me as the first of a wave of reinforcements."

John let out a huff of air that might have been a scoff. One she wasn't going to take personally. She wanted John and the other townspeople not to see her as anything but a friend of Lyle. Her reputation wasn't something that was just based on her kills. Some idiot propaganda officer had tried to make her into something she wasn't before. It hadn't turned out well.

"This doctor buddy of yours, how much do you know about him?"

"He's a scientist. Studies mushrooms. Doesn't see well or shoot well. Flirts a lot. He's harmless."

"Lyle said the same thing about Siena," John said.

"What do you mean?"

"I think Siena was working for Contesti."

She shot him a glare and lowered the cloth. "Are you suggesting that Contesti anticipated me coming back and somehow orchestrated my acquaintance with Logan?"

"Lyle said you were a smart girl."

She grimaced. "He said no such thing. For one, he would have used the word 'bitch.'"

"And 'smart.' That being the operative word."

She sighed. She could not imagine Logan as some deep agent. Although if he was one, he wasn't just good—he was amazing. She opened her mouth to tell him exactly that but the sound of pounding feet coming up the porch steps interrupted her. It was followed by another pair of steps and knocking.

John looked out the peephole and opened the door.

Logan and Maeve came through. Outside, the rain had turned into a sort of misty drizzle and in the distance, someone made a gong ring out. The air was so wet it muffled its report. Maeve shook out her coat and hung it up along with her hat.

"Where are the robots?" Talia asked.

"They're programmed to patrol the perimeter at this time of day," John said. "Not that it'll do any good."

Maeve made a face as she crossed the room and took hold of Talia's chin. "That looks like it hurts."

"It does."

"I hope you gave as good as you got," Maeve said.

Talia shrugged, tapped the fingers of her prosthesis on the tabletop. She'd been afraid to punch with that hand ever since she'd gotten it. It may have weighed the same as her missing flesh, but it had no fleshy parts to cushion a blow. Even when she'd punched Rhodes, she'd used her left hand.

"Well, did you get what you needed?" Talia asked Logan.

"Yeah, about that," Maeve answered instead. "Did you know he's working the formula from memory?"

"No, I did not." Talia panned her gaze from Maeve to Logan.

He had the good sense to look sheepish. "I have a very good memory."

"Ah-ah-ah." Maeve made a scolding, side-to-side motion with her forefinger. "Let's be specific here, Professor."

Logan took his glasses off and wiped them down with a dry

handkerchief from his front pocket. He did so in silence. Twice. When he reseated the glasses atop his face he merely smiled.

"He got a passing glance at something in a journal a few years ago," Maeve said.

"That must be a helluva memory," John said.

"It is," Logan said proudly.

Talia's jaw clicked shut. "Maeve, you know stuff. His kind of stuff, right?"

Maeve crossed her arms. "Well, I watched him make it. The stuff he had in that trunk... do you have any idea what he had in there?"

Talia shook her head.

"Well, if I didn't know any better, I'd say he was aspiring to be an embalmer."

"Are you?" Talia asked Logan.

"Family business. My father was a mortician. Some of the tools of the trade overlap. Others, well, they have sentimental value."

"Very convenient explanation," John said, but he was looking at Talia.

"So, what do we have?" Talia asked.

Logan reached into his coat and pulled out a small wooden box. He set it down on the table and flipped up the lid. A syringe, the old-fashioned kind with metal thumb- and finger-rings, rested inside, filled with a yellowish-green liquid.

Her skin crawled at the size of that needle. She didn't want it anywhere near her. It was huge.

"It's an antagonist," Logan explained. "It's going to make it so hypnolin doesn't do anything for him, except maybe make him really sick. He's not going to be happy—in fact, he's going to be miserable—but he won't be prone to suggestion."

"How long does it last?" Talia asked.

"A few days."

John came closer, looked at the box. His eyes went wide, and he gulped hard enough that she heard it. He tossed a look over his shoulder at the holding area.

"Even if it works," John said, "is that going to be long enough? He's been on it for months."

"It works. I can tell you that for sure," Logan said.

"That," John said pointedly, "is a lot of certainty for someone who saw the formula in a journal."

"I looked up the formula because I saw how well it worked."

"Saw?" Maeve asked.

"Clinical trial."

"Saw a report, you mean," John said, still skeptical. He kept looking into the other room like he was waiting for Lyle to rise from his stupor.

"So why aren't they using this to cure all the hypnolin addicts?" Maeve asked.

"It's still waiting for approval," Logan said matter-of-factly. "Maybe in ten or twenty years, after it's made it through all the bureaucracy back on Earth, you'll see it being used here."

Maeve said something under her breath as she reached into the box and picked up the syringe.

"What are you doing?" John asked.

"Well, I'm not going to wait ten or twenty years, if that's what you're thinking, and I'm not going to debate it any further. You guys hold him down. I'll give him the shot."

"What if it kills him?" John asked. He looked, and sounded, genuinely afraid. Not just concerned, not just skeptical, but terrified.

"Then I guess Dr. Temonen here will be looking for a new job," Maeve said.

"I'm not that kind of doctor."

"Rest assured," Maeve said, "if this kills Lyle, no one will ever assume you are one again."

"Maybe we should ask L—"

"It's my call, John," Maeve said.

"How is it your call?" John asked, eyebrows drawing together in a frown.

"I love him. And while I have my doubts about this concoction, I'd rather give it a try than stand by as he slowly kills himself. Ever since that Siena bitch got her claws into him, I've been kicking myself for not doing something. Well, I'm not going to wait until he blows his own brains out. You going to help me or am I on my own?"

For a moment Talia thought that John was going to back out. She could tell that this was personal for him, somehow, although she wasn't sure why. There was old pain in his eyes, the set of his shoulders, like guilt was riding him and had been for a long time.

He met her gaze and nodded. "Where does it go?"

"Backside, I think." Maeve threw a questioning look at Logan.

He nodded.

"I'll take one arm," John said. "You"—he pointed at Logan—"take the other. Talia, think you can pin his legs down?"

"I should be able to do that, yes."

An image of her boot on Lyle's ass formed and lingered for a satisfying moment.

John and Logan didn't even bother lifting Lyle off the floor. He'd crumpled onto it after falling into the bars and just slid down onto the soaked rug where he'd been lying the entire time. The men repositioned him so that everyone could fit inside the cage.

Lyle let out a muffled groan. Drool and snot poured out of him, coating his whiskers.

"I don't like his breathing," Maeve said as they moved him into position.

Logan knelt at Lyle's side and John mirrored him. Talia straddled his legs, pinned his thighs to the floor with her hands. Standing with her boot on his ass just wasn't going to do it, no matter how much she liked the thought of it.

"I think we're ready, Maeve," she said.

Maeve pulled at Lyle's waistband, bared a cheek, and plunged the needle into it.

The muscles in Lyle's thighs tightened under Talia's grip and his calves spasmed under her bottom.

Maeve stepped back, holding the needle up. "That's it." She looked and sounded surprised.

"I'd leave the room now, if I were you," Logan said.

"He's out. He's fine." Maeve sounded very sure.

"No, I'd really like to leave this room. But ladies first." There was warning in his eyes and voice and the way that he was bearing down on Lyle like he expected to be thrown off.

Talia and Maeve made it into the front room just as Lyle made a loud sound, not quite a scream.

Logan stumbled up and out, with John skipping after him. They latched the cage shut as Lyle rolled over and let out a blood-curdling wail.

John wiped at his brow. "This normal, Doc?"

"I think so."

"You think so?"

"Well, it hurts. Some subjects reported that it felt like their veins were on fire."

"Failed to mention that didn't you?" John said.

"Some subjects, not all," Logan said defensively.

"What else can we expect?" Talia asked.

"A small number of subjects became violent, usually for a few minutes, and then they passed out."

"And then?" Maeve asked and bit her lip as she looked at Lyle's prone form. He'd gone fetal and was groaning like a man with his belly on fire. His face contorted, turned red. He whimpered and twitched like someone was kicking him.

"He's not going to thank you when the pain comes back and nothing works to alleviate it."

"What do you mean by nothing?" John asked.

"Nothing. That's part of the other reason it's going to take awhile to get approval. The antagonist makes all pain-relief ineffective. At least for awhile."

"Should've told us that," John mumbled.

"It wouldn't have mattered," Maeve said as she turned away. "I'd still have done it."

"I need a drink," John said as he grabbed his hat and shotgun. He took one of the portable radios too, slipped it into a clip on his belt without testing it.

He stalked past the whiskey bottle on the desk, left the door ajar, and called for the robots to follow him.

"You made the right call, Maeve," Talia said as she patted Maeve's shoulder.

Maeve brought her hands to her face, hunched her shoulders, and leaned into Talia.

She let her cry.

CHAPTER TWENTY-SIX

JOHN DID EVENTUALLY COME BACK, ALTHOUGH IF HE'D HAD anything to drink, Talia could not smell it on him. They took turns keeping an eye on Lyle, making sure that he was breathing.

"A deep sleep is normal," Logan said. "Some subjects were unconscious for close to twenty-four hours. Of course they had IVs, so maybe..."

The door rattled as Maeve reentered the jailhouse. "Did someone say IV?"

She was holding up a glass bottle with rubber tubing hanging from it.

John turned a little green as he watched Maeve poke around Lyle's veins. She wrapped a bandage around the needle protruding from the arm.

"This needs to stay wrapped," Maeve said. "Consider it your job to keep it that way."

"Sure," Talia said.

"No problem." Logan's tone belied his words.

"Talia," Maeve said, "on the coach you mentioned something about teaching Logan how to shoot."

"You don't know how to shoot?" John gave Logan an incredulous look.

"Not much call for it in Sakura," Logan said defensively.

"Our things are still over at Maeve's place," Talia said. "But yes, I'd very much like to take Logan out, maybe practice some of my long-range shots as well."

Like anything, it was a perishable skill.

John scratched his head. "All right. I have a place I think will work. Bit of a drive out though. I'll bring the wagon around. Come, boys."

DespairBear and CorgiSan had been sitting on their charging mats in the front room. John picked up one of the shotguns hanging on the wall and loaded it.

"Wait?" Logan said. "Do you just leave the jailhouse, you know, unattended?"

"We don't have anyone under arrest. Besides, Maeve is going to keep an eye on Lyle and I'm tired of being cooped up. Aren't you?"

Maeve reached into a pocket, pulled out a metal key and tossed it at Talia. "Lock the shop back up when you're done."

John pulled the wagon to the front. Both of the robots were sitting next to John like it was the place they usually rode.

"In the back, both of you," he directed the dogs.

With what Talia could only describe as reluctance, they jumped into the back. Talia took her place next to John while Logan hopped in with the dogs. They cuddled up to him, one on each side, and CorgiSan settled his chin on Logan's thigh. DespairBear propped his front paws on the side rails and put his snout into the wind.

They stopped by Maeve's shop. It only took a few minutes to load Talia's trunk into the back.

They crossed several streams, all swollen by the recent rains. "Something doesn't make sense to me, John."

"And what would that be?" He urged the horses on.

"Why not just outright kill him? Why go through all this drama of getting Lyle hooked on hypnolin?"

"You mean Contesti."

"Yes. I mean, it's possible that this woman had nothing to do with Contesti, right? That she was just trying to help Lyle deal with the pain. If she had been kidnapped by Contesti's men, or even if she'd gone there willingly—for whatever reason—but not been allowed to leave, then had to deal with Lyle getting hurt because of that. It's shitty, but I can see her deciding that this wasn't the life for her."

"You weren't here."

"Fair enough. Why do you suspect her?"

It was like she'd opened the floodgates. She didn't think he was capable of so many words, so long a story. Over the next hour he told her about all the times he'd seen Siena Blade talking to Contesti's men, how often he'd told himself that it was nothing because he didn't want to ruin things.

He told her of the time he'd followed Siena and been caught. How she'd pretended to be hurt by his lack of trust. At first, he'd thought it was genuine, she'd been so convincing.

"She'd always had a good reason, you know." He cleared his throat and hawked spit over the side. "I should've trusted my gut."

"All right. Which brings us back to why set Lyle up?"

"Contesti knows that the murder of an elected official will draw the wrong kind of attention from the planetary authorities, such as they are. Maybe give credence to any accusations of impropriety regarding any claims or filings, of things being done under duress. That's still a thing here. Earth may not see it that way, but Sakura does. As long as there is anyone to testify that there was duress, anything signed while under duress is null and void."

"A sheriff who's an addict or a drunk on the other hand," Talia said, "is not likely to attract the attention of planetary authorities."

"Not only that, but his testimony on the matter of duress, even if he is still alive to give it, won't matter," John said. "Contesti may be an evil, greedy bastard, but he's smart. Despite his posturing with the hired guns, he's kept it all under control. Apparently he's decided not to assassinate Lyle outright, just render him ineffective."

"A disgraced, ineffective sheriff is better than a dead one," Talia agreed. "At least for Contesti."

"Exactly."

"What about the territorial government? Surely you're not on your own out here."

"We have a marshal making rounds, but he has a lot of territory to cover. Not just Tatarka, but the other islands in the chain as well. Marshal's office is supposed to check in every few weeks, but they're shorthanded and everybody knows it, especially people like Contesti."

He had driven them into a relatively flat area ringed on one side by hills. Clusters of young trees dotted the landscape, mostly near streams.

"And here we are," John announced.

He jumped down and undid the latch on the back of the wagon. The robots rushed forward and butted up against his hands. "Survey mode. Load and execute queued protocol fifteen-beta."

The robots jumped out of the wagon and took off, heading for the hills.

"There are some caverns I've been meaning to have them map," John explained.

Logan helped Talia lower her trunk. The shotgun and rifle were nestled inside, wrapped in the clothing she'd bought.

"How do you retrieve the data?" Logan asked.

"Back at the house. They download to a computer."

"You have a computer?" Logan was almost bouncing on his heels.

"It's an isolated system. Not like what you're thinking, son."

"Why? Why not get a real computer? If you have the power source—"

"Because those things come with the kind of software designed to chain you to Earth. They all require I connect to the satellite over Sakura on a regular basis. Not only don't we have the means to do so, we don't want it."

"Very provincial, but okay. How do you get the data to Sakura then?"

"Anyone in Sakura who wants the data buys a thumb drive. I ship it out and hopefully, in a few weeks, they get it in the mail. The locals buy paper maps."

John watered and hobbled the horses, while Talia dug through the trunk. She handed Logan two ammo boxes, one for the rifle and one for the pump-action. She hung a pair of passive light binoculars around his neck.

Talia hoisted both of the long guns over her left shoulder. "Ready."

John led them downslope along an animal path and into a gap between two hills.

"We're in luck," John said as he forged ahead. "Didn't get flooded here. The gap up ahead. Good flat land with a mountain for a backstop."

"Oh, mushrooms," Logan said.

"Later, Logan," Talia warned.

"But—"

"Later. They're not going anywhere." She turned to make sure he was following.

"John, do we have to worry about dynamite trees here?" she asked, eyeing the increasing number and size of the trees up ahead. She'd never look at crowded trees the same way again, she was sure.

"No, the most dangerous things here are these," he said, stopping and picking up what looked like a horse apple.

The bumpy, greenish-orange spheres littered the ground and were about six inches in diameter.

"We call them ghost apples," John said, "because they're a ghost of evolution, an evolutionary anachronism."

"That means that it came about as part of coevolution with another species that became extinct," Logan added helpfully. "It means that it has no use. Animals don't eat it." He picked one up, flipped up his sunglasses, and examined it.

"Careful, Professor," John said.

Logan looked up, excitement in his eyes. "Does it secrete poison?"

"No. Just a type of sap."

Logan reached into his pocket, pulled out his notebook and pencil and made a note.

Talia was about to ask John how much further when CorgiSan came barreling down the gap, barking insistently. He zoomed past Logan and Talia, barely missing Talia's boot and ran circles around John.

"What's wrong?" Talia asked.

"I'm not sure."

"You can't communicate with them?" Logan asked.

CorgiSan was nipping at John's calves, pushing him back the way that he'd come.

"I lost the tablet awhile back. Still waiting for a replacement." John set off back up the gap, CorgiSan at his side.

They followed the robot past the horses and up a hill before they reached the entrance to a cave. CorgiSan's barks echoed as he entered through an opening about twenty feet wide and ten feet tall.

"Wait here," John said and followed CorgiSan in. The robot had stopped and was looking at them expectantly.

Talia could make out John's silhouette as he looked around. Light still reached into the cave mouth, but it was undoubtedly darker within, and the afternoon sun was not going to work in their favor.

"Aw, hell," John said as he came back out and reseated his hat.

"What's wrong?" Talia asked.

"DespairBear. He probably got stuck somewhere. I need to go back to the wagon, get some rope, a few lanterns."

"What do you want us to do?" Talia asked.

"Wait for me. Whatever you do, don't go exploring." He looked pointedly at Logan. "Especially you."

"I'm no spelunker," Logan said.

"No, but you're going to get distracted looking for fungi, and then I'm going to have two to rescue."

"Am not."

"No problem," Talia said. "We'll go back downhill. I'll have Logan practice with the shotgun."

CorgiSan followed them and ran circles around John's feet, herding him back toward the cave.

"I know, buddy. I know. I need some rope. I'll be right back."

CorgiSan sat and let out an electronic whine.

When they were about ten paces away, he got up and followed John back to the wagon.

Talia picked up a couple of the ghost apples lying about and set them up atop some nearby hedges. She had Logan do the same, spacing them out over several hedgerows, some farther out.

She brushed out some brambles that had attached themselves to the scarf she'd tied around her neck and stuffed into her cleavage to keep any hot brass from landing there.

She had Logan practice loading and unloading the pump-action. He did it perfectly.

"You *are* a quick study."

"I tend to be, despite the eyes."

"All right," she said. "Let's try this. Just point and shoot."

"Really?"

"Bring it up to your shoulder like I showed you. Point the gun at your target as you look down the barrel. Don't worry about the sights."

He fired a shot at the nearest ghost apple. It didn't explode, but he'd hit it. Tiny holes bled a white substance.

"I did it!" He lowered the gun, set the safety.

"You sure did." She patted him on the back. "Let's try the next group."

It was only a few feet farther. It took about twelve shots to determine that he was fairly accurate at a middle distance, maybe about ten feet to twelve feet.

"Do you think that's good enough for me to carry?" he asked.

"I'd prefer you give it a few more sessions."

CorgiSan's barking warned them of John's return. He was carrying a coil of rope wound around his torso. He'd also brought a bag that rattled and three Davy lamps. She took one and Logan took the other.

"You can probably leave the guns here," John called over his shoulder. "We'll pick them up on the way back."

Logan held the lamp up, a puzzled look on his face, and ran uphill after John.

"Why the mesh?"

Fine copper mesh enclosed the Davy lamp's main chamber.

"Lets air and methane in, keeps the flame from escaping though. That way it can't propagate and ignite."

"And these markings?" Logan was referring to slashes cut out along the two metal pieces that partially covered the mesh on two sides.

"That's to tell us if there's been a change in the air. It flares in the presence of flammable gases and fades in the presence of asphyxiants such as carbon monoxide."

"Oh, interesting." Logan pulled out his notebook. "What's the fuel source?"

"Vegetable oil. Why?"

"Just curious." He made notes until they stopped in front of the cave mouth.

CHAPTER TWENTY-SEVEN

COOL, MOIST AIR BILLOWED AROUND THEM.

CorgiSan was already inside the cave, pacing and barking impatiently, disturbing the bats within. They would chitter and shift, like annoyed sleepers.

John had stopped to light the lamps.

"I'm coming, boy, I'm coming," John groused.

"How can we help?" Talia asked.

"Don't become someone in need of rescue," he said again as he moved into the cave.

In the distance somewhere, water was dripping. The ground near the entrance was a mixture of grasses and moss. Decaying wood littered the cave floor. As they moved further in, it became sandy, then rocky with moss climbing the wall. Some of it glowed.

"Oh, bioluminescence!" Logan was already heading to take a closer look. "They glow because of a chemical reaction called luciferin. Did you know?"

"No, Logan, I didn't. Try to keep up please. I don't want to lose sight of John or get lost in this place."

"Some of these release toxic spores. John!" he called down as he ran into the cave.

John turned around, an annoyed look on his face.

"Toxic spores," Logan repeated. "Some of these bioluminescent species release spores toxic to humans."

"How toxic?" John asked. "I didn't bring respirators."

Talia could hear CorgiSan's barking but it was hard to tell what direction it was coming from as it bounced and echoed.

"Can we go back for them? Come back for DespairBear?"

"No." John's tone said he wasn't going to argue this.

Logan threw Talia a beseeching look.

She untied her cleavage-saving scarf. "Will this do?"

Logan made a face as he fished out a bandana. He held it up to the lamp. "Slow it down, maybe. Just stay away from anything that looks like it might be a mushroom."

"No problem." Talia tied the scarf around the bottom of her face.

Reluctantly, John pulled a shemagh out of his bag and wrapped it around his head and face. "Satisfied?"

"Oh, that's nice. What is it? Where do I get one?"

John ignored him and resumed his trek.

"What did I say?" Logan asked as he tied the bandana behind his head and tucked the free end into his shirt.

"He's just worried about DespairBear. Don't take it personally."

"It's just a robot."

"Not to him."

She stepped around rocks, boots splashing in tiny rivulets running down toward the inside of the cavern. Farther in, the ceiling dripped, and the air became mustier, earthier. There was definitely an undertone of mold, although it cleared up as the rivulets converged to turn into streams.

Now that she was looking for them, she spotted clusters of mushrooms, bioluminescent ones and not. She raised her lamp in the direction of a cluster and the light revealed a cloud around it.

"See," Logan said. "Spores."

"Toxic ones?"

"Think so. Can't tell without getting closer."

Up ahead, John's lamp flickered.

She followed through twists and turns, occasionally glancing behind her. Logan was just a few steps behind, carefully navigating a cavern floor made slick by slime and running water. The cavern widened, giving way first to stalagmites and stalactites.

The light around her changed. She turned and found out why. Logan had fallen behind, was kneeling down by a rock, collecting samples.

"What are you doing? I thought you said to keep away from mushrooms."

"Soil sample," he said. "It'll just take a moment."

The sound of water falling somewhere was like a white noise. She noticed it now that CorgiSan had ceased his barking. She'd lost sight of John's lamp. Her heart kicked up a notch. She was certain she'd not missed any turns.

If they got lost, she'd strangle Logan. Her prosthesis twitched in response, making the lantern sway. She forged ahead.

The cavern floor turned rocky, then sandy, like one might find on a beach. The sound of water falling was far more distinct as she emerged into a larger space where the stalactites and stalagmites had merged to create columns. John had set his lamp on the ground and was using CorgiSan as a stepstool, driving a hand drill into the ceiling above. He was standing next to an opening, a rather large pothole right below a series of gours—small, stacked pools into which water was falling from a swallow hole leading to the surface.

"What are you doing?" Talia asked.

"Drilling a hole for a bolt," John said. He'd stopped to wipe the residue that had fallen into his eyes.

Logan joined them. "I can do that for you if you like," he offered.

"Thanks, son, I'm almost done."

Talia looked down into the pothole. An underground stream flowed about ten feet below.

"DespairBear is down there," John said. "About two feet underwater. If you look really carefully, you can see his emergency lights strobing."

Talia squinted into the darkness as John hammered a bolt into the hole he'd just made.

"Ah, I see. Is he stuck?"

"Probably. More likely, he surveyed the bottom of the stream bed and got to a point he couldn't pass through. So he returned to where he fell in. Hand me the rope, will you?"

Talia did and he passed it through the bolt, jumped off CorgiSan's back, and brushed off all the rock residue that had accumulated on his shemagh.

He looked Talia up and down.

"You know, you're smaller and lighter than I am. This would go a lot quicker if I can lower you down than if I do this on my own."

"Sure, I can do that. Do you have a harness?"

John bent down and rifled through the sack. He handed her a seat harness, took out a canteen and drank. He offered the canteen to Logan as Talia stepped into the harness and cinched it tight. She took off her hat and remade her ponytail into a bun.

Logan had taken a drink and wandered over to the gour. It looked like he was collecting samples again.

She took a drink from the offered canteen.

John hadn't bothered to redo his shemagh. He checked the harness and attached the rope. "I don't see any mushrooms or plants around here, do you?"

She pulled the scarf down and flashed him a smile. "Once I get down there, how do I get him out and up?"

He handed her another harness, one that had been obviously custom made. "Not the first time this has happened. You ready?"

"Yes, I think so." She checked the harness again.

"Here we go."

She placed her left foot on one side of the pothole and strained to reach the other side with her right. John had attached her lantern to the rope above her and improvised a belayer's harness with the free end.

He put tension on the rope.

Slowly, she brought her feet together. Down she went, a slow descent, right through the pothole. Its walls were uneven, but smooth. The underground river was still several feet below her when she broke through the pothole's bottom. She slipped into the water. It was chilly, almost cold. DespairBear's emergency strobe was clear now, under the rushing water. It made a deafening noise as it flowed around her.

"All right, little guy. Let's get you out of here."

She was unreasonably grateful for the fact that he was not a real dog. A real dog would have died. Yet, she could see how John had become so attached to them, why he called them "boys."

She worked the robot harness open and reached down into the water, careful to use her left hand. She didn't want to lose the harness to the pull of the water. The robot was deep enough under than she had to take a deep breath and go under to reach under him. His legs were stuck in the soft sediment. Her own feet were slowly sinking into it.

The light coming down from the lanterns was weak. She blinked, hoping it would make her eyes adjust faster to the underwater murkiness.

She felt around, ended up petting the robot. The water was making her shiver now, and it felt like her boots had sunk in past her ankles. She scooped some of the silt away, driving it from the leather, but the water pushed it back.

Talia slid the harness under DespairBear's torso, pushing it through the silt. It must not be that deep or he would have sunk further.

She worked the first snap closed behind his front pair of legs, then moved to the rear. A pair of handles were part of the harness, and she grasped them with both hands.

She pushed up, heaving and straining and pulled DespairBear loose. The motion made her boots sink to the bottom, hitting rock.

"I've got him," she called up.

The rope tightened and she was jerked upward. For a second it felt like she might lose her boots, but they came up, water spilling out of them.

As John pulled her up through the pothole, she had to shift DespairBear so he wouldn't bump up against the edges.

God, she was cold. She couldn't wait to get back out into the sunlight.

John's smiling face appeared as she cleared the top of the pothole. Bandana around his neck, Logan was lending a hand with the rope. At John's nod, Logan let go of the rope and reached out to grab DespairBear. He set him down and CorgiSan trotted up, nudging the other robot with his snout.

John grabbed Talia's hand and pulled her forward.

"Nice job," he said. "Why are your teeth chattering?"

She grabbed the shemagh from around his shoulders and used it to wipe her face and dry out her hair.

"Because I'm cold."

"Is he recoverable?" Logan asked. He'd been poking at DespairBear, despite CorgiSan pushing him away.

"Should be," John said. "He powered down to save energy. Weird glitch on that one. Can't get him to take a full charge. No logical reason for it. I've checked all the circuits and everything is fine."

"Maybe he's watching his figure," Logan said. He was sitting cross-legged next to the robots. He reached out to pet CorgiSan, but apparently the robot wasn't in the mood for play. Instead he returned to DespairBear's side and whined.

"Now comes the fun part," John said.

"I'm almost afraid to ask what that is," Talia said. "And does it involve going back into the sunlight so I can stop shivering?"

"Someone gets to carry DespairBear out. And by someone, I mean Logan."

"Why me?"

There was an evil twinkle in John's eyes. "Convenience. Mine, to be clear."

After rescuing DespairBear, John drove them back to Maeve's to pick up Logan's trunk. Then he drove them to a friend's boarding house, made introductions, and left them there, insisting that he'd rather work on DespairBear without further distractions.

Talia changed out of her damp—but no longer dripping wet—clothes. Wearing fresh boots, she and Logan walked back to the jailhouse to relieve Maeve. Reluctantly, she had allowed herself to be relieved and gone back to the shop with promises to come back with food.

Lyle was still asleep, snoring loudly in the back. He looked like Maeve had cleaned him up a bit because his beard was no longer coated in dry snot.

The radio made a squelching noise behind her. She turned around. Logan was fiddling with the dials.

"Sorry. I'm trying to figure out why this thing isn't working that well."

"Just don't make it worse," she said.

The front door swung open.

"You two still here?" John grumbled.

"How are the robots?" Talia asked.

"DespairBear booted up just fine. I now have a new map of the underground riverbed. Thanks for all the help, both of you." John reached for the coffee pot and poured himself a cup.

"What about the data on the cavern they were mapping?" Logan asked. "Oh, and I've been meaning to ask, can you start having them map the locations of mushrooms?" He'd stopped fiddling with the radio and set up his sample bottles on the desk.

"Good data by the look of it. I know they don't look like

much, but they really are good at their jobs. As for mapping mushrooms, well, yes. It would take some programming. Why?"

"I have an interest. It would help me with my data analysis. Perhaps help me confirm my theories."

"Before I forget." John made a face as he swallowed some coffee. "Guess who I ran into on the way here?"

Talia raised a brow. "A man with a rather unique scar?"

"Got it in one. Looks like Contesti's reinforcements have arrived."

"His name is Jerod Rhodes," Talia said. "He was the one who was recruiting for Contesti in Sakura, the one who said he was going to take Lyle out."

"You know that Lyle won't appreciate you thinking he needs your help. Even if he does."

"What do you think, John?" Talia asked. "That I should stay out of it?"

"No. Lyle is more than a friend. I can see that."

"I didn't come back just for Lyle," she said.

"Why then?"

"I owe the Haricots."

He studied her, the skin around his eyes wrinkling. "You know that the martyr complex has gotten a lot of people killed."

"It's not a martyr complex," she said and took a sip of her coffee. "It's survivor's guilt."

The only thing worse than dying was living with the knowledge that others had died for you, because of you. She'd thought her scars healed, right up until Elias Haricot's life passed right through her hands, and somehow opened up all her old wounds as well as awakened all the ghosts that haunted her.

It hadn't affected her as much the first time she'd lost someone, the first time someone had died instead of her, and that too carried its own price—the fear that she'd become indifferent to it, the guilt that—

"Let me out!" The shouting was coming from the back.

Logan had taken his little collection of specimens and stuffed them back in his pocket. He stood up and set about making more coffee.

"It's not locked," Talia called. She crossed the room so Logan could pour her a fresh cup. Sometimes fortifications really were best in liquid form.

Lyle stumbled forward, leaning first on the cage door until it gave way, then the wall, then the door jamb. His right hand was clutching at his lower back as he wavered in the threshold.

"Who did this to me?"

"I believe I'm the one to blame," Talia said.

He looked up. His hair was plastered to his scalp, and he smelled awful.

His eyes were unfocused at first, then seemed to home in on her face. He let go of his back long enough to run his fingertips over his swollen knuckles.

"Did I do that?" he asked her as he dislodged Logan from his seat. He lowered himself into the chair and rummaged through the drawers of his desk.

"Yes, you did." She spooned some sugar into the cup and mixed it in. The three of them stood almost shoulder to shoulder, cups in hand, facing Lyle as he pulled at drawers, rummaged through them, then slammed them shut only to start over again.

"Where is it, John?" Lyle demanded, his voice shaking.

"The outhouse. Where it belongs." John flashed a smile and blew on his coffee.

Lyle took a deep, rattling breath. Then another, hands shaking as he formed them into fists. His gaze bounced from one to the other, eyes flashing with anger.

"Who the hell are you?"

"I'm Loga—"

"Never mind." He slammed the top drawer shut again, this time on his left thumb. He swore as he raised it to his mouth and bit down on the insulted knuckle.

"Coffee?" Logan asked, offering a cup.

"No, I don't want any fucking coffee." He pushed himself up, caught himself on the edge of the table and almost doubled over.

He stumbled out into street, cursing a blue streak that faded behind him.

"When did his back start hurting again?" Talia asked.

"Rescuing his so-called wife," John said. "At least that's what he said. Wouldn't let Caspar touch him though."

"Lower right?" Talia asked just to be sure they were talking about the same thing.

"Yes. How did you know?"

"Old war injury. Lyle was hurt on a mission. The doctors couldn't quite fix it, warned him about reinjuring the site."

"Don't you find that interesting?"

She answered with a quirk of her eyebrow.

"That he would reinjure the exact same spot," John clarified.

"Maybe."

"So maybe John isn't so crazy, after all," John said. "Maybe John is suspicious of people for a reason."

"Since Rhodes is in town, I'm thinking maybe we should go after him." Talia set her coffee down. "Just in case."

CHAPTER TWENTY-EIGHT

TALIA TOLD LOGAN TO STAY PUT. SHE DIDN'T WANT HIM GETTING in the way and had told him so when he objected. Despite the crestfallen look, he'd remained behind.

It was becoming obvious that the map of Tsurui, the one she'd committed to memory, was outdated. Talia followed John down the winding street and over bridges to one of the grander buildings—a trilevel structure with a waterwheel and a bright, red torii gate. Willows and plum trees lined the stream leading to it. Light spilled out of the large windows and several people were crowded around the entrance itself, looking in from the wraparound porch.

John pushed his way through the gathered spectators, mostly townspeople by their clothes and reluctance to enter. He flashed a badge she hadn't realized he had. Instead of returning it to his pocket he hung it off his neck like a talisman. He just didn't project the kind of bravado that would turn it into a shield.

She followed, tilting her hat down over her face a bit and flipping up her coat's collar.

Within, Contesti himself was sitting at the head of a long table, fingers steepled thoughtfully in front of him. Dame Leigh stood at the other end of the table, clutching the rounded top of her cane in a viselike grip. Smaller tables and accompanying chairs were scattered in the center of the room. A bar with taps and shelves of liquor bottles behind it took up the back wall. A small door led into what was probably a kitchen or storage room. Stairs led to the upper levels.

Several of Contesti's men, including Rhodes, were casually leaning against the bar itself or were half perched on the barstools. They were all armed, holsters in plain view. Their smiles, the ease of their body language, suggested amusement.

The bald, squat man behind the bar brought out a small bottle, the kind that one would expect to hold medication. Bare head gleaming in the warm lights, he set the bottle on the lacquered surface, pushed it toward the edge.

"Is this what you want?" the bartender asked.

At first Talia wasn't sure who he was talking to. His gaze was aimed at the middle of the floor and a table was blocking her view.

A hand came up from below, grabbed the edge of a barstool. It belonged to Lyle, who used it to help prop himself up. He winced as he stood, still pressing a hand over his back. He seemed oblivious to the crowd that had gathered, and she wasn't sure she wanted to know how he'd ended up on the floor in the first place.

Talia darted a glance at Dame Leigh. The matriarch's face projected unbridled disgust and there was an edge of desperation in her eyes as her gaze met Talia's.

"Oh good, the gang's all here," Rhodes said. He seemed quite delighted as he straightened up and adjusted the string tie at his throat.

"Has everyone met Death's Handmaiden?"

John moved out of the way and Talia wished he hadn't. She caught fear and confusion as he cast her an apologetic look, which made him smart and sensible. Fear would eventually catch up with her later, after it was all over. It wasn't an undesirable trait, the delayed reaction, but it sure was unpleasant once it hit.

She tilted the hat up and stepped around the gaming table. Someone had spilled something on the floor, and it looked like Lyle had slipped in it. As for Lyle himself, he had eyes only for the bottle under the bartender's pudgy finger. Hypnolin no doubt. If Lyle was even aware of Talia—of anyone, of anything—he gave no sign. He was licking his cracked and bloodied lips like a man dying of thirst.

That vile scent of desperation and fear, of pain and human

waste, spread its tendrils around the room, mixed in with the smoke from lamps and pipes. It made Talia want to wretch.

"We were just introducing everyone to the... sheriff," Rhodes said, making the last word sound like some kind of insult.

Laughter rolled through the crowd, even the townspeople. After it stopped, the echoes of it lingered in the air, adding to the already foul stench.

"Time to go, Lyle," she said.

"Please," Rhodes said, "Sheriff Monroe, sir... don't forget your bottle."

He was looking at Talia as he said it, his eyes full of challenge, his face hard. He was obviously playing mind games, posturing for the crowd. It wasn't so much arrogance, as tactics. A martyr was no good to them, no good for Contesti. Clearly, they needed to bring Lyle down and do it as publicly as possible while at the same time making it look like it wasn't their doing at all.

Well, she'd never thought either of them, Contesti nor Rhodes, stupid. The rest, however...

"Lyle, let's go," she said.

"Maybe you should dye your hair. Makes it easier to boss him around."

She darted her gaze to the source of the mockery. It was the thug from the boat, the one with stark red hair, whom she'd dubbed Dye-job.

"Wanna let me try?" he said, coming forward, preening as he imitated a feminine sway of the hips and batted his eyelashes.

Amused chuckles and wolf whistles escorted him toward Lyle as he played at being a woman, pushing his lips out in a pout, fanning himself.

"Lyle, oh Lyle," Dye-job said in a falsetto. "Help me, Lyle."

He rose up on his toes, struck out his ass and chest, imitating a woman's high-heeled walk, blowing kisses as he pranced around Lyle.

Touch him, and I'll end you.

Her temper. She reined it in. Cold calculation routed out the heat rising in her veins.

If Lyle was aware of the ridicule, it didn't seem to matter to him. His gaze was still locked on that bottle, focused and unrelenting like a laser beam. It was a wonder he hadn't already grabbed it, swallowed it down.

Dye-job continued to play to the catcalls, playing up the persona and high-fiving his buddies—not just the boat thugs, Ponytail and Tattoo, but others—as he passed them.

Talia gritted her teeth, gaze darting from one thug to another. There were too many of them. And as long as they were laughing, they were unlikely to act. But the mood of crowds, of mobs, was a fickle thing.

"Lyle. Out. Now."

In the edge of her vision, she caught Lyle snagging the bottle off the bar, clutching it in his hand, tucking it to his chest. He was right behind her—she could feel the heat of his body, smell his stench, hear the rasp of his breathing.

Move, Lyle, move. Why wasn't he moving?

More laughter.

"I thought you weren't taking sides, Ms. Merritt," Contesti said in his soothing, cultured tones.

"I've changed my mind," Talia said.

"If this were Earth, I would file a complaint against your license," Contesti said.

"Good thing this isn't Earth then. Paper cuts are so annoying."

Contesti smiled. "So they are. They do have a way of accumulating though, do they not, Dame Leigh?"

Color rose in Dame Leigh's cheeks, not the color of embarrassment, but of anger. It was the tautness of her body, the way she looked at Contesti, that gave it away for what it was.

"Dame Leigh, would you mind giving me a hand with Lyle?"

Whatever Dame Leigh was doing, she didn't look like she wanted to be here. And she was alone and, with every passing moment, looking like she wanted to be here even less than Talia herself.

Moving like a much younger woman, Dame Leigh slid behind Talia and pulled Lyle toward the door. John followed. Good. She wanted the room cleared of anyone she cared for, anyone she might have to answer for. She wanted it clear of her people.

Rhodes raised a glass to his lips and stood.

"Ladies and gentlemen, I propose a toast to our resident celebrity. A woman with three hundred and one kills to her name. To Izanami."

Izanami. A deity who invited humans toward death. How quaint. I expected something more original.

Rhodes raised his glass, but no one else joined him.

He didn't drink though. Just kept those cold, golden-green eyes on her as he stood.

Him calling attention to her reputation and giving her yet another moniker, she had not expected. He wasn't praising her. He was casting her in the worst possible light—a murderer, a hired gun. A demon.

The fingers of her phantom ached. Itched. Burned.

"She was amazing. Is amazing. Look at her, ladies and gentlemen. She is like ice."

Moving closer, he brought the glass to his lips, tilted it back, just enough for the liquid inside to graze his lips. He made like he was swallowing, but his lips had remained sealed. Steady as a rock, he was. Steady and sure. And stone-cold sober.

What are you playing at, Rhodes?

"Three hundred and one, Miss Merritt. We never did get to celebrate that last one. A boy, wasn't he? A poor, confused, sick boy."

He was close enough to touch now. His gaze lingered on her right cheek, still purple from the punch she'd taken.

"What is your count, Mr. Rhodes?" she asked.

His lips stretched into a smile. He swirled the glass in his hand. Round and round the liquid went, edging up the glass almost to the rim.

"Depends on how you tally it," he said. "Izanami."

He was close now, close enough for a kiss. He smelled of aftershave and cigars, of woodsmoke and musk. Under different circumstances she would have leaned in, savored it, given the sweat pebbling on his cheek a taste.

In her mind's eye she saw two outcomes. One where Talia Merritt rode him to exhaustion, made him beg for release. And another where Death's Handmaiden slipped a blade between his ribs and through whatever passed for a heart. For a moment that duality merged and the room around them disappeared.

He held her gaze. Did he see it, the desire in her eyes, the cold, calculating killer living inside her, the one he called Izanami, the one others called Handmaiden, the one that only answered to Death, vying for control, wrestling Talia for its moment? Was he summoning her on purpose, tempting her?

"It looks like we're going to have to dance sooner or later," Rhodes said.

Dance. He didn't mean to music.

"But not tonight," Talia said.

"No, not tonight."

The hardest thing about the trek back to the jailhouse was not looking back to check and see if they were being followed. She didn't have to understand all the nuances of the game that Contesti and Rhodes were playing to have it raise the hairs on the back of her neck.

Sight lines formed and shifted as she and John turned corners. He had sent Dame Leigh and Lyle ahead and waited for her. She appreciated the gesture, even if it was wasted. By the look of him, he wouldn't have been able to do much.

"Sorry about that," John grumbled.

"Sorry about what?"

"About not... Look, I only pinned this badge on because I was trying to take care of Lyle. I thought... I thought..."

"It's all right, John. We're alive. You did fine."

"We're alive because Contesti can't be seen as anything but a benevolent despot. Because he can't afford for the planetary authorities in Sakura to take note and intervene. Not because of anything we did."

"That's true, but it doesn't matter."

"How does it not matter?"

"Because they didn't goad us into doing something stupid. It may not look, or feel, like much of a victory, but it is. Hopefully the spectators saw that Lyle's friends remained loyal to him, that he was a sick man who needed help and was being ridiculed for his illness. An illness brought on by the noble act of rescuing his wife."

She kept the "I hope" to herself.

John shook his head. "I need to go check on my boys. They've been charging and I... I need to go check on them."

"Go ahead," she said, thinking that he certainly didn't need her permission. He was the one with the badge, not her, but then again leadership was as much a mindset as anything else.

Damnit, Lyle. I don't want this.

John broke left at the next bridge and headed down the cobblestoned street with its huge flowering trees.

Another bridge took her over one of the larger streams, its gurgling swollen by the recent rain. Had the circumstances been different, it would have been soothing. As it was, she slowed as she approached the blind corner, but no one was waiting, no one was lurking in the shadows.

The jailhouse was still framed by the same old trees, still had unlit lanterns hanging off its eaves, and the steps still squeaked as she mounted them. The bellpull, with its thick cords twisted together into a bundle as thick as her wrist, hung next to the bell hanging from the ceiling.

The front door was slightly ajar, the slit between door and frame flickering, betraying its source—the fire in the wood-burning stove.

Inside, Lyle was huddled in a corner, the bottle tucked up against his chest. He was shaking and sweating. Dame Leigh stood between him and the door, hat hanging down her back.

Logan had taken one of Lyle's shotguns and disassembled it. A magnifying glass sat among the tangle of screws, pins, and springs, each one lined up by size. Had Lyle been sober, he'd be screeching. Doctorate or not, Logan was really like a kid. Fortunately, the rest of Lyle's arsenal—two rifles and another shotgun—were still in their racks.

She darted a look at the radio. Well, at least he hadn't decided to disassemble it. Or at least she didn't think he'd had time to—

"Lyle, let me call Caspar," Dame Leigh was saying. "I'm sure he can help you."

"No." He shook his head. "I'll be fine. I just need..."

Lyle lifted his gaze. His eyes widened as they passed over Talia. Was he seeing her or someone else? Something else? Comrade-in-arms? Friend? Rival? He'd seen both sides of her, seen deep into her soul. As well as anyone, he knew what she was, who she was, so why the surprise? He looked down at the bottle in his hands as if it had just appeared there.

"I just need..." passed his lips once again.

"Let him have it," Logan said.

Dame Leigh frowned at him. "Who are you again?"

"Never mind," Talia said. "Let him have it."

Dame Leigh's incredulousness crested as her gaze bounced between them. She pursed her lips, making the lines that betrayed her age stand up.

"Very well, Ms. Merritt. But things are going to get worse, for all of us, if he doesn't get his act together. Or have you come to take over, do his job for him?"

"I don't need her to do my job," Lyle said as he slid up the wall he'd been leaning against.

"They grabbed me off the street, Sheriff," Dame Leigh said. "Made me go into Contesti's club."

"Will you be safe going back? Do you want an escort?" Talia asked.

"No. Now that I know they've upped the game, I'll be more… vigilant."

"How is Sam?" Talia asked.

"Still calls out for his brother," Dame Leigh said. "How's your head?"

"Still attached," Talia retorted, returning the iciness of Dame Leigh's tone.

"Excuse me," Dame Leigh said. "I need to get back. And thank you for your help, Ms. Merritt. I won't leave my land without an escort in the future. I was hoping it wouldn't come to that, but so be it."

"Will that be enough?" Talia asked. "Perhaps you should hole up. Stay where it's safe, until this is over."

Dame Leigh let out a bark of laughter and tapped the tip of the cane into the wood.

"Out of the question. First of all, this has been going on for years. It might go on for years more. Second, I will not concede this ground, nor any other, now or ever. Third, if you think they won't eventually come after me, after us, regardless of whether or not we 'hole up' then maybe you should pack your bags and go back to Sakura right now. You are far too naïve to be here."

She tucked the cane under one elbow and pulled her hat up to the top of her head. She was the picture of matronly determination, of stubborn pride, and motherly disappointment as she cast Lyle one last look.

"I will send Caspar anyway," she whispered as she turned to face Talia.

They exchanged nods of understanding. Dame Leigh pulled the door shut behind her.

"That's not how you clean a shotgun," Talia said, indicating the disassembled firearm.

"I wasn't cleaning it," Logan said defensively. "I wanted to see how it worked?"

"Really? You needed to take it all the way apart for that?"

He shrugged. "I can put it back together."

"I would, if I were you. Before Lyle notices."

Lyle was still looking at the bottle as if he wasn't quite sure what it was. He seemed completely unaware of Logan's presence. Confusion was part of hypnolin's effects, but this looked like something else. Obsession maybe. Carefully, he set the bottle down on the table and backed away from it. Then dropped into the other chair and pulled at the stopper.

"Go on," Talia said, crossing her arms. "I won't stop you."

His gaze rose to hers. "You know what pain feels like, what it can do to you."

Yes, she did. All too well, which made her less sympathetic than he was apparently expecting. She'd tried not to judge him. Especially since it looked like his so-called wife had gotten him hooked. It was what had earned him as much grace as she'd given. But it was running out.

"What happened, Lyle?"

"They laughed at me." He said it as he swirled the liquid in the bottle around.

It wasn't what she'd meant, but she should know better than to start a deeper conversation with an addict.

"They've been laughing at you for weeks, months."

The muscle in his jaw pulsed. The look in his eyes was no longer haunted. It was angry. His hand wrapped around the bottle. High on something new—defiance—he looked right into her eyes as he lifted the bottle to his lips and drained it dry.

He slammed the bottle down, making all the gun parts rattle. Lyle kept looking at her. He was waiting. Waiting for it to hit. The clock on the wall ticked, the seconds turning into minutes.

The sound of Logan reassembling the shotgun intruded, little clicks and clatters as he brought metal and wood components together. She'd never seen anything like it—the precision, like a film run in reverse, without any hesitation or doubt, he looked like he'd done this a thousand times before.

Lyle leaned in Logan's direction.

"Who are you?" Lyle asked.

"Logan." Bigger components took form as he worked, drawing Lyle's attention as well.

Lyle looked up at her. "Who is this?"

"Friend of mine."

Logan lined up the left- and right-handed cocking pins, working with a dexterity that would have impressed Lyle. But Lyle's attention was no longer on the gun taking form in front of him. It was back on the empty hypnolin bottle.

A knock at the door made them turn toward it.

Maeve came in, the concern on her face turning into disappointment when her gaze landed on the empty bottle in front of Lyle.

"I heard what happened," Maeve said. "Is everyone all right?"

"Fine. Everyone is perfectly fine," Lyle said, the muscle in his jaw pulsing under the stubble.

"How are you feeling, Lyle?" Talia asked.

There was a part of Talia that didn't want Lyle to suffer, and a part of her that still wanted to kick his ass. She was going to have to find a way to vent her rage and frustration soon or it was going to have its way with her.

"Sometimes I need more," he said. He was still sweating, but the curiosity he'd summoned for Logan's existence and the reassembly he was performing seemed to be slipping Lyle's grasp.

Maeve went up to him, ran her hand along the side of his jaw.

"Let us help you," she said.

He squinted at her, raised his hand to return the gesture, tracing down her face to her hair.

"Sien—" His hand froze. He blinked. Blinked again. The gentle look on his face faded, hardened. "I don't need help. What I need is another dose."

Maeve pulled away. Talia had no doubt she was on the verge of tears. No time for those though. Not yet.

Lyle put his palms on the table, pushed up to a precarious stand betrayed by the tremors in his forearms. He looked around. "Where's my hat?"

Talia grabbed a hat from the coatrack and flicked it at him. The old Lyle would have caught it. But his reflexes were shit because it bounced off his chest and landed on the floor in front of him. He stared at it as if it would come alive and bite him.

"Hallucinating?" Talia asked. "Hard to say, isn't it? What are you seeing, Lyle? Is that really a hat?"

He snagged the hat, put it on his head. "It's just not *my* hat, that's all. Doesn't matter. A hat is a hat."

Talia crossed her arms and leaned up against the support column. "Sure it is, Lyle. Sure it is."

"Where's John?" Lyle demanded, one hand working that spot on his back, the other still shakily supporting him as he pushed up using the table edge for support. The muscles in his forearm stood up like cords of rope, straining against loose, tanned skin.

The radio came to life with a hiss. "Talia? Lyle? Is anyone there?"

Maeve picked up and keyed the mic. "This is Maeve. What's wrong, John?"

"We have a problem." A pop and hiss followed. "Looks like one of the Haricots got tangled up with some of Contesti's new henchmen."

"Where are you?" Maeve asked.

"The temple, just south of the fountain."

"Do you know where that is?" Maeve asked Talia.

"Yes." Talia grabbed one of the rifles from the rack, slapped a magazine into it, and made for the door.

Logan had taken it upon himself to grab a radio. "I'm coming with you," he insisted. "I'll stay out of the way, I promise."

"Wait for me." Lyle was still using the table to hold himself up. He took a step forward. Had Maeve not been there to catch him, he'd have gone down.

Talia stopped to throw a glare over her shoulder and said, "Why?"

PART THREE

CHAPTER TWENTY-NINE

DESPAIRBEAR GREETED THEM A BLOCK LATER. BEHIND TALIA, Logan was fiddling with the radio's controls.

"You know how to use that thing?" she asked.

"Yes. It's not working though."

"Jamming?"

"These aren't military units," he said. "They're not even police units. They're very early, very basic civilian models. Line of sight. I was checking them out while I waited for you. Their batteries don't charge fully, and they drain too quickly. Old or bad batteries, probably."

"Well, be sure to tell Lyle, when he's sober."

"Tell me what?" Lyle was wheezing as he joined them. He seemed to have less trouble standing upright once he was in motion. Standing still was more of a challenge by the look of it as he leaned into one of the posts holding up the covered walkway. A rifle was slung over his shoulder right atop the dirty shirt clinging to his sweat-soaked back.

Fingers fumbling, he even managed to load it, although not on the first try.

"Go back, Lyle."

"I'm the sheriff here." His voice was steadier now.

Elliott's words about wearing her heart on her sleeve echoed in her ears as she turned away so he wouldn't see her face.

At least Maeve had had the good sense to remain behind.

Once the shooting started, if it started, Talia wanted as few distractions as possible.

They passed the *kitsune* fountain and continued down the street. It dead-ended with a flight of stone steps bracketed by an orange-and-black torii gate. Manicured shrubs, arranged with military precision, spread out on both sides of the gate and up the hill.

DespairBear practically slithered up the stairs and joined CorgiSan, who was sitting beside John. He was crouching behind the purification trough. He made a hand gesture, and the robots went into a down-stay, ears pricked forward, just like real dogs.

Keeping low, Talia sprinted up the stairs and sank down beside John. Little more than a stone pool, the trough nevertheless provided decent cover. The bamboo dipping cups resting on the ledge were cracked and broken, the water brackish. Even so, the wood canopy above them was solid enough to cast a large shadow in which to hide.

"Radio not working, I take it?" John said.

Logan and Lyle had made their way up. They squatted beside them, both of them wheezing from the effort.

"Told you," Logan said. The radio gave off a pathetic squelch as he turned the knob and shut it off.

Talia surveyed their surroundings. Decorative stone lanterns lined the path up to the temple. Beyond the lanterns, there were two small buildings, one on each side of the road. One was a covered stage. The other had probably served as an administrative building before the temple had been abandoned. A wall covered with wooden wish and prayer plaques fronted the stage.

The road ended with a pair of stone guardians—both *kitsune*—that stood in front of the oratory. Beyond it, the shrine itself waited, a tall, imposing building surrounded by a half-demolished fence. Both oratory and shrine looked like they needed mending, particularly the oxidized-green roofs. There were more missing and damaged tiles than intact ones.

John was looking down the path, but Talia couldn't make out what he was frowning at.

"What's going on?" Talia asked.

"Sam Haricot got himself shot."

A sinking feeling formed in the pit of Talia's stomach. Her fingers tightened around the rifle.

"The twelve-year-old?" she asked. She had to make sure.

"Apparently he'd heard that they'd forced Dame Leigh into the club. Hadn't gotten word yet that we got her out, so he rode into town to rescue her. Took a shot at one of Contesti's new hires, the asshole with the red dye job. Asshole and two of his friends shot back."

She would bet her cryptochip that she knew who his two friends were.

"Is Sam dead?" she asked.

"I don't think so. Wounded, last I heard. The doc is tending to him back at Haricot House."

"Why are we here, John?" Lyle repeated, wiping at his brow.

His eyes were glassy, but at least he wasn't shaking, not that Talia could see anyway.

"They were standing over the boy, having a bit of fun with him as he tried to crawl away. I challenged them. They took a shot at me and ran this way."

"Took a shot and missed?" Talia asked.

"You thinking they missed on purpose?" John asked.

For a man who'd been afraid to step into Lyle's role earlier, he was very calm about being shot at. But then again, some people were that way—more afraid of responsibility for others than for their own safety.

"Why would they come this way?" Logan asked.

"No one comes here," Lyle said. "At least, not anymore."

"It's a great place to lure us in," Talia said. "Pick us off as we come running after them."

"That's what I was thinking too," Lyle said.

"Far enough off the main road as well so there would be no witnesses or civilians in the crossfire. Either they're very clever thugs or . . ."

". . . someone smart is directing them," Lyle finished for her.

"Maybe," she admitted. "They had no way to know that Sam would take a shot at them."

"Doesn't matter," Lyle said. "John, can you send your boys out to draw their fire?"

"I hate to use them like that, but yes."

"We need to get closer first," Talia objected.

"I'll take the stage," Lyle said. "You get the admin building."

"You sure you're up for that?" she asked.

"I may not be able to do much, but I can crawl."

"You're no good to me dead."

"I'm no good to you alive either," he said and surged forward before she could stop him.

A shot rang out as he threw himself on the ground between the fountain and the stage. The grasses were about a foot tall, the flowers prolific, but his motion through them gave him away.

Talia swore as she returned fire, but the angle was all wrong. She got off five shots, mostly covering fire that left behind a haze of gun smoke to curl around her muzzle. John whistled and DespairBear sprinted forward. He zigzagged through the stone guardians lining the road like he was running weave poles on an agility course. He didn't draw fire until he broke across the field between the wish and prayer walls.

By the time Talia finished reloading, both robots were on the other side of the oratory, circling it, running figure eights around it and the shrine.

Lyle was hunched down behind a crumbled stone wall.

John's whistles rang out in short, loud bursts. CorgiSan changed his pattern, running from one end of the temple grounds to the other, but Contesti's men were no longer firing on the robots. Unless the robots were a threat, they were mere distraction, and she wouldn't have expected Dye-job or his friends to waste any ammo on them once they figured out they weren't military models that could return fire.

She gave Lyle the signal to cover her. It took him longer than it should have, but he acknowledged it.

"You two," she said to John and Logan, "stay here. Let us take care of them. Am I understood?"

As soon as Lyle took his first shot, she aimed herself across the walkway, landing with a painful jolt that took her hard in the shoulder. Rifle tucked up against her torso, she pushed up, sprinted.

Over gasping breaths, she counted the shots—three, four, and five, delivered rapid-fire. She took position behind the collapsed veranda of the admin building.

It gave her a clear line of sight to the shrine. One of Contesti's men lay prone on the sloping roof, head barely visible behind the protruding barrel of his rifle. She aimed, fired, moved.

The robots did another run, drawing one shot from the interior of the shrine itself. Another shot rang out from one of the many broken windows. It hadn't been aimed at the robots or her.

John had said that there were three of them.

Adrenaline coursing, she risked exposing herself by darting closer to one of the smaller, crumpled auxiliary shrines paralleling the oratory. The stone base and statue were barely big enough to hide behind. It wouldn't be the first—and undoubtedly not the last—time that her smaller size would be an asset.

A shot rang past her head, making her ears ring.

Another answered it, Lyle protecting her.

Scraping up against the stone, she aimed for the target on the roof, but it was gone. The ricochet of a small rock off the crumbled statue echoed. Lyle had moved forward, was crouched behind a statue overgrown with vines. He signaled that he was moving forward.

She returned an empathic no. A shot rang over their heads, making her draw in on herself again. When she looked back up, Lyle was gone. Either he had not read her signal or he didn't care.

Bursts of whistling rang out, a steady staccato like a code.

A hiss that sounded like a gas leak triggered her instincts and made her hold her breath. Frantically, she looked around.

CorgiSan's paniers had opened up and deployed a dozen balloons. Not the kind that were connected by string, but the kind that made him look like he was wearing a puffy coat. Slowly, they inflated, for some reason making the robot's rear end float up first. His legs made walking motions as the loft of the front-end balloons caught up with the rear-end balloons. The robot looked like he'd been swaddled in giant cotton balls.

She heard laughter from the shrine, followed by a curse. CorgiSan floated upward slowly, spinning leisurely in the wind. The nozzle on his rear end fired brief spurts of thrust. He was maneuvering so that the expanding balloons were effectively blocking the line of sight from the shrine's roof.

Shots rang out, missing the balloons they were undoubtedly aimed at.

Gotcha! All three of them were inside the shrine. A part of her still wanted to check the oratory to make sure that there weren't more of them. Just because John had believed there were only three didn't mean there weren't others.

She caught sight of Lyle running up the steps. He kicked the doors in and disappeared within.

"Oh hell."

This was no way to make an entry.

Leading with her rifle, she moved forward, firing at the positions she'd seen shooting at CorgiSan, but to no avail. The lack of return fire suggested they had moved.

The doors were still swaying back and forth on damaged hinges as she ducked under the eaves and shouldered her way in.

The interior was lit by pools of light falling through the damaged roof. Dust swirled, making the shadows move. A ladder with missing rungs led up to the roof.

The tattooed thug from the boat was lying in a pool of his own blood. Lyle had shot him in the face. The one with the ponytail was trading blows with Lyle, and Dye-job was up in the rafters, pistol aimed at the fighting men.

She dropped to one knee, raised the rifle, sighted in on his center of mass, and fired. The pistol clattered to the ground and Dye-job's body followed, landing atop it, with a thud that sent up a cloud of debris and broke the rotting wood panels of the flooring.

Talia rushed forward, scanning the interior for other threats, and knelt by Dye-job's body. She kept her rifle on him, but he didn't move, and he didn't look like he was breathing either. The exit wound coming out of his back registered for what it was—terminal—and she lowered the rifle.

Lyle had Ponytail pinned to the floor and was punching him in the face again and again like he wasn't actually aware of the fact that his target was no longer conscious.

He undoubtedly had more pent-up rage than she did, so she let him get in three more blows.

"Lyle," she whispered.

He froze, his elbow pulled all the way back.

"Is he dead?" he asked.

She came to stand by his shoulder and leaned down. Ponytail's face looked like hamburger, all bruises and blood, and he wouldn't be opening either his eyes or his jaw any time soon by the look of it.

"Maybe," she said. "Either way he can't feel it, and if you kill this one too, there's no one to testify as to who sent them."

"I know who sent them. So do you."

"Is that enough?"

He got one more punch in, winced at the impact of it, and took a step back, hands clenched as if he wanted to do nothing but hit Ponytail some more. She couldn't say she blamed him. She certainly did.

"They could've killed Sam," he said.

"But they didn't."

"That is their plan, you know. Kill all the Haricots. That way no one will be left alive to challenge Contesti on how he acquired his new patent."

"So kill him. I won't stop you."

She meant it too. If she had caught anyone midrape or midmurder, she wouldn't need a judge or jury's sanctification either. Surely killing Giuseppe Priser was proof of that. Death's Handmaiden reared her head deep inside Talia's psyche just long enough to give a satisfied nod.

Lyle deflated. He shot her a look of pure malice that faded into shame. Well, at least he still had his conscience. One of them should, anyway.

Ascending footfalls made the stairs squeak. They both turned and Talia raised her rifle, but it was only DespairBear. He aimed those mismatched "eyes" around the room.

"Can John see what they see?" Talia asked.

"No," Lyle said. "Not in real time, just playback. I think John lost the tablet that allowed him to do that some time back. Hasn't been able to get a new one."

Talia pushed the shrine door outward. One of the doors came off its hinges and toppled to the floor as she waved.

"All clear," she shouted.

"What are you going to do?" she asked over her shoulder.

"I'm going to arrest Contesti."

CHAPTER THIRTY

COVERED IN MUD AND ABRASIONS, SHOULDER SMARTING, TALIA followed Lyle into Contesti's in-town club. According to Lyle, he'd built it shortly after Talia had left town. Speculation as to why had been a major source of gossip: some said it was because he wanted an in-town presence; others had expected him to run for mayor or sheriff or believed that it was in preparation for the territory's recognition and subsequently his ambitions to run for governor; Lyle himself thought it was to make it easier for his men to keep an eye on things, something they undoubtedly couldn't do from Contesti's isolated estate.

They'd agreed that the best course of action was for John to take Ponytail back to the jail, call for Caspar, and keep the thug locked up. The bodies of Tattoo and Dye-job would have to wait. What could not wait was arresting Contesti while he was in town. Extracting him after he went back to his own estate was not something she and Lyle could do on their own.

And with the uncertainty of exactly when the marshal was going to return, Lyle wanted to make sure Contesti couldn't flee. Between the airfield on his estate and his power and influence, it would be easy for Contesti to slip away to Sakura or anywhere else.

The crowd had cleared from the earlier spectacle, giving the place a deserted feel. Even most of the hired men were gone, much to Talia's relief. That badge of Lyle's was only going to carry them so far.

"You sure you want to do this?" Lyle had asked her.

"I'm sure," she'd said.

Contesti and Rhodes were seated at the large table, the remains of their dinner cooling as they smoked cigars and sipped scotch. It was the ease of their manner, glimpsed through the window for a moment as she climbed up the porch steps, that told her that Contesti probably hadn't ordered Dye-job to go after Sam. If he had, Contesti wouldn't just be sitting here, waiting to be arrested.

Or maybe he was betting that Lyle was high on hypnolin.

As for Lyle himself, he looked steadier than he had all day. On occasion he would tense up and his pallor would change, the blood draining from it like he was in pain, and then he'd catch himself and pretend that he wasn't suffering.

He pushed the door open with his rifle, aiming it at Contesti who looked up with barely a raised brow. It was Rhodes who tensed, his hand drifting to his sidearm until Lyle swung the rifle his way.

Talia aimed hers at Contesti. "If you move, Rhodes, I will end your boss."

Rhodes swallowed, looked at his boss for confirmation.

"It's not a problem," Contesti said, leaning back in his chair, taking a slow puff off the cigar. "You'll see."

"I'm arresting you for the attempted murder of Sam Haricot," Lyle said, his voice steady, his stance firm as he lowered the rifle.

"No, you're not," Contesti said and pulled the cigar out of his mouth, made a smoke ring, and watched it drift up to the ceiling.

There was something in Contesti's voice, not just an arrogance, but a certainty that was far beyond that of a man used to giving orders and having them be obeyed.

"You heard the man," Rhodes said, but his voice held doubt.

"Shut up, Rhodes," Lyle said, still facing Contesti.

"How's your back?" Contesti made another ring, lofted it off his tongue, and blew it toward the ceiling.

Bastard. Nothing like suggestion to bring back something that Lyle was ignoring.

"Stand up," Lyle insisted.

"Go back to your office, Sheriff. And take that bitch with you."

Lyle's face twitched. He fired a shot past Contesti's ear, aiming it right into where the eaves crossed.

Rhodes drew his revolver and aimed it at Lyle.

Talia pivoted, putting him in her sights. He was a silhouette, perfectly framing the sights, and at this range, even if she missed his heart, she'd hit other parts of him. She could hear blood coursing, the squeeze and release of muscles. Her own probably, but it might as well be his. They were that close, his gaze meeting her across the length of the barrel.

His eyes. They took on a hard glitter.

"Drop it," she said.

The sound of the revolver clattering to the floor was both loud and muffled as adrenaline distorted time and sound and sight.

"The other one too. Drop the belt."

Again, he complied, his golden-green gaze never wavering.

"You can't kill me," Rhodes said. "I've done nothing wrong."

"Death doesn't need a reason," Talia said in her iciest tone. "She wears no badge."

"Sheriff, time to go," Contesti said. "Put your gun down. Put it down now."

Out of the corner of her eye, Lyle stood like a statue. But he hadn't obeyed. And she could tell that it was costing him.

"Miss Merritt," Rhodes said. "It's just a matter of time before your friend does as he is told. You know that, don't you?"

They were expecting the hypnolin in his system to make Lyle pliable, obedient.

"What happens when Signore Contesti orders him to kill you, Miss Merritt? Think about that." His voice dripped with smug satisfaction.

"Did he not tell you about the time he came in here and I had him put his own gun against his head?" Contesti asked.

Talia remained fixated on Rhodes.

"Turn around, Rhodes. On your knees," she said as she kicked the revolver one way, the gun belt the other.

Slowly, he laced his fingers behind his head, turned around. Dropped.

"Who's the obedient one now?" she whispered.

Rhodes tilted his head toward her, a smirk on his face. "Wait for it. Wait and see what has become of your so-called partner."

"I said put it down, Lyle." Contesti again, his voice going low, menacing.

In her peripheral vision, Lyle's hands were no longer steady. Tremors traveled over his skin, down from his elbows to his fingertips, a visible wave. His shoulders slumped. It was like watching dominos topple as Lyle took an unsteady step forward and then another.

She wanted to catch him, to pull him away, drag him from this place, but for Rhodes. Rhodes was the real threat, not Contesti. Rhodes would be protecting his boss from a sheriff with a drug problem, a man who couldn't be trusted.

It felt like her heart was going to fracture at the sight of Lyle complying, of him giving in. He looked like he was going to fall at Contesti's feet.

Contesti seemed to think so too. A triumphant smile formed on his lips, made his eyes flash.

And then Lyle's fist came up and connected, sending Contesti and his chair tumbling backward.

Thuds followed, Contesti's head impacting with the ground.

"Hear that?" she whispered in Rhodes's ear. "That's my boss beating the shit out of yours."

He looked up at her, eyes flashing with disbelief. "That's not going to look good. For your boss, that is."

She was tempted to wipe that insolent look out of his eyes by introducing his face to the buttstock of her rifle. Or the ceramics in her prosthesis.

"You're under arrest for attempted murder," Lyle was saying. He hauled Contesti up. Lyle hadn't done nearly as good of a job with Contesti as he'd done with Ponytail, but he had given him a black eye, a busted lip, and a cut on the cheek. Blood stained Contesti's fine white shirt.

Lyle cuffed Contesti's arms behind his back. She heard the cuffs click and then click again.

Contesti spit blood on the floor, leered at Talia. His gaze found Rhodes.

"What am I paying you for?" he demanded.

"Am I fired?" Rhodes asked over his shoulder.

"No. Get me out of jail."

"Careful there, Signore," Lyle said, flexing his hand like it hurt. "Bad things can happen to you now. Accidents. Getting shot while trying to escape. Those kinds of things. You know the kind of state I'm in. You might not even make it to the jail if anyone takes a shot at me. No telling what might happen."

"You hear that, Rhodes? Sheriff is threatening me."

"I hear him."

"Well then?"

"I'm sorry, but you're going to have to go with him. For now." Rhodes looked up at Talia. "But don't worry. I'll get you out."

Lyle pushed Contesti out the front door.

"Did you know about Sam?" Talia asked, pressing the muzzle of her rifle to the back of Rhodes's head.

"No."

"If you had, would you have stopped it?"

His silence answered for him.

"Well, at least you're not a liar," she said.

A smirk pulled at his scar.

Talia wet her lips. "I'd be very careful about what you do next, Rhodes. The only way to keep your boss alive is to let the marshal take him. You do understand that, don't you?"

"I doubt Contesti sees it that way."

"Whatever he's promised you, you can't collect if he's dead. This isn't Earth. Things don't work that way here. Make sure the others understand that too."

"When did this become so personal for you, Izanami?"

"When you involved women and children."

"How archaic. You're a woman, no?"

"No, I am Death."

Alone, Talia approached the jailhouse, Izanami's voice and tone—"I am Death"—echoing in her ears. She'd always known she had a dark side, just like everyone did, even if few recognized or acknowledged it. Even fewer had it as a persona, even if it was one that had been created for her, first by the propaganda, then by the reputation it had spawned. That reputation, that shadow that she could not outrun, had always had a name—many in fact—but never a voice.

At first she'd thought Rhodes's use of Izanami as nothing more than a way to cast her in a bad light. There were enough people in Tsurui to whom that moniker would have some meaning. As diluted as the culture of old Japan had become—here and on Earth—names still had their own sort of power. On Earth, Westernization had allowed a death god to enter Japan, given the *shinigami*—supernatural creatures sometimes described as monsters, other times as helpers, but always as creatures of darkness—a human nature.

Some had blamed *shinigami* for leading people to their deaths, usually by suicide. Others saw these demons as merely guides who invited men and women to take the road toward Death. For her, the *shinigami* had merely been an expression for the fleeting nature of life. But Rhodes had chosen Izanami, a very specific deity—the goddess who gave humans death.

Did he not know that those who knew her name also knew her as *Izanami no mikoto*, a goddess of creation? Which one was she truly embracing, the goddess of death or creation?

She hadn't been able to resist playing off Rhodes's name for her, letting him think that it was true. Would it intimidate him? He didn't look like the kind that was easily unnerved.

Chills crawled up her spine.

She shook them off, making the guns she'd taken off Rhodes shift. Still in their holsters and accompanying belt, they rode her shoulder, balancing out the weight of her rifle.

She had no doubt that Rhodes would have others. The question remained if he'd been in town long enough to establish himself as Contesti's second-in-command, if Contesti's hired guns would obey him.

Rhodes wasn't the kind to betray his boss. Of that, she was sure. He wasn't in this just for the money. And that was the problem. She thought she'd had him figured, but she was beginning to have doubts. Men who did things for money were easier to control than men who did things for power or reputation. Or because they thought they were right.

She knocked on the jailhouse door. "It's Talia. Let me in."

The door swung open to reveal a wide-eyed Logan. She hung Rhodes's gun belt on the coat rack.

"Where's Lyle?" she asked.

"In the back," John said from behind the desk. He had CorgiSan standing atop it, the deflated balloons draping over his torso like a cape. Electronic eyes swiveled in her direction. The way that the segmented muzzle was configured looked too much like a canine smile as John covered the punctured fabric with adhesive patches that gave off a chemical scent when pressed with a glowing iron.

In the back room, Lyle was dry-heaving into a bucket. Ponytail was passed out in one cage. Contesti was pacing the other. He stopped and grabbed the bars when she came in. The swelling was puffing out his gaunt features nicely, making one side of his face look younger despite the purple coloring.

"Your friend isn't doing too well," Contesti said. "I have what he needs."

"Your friend isn't doing too well either," she said, gesturing to Ponytail.

"Not my friend. I didn't tell him to do anything."

"He's one of your hired guns, isn't he?"

"I paid Rhodes to recruit men. I know nothing else about those three."

She smirked. Three. Of course he knew nothing. Just how many men had been sent, or allowed to go off on their own.

"That your story?" she asked.

"It's the truth."

"We'll see what he has to say when he wakes up."

Lyle dry-heaved into the bucket again. Her stomach knotted in sympathy. She knew just how hard that had to be on him, particularly if his back was hurting.

She knelt beside him. "Can I do something?"

He shook his head. Sweat was dripping off him in rivulets now. She wrinkled her nose, patted him on the back, and returned to the front room.

A young woman was standing by the door. She looked about twenty, tanned, her split-skirt patched in places, her blonde hair wild like she'd ridden here with it loose behind her and the wind had tangled it.

"This is Cora," John said. "Elias's sister."

Of course she was. Who was Talia going to have to face next? Elias's parents?

"Dame Leigh sent me," Cora said. "Caspar got the bullet out of Sam's shoulder. He's going to be fine. She thought you might want to know. That it would make a difference."

Patting a damp towel to his face, Lyle entered the room. "Good news, then. What did Sam say about the men who shot him?"

"Sam was unarmed," Cora insisted.

"What was Sam thinking?" Lyle asked. "A kid like him, going after three thugs by himself. Unarmed."

"He's just turned thirteen, Sheriff, or don't you remember? That's something of a milestone for us. He's technically an adult now. He heard they'd taken Dame Leigh. He was scared, afraid of losing her too. It's not like there was much chance of you stopping them, was there?"

"Well, we have the men responsible. Two are dead. The other one, we're holding."

"Contesti? He's here?" Cora asked.

"My, news does travel fast, doesn't it?" Lyle said.

"We monitor their communications. They monitor ours. Sometimes we get lucky and learn something useful."

"Tell Dame Leigh that I'm charging Contesti with attempted murder."

"Will it stick?" Cora asked.

He shook his head. "Don't know. That'll be up to the marshal. And once the lawyers get involved, who knows."

Tears welled in Cora's eyes. "Can I talk to him?"

"Talk to whom?"

"Contesti."

Lyle put his hands on his hips. "Sure. You can talk to him from here."

"No," she said. "In private. I'd like to talk to him in private. Sheriff."

He made a self-deprecating sound. "Yeah, Contesti tried that too. That suggestion thing. Didn't work, I'm afraid."

Her eyes went wide. "Please."

"Talia," Lyle said, "would you mind checking the young lady for weapons."

Talia moved toward Cora, but the young woman held up a hand and stepped away. "Never mind."

"Never mind?" Lyle said. "You thinking you can murder a man in my custody?"

"It wouldn't be murder," Cora said, raising her chin.

"Go home, Cora. Tell your family we have it under control."

Her skeptical gaze swept them, found them wanting.

"Lots of people in this town wouldn't mind it if something happened to Contesti. The same kind of something that's been happening to anyone who opposes him long enough. If you take my meaning."

"I do," Lyle said.

Skepticism moved aside for contempt, the kind that could only be projected by youth confident in its unwavering belief that it knew everything. That everything was simple and clear, that the world wasn't made up of grays. Talia saw it stir within Cora's eyes as it had stirred within her, oh-so-long ago.

"Logan," Lyle said, "would you mind escorting Miss Haricot to the edge of town."

Talia opened her mouth to object but Logan perked up and rushed forward. And then it hit her. Logan wasn't being sent along to protect Cora as much as he was being sent along to keep an eye on her, maybe let her cool down.

Cora let him open the door for her, strode out with a reasonable imitation of Dame Leigh.

"She's going to eat him alive," John said.

"He'll be fine," Lyle said. "Cora is a nice girl, despite that little show she just put on."

"Was it really that easy to get you to obey?" Talia asked.

A burst of red colored his face, washed down his neck.

"Was it?" he asked John.

"Afraid so. Good thing you don't remember all of it."

"How's the pain?" Talia asked.

He looked down at his hand. It was swollen. He was favoring his right side too.

"I've had worse," he said, but the bravado didn't reach his eyes as he picked up his rifle.

"Where you going?" she asked.

"We used to do a patrol about this time of night. I think it's time I started showing people that I'm back on the job."

"I need to finish working on CorgiSan," John said as he carefully folded the freshly patched balloon back into one of the robot's paniers. The remaining balloons looked like they were going to need a lot more mending.

"I'll go with him," Talia said.

Lyle opened one of the desk drawers. For a desperate moment she thought he might be looking for hypnolin again, but he pulled out a badge in the shape of a shield. An outline of Tatarka was inlaid at its center.

"I'm no cop," she said.

"I know. Take it anyway."

She used the clip to hang it off her belt. "Pretty target."

"That it is," Lyle said.

CHAPTER THIRTY-ONE

EVENING WAS WELL ENOUGH ALONG THAT IT WAS WRAPPING Tsurui in mountain shadows. Shirubarādo, Gōruden's silver companion had just crested the peaks, making the stars fight for the right to be seen. Just like Earth's Moon, Gōruden's satellite was responsible for the planet's suitability—the tides, the protection it had provided from meteors over billions of years. And just like Earth's Moon, it went through its phases, waxing and waning. Soon it was going to turn into a sniper's moon.

Some of the storefronts were closing, shutters being drawn across the partitioned windows. The wind shifted, bringing the scents of restaurant row with it.

The place should have smelled of rice and fish, of pork and miso. Instead it smelled of beef and potatoes, of pasta and cheese. No, this wasn't the place in her memories, the place where she'd grown up surrounded by a loving family, but it was close. Close enough to make her heartsick. Close enough to make her want.

Her stomach grumbled, both reminder and complaint that she'd given it nothing but coffee and adrenaline for far too long.

"Think you can keep some food down?" she asked Lyle.

For the first time ever, she'd slowed her pace to accommodate him. But at least his sense of balance seemed to be returning. He was staggering less, trading that lurching half walk for the stiffness of pain.

"Maybe," he said. "Maybe some broth."

He rubbed at his chest like a man with heartburn and then looked down at himself.

"I need a bath."

"Yes. Yes you do."

He shot her an unamused look. "Think you can bear it long enough for us to eat, or should we head to the onsen now?"

She wrinkled her nose. "I'm more worried about what you're going to do for the restaurant's business."

"Good point."

He turned toward a food stall rather than a restaurant. The menu was scribbled in chalk on a slate board. Half of it was Italian food. The other half, Asian. The kid who came up to the counter looked like he was the beneficiary of both those inheritances. Dark eyes with a hint of epithelial fold, dark hair that looked like it was going to explode out of the headband keeping it off his forehead, olive skin and high cheekbones.

He called their order to the back.

They settled in to wait under the awning. Talia leaned against one of the sturdy poles holding it up and pulled the glove off her prosthetic. Already, the fabric was threadbare and torn. It was covered with stains that looked like blood splatter, smudged dirt and grass, and other things she couldn't identify.

"I've been meaning to ask, how is your prosthesis?"

She tugged the damaged glove off and tapped her phantom's fingers against the counter.

"The prosthesis itself is fine."

"But?"

"Cyberneticist in Sakura said I need to have the implant controlling it replaced."

He winced.

"How much is that going to cost?"

"More than I've got."

"What happens when it stops working?" he asked.

"I figure out how to live without it."

"Contesti's offer would have gotten you there, though…" He looked miserable when he said it.

"And then every time I looked at it, used it, I would be reminded that the price I paid for it was too high. That I had sold not just my arm, but whatever was left of my soul. No thank you."

"Don't let him get inside your head," Lyle said.

"What do you mean?"

"Rhodes called you 'Izanami.' He calls you that because he knows what you can do. Wants the others to be scared of you too, because he's afraid of you."

She scoffed. "No, Lyle, he's not afraid of me."

"He's not?"

"I wish he was afraid. He might decide that Contesti's money isn't good enough then. No. This is something else. I've spent the last seven years watching his kind in Sakura. I was thinking that he was here to prove himself, but now, now I'm not so sure."

"I've seen you in a sniper's duel," Lyle said. "He hasn't."

"It's not going to be a sniper's duel."

"No?"

"Snipers hunting each other happens in the shadows," she said.

"You think he's going to want to put on a show?"

"Yesterday, he might have, yes. Today, I'm not so sure. After all, I made him look bad in front of the man he was hired to protect. Ruined his reputation, such as it was."

"Sheriff," the kid behind the counter called. He passed two bowls to them.

Lyle's was clear broth, the steam rising in tendrils through the small opening of the bowl's cover. Hers was filled with chicken and noodles swimming in Alfredo sauce. A breadstick bridged the bowl, and a pair of chopsticks were stuck into the noodles at a rakish angle.

Lyle reached into his pocket, pulled out some coins.

The boy counted them, handed one back.

They set their food atop the high table just outside the awning and sat on the high stools to enjoy the ambiance of the evening.

Several people walked by, did a double take. For once it wasn't at the woman with the cybernetic arm. Lyle waved and greeted them by name.

He must have been pacing himself because he sipped cautiously at his bowl.

She had missed this, eating in companionable silence without the need to make idle chitchat. Most of the people in Sakura seemed unable to spend more than ten seconds in silence and couldn't abide a meal that wasn't filled with inane chatter.

By the time she was wiping her bowl clean with the last of her breadstick, Lyle had reached the bottom of his. His color was better, and he was no longer hunched over his belly like it was on fire.

"Are you going to tell me what happened?" she asked.

"With Siena?"

"Unless you married another redhead I don't know about."

He wiped at his lips with a trembling hand.

"She was my type, but you already know that."

"How come you went for her instead of Maeve?" she asked. She really needed to know. Something about John's crazy theory that Siena had been a plant was beginning to make all sorts of sense, although she wasn't sure why.

Another couple strolled by walking a Great Dane, the woman in a Victorian-style dress that looked out of place with the gun belt gracing her hips. How did she draw from that thing without the gun pulling the holster up? On the man the lower strap would hold his holster in place, but on the woman... Was there some way to anchor that?

Lyle tipped his hat at them.

"Because I promised Simon that, if anything ever happened to him, I'd see Maeve settled away from here."

"Oh? Why?"

"Because it's a dangerous place to be. Simon liked taking risks. But he hated that Maeve followed him out here. He wanted her safe in one of the larger towns but couldn't convince her to leave. And after she miscarried, he almost quit his survey contract. Maeve insisted he finish it out, and that's how he got himself killed."

"Does Maeve get a say in all this?" Talia asked.

"I'd say she's had more than a say, wouldn't you?"

"What do you mean?"

"If she would have let him quit, they would have gone back home and he'd still be alive."

"So, plenty of guilt to go around then," Talia said. "She feels guilty because he stayed on a job she insisted he finish. You feel guilty because he died, leaving her alone, and even though you want her—"

"What makes you say that?"

"Don't you?"

He pulled his hat off, ran his hands through his hair and lowered them again. They were shaking.

"Yes, I do. I thought I was hiding it well enough though."

She shot him a wan smile.

"I screwed up with her, didn't I?"

"Yes you did."

He cradled his face in his hands for a moment. When he lowered them, he looked lost and confused, desperate even.

"After what I've done, how do I . . . approach her?"

"Apologize. Profusely. Tell her how you feel."

He groaned. She knew him well enough that she expected it, welcomed it. He was not one to talk about his feelings. It always took a pry bar to get him to open up. He preferred action. She had no doubt the action of making an apology would be the easier task.

"Lyle, you deserve a happy life, just like everyone else."

"Do I? A man who let himself be hooked on hypnolin because a pretty girl smiled at him? Why did these people let me keep my job after I showed them what kind of fool I really was?"

"Maybe they're more forgiving than you are."

"Maybe they're just desperate."

She wanted to deny it, but couldn't. Maybe they were. She hadn't been here long enough to know the situation well.

"I never suspected hypnolin, you know. She was . . . well, loving, attentive, exciting. Better than I deserved. Hypnolin doesn't just make the physical pain go away. It . . . it makes everything easier. It helps you function better, when all that pain is gone, when you're no longer devoting so much energy to dealing with it, hiding it."

"But?"

"Ah yes, the 'but.' There is a threshold after a while. Once you cross it, the pain is gone but other things as well. I think Caspar called it 'executive function.' It takes that too. You feel lost. There is no one to tell you what to do; no one to tell you to eat, or drink, or bathe. Even the simplest decisions become too overwhelming and it's just easier to not do anything. Hypnolin not only makes you pliable, it makes you dependent. You want to be told what to do, how to do it, when to do it. Just shut off your brain and let others think for you."

"What happens if you stop taking it?"

"The pain comes back stronger. It's your mind tricking you into taking more. And you will falter, eventually, because it consumes you from the inside out, until all that matters is ending it."

He looked into her eyes. "Contesti asked for my revolver. I handed it over. Didn't even think to deny him. He returned it to me. Told me to put it up against my head. So I did. Told me to pull the trigger, so I did. And every time I did, I thought, yes, the next one, the next one is going to end it all. I'll be free."

Her heart ached in her chest like it had been stabbed. "Lyle, you don't have to—"

"Yes, yes I do. Because I need for you to know how compromised I am. It wasn't a one-man Russian roulette. He'd reloaded it with spent rounds. All of them. He didn't want me dead. He told me so. Not yet, he said. Not until he won. He wanted me to live long enough to see him win while I was left with nothing."

He paused then, his eyes taking on a faraway look.

"I lowered the gun," he continued, "fell to my knees, and wept. I don't know how long I was there, wallowing in misery, wishing I had the 'executive function' to grab his gun instead. He knelt down beside me, pried the gun from my fingers, placed a bottle of hypnolin in my hands.

"It was like the sun had parted the clouds, like a choir of angels was singing. I couldn't get it in me fast enough. And as soon as I emptied that bottle, I wanted another.

"He mocked me then, even as he gave me a second one. 'Easy now, not too much. We don't want you ending it prematurely. Let's dole it out on the schedule that Siena gave us.'"

Talia closed her eyes to keep the tears that had been building up contained. She put her hand on his.

"I'm sorry."

"I don't want pity."

"It's not pity," she said. "It's compassion."

"I told you this so you would understand what you were really getting into."

"I do, Lyle. And I'm still going to stay and see it through."

"Why?"

"Because it's what friends do."

Given the state of Lyle's hygiene, Talia did not expect him at the Full Moon onsen's soaking pool for awhile. He would have to spend some time scrubbing. She stowed her clothing in the basket right atop her gun and set it down within reach.

Paranoid? Not me.

She couldn't remember seeing any women among Contesti's thugs, but that didn't mean he didn't have any in his employ. And if Contesti was as concerned about appearances as he'd been signaling, then perhaps Rhodes would be cautious as well.

Nevertheless, Talia left her prosthesis on this time.

She sat down on one of the stools underneath the low shower head and scrubbed herself and her hair clean. The water sluiced into the seam of her prosthesis where she had no sensation. It made her phantom feel like parts of her forearm were numb. Right on cue, the phantom-implant connection "filled" things in by making it feel like ants crawling.

Talia fought the sensation by staring at the prosthetic, making her brain take note of what her eyes were clearly seeing—no ants. It was just water. Water disappearing into the prosthesis as if it was sinking into her nonexistent skin, slipping underneath the nonexistent fascia, the absent veins, and tendons and bones.

Her mind resisted. Some people insisted that you were in control of your own thoughts, and hence, your own happiness and health, as if it was merely a matter of willpower.

But it was a lot of work. A lot of retraining of the mind, the body, and everything that connected them.

Steam rose around her, fogging up the mirrors and room, but by the time she was done, she felt better. The wood planks creaked underneath her bare feet as she picked up the basket and carried it with her to the soaking pool.

Two women, a blonde and a brunette, were already there, chatting amicably in low tones. They eyed the basket but said nothing about the breach in decorum. Let them think she was being rude, or a rube. Better to have her gun and not need it, than need it and not have it.

She set the basket down by the pool's edge and took the steps down into the hot water, going slow as to allow herself to acclimate. The heat sank into her aching muscles like a balm.

"Nice, isn't it?" the blonde woman asked.

"Very."

"I'm Nancy," the brunette said. "This is my cousin, Paula."

"Talia Merritt. Nice to meet you." She lowered herself to the seat cut into the rock.

"We know," Paula, the blonde, said. "Maeve's friend."

The hairs on the back of Talia's neck rose. Annoyed, she reached up and smoothed them down. "You know Maeve?"

"She said you were here to get rid of Contesti and his men." The way that Nancy said the word "men" was filled with disgust.

"I'm just here to help my friend," Talia insisted. "You don't like Contesti?"

Paula made a face like she'd bitten into a lemon. "We don't like Signore Contesti, and his men are swine."

"And you've already killed two of them," Nancy said. "For this, we are—"

"I didn't kill them," Talia said.

"Do you think they will leave now?" Paula asked. "Now that Contesti is under arrest? It's been nice to have so much new business, but..." She shrugged.

"I don't know," Talia said. "No one does."

"Do you think that since they shot Sam Haricot, that we are in danger too?" Nancy asked.

"Everyone is in danger," Paula insisted. "I've been trying to explain that to my cousin here"—a poke at the brunette's shoulder—"but she won't listen."

"If it was up to you, we'd be hiding at home," Nancy said. "Hiding under our beds, too scared to go out for fear of being shot."

Paula made a face and stuck out her tongue.

Nancy laughed and splashed some water at her. She turned from her cousin back to Talia.

"What do you think?" she asked, her tone serious now. "Should we be hiding?"

There was a part of Talia that wanted to tell them to stay home. The fewer people that were out and about the less likely they were to get caught in the crossfire, but if she confirmed their fears, those fears would grow and spread, maybe even become a self-fulfilling prophecy.

"Signore Contesti seemed to be more concerned about those taking sides, openly opposing him," Talia said instead. She cleared her throat. "What is it that you ladies do, anyway?"

Nancy's lips quirked up into a smile. "I design and make clothes. Paula here cuts hair."

"And you've tangled with Contesti's men, how?"

"They don't like it when we say no," Paula said.

"Have they—"

A shot rang out.

The women flinched and Talia bolted out of the water. She had her 1911 in hand as she sprinted for the source, the other side of the changing room.

Lyle was the only man inside, buck naked, standing with his shoulder braced up against a column, looking out into the night, his pistol in hand. Blood ran down from his right calf to mix in with the water flowing around his feet.

"What happened?" Talia asked.

The onsen hostess ducked her head in and ran screaming the other way when Talia pointed her gun at her. She lowered it as soon as she realized the woman was no threat, but wasn't going to blame her for running away. She certainly would have.

"Coward slashed my leg and ran," Lyle said. "I think he's gone though. Went down the side of that hill, right into the gulley."

"Did you get a good look at him?" She looked around the entry leading to the pools but there was no one there. The bushes were disturbed, their branches bent and broken where someone had gone through them.

"No, I didn't get a good look at him. Had soap in my eyes."

She bent to check out his leg. It was a deep slash, one that looked like it had gotten muscle as well as skin.

"Let's talk to the hostess," he said. "Find out who came in after us."

She made toward the door leading to the lobby.

"Talia," Lyle said. "Clothes first, I think, don't you?"

Oh, yes. Clothes. Heat crawled up her face as the rest of her cooled with the water evaporating off her skin.

"What? You don't think a naked cyborg running through the streets after Contesti's goons is what we need right now?"

"It's your call, Talia. I'll back you up."

She scoffed. It was good to see that the old Lyle was still in there, under all the pain and guilt.

CHAPTER THIRTY-TWO

EVEN THOUGH LYLE HAD LOST WEIGHT IN THE LAST SIX MONTHS, Talia struggled to hold him up as she and Paula helped him get from the onsen to the jailhouse. The hostess hadn't been as helpful as they'd hoped. She hadn't admitted anyone into the onsen after Talia and Lyle, which meant that the attacker had snuck in, probably the same way he'd run out.

Talia, Nancy, and Paula had dressed so hastily their clothes clung to them, their hair dripping down their backs. Every time the wind gusted, it made Talia shiver.

Nancy had taken off to get Maeve and see if they could reach the Haricot's doctor. The hostess had given Lyle a robe and sandals to wear. She'd also wrapped his calf tightly, but the bandage was now soaked and blood was dripping down his leg. Paula was awkwardly balancing Lyle's shotgun on one shoulder. He'd stuck his revolver in the robe's pocket, but Talia doubted he'd be able to reach it and draw if they were attacked.

They crested the hill leading to the jailhouse.

"Well, that was fast," Lyle said.

"What was fast?" Talia asked.

"That's Caspar's horse."

A gray mare with a black blaze on her nose was tied out in front of the jailhouse.

"I can make it the rest of the way," Lyle insisted. He took his weight off their shoulders. Blood gushed down to his ankle, and he made it the last few steps. He faltered and reached out, catching the thick length of rope hanging from the rafter. It caused the bell to ring.

"I hate this thing. Why is this still here?" Lyle asked, leaning one hand on the door and swatting at the rope. It only made the bell ring again. "Damn it, John, why is this cursed thing still here?

The door swung open on a wide-eyed John. "Damn it, Lyle, what—"

He blinked, no doubt at Lyle's attire. He swung his gaze down, saw the leg. Then he found the women standing behind Lyle.

"What happened?" He moved aside and held the door open. He was holding a mostly empty whisky bottle at his side.

Talia took hold of Lyle's elbow and guided him into the chair behind his desk. CorgiSan was still atop the desk, in a down-stay, a single balloon still spread out atop him like a saddle.

"Someone came at me with a knife," Lyle said.

"Where's Logan? Isn't he back yet?" Talia asked as she helped Lyle prop his leg up on the table.

"Yes, he got back just fine. Cora didn't suck the life out of him or nothing. Was kinda disappointed myself."

Talia gave him her annoyed matron face.

"Fine," John said, setting the bottle on a shelf. "No sense of humor. Noted. I sent him and DespairBear to Maeve's for supplies. He should be back soon."

Caspar slipped into the front room from the holding area and shut the door behind him. His long hair was pulled back into a queue, unbraided, but cinched tight with plain ribbon in several places. His eyebrow rose a fraction at the sight of Lyle's newest wound.

"Hello, Doc," Lyle said. "Don't take this wrong, but why are you here?"

Caspar crossed the room and unwrapped Lyle's bandage.

"Let me take a look at your wound first."

"Fine," Lyle said. "John, you mind telling me what's going on?"

John scratched at his head. "When I went to check in on the ponytail guy back there, he didn't seem to be breathing. I gave him CPR, but..."

Caspar's probing fingers made Lyle wince. "Your prisoner is dead, by the way. Looks like he suffocated."

Lyle's gaze met Caspar's.

"Don't insult me with those eyes, Sheriff. If I was out for blood, I'd have killed Contesti, not his henchman, made it really easy for all of us. The fact that he is still alive and well should earn me sainthood."

"Saint Caspar," John said. "Has a ring to it."

"Sorry, Doc. I just . . . I guess I'm suspicious now that I'm coming off a fresh knifing."

"About that, Lyle," Talia interjected. "It's rather convenient, don't you think, that one of Contesti's men only wounded you."

"What do you mean?" Nancy asked.

"With Lyle dead," Talia said, "we are down one. With Lyle wounded, we need others to help take care of him. And with Lyle hurt, he's more likely to . . . well, want something for the pain."

Lyle opened his mouth like he was going to object but shut it with a snap.

Caspar reached into his doctor's bag, drew out a syringe that wasn't quite as big as the one that Maeve had used on Lyle, but it still made his eyes go wide.

"This is a very deep cut. I need to clean your wound before I stitch it back up. This is for the pain." Caspar drew a clear liquid into the syringe.

"Can I talk you into letting me get dressed first?" Lyle asked.

John opened a cupboard, reached inside and brought out a stack of neatly folded clothes. A knock on the door made Nancy shuffle away from it.

Paula and Maeve entered.

Maeve rushed at Lyle, put her arms around him. Kissed the top of his head and just rested her cheek next to his for a moment.

If she and Lyle had been alone, Talia would have said something like, *Look how Maeve rushed to your side. Look into her eyes and apologize. You probably won't even have to grovel. She just needs to hear you say you're sorry, that you do love her. Just three little words, Lyle. Say them!*

Logan came in behind them, carrying a whiskey bottle—the aforementioned supplies, no doubt.

"What's going on?" he asked.

"Great. The gang's all here." Despite the sarcasm, Lyle was beaming as he sat there with Maeve's hands resting on his shoulders.

Lyle sent Paula and Nancy away with his thanks and promised to look in on them. John took CorgiSan off the table and set him up on a charger. The robot settled on the charging pad with what could only be described as contentment. Or as much as something like that could be applied to a machine. John made an excuse about needing some air as soon as Caspar took up the syringe again. DespairBear trotted out after him.

Caspar numbed up Lyle's leg with efficient, expert motions. Lyle limited himself to a heartfelt wince and the occasional huff.

"Give it a few minutes," Caspar said and laid his suture kit out on the table.

Logan helpfully offered to boil some water.

"Maeve," Lyle said, "after we're done here, I need you to go back to your place and keep a low profile."

She looked down at him. "Why?"

"Both Nancy and Paula seemed concerned about Contesti's men," Talia said.

"I'll talk to them," Maeve said. "I don't think it's a good thing for them to be spreading panic."

"They shot Sam Haricot," Lyle said.

"Contesti and the Haricots have been feuding for years. As far as I know, the only time Contesti has done anything to anyone is if he was feuding with them."

"Still, I'd rather not have you caught up in it, not with this Rhodes guy running things now."

"He's right, Maeve," Talia said. "He could use you against us. And after tonight, I think we need to be more careful. Maybe even stay put until this marshal of yours comes in to take custody of Contesti."

"All right," Maeve said, but her tone said she didn't like it. "I'll be careful."

It wasn't a promise to keep a low profile. A detail that Talia almost pointed out.

"Did Contesti murder his own man?" Talia asked instead.

"He denied it when I asked him." Caspar was pouring the heated water into a basin. He tested the water's temperature. "He actually told me the sheriff did it."

Lyle let out something like a scoff or a cough.

"That man was alive when we left," Lyle said. "Ask Talia. Ask John."

"I don't doubt you, Sheriff," Caspar said as he scrubbed his hands with soap and plunged them into the hot water.

Logan handed him a towel.

"Ouch," Lyle said when Caspar poked his leg.

"Truly?" Caspar asked. "You can feel that?"

"Not just feel it. It hurts."

Logan raised his hand like he was in a schoolroom. It crept up slowly above a hunched shoulder.

"What?" Lyle said, aiming his ire at him.

"The hypnolin antagonist. I told you that this was a side effect." He lowered his hand and gave them a sheepish shrug.

"You'll have to tell me about this antagonist." Caspar prepared a second dose and gave it to Lyle. "In fact, I insist on it. When can you come to our place? We have facilities as good as any in Sakura."

Logan straightened and his face lit up. "Really?"

"Really. I think an exchange of information would be mutually beneficial, don't you?"

"All right, dok-tors, that second shot didn't do anything either, so shall we just proceed?"

"Logan," Talia said, "why don't you take Maeve home and bring back some food for us and the gentleman in the back."

"Consider it done." Logan looked eager to escape.

"All right," Maeve said with some reluctance.

"He's going to need crutches," Caspar said.

"Crutches as well. Will do." Maeve closed the door behind them.

Lyle groaned. "Can we get this over with?"

He reached for the whiskey, took a fortifying gulp or two.

Once again, Talia found herself holding Lyle down as he swore and cursed. She was glad that Maeve had left. He would have put on a brave face, much braver than the one he was putting on now as he squeezed her prosthetic hand for all it was worth. He dug his nails into it, and had it been flesh, she had no doubt he'd have drawn blood.

"Just two more stitches."

"You said that two stitches ago," Lyle complained. His face was red with strain, and he must have bitten the inside of his cheek because there was blood on the seam of his lips.

Talia was no expert, but it looked like Caspar wasn't having to just stitch up skin. He was having to stitch up muscle first, then close the skin around it.

Caspar put in four more stiches, cleaned the wound again, and wrapped it up.

"Make sure he stays off that leg as much as possible. If he doesn't, you have my permission to use the crutches to beat him."

"Thanks, Doc," Lyle groused, reaching for the bottle of whiskey Logan had brought back.

"Does that help?" Caspar asked.

Lyle took another deep swig. "Nope. Not a damn bit."

"Interesting." Caspar wrapped up his tools and set them in the bag.

"What will you be putting on Ponytail's death certificate?" Talia asked.

"Suffocation. Cause unknown." He zipped up the bag. "But, regardless, Contesti will call foul."

"If I killed that man, I want to know," Lyle said, swiping at some blood and whiskey that had dribbled down his chin.

"I find it interesting that he insists that he didn't even know the man's name," Caspar said. "I guess I'll have to ask Rhodes. Anyway, it's entirely possible that the beating damaged his airway, that the subsequent swelling compromised it, and that at some point he simply stopped breathing. It's also entirely possible that Contesti reached through the bars and helped him along, perhaps when John let him out to use the facilities. I'm no medical examiner, therefore my report will simply say 'Suffocation. Cause unknown.'"

"Caspar," Lyle said, "*I* need to know."

He buttoned up his coat and straightened his shoulders. "I don't know, Lyle. You might have."

"All right, Doc. Thank you."

"I will have someone collect the body. We don't have the means to store it for the marshal. That works both in your favor, and his." Caspar indicated the holding area where Contesti was pacing back and forth.

"May I speak with you?" Caspar asked Talia.

Talia escorted Caspar onto the front porch. Even before she was out the door, her gaze drifted to the roofs, the eaves, the dark corners, the shadows. A few eyes glittered back at her. Bats. Hanging from the eaves.

I'll get you out, Rhodes had promised Contesti.

Unlike the urban landscapes devastated by war, there were no piles of debris and the only things that fluttered across the cobblestones were leaves. Tsurui was tidy and neat, and she wanted to keep it that way.

The wind stirred her still-damp hair, slid along the damp clothes. She pulled the coat tight around her.

Caspar opened up his mare's saddlebags.

"Were you able to get to a cyberneticist in Sakura?" he asked.

"Yes." It came out warier than she'd intended.

"Care to tell me what they said. Perhaps I can help."

Talia couldn't come up with a polite way to say it was none of his business but didn't want to alienate their only doctor either. And there was no reason to think that Caspar had anything but her best interests in mind.

"Look," Caspar said as he put his bag away. "It wasn't your fault that Elias died. I did a thorough autopsy and no one but a trained medical professional would have done it differently. I explained that to Sam, and he is supposed to come and apologize to you for his actions. Making amends for such things is part of his coming-of-age ritual and I—"

"It's probably best that he stay out of town, at least until we get Contesti turned over to the marshal. Besides, he's just a boy. I don't blame him for . . . for what he did."

"He is thirteen. In our eyes, he's no longer a child, but a man-in-training and is now expected to act as one. We don't let them be children until they are twenty-something and expect an adulthood switch to flip on just because an arbitrary date has been reached."

"I understand, but—"

"Do you?" His voice was harsh, unwavering. "Then when he comes to apologize, you will treat him like a man who attacked you and has come to make amends."

"What do you expect me to do?"

"That depends. How is your prosthesis? Is it damaged?"

"You know that it's not the prosthesis, don't you?"

Caspar nodded, his lips flattening into a line. "I've been educating myself, just in case. And I was afraid that might be the real problem. Well, know this, the Haricots will make it right."

"I don't think anyone can make it right," Talia said, "and I don't mean that in a vengeful way. I mean that an implant can only be had from Earth. It's not something you or anyone else can repair. The cyberneticist in Sakura made that very clear."

Caspar put his foot up in a stirrup and pushed himself up. He patted the mare's head and clucked his tongue as he seated himself in the saddle.

"We stand to make a lot of money from our project here," Caspar said. "I think that we will be able to afford to replace your implant."

"That puts me in a bind. Some might say my objectivity here is compromised, that I have a vested interest in seeing Contesti arrested."

"So it does. Bitch of a situation, isn't it, but it changes nothing."

"As soon as Lyle doesn't need me anymore," Talia said, "I will go back to Sakura and figure out a way to pay for my own implant."

"No wonder Dame Leigh likes you," Caspar said, looking down at her. "You two are cut from the same cloth. Stubborn, arrogant, proud."

"I guess I'll take that as a compliment."

"Don't. It wasn't meant as one."

The undertaker turned out to be a woman named Shanon Koscielny. Middle-aged and tanned with a hook nose and dressed all in black, she had two young men as assistants. A scarf of some kind covered her hair and she showed up just before midnight.

Lyle had fallen asleep on the cot and was snoring up a storm. He stayed asleep as Madame Koscielny and her men put Ponytail's body on a stretcher and carried him outside to a waiting wagon.

"Name of deceased?" she asked in a nasally voice and an accent so thick that it took Talia a second to decipher what she was saying.

"Ask Signore Contesti over there," John said.

Contesti was sitting on his cot. His clothes were rumpled, his hair plastered to his head. He'd smoothed it back of course, but dirt and sweat weren't nearly as enhancing as pomade. Eyeing Talia, he scratched at his scraggly cheek. The definition of the pencil-fine moustache was gone, crowded out by a day's worth of unruly growth. The goatee hadn't been absorbed yet, but it no longer looked like refined grooming, just a patch of extra-long hair.

The eyes, however. The eyes were cold and dark. Reptilian.

"I don't know who that man was," Contesti insisted.

"That is three John Does," Madame Koscielny complained. "All in one day."

"So it is," John said.

She shot him a look. "John Does are buried at town expense."

"I do know that, Madame. Would you like me to make up a name instead?"

She twisted her face. It made the lines stand out. She pulled a pad of paper out of her skirt pocket, along with a pen and scribbled, then handed John a ticket.

"Thank you. I'll put it with the others."

The undertaker marched out and spoke to her men in a language Talia did not understand—Polish maybe. John followed her out.

"Did you kill that man?" Talia asked Contesti.

"Don't be ridiculous."

"I want to believe you, Signore, I really do," she said. "But I don't."

She pivoted for the door.

"Wait," Contesti said.

It brought her to a stop. She didn't turn around. Logan and John were standing in the doorway watching her, watching Contesti.

"Rhodes wants you."

The world shrank to just her and the man in the cage. A man she had at her mercy. A man who deserved none. She should gut him, send him back to Rhodes as a corpse. Would he thank her for it?

"He's obsessed with Izanami," Contesti added as if that explained anything.

"Izanami is a myth, a legend. She's not real."

"To him she is. Has a real hard-on for her. For taking her."

"Taking her where?" Logan asked.

John groaned and rolled his eyes.

"What did I say?" Logan stammered as John pulled him out of the doorway.

The door swayed on its hinges a bit before closing. Talia waited for the hairs on the back of her neck to lie back down.

A reptilian smile had formed on Contesti's face, made lurid by the bruises, the blood. In the shadow of the threadbare lamp, his face was somehow sinister, threatening.

I'm tired, that's all.

He hadn't really changed. He was still the same refined dandy, a man who didn't like to get his hands dirty, a man who thought he was a force for good, who knew right down to his soul that he was better than everyone else around him.

Don't let him get inside your head, Lyle had said. And he was right. Battles were won and lost there. Contesti knew it. So did Rhodes.

She slammed the door shut behind her.

CHAPTER THIRTY-THREE

TALIA AND LOGAN RETURNED TO THE JAILHOUSE THE NEXT morning. The front door was locked, an improvement over its usual condition. She knocked and waited.

"They're probably still asleep," Logan said, stifling a yawn.

She was about to say, give them a moment, but he took hold of the bell-pull and shook it. The metal band at the top hit the bell. The sound traveled quite nicely in the chill, morning air, making the horses stabled down the street neigh. Dogs barked. Something that sounded like a rooster answered.

"Well, now everybody is up," she said.

The door flew open, revealing a crumpled John and his bowie knife, held at shoulder level, ready to come down.

"Damn it. Never ring the bell." Slowly, he sheathed the knife.

"If you don't want it rung, why is it here?" Logan asked.

"To signal an escape. Sheriff's been wanting it gone and you're not helping."

Logan stepped past John. "He's the sheriff. Shouldn't he get his way?"

Talia followed him in and John locked the door behind them.

"And for that," Lyle said, "I'm not going to throw anything at you for waking me up."

He was siting atop the cot where he'd spent the night. There was a bedroll on the floor as well, probably John's. DespairBear was in a down-stay on the bedroll and CorgiSan was humming on his charger. Actually humming, although that might have just been the charger itself.

John maneuvered around the bedroll and set about making coffee.

Lyle rested his elbows on his knees, head between his hands.

"How are you fee—"

"Don't. Don't ask." He grabbed the crutch lying by the cot and stood. He stuck it first under one arm, then the other.

"It goes on the opposite side," Logan offered.

"Does it now? Excuse me." Lyle put his weight on it and groaned. He switched it as he maneuvered around DespairBear and then two steps later, as he went into the holding area.

"How is he?" Talia asked.

John blew out a breath. "Worse than he's letting on. After you left last night, he woke up for a bit. When he wasn't tossing and turning he was having nightmares. I don't think he got more than an hour or two of sleep."

"And you?"

"About the same," he said rolling up his bedding. He nudged DespairBear off. "You, get on your charger. I don't need to be chasing your ass down again because you ran out of juice."

DespairBear made a noise like an electronic huff and edged onto the charging mat. His did not hum.

The kettle whistled and John rushed to pour the water over the waiting grounds. He poured four cups.

"Sorry, no sugar, no milk."

Talia took the offered cup. Logan did too. He sipped. She didn't. Black coffee was something she saved only for the direst of emergencies.

"He seems to be doing better," Logan observed.

"That stuff you gave him, it seems to be . . . well, I've never seen anything that worked on an addict like it."

Logan shrugged. "There might be a placebo effect to it as well."

"Or," Talia said, "he's not letting on how much he's struggling with it."

"And it hasn't been very long either," Logan said. "Time will tell."

Lyle returned wearing a fresh shirt and wiping his face with a towel. He too reached for a cup and made a face.

"John, do you think you could stand another shift? I need to check on Maeve. Grab some breakfast, that kind of thing."

Maybe talk to her, apologize, grovel, that kind of thing. Talia bit down on her lip to keep the thought from being spoken.

"I can," John said. "But I'd like to do it alone, if you don't mind. Maybe catch some sleep this time."

"Yeah, sorry, about that." Balancing on his good leg, Lyle put on his gun belt, slipped into his duster, and reached for his hat.

"I'd like to come along too," Logan announced. "Your radio. I think I saw something in Maeve's shop that might help me fix it." He set the cup aside. Talia placed hers next to his.

"Would that something answer to the name of Cora?" John teased.

Logan turned beet red. It was like watching a mercury thermometer fill with color. Talia almost felt sorry for him.

"No," he said unconvincingly.

"That radio is a lost cause," John said. "I know because I'm the one who's had to scavenge parts for it, improvise parts for it, and I've given up."

"Why not just order replacement parts?"

Talia thought that John was going to strangle Logan.

"Don't you think we've tried? We can't get them fast enough. I've had some components back-ordered for years. I could have ordered a whole new radio from Earth and it would already have gotten here."

"So why didn't you?"

Talia made a warning sound, a bit like a hiss. Lyle put his hand on her shoulder, kept her from getting between them.

John advanced on Logan, pointer finger first.

"Because I didn't know two years ago that it would take two years."

Logan raised his hands in surrender and took a step back.

"All right," Lyle said. "Time to go, I think. Let John get some sleep. I'd say he earned it."

He switched the crutch again and grabbed Logan by the back of his collar, aimed him at the door, using him as support. He didn't let him go until they were on the porch, wind pulling at their coats.

"I didn't mean to offend him," Logan said.

"I know. He's tired. Don't worry about it. He'll have forgotten it by tomorrow."

"Where's the wagon?" Talia asked.

"Down at the stable. Why?"

"Because I'm not letting you ride horseback. Caspar said to stay off that leg. Or do you want a beating?"

He sneered. "Fine."

It was a testament to how much pain Lyle must actually have been in because he didn't argue further. The strain of it was clear by the time they made it to the stable and hooked up the horses. He did insist that he drive, and she allowed it. Logan climbed into the back without argument and had his nose in his notebook within seconds.

"Do you really think they would go after Maeve?" Talia asked as he pulled into the street.

The clop-clop of the horse hooves was like a timer counting out his hesitation.

"I thought a lot about what you said last night, about them sending someone to wound me. They probably don't know about Logan's concoction, but they might just think Maeve is responsible since this would be her area of expertise."

"She did help him make it."

"Logan," he called over his shoulder. "You said your concoction only worked for a few days. Anything more specific than a few?"

"It depends on how long you were on hypnolin, the concentration, your own metabolism. I couldn't account for it all, but made some guesses, so no, not really. I erred on the side of a stronger dose, given the circumstances. You probably have at least a couple more days. But probably not more than three."

"It'll have to do." He brought the horses to a stop to allow a woman with a bakery cart to finish crossing the street.

"Thank you, Sheriff," she called to him. "Good to see you're up and about."

"You're welcome. Have a good day."

Talia's gaze drifted to the tops of the shops and homes, the canopies of the cherry and plum trees.

"Still seeing sight lines?" he asked as they rolled forward.

"Yes. Do you?"

"No. Not anymore."

"Is that good or bad?" she asked.

"Not sure yet. Will let you know when this is over."

She scoffed.

"Or sooner. If they hurt Maeve."

There was something in his voice, fear and anger perhaps. Whatever it was, she wanted—needed—to know.

"Tell me."

"Do you remember Beamer?" he asked. "We found him up against a wall, gutted. They'd pulled out his intestines. It looked like he'd tried to gather them back into his belly."

She closed her eyes, looked away. "I remember. Somehow, despite all of that, he wasn't dead."

"Do you remember the way his eyes begged?"

"Yeah. They took his tongue. It was nailed to his chest. You took his hands in your own, murmured a question. At the time I didn't realize what it was. I was looking for his bleed kit as if that would've helped."

"What did I ask him?"

"You asked him if he wanted you to end it. He nodded. You stood up, pulled me back, forced me to my feet. And then you fired a single, merciful shot. But this isn't war, Lyle. They are not going to do that to Maeve."

She looked at him, silently pleading that he agree with her. Because if he didn't, she wasn't sure she'd be able to stop him.

"Here we are." He pulled the wagon in front of Maeve's shop and set the brake.

"Lyle. They are not going to do that to Maeve."

"I'm not afraid of them doing that to Maeve. I'm afraid of me doing that to them."

She made a soundless "oh." Well, she had a dark side. Why shouldn't he?

Logan had jumped out of the back and helped him down. Lyle stuck the crutch under his arm.

Once inside, Lyle hung his hat on a peg. Maeve came out from behind the counter and pulled him into a hug. He turned it into a kiss. She melted into him.

He pulled her outside, making the shop bell ring as he let the door shut.

They spoke.

Talia couldn't hear them or make out what they were saying, so she supplied her own dialogue from gesture and expressions.

Lyle: I'm so very sorry.

Maeve: For what?

Lyle: You know, for being an ass, for ignoring how you feel, for putting duty to Simon above what you wanted.

Maeve: Oh, Lyle, you're so bad at this.

Lyle: Look, I'm trying. Do you want me to get down on both knees and beg for forgiveness?

Maeve: Well, that would be nice. Do you think you can actually get that far down or make it back up?

Lyle: For you my love, anything. Anything at all. Here, help me get down. Will one knee do? Or would you consider that an insincere form of groveling?

Maeve: Oh stop it, you big lug. You know that I'm not that kind of girl.

Lyle: So what kind of girl are you?

Talia stifled a giggle at the obvious corniness of her own imagination.

While she'd been indulging her sense of drama, Logan had sauntered up to Cora and leaned back into the counter, resting his elbows on the surface.

Talia wandered around the shop, drifting closer to Logan and Cora, feeling very much like a fifth wheel. It was an altogether too familiar feeling, and it didn't seem to be getting any easier to bear.

"How long do you think it'll take Maeve to come up for air?" Logan asked.

Talia snuck a look outside. Lyle and Maeve were in the middle of a very passionate kiss.

Cora giggled. "Another minute."

"Think we can beat that time?" Logan asked, throwing a look over his shoulder.

Cora blushed and shook her head. "I need to put some stuff up in the back."

"Let me help," he said and followed her.

Talia almost said, "Get a room," but bit down on it and looked around the shop. It was as tidy and neat as she remembered it, its multitude of shelves free of dust and clutter, everything neatly arranged into sections, every jar, box, and bottle labeled. And on the wall behind the register, something new. A picture of Maeve's dead husband, Simon. And below it, his katana.

Outside, they must have broken their kiss because she heard whispering.

"I'll be all right, Lyle," Maeve insisted. "I'm armed, and Cora is almost always here. Mr. Manetti across the street checks in on me regularly. So do his delivery boys. Nicolson next door, too. And I can't shut down. Too many people here rely on what I make, and I've got perishables I must dry and process."

"You can do that in the back, even with the shop closed."

"I am not going to hide. Period. End of argument." Maeve pivoted on her heel and came at Talia, arms wide open.

"Thanks for making him ride in a wagon," she whispered into Talia's ear.

"You're welcome," Talia whispered back. Lyle was watching them from just inside the door, shaking his head.

He moved aside for an elderly couple entering the store.

"Sheriff, I didn't know you were..." the elderly woman trailed off.

"Sober?" Lyle said. "Yes, Mrs. Hogan. I am. How are you?"

"We're here to see Mrs. York," her companion announced as he thrust his hand out. "It is good to see you, Sheriff. Up and about. Sober."

Lyle shook his hand.

"Clean," Mrs. Hogan added with a smile. "You do clean up nice, Sheriff."

"Why thank you, ma'am. I do appreciate the compliment."

Maeve took over and shepherded them around the store. Lyle hobbled over next to Talia, leaned against the counter, and rubbed at his leg.

"You going to make it?" Talia asked.

"Not like I have a choice."

"I think I'm going to check on Logan." She moved into the gap between the counters but Lyle blocked her with his crutch.

"Don't. He's impressing Cora. Let him. That's why he lied about needing radio parts from an apothecary's store."

She let out a sigh. "You're not the one who usually picks up on these things."

"Yes, well, I too was a young man. Once."

They moved aside for Maeve and the Hogans. She rang them up, wrapped up their purchases, and was escorting them to the door, when it opened, seemingly on its own.

"Oh dear, it's that little robot dog," Mrs. Hogan said as Despair-Bear threaded his way around the couple. The way he bounced along in his netting, freshly decked out with twigs and paper and lily leaves, he looked like he'd rolled around in the street.

Maeve finished ushering the Hogans out.

"He's got a note dangling from his neck," Lyle said when DespairBear sat down by his feet. "Would you mind? I'd rather not squat right now."

"Sure." Talia gave DespairBear a friendly pat. He leaned into her hand appreciatively. A scrap of fabric had been cut into a makeshift ribbon and been used to tie the note around his neck. Primitive, but effective.

She handed it to Lyle. His face darkened.

"What is it?" Maeve asked.

"John got a tip from the post office. They have a package for Rhodes. The label on it—a cancan girl wearing a geisha wig—piqued the mailman's curiosity. Thought we might want to know."

"Candy's Gun and Toy Shoppe," Talia said.

"You know it?"

"Yes. Candy herself is the decent sort. Very proud of her stock. At first, she thought I worked for Rhodes. Got a bit nippy about a special order she thought I was there to pressure her for on his behalf."

"What special order?" Lyle asked.

"An antimatérial gun."

"Well damn."

"What's wrong?" Maeve asked.

"An antimatérial gun will shoot through a stone wall," Talia explained.

Maeve's eyes went wide. "The jailhouse."

"Well, Rhodes did promise Contesti he'd get him out. That would do it." He was scribbling on the back of the note with a pencil he'd retrieved off the counter. He reattached the note to the ribbon and handed it to Talia.

She put it back around DespairBear's neck.

"Take it back to John," Lyle ordered.

DespairBear barked once. He trotted up to the door and pushed it open with his head.

"I have to go too," Lyle said and pushed away from the counter with a wince.

"I don't think you're in any condition to go chasing anything down, Sheriff," Maeve said.

"Sheriff is it?"

"Lyle. Please."

"You and I," he said, pointing a finger at her, "we're going to talk about being a sheriff's wife, just as soon as I get back."

She hit him on the shoulder. "Oh, that's a helluva way to make a proposal."

Talia wasn't sure if Maeve was more annoyed or surprised. She was glowing, that was for sure. Whatever Lyle had said, he'd made it good and not wasted any time. Good for him.

Lyle snuck in a peck to Maeve's cheek and headed for the door.

"I'm coming with you," Talia said.

"No," he said, "you're not. I'm just going to the post office. Bringing you along will look suspicious, like I'm there for something other than my usual stop. I'm just going to have a look inside that box before it's picked up. If it's what you think it is, I'll see that it gets misplaced or delayed or something."

"Commandeered?" Talia said hopefully.

"Maybe."

"What are we commandeering?" Logan was holding on to Cora's hand as he led her back into the store.

"Nothing," Lyle said backing into the door. "You two can find your way back, right?"

He didn't wait for an answer though.

"Talia," Logan said, "I'd like to take Caspar up on his offer of a tour of his facilities. Need a guide. Cora can't do it, but she did offer her horse to me. Maeve, can Talia borrow Rosie again?"

"Wow," Talia said. "Had that one planned out already. You sure I can't take over for Cora here instead?"

"No, ma'am," Cora said. "I have about twenty deliveries to make and you don't know the town that well."

"Maeve, you all right with this?"

The question seemed to pull Maeve out of some deep thoughts. "Yes, yes, take Rosie. I have a ton of perishable stuff I have to deal with today."

She cast a worried glance at the door.

"Lyle knows what he's doing," Talia said.

"Sure. Yes." A forced smile. "I'm sure you're right."

"Come on, Logan. Let's go see this mysterious space cow operation."

CHAPTER THIRTY-FOUR

EVEN THOUGH IT HAD BEEN MORE THAN SIX MONTHS, TALIA HAD no trouble navigating from Tsurui to the Haricot lands. She did have a map tucked into her coat, but the hill- and mountainsides were barer now that autumn was so well along and the path was obvious.

Maeve's shotgun rode in a saddle holster. She'd insisted.

Rosie tossed her head, making her tack jingle. Roscoe came up behind her with Logan aboard. Cora's horse had the most unique coloring Talia had ever seen. Most of its body was a gorgeous silver or gold tone—depending on the light. But the silver coat had so many dark points that the mane, tail, and legs were black. The actual name for it had been on the tip of her tongue for a while.

They had taken the back way, the one that would lead them to the Haricot graveyard first. She had been seized by the urge to visit Elias's grave. It seemed only right to pay her respects.

The buckskin glove was making the skin between her left thumb and forefinger itch. She pulled it off and gave the skin a scratch.

"Silver buckskin! That's what it's called."

"What's called?"

"Roscoe."

"He is a pretty horse, isn't he? Pretty horse for a pretty girl." He leaned down to smooth the horse's neck as he said the singsong words.

"Smitten, aren't we?"

"He is a pretty horse."

"I meant Cora."

He smiled, reddening only slightly this time. "How much farther?"

"Not sure. First time I've come this way."

Logan threw her a questioning look as they followed the turn of a switchback.

"You'll see." She spurred Rosie on.

A bird called in the distance and it echoed off the rock wall to their left. The wind drove her scarf up into her face and she pulled it away, tucked it back into her blouse.

Five minutes later the mountain path became a hill path and ten minutes after widened into what one might call a road as the land flattened. A torii gate fronted the graveyard, rising out of the ground on thick beams that had been painted black. Berms surrounded the graveyard on three sides, enclosing it as if it the Haricots were expecting the land's embrace to limit its size.

Talia stopped counting the markers when she reached thirty. Most of them were made of native rock: boulders chosen for a partially flat surface onto which an inscription could be made; thick slabs with rough edges in either a vertical or horizontal configuration; a few bevel and grass markers as well. A wide path cut through the center of the cemetery and smaller paths branched off it. Lilies grew wild wherever they could take root, and the late-blooming ones still had flowers.

Talia dismounted, took off her hat, and led Rosie through the tidy paths. Logan dismounted too, but he didn't follow her. He was fishing in his coat pockets, probably for his handy notebook and pencil.

It wasn't that hard to find Elias's grave. There had been time for grass to grow over it, but the marker wasn't as weathered, or perhaps it was just random luck. She cringed at the dates. Sixteen was too young.

Beloved son and brother seemed too short of an epitaph.

She brushed at the top edge of the marker, came away with a layer of dust. It didn't cling to the prosthesis for very long, merely slid off the pore-doped ceramic, and something like a stab lanced through her chest.

She held on to that pain a bit before letting it go. She pulled off the glove and dragged the fingers of her left hand through the dust. Sweat kept it on the skin and she rubbed it between the fingertips, feeling the grit and graininess of it for a few precious seconds.

"I'm sorry. I wish I would have known what to do. You deserved a long and happy life. You deserved... more."

She swallowed the fist that had formed in her throat, waited for the ache in her chest to stop squeezing on her heart so her lungs could make air move again.

"Forgive me," she choked out, blinking back tears. They were threatening, oh yes, and if she let them flow, she wasn't sure she could stop them. Maybe she shouldn't. Maybe she should just shed them, but if she opened the floodgates—

The sound of galloping horses jerked her out of her misery.

She came up, gun in hand, whirling in the direction of the noise.

Two riders mounted on brown horses were coming down the road at a gallop, the hooves kicking up chunks of earth and grass behind them.

They split off, one coming at her, the other at Logan, who looked like he had been digging around behind a gravestone that backed up to the berm.

Talia grabbed Rosie's reins and strode toward Logan, who looked up, stood, and raised his hands. They were both covered in dirt like he'd been using them to dig.

She didn't recognize either of the men. As they slowed, one of them had taken his shotgun and laid it out across his lap. He took his horse up the berm and loomed over them, a tall, dark silhouette that blocked out the sun. The horse shuffled its feet, tossed its head.

The other man had circled around and came up behind them, placing himself between Talia and any escape route, boxing them in between graves and berm.

Talia took a calming breath and then another, gauging distances and angles, checking for other riders, other threats. She saw none and blew out a breath.

It wasn't the reception she'd hoped for, but this was their land. Their dead. She could understand their—

"What are you doing with Cora's horse?" the one with the shotgun demanded. His gray duster flapped in the wind, making a snapping sound. A matching gray hat kept his face mostly in shadow, revealing only a trim beard.

"I'm Logan. Cora lent him to me."

"Did she now? And why would she do that?"

"We're friends an—"

"Like hell you are!" That from the man behind them.

Slowly, Talia turned to face him. His hat didn't obscure his features as much and she almost didn't recognize him without his goggles. The man had been there when she'd brought Elias in. She'd never gotten his actual name. Goggles was going to have to do.

"Remember me? Talia Merritt."

His eyes went wide and his scowl deepened. "You, I remember. Doesn't make him *or you* Cora's friends. Much less friends enough to lend you Roscoe."

"Well, she did," Talia said patiently.

"What are you doing here?" the other man asked.

"Came to pay my respects," she said, indicating Elias's grave. "On our way to see Caspar. He invited Logan. Call him and ask."

Goggles's scowl didn't waver.

"Why are you digging up our dead?" the other man asked.

"Digging up?" Logan's voice had that quaver that might be guilt or fear. "No, no, I wasn't digging up anyone. There's some fungal growth underneath this piece of wood and I was just trying to get a sample."

Carefully, he reached for the sample case on the ground. He brought it up, opened it, and showed them all the little bottles he had lined up within.

Skeptical, the man leaned down to take a closer look. His gaze flickered over the samples and continued downward to the ground, to the small trowel Logan had been using, the piece of dislodged wood, obviously pulled up from the ground.

"We don't like strangers digging up dirt," the man said. "Not around the graves. Not anywhere."

"I'm sorry," Logan said. "I didn't know."

The man gave him another once over. "You armed?"

"No sir."

"She is," Goggles said.

"Take her guns. Then we'll take them back to the house."

Goggles grabbed Maeve's shotgun from the saddle holster.

Rosie protested with a rumble and edged away a bit, but he had a long reach and compensated easily.

"Your sidearm, please."

"Is that really necessary? You know who I am."

"I know you filled one of these graves, lady. Give me your sidearm and your blade if you want to see Caspar or anyone else. Otherwise, I'll be happy to escort you off our lands. Your choice."

He enjoyed that last, she could tell.

She handed him her pocketknife first. When she reached behind her hip, the other man leveled his shotgun at her, so she slowed, prying the 1911 loose and bringing it out slowly, flipping it around and handing it to Goggles with the muzzle pointed down.

He took it, shoved it into a saddlebag along with her pocketknife and glared at her. "Is that *all* of it?"

"Sorry, I left my howitzer in my other pants."

Talia did not like being unarmed. It made her twitchy. Her phantom's fingers trembled, which made the prosthesis respond in kind. Her heart rate was up. Her alter ego kept threatening to surface, pushing at Talia's mind from the depth of her subconscious as her hyperawareness kicked in.

She fiddled with her glove as they waited outside of one of the big hangar-like buildings.

They were far enough away from the livestock enclosures that the smell was not overwhelming. A fecund scent lingered, nonetheless, mixing in with that of compost, especially as the winds shifted.

Most of the herd was out in the open pasture. The big house at the center of the compound seemed to be closer than she remembered it. Her scalp itched and she scratched the patch at the base of her skull with her prosthetic. Without nails, it wasn't nearly as satisfying. She turned her head to the left and brought up her left hand to do job instead.

Ah, yes, much better.

When she'd had fingernails on her right hand, she'd picked at the polish once it started chipping. Her prosthesis didn't allow her to do that though. Her manicure remained nicely intact even if it was showing signs of wear.

She made a very unladylike snort at her fingertips.

When the hangar door opened to reveal Otto, Talia almost called out his name.

The man with the gray duster and hat, leaned down to speak to Otto sotto voce. Otto nodded, grunted, nodded again.

Finally, he came forward and looked up at Talia.

"It's nice to see you again, Miss Talia," he said, that deep voice rumbling in his chest, soothing her.

She shook herself. Forced a smile. "Nice to see you too, Otto. Caspar invited Dr. Temonen here to the lab. They want to talk shop. It's why we're here. The only reason we're here."

"Given what's happened to Dame Leigh, to Sam, I'm sure you understand our caution, Miss Talia."

"I do, Otto. I really do. I'd just feel a lot better armed. You know how it is."

He took a deep breath. Sighed. Nodded to Goggles.

Reluctantly, Goggles dismounted and returned her knife and gun. He shoved the shotgun into the saddle holster as well, and Rosie moved her front hoof and shifted her weight, making him yelp as she got the front of his toes.

To his credit, he didn't do anything to her. Maybe he was used to it.

Talia patted Rosie's neck and refrained from telling her she was a good girl and that there were apples and carrots in her future.

"Come on in," Otto said. "We'll take care of the horses for you."

Rosie wasn't particularly happy, casting a backward glance as Goggles led her and Roscoe away. Roscoe hip-checked her though, apparently enough of a distraction to make her pick up her pace and hip-check him back.

Talia followed Otto and Logan inside. Cold air hit her face and it took her a second to recognize the change in pressure—positive pressure.

"Please leave the hats and coats," Otto said, indicating shelves and hooks for use. "Caspar likes things clean."

Logan pulled his notebook and sample case from his coat before complying. They left the riding gloves and Talia threw her scarf on the pile as well.

Otto led them through a strip curtain. Air blew down on them, sending dust swirling to the ground where it was sucked into channels and pulled out of sight.

A washing station was next. She was glad to have the opportunity to wash her face and scrub the dirt from underneath her fingernails.

"Love the color," Otto said. "It suits you."

She flashed him a grateful smile, wondering if the mild flush creeping up her neck was going to turn into a blush.

Dirty water sluiced into the sink, swirling under cold, harsh, fluorescent lights.

"Quite a set up you have here," Talia said. "What's your power source?"

"Kerosene."

Otto swept them into the lab. White walls, white tile on the floors, bright lights from above, illuminating an expanse of high tables and shelves so orderly that it made Maeve's apothecary look messy.

Sinks and fume hoods, glassware of the scientific kind, machines that she could not name, full of status lights. The whir of a centrifuge as it came to a stop stood out against the backdrop hum of scientific efficiency.

Caspar himself, tall and thin in a white lab coat that clashed with his boots and jeans, lowered a pair of safety glasses from his face.

"Ah, finally!" he said.

"I'll leave you to your work." Otto retreated back into the hall.

Like a moth to flame, Logan was drawn to the computer sitting atop a workbench. "Is this one isolated too?"

"Sure is," Caspar said, shoving the safety glasses into a pocket. "Best way not to get hacked."

Logan's excitement turned to disappointment.

"Homesick?" Talia asked.

He shrugged. "I get it. I really do. And I'll get used to it."

"So, the samples?" Caspar asked. "Is that what you have there?"

"Oh yes." Logan and opened up the sample case. "Some I collected on the way here. Others in the caverns. I've been collecting when I could. And this last one is from the graveyard. I've had a chance to look at some of them through a passive light microscope, but I'd love a look via your equipment here."

"Sure, no problem. I don't see why not."

"What can you tell me about the mycelium in the area?" Logan asked.

Caspar picked up the sample bottles and checked the labels. "Not much, I'm afraid. Not my area of expertise. I'm really just an MD. The geneticists might be able to help, but what we could use is someone like you."

"Here?" Logan's eyes went as wide as saucers. He looked around with fresh avarice rising in his eyes.

"I can get you some lab space. You share your data with us, and we in turn, share ours. At least data related to the soil and plants and such. The nonproprietary stuff, initially. We've found fungi with active paternal and maternal nuclei. The proprietary data, eventually, depending on how things go. You'd have to sign some nondisclosures, that kind of thing."

Logan's gaze bounced from Caspar to Talia. The unspoken "Can you believe this?" was clearly there.

She answered with an encouraging nod. Not that he needed her permission, but he did seem to want her blessing. Or perhaps her endorsement.

"The Haricots are good people, Logan," she said just in case.

"Why thank you, Miss Merritt." There was no malice in Caspar's voice, just a dry amusement.

They seemed to forget about her as they transferred the samples from the case to Caspar's trays, put them under microscopes, and chatted about extracting DNA. She wandered about the lab, only peripherally listening as Logan went over his theory about the fungal blooms being responsible for the die-offs that had led to failure of Neo Bravo, the first colonization effort, in the islands.

"That's very interesting," Caspar said. "I'll pass that on to my partners. Or perhaps you'd be willing to discuss it with them."

"That's why I came out to Tatarka. There've been changes in the mycelium samples I've been getting back."

"What kind of changes?"

"Maybe a new sort of bacteria. Fungi can feed on bacteria, you know. Like the ones that I collected from the cavern. I'm fairly certain some are thriving on the bacterial growth."

"Hmm..." Caspar leaned up against one of the tables, considering. "I believe we made some changes to the cows, to make their blood-borne pathogens more resistant to the predatory bacteria passed on by the local bats—a Tatarkan subspecies of vampire bat. It's reduced the epibiotic predation by the bacteria passed into cow blood by the bats."

"Predatory bacteria?" Talia asked, curiosity piqued.

"In this case, the bacterium from the bat—we call it the predator—was attaching to a larger bacterium, the prey cell, in the cow's blood, puncturing it, and feeding on the interior. The cytosol, I believe. The result was less bacteria in the cow's blood, and thus in its waste."

"Why would you want to *reduce* the amount of bacteria in the cow's blood?" Talia asked.

Caspar smiled. "I'm sure you've heard all the rumors about space-cow poop."

"So Maeve said. I thought she was joking."

"Not joking. Just not the full story."

"Is that why your men were so prickly about my collecting samples?"

"I think they're prickly about the trespassing, the shooting, and so on. And stolen cows, not that it'll do you any good." Caspar went on about how all the original genetic tweaks were done on Earth and the rest by selective breeding, so that only they had the key to which cows embodied which changes.

"But you can't control the genetics postbreeding," Logan said.

"Don't have to. Old man Haricot wanted some randomness introduced. But without the original blueprint, it'll be almost impossible for anyone to reverse engineer the process."

"Hence Contesti's frustration," Talia said.

"Signore Contesti made a lot of assumptions. Erroneous assumptions. We are happy to leave him... unenlightened. Now, about this hypnolin antagonist you prepared for Sheriff Monroe. That is something that I am most eager to discuss with you, particularly its manufacture. Have you given him a second dose?"

"No, not yet. He didn't ask."

"Perhaps we should prepare one just in case. Did you bring—"

Otto cleared his throat, making them all whirl toward the door. Talia could have kicked herself for not noticing.

"Dame Leigh requests your presence at the house, ma'am."

Talia took a deep, bracing breath to ease the trepidation that had formed like a stone in her belly.

Intimidated? No, not me.

CHAPTER THIRTY-FIVE

OTTO DIDN'T TAKE TALIA TO THE FRONT OF THE HOUSE, BUT TO one of the surrounding "cottages." She'd counted six of them upon approach, smaller homes, some connected by covered walkways, others by uncovered ones. They seemed to spiral outward from the main house.

The wood planks creaked under Otto's weight. The walkway was built over a bubbling brook that cut a serpentine path through what one might call the backyard—a very generous backyard.

The covered deck followed the brook for a bit and connected to a veranda. Off the veranda, an artificial pond surrounded by rocks hosted water lilies. A young doe was in the pond, water swirling around all four legs, as she munched happily on the lily pads themselves, flicking one ear and then another as she looked up at Talia.

Dame Leigh was seated on a rocking chair on the veranda, her cane propped up within reach, her lap covered with a tapestry. She was bent over it, glasses perched on the tip of her nose, working a needle and thread into the canvas. The decorative comb she used to control her bun rose above her hair like a fan, casting a shadow that looked like a crown. Beads jangled within the cutouts of the fan shape, sending sparkles and reflections in all directions.

"Caspar told me that you refused to accept our help in acquiring a new implant." Dame Leigh didn't look up. Instead she leaned to the side, aiming her nose over the table by her left elbow. A sheet of paper was propped up on a book holder, held in place by a decorative wood clip.

"I've just come off a seven-year indenture, Dame Leigh. You'll have to forgive me for not wanting to sell any piece of myself off to anyone."

"Sell a piece of yourself? How?"

"It would compromise the integrity of what we are trying to do here, don't you think?"

"Compromise it how?" Her deep, blue gaze rose up to meet Talia's.

"Make it seem like I had a vested interest against Contesti."

"Don't you? Just on the principle that he lied to you about the situation here, tried to set you up against Lyle, the man you spilled blood with—your mentor, your friend. Contesti threatened you for coming back to help him. Set Lyle up to take a personal and professional fall from which he may not recover. Would anyone blame you?"

"You know about Siena then? About the hypnolin?"

"The hypnolin. Your young scientist has a cure, no?"

"Not a cure exactly," Talia said, wishing it was exactly that.

"He is better, though, Lyle that is. No longer lumbering around town, I hear, sometimes sober and capable, sometimes not knowing who he is or what he should be doing."

"Yes, he is better," Talia admitted. "And he'll be staying that way."

"Good. Now back to my original question. Would anyone actually blame you for having a vested interest against Contesti? And why do you care what others think?"

Talia flexed her prosthesis. Its movement didn't go unnoticed. Not by those penetrating, blue eyes or the experience behind them. Dame Leigh must have known that it wasn't just about what others thought.

"People judge. They say that they don't, but they do. They can't help themselves. Judging what they see or what they think they see," Talia began. "There's a reason Signore Contesti wears all those fine clothes and takes on all those fine manners. He wants to present an image to the world. One in which he wears a white hat. Same with Rhodes. War hero. White hat. Because heroes wear them. Heroes walk in sunlight. They fight in the open, face-to-face. They show themselves to the enemy, perhaps even in the town square for all to see.

"Someone like me, well, people don't see as a white hat. Not even if I were to don one. I could wear nothing but white, and my actions, who and what I am, would still define me because I can't keep up appearances like... like the rest of you.

"When they look at me, they see someone who makes them shiver because I don't deal death from the front."

Talia took a deep breath. And another. Dame Leigh waited patiently as if she knew that there was more, her mouth pulled into a considering expression that suggested understanding.

"Worse, they see a murderer-for-hire," Talia continued "Not someone who protects her friends, her comrades, her people. They don't see self-defense or defense of another. They don't see all the people I saved by taking a life. All they see is that I deal in death and that I do it again and again, and unlike them, I go on as if it never happened. Even the ones who know the difference between killing and murder, know it's just a line. A very fine line. And they can't help but wonder if I've already crossed it. It is so very, very thin, that line."

"It is, Miss Merritt. And I know that you haven't crossed it."

"Do you? How?"

"You brought Elias back to us so we wouldn't have to wonder what happened to him, perhaps jump to the wrong conclusion and think it had been Contesti's people and who knows what that would have led to. You couldn't save Elias—no one could have, we know that now—but you saved other lives by bringing him back, and risked your own life to do it."

"I try to do the right thing, ma'am. That's all."

Dame Leigh looked into Talia's eyes like she was determined to see into her soul. She came closer and Talia blinked away the image of *Sobo* staring at her through those blue eyes. Dame Leigh's hand drifted to Talia's cheek, like she was going to cup it as if she were a child.

Talia flinched back before Dame Leigh could complete the motion and she pulled away, disappointment in her eyes.

"Otto," Dame Leigh said. "Would you excuse us please."

"Yes, ma'am."

Footsteps betrayed his departure. Talia's gaze followed him back to the main house.

"May I have a better look at your arm?" Dame Leigh asked.

"What would a better look tell you?"

"Indulge me, will you? Just this once."

A smile spread on Dame Leigh's lips as she took Talia's cybernetic hand in her own. Dame Leigh's hands were warm and dry, the fingertips not as rough as a few spots on the palm. There was a slight sewing callous on her forefinger.

She looked the prosthesis over, pushed down on Talia's palm. Reflex made her cup her hand around the motion. The rubbing motion didn't translate well. The phantom sensation that was the movement of skin over muscle was off, like her prosthesis was only registering the muscle but not the skin, and the phantom was.

That signal degradation that Frowst had talked about. It must be.

"It is remarkable," Dame Leigh said. "Doesn't feel like flesh, despite its appearance. Why the black and gray? Why not flesh tones?"

"So that I won't forget."

She let Talia's hand go. "So that others won't either, though, correct?"

"They don't like being fooled. They don't like reaching out thinking it's flesh and finding ceramic instead."

"Ah. I can see that. Permit me one more thing." Dame Leigh picked up the needle she'd been using.

Talia nodded.

The prick was gentle, experimental. The tip of the needle against the tip of her forefinger, as if she wanted a drop of blood. Her phantom anticipated the prick, the pain, the blood so much that Talia couldn't help but look away. Her gaze caught the pattern on the paper, what she had thought was a pattern for the tapestry, but it was unlike anything she'd seen for needlepoint. Instead of a multitude of symbols crowding each other on a ten-by-ten grid, it was a string of ones and zeros.

"Can you feel that?" Dame Leigh asked.

"Yes."

"Does it hurt?"

"No."

"You're a poor liar, Miss Merritt."

Talia pulled away and Dame Leigh stabbed the needle back into the tapestry.

"You do lovely work, Dame Leigh." Talia picked up the tapestry, pulling it closer to look at it. The stitching was tight, precise, the tapestry more than half complete, with a beaded edge in progress on the complete side. On the uncompleted portion she was switching out the thread to complete ten-by-ten squares one at a time by the look of it. And none of the grids matched that string of ones and zeros by alternating between just two colors.

"It helps me relax. Keeps thoughts of lawsuits and court filings and financial provisions and all sorts of political nightmares at bay, at least for a little while."

Dame Leigh took hold of her cane like she intended to leave.

Talia turned at the sound of approaching footsteps. They startled the doe too. She jumped out of the pond and disappeared into the bushes and trees abutting the garden.

Otto was back, Sam at his side. He had grown, not only in height, but in size. He'd filled out a bit. His shoulders were broader, arms heavier.

A blue checkered shirt betrayed the bandages still wrapped around his shoulder. His arm was in sling and his face showed fading bruises. One side was still swollen, particularly around the jaw and cheek. Stitches decorated the eyebrow above his left eye. He was going to have quite a scar there by the look of it.

"Please let him just do it," Dame Leigh whispered from behind Talia. "Let him just get it all out."

Sam came to a stop in front them. Otto had fallen behind and was leaning on the rail, looking down into the pond the deer had vacated as if it was far more interesting than anything else around him. Lucky for him. Awkward moments weren't Talia's thing either.

"Grandmama," Sam said.

"Good afternoon, Sam." Dame Leigh made a small circle on the wood deck with the tip of her cane. "Would you like me to stay or go?"

"You can stay."

"Get on with it then."

Sam threw his shoulders back, and popped out a quick, shallow bow, aiming it at Talia.

"Miss Merritt, I hurt you. I'm not going to pretend that it was an accident or that I didn't mean it. I let my anger, my ignorance, my emotions control me. I acted thoughtlessly and carelessly, and it resulted in a grievous injury to you.

"Those were the actions of an impotent child. One who had

to learn, the hard way, that his actions have consequences he can't control—"

Dame Leigh cleared her throat.

"I had to learn the hard way that *my* actions have consequences *I* can't control and that I must temper my decisions with that in mind. Going forward, I promise to do a better job. With my anger, my emotions. I will think before I act. I will be more careful. I won't let ignorance guide my actions. I apologize and humbly ask for your forgiveness."

His gaze never wavered.

It made it harder for Talia. Her eyes were filling with tears. She hated them. Even these tears. They pooled in her throat right now, threatening her ability to respond.

Her hands were trembling. Both of them. She pushed her fingers out along the seam of her jeans, hoping it would make them tremble less.

"I accept your apology." She swallowed. "I forgive you."

The entire ride back, Logan talked about the wonderful things he'd seen in the lab, how much of a genius Haricot must've been to create the initial batch of cow embryos, how he wished he had a computer with which to pull up all the background information he needed.

It was midafternoon by the time Talia and Logan returned Roscoe and Rosie to the stable. They walked the horses to allow them to cool down before bringing them into the barn. Cool water and shade awaited.

Talia let Rosie get her fill before taking her into her stall and flipping the reins over the horse's head. She removed the bridle and secured the halter.

"I still owe you an apple, you know," Talia said as she leaned her forehead against Rosie's neck.

Rosie nodded and let out a throaty huff. She shifted her weight into Talia, putting her into a horse hug. Talia took a deep breath, grateful for the uncomplicated scent of horse sweat and hay and sunshine. She passed her prosthesis over Rosie's coat, gliding the tips of the fingers over the needlelike hairs there.

The phantom's skin floated between prosthesis and horse, almost visible in her mind's eye. The amount of conflicting information continued to grow. As long as it was only tactile, it was tolerable.

She drummed her fingers on the horse's side. The motions all flowed in perfect sync. She sighed in relief. Movement was uncompromised.

"You've been very quiet," Logan said from the next stall. He'd finished tacking up Roscoe. "Did something happen?"

"Yes." Talia grabbed Maeve's shotgun from the saddle and passed the strap over her shoulder. She headed for Maeve's.

"Did it have anything to do with the grave?" Logan asked as he followed.

"You're a smart kid, Logan."

He snorted. "You're just avoiding the question."

"What do you know about binary codes?"

They passed under a maple tree with low branches that reached down in front of them. They ducked under it.

"Ones and zeros. It's for computers. That's how they actually process information. They turn everything we put into them into binary. Our numbers, our letters, pixels from photographs, frequencies from sound, all sorts of input, essentially is nothing but binary. Why?"

They nodded to a couple strolling by arm in arm, and to a vendor rushing past with a covered cart in front of him. The scent of chicken was like a cloud around him as he went past.

It sent her stomach grumbling, her mouth watering. She looked over her shoulder and considered flagging him down, but Logan had pulled ahead of her.

"Passwords?" she asked as she caught up with him.

He was probably eager to get to Maeve's.

"Sure," he said. "Passwords are nothing but characters from a keyboard or a spoken phrase. Even a retina scan is encoded in binary, one pixel at a time. Why?"

Maeve's sign rattled above them, driven by the wind. "We should get back to the jailhouse. Find out what Lyle learned at the post office. Maybe relieve John."

Logan held the door open for her and the shop bell rang them in. The scent of spices and soap and flowers was thick enough to taste. Not unpleasant at all, but unexpected.

Maeve poked her head into the front. She had her hair wrapped up in a net and was wearing a canvas apron. Her sleeves were rolled up past her elbows, her hands covered in what might have been flour or talc.

"Oh, it's you. Come on back." She sounded tired, distracted.

They put their coats and hats on the coatrack.

Talia returned the shotgun to its shelf behind the counter. She passed her hand along the katana's scabbard, enjoying the tactile smoothness as it flowed along the prosthesis and into the phantom despite the degraded signal. Home, it said to her, as clearly as if it had spoken.

She should have brought her own *daishō* just like she'd planned. Even if she never did anything with it again, it would have been worth having just for how it evoked those memories.

"Maeve," Logan said, "when are you expecting Cora?"

"She's still running errands," Maeve said from within. "I'm not sure, to be honest. She doesn't usually run them on foot. It may take her the rest of the day."

"Oh," he said, lingering in the doorway. "Can I help?"

"Sure, I need you to sort and label the mushrooms in that box over there." Maeve pointed a powder-coated finger at a crate on a workbench across the room. The bench itself had been set up for sorting, trays stacked neatly, along with labels and a log.

Logan rummaged through the crate, assessing the contents with an eager, expert eye. "Any particular order, placement?"

"Just sort them out for now."

"Where did you get these?" he asked.

"Foragers trade with me for finished products."

The crate was filled with all sorts of things that Talia wouldn't have thought a mushroom—ball-shaped, lobed, nest-shaped things; some that looked like bark or crust; a particular one resembling coral; star and trumpet shapes; phallic ones.

Logan was looking them over in that close-eyed way of his, as if he was doing far more than sorting, so she left him to it and wandered to the next table.

A terrarium had been set up. Half full with mulch and dirt, it sat shaded from the lights above by a canopy. Sometimes the dirt would move or pulse. The millipedes.

She shuddered and wandered back to Maeve's table.

"Have you heard from Lyle?" Talia asked.

"No. And I am worried about him. It seems like such a long time to be gone for a run to check on that package. But if something big happens, word does get around town. I think if something bad had happened"—she swept at her forehead, streaking it with powder—"I would have heard."

"We'll go check on him next. I'll send word," Talia said.

"In that case, I made some food for the jailhouse," Maeve said. "It's in that basket over there." She gestured with her chin as she poured measures of powder from a sack into smaller jars set atop a scale. "You better take it over. I have no idea how long it's been since they've eaten and if Lyle is there, someone find a way to let me know so I don't worry and tell him I would have wanted to know sooner."

"I guess that's our cue to go," Talia said. She looked at Logan. "Do you want to wait here for Cora?"

"No, no, no," Maeve said. "John needs respite. You guys go relieve John. Make sure he hasn't been ignoring Contesti or worse, paying too much attention to him. They'll drive each other nuts, those two, and I don't want John being tempted to settle the whole Contesti-Haricot imbroglio on his own."

"Would he do that?" Talia asked.

Maeve brought her right ear down to her shoulder as if she was scratching an itch.

"Food would really help mitigate the chance. You know how they get when they're hungry. Or thirsty. I put some beer in there too, and it's still got a bit of chill to it."

"I can take a hint." Logan wandered over to the basket, peeked inside, pulled out a beer and popped it open. "Nice."

Talia worked Maeve into a half hug, not really caring nearly as much about getting dirty as Maeve seemed to be. "Will you be all right? Want us to lock the front door?"

"No, I'll be all right. I'm waiting on two more deliveries and then I'll lock it and come by the jailhouse. I'll be fine. Go. Go. Food's getting cold, beer's getting warm."

"Can't have that."

CHAPTER THIRTY-SIX

"FINALLY, REINFORCEMENTS!" JOHN SAID AS TALIA AND LOGAN shut the jailhouse door behind them.

The jailhouse desk was littered with radio parts, wires trailing from desk to wall. John's fingers were gray with soot and his face smudged.

A bark from below earned CorgiSan a pat on the head from Talia and he settled back down on his humming charger. DespairBear nudged Talia's boot, got a similar pat and then trotted back under the desk.

John ducked his head. "You. Back on the charger."

DespairBear let out an imitation of a doggy snore and ignored him.

John pushed him out with his boot, making the metal of his chassis scrape against the carpet. DespairBear shook himself and found a spot out of John's reach and sat down with no small amount of defiance.

Logan put a bottle of beer in front of John. "Maeve's?"

"Of course."

John wiped his hands on his shirt, twisted the top off and chugged half the bottle before coming up for air.

"How's Contesti doing?" Talia asked.

"He's alive," John said as he picked through the basket. He and Logan set about dividing the spoils. Talia had a feeling that if she didn't intervene, neither she nor anyone else was going to get fed, so she snagged three of the paper-wrapped sandwiches, put one in the icebox for Lyle and one for herself, and took the third one—along with a bottle of beer—through the holding area door.

"No glass, Talia," John said around a mouthful of food.

"I'll pour it into his cup," she said.

Contesti eyed the food and drink.

She set the beer bottle down on the platform in the middle of the cage room, opened it, and poured it into a steel cup. She handed it to Contesti.

He reached through the bars for it, long pianist's fingers extending. "Thank you, Miss Merritt."

She passed him the sandwich too. He set it down on the cot and sipped the beer awkwardly from the mug.

"How much longer am I expected to linger in these . . . conditions?" Contesti asked as she turned to leave.

"Until the marshal returns."

"You have no idea when that will be, do you?"

Talia shrugged off his attempt to goad her and moved back toward the door. She knew—and Contesti must as well—how unreliable travel was here.

Her hand was on the handle.

"You don't know what you've gotten yourself into, Miss Merritt."

She whirled on him but stopped herself from going back up to his cage. If she did, there was no telling what else she might do. An unarmed man in a jail was not a threat.

Tell that to Ponytail.

"You went to see Dame Leigh," Contesti said calmly, those reptilian eyes flashing.

"Whom I see is none of your concern, Signore."

"You can't win this. You must know that. Dame Leigh and the Haricots don't have the political connections I do."

"You know what, Signore, I don't care. I don't care about you, or your political connections. Nor do I care about your power and money."

"What do you care about, Miss Merritt?"

"My friends. This place. I sold seven years of my life for a ticket here, to have freedom, finally, from people like you."

"People like me make the world go around. You can't get away from us. We made this all possible. The spacecraft, the wormholes. That prosthesis you wear. We are the movers and shakers, the ones who look at the big picture, a picture your kind can't even begin to fathom. What are you without us? A cripple at best, dead at worst."

She shook her head. Like all of them, he imagined himself as the reason for everything good.

"A free cripple, a free corpse," she said. "Both better than what you think you're offering. Good afternoon. Enjoy your sandwich."

She slammed the door behind her with a little bit more force than she'd intended.

Logan had replaced John in the chair behind the desk. He was fiddling with some radio component, blowing dust out of it with a bulb syringe. The dogs were gone too.

"Where's John?" she asked.

"Took the SONS to go looking for Lyle."

"He's still not back from the post office?"

"No. John says it's not that unusual. No telling who called on him, where he had to go after the post office. Said not to worry until we know there's something to worry about."

She made a noncommittal sound and picked up one of the radio components. It might as well have been something out of a museum.

"John did ask me to ask you to go to the onsen, check out if Lyle might be there. Yui—that's the onsen lady's name, right?—she was supposed to send word if he came in, but..." He gave a helpless shrug.

She grabbed a sandwich and beer out of the icebox and popped off the cap. Maeve's beer washed down with ease.

"All right."

She finished off the beer and sandwich on the way to the onsen. Most of the townspeople walked past her without acknowledging her greeting. The sound of barking interrupted her consideration of sightlines but it was someone's dog, not one of John's SONS.

Several people were leaving the onsen as she approached. A man with a height and physique that made him look like a small tank held the door open for her and tipped his hat. She thanked him and stepped inside.

Yui looked up from behind the counter where she was folding towels.

"Good evening, Yui. Has Lyle been here today?"

"No, Miss Merritt. Haven't seen him. I would have sent word."

"Busy day?" Talia asked.

"Was," Yui said. "Empty now. Unless you plan on a dip."

If Talia hadn't caught her reflection in the mirror on the wall, she would have said no. But her face was smudged and her hair looked like she'd rolled around in the dirt, and she undoubtedly smelled like Rosie.

Instead she said yes, took two of the offered towels and told herself she'd make it quick. She slid the shoji door aside, entered the changing room, and grabbed one of the baskets for her clothes and gun.

The lamps were turned up high, creating pools of warm flickering light on the freshly scrubbed tiles. The minerals from the natural pools beckoned, making her reconsider a proper soak.

It took about ten minutes to get the water running through her hair to run clean. It sluiced down her chest, over the cryptochip hanging around her neck, through the long strands that curled around her breasts. Now that she was out here, maybe she should consider cutting her hair again. As a disguise to make her not look like her old military pictures, it didn't seem to be working. She scrubbed shampoo into it, pulling the curtain of her hair forward over her face, and running her hands through the slick coating of bubbles. She took a deep breath and closed her eyes as she ducked her head under the low tap.

She came back up, flipped her hair back. The room seemed darker as she rinsed the shampoo out of her eyes. She blinked them open.

Shit. The room *was* darker. Through the shoji doors the lamps in the hall still flickered, but the changing room itself, it was dark.

The sense of wrong hit her, but not in time. She lunged for the basket she'd placed just out of reach on her right to keep it out of the water. Caught movement from the corner of her left eye. It made her turn her head that way. Her prosthetic fingertips came down on the edge hard enough to tip the basket over.

Hands grabbed at her. Someone kicked or pulled the stool out from underneath her as she scrambled away. Her right hip hit hard against the tiled lip edging the drain. A fist tangled in her hair, gave it a yank, the momentum of having her head wrenched the other way taking the basket and her gun forever out of her reach.

Her prosthesis connected with a wall of armor-covered chest

so hard that, had her hand been flesh, she had no doubt she'd have broken it. The pain was that intense, making her see stars.

The large man who'd opened the onsen door for her knocked the air out of her lungs and wrestled her down to the ground. He pinned her arms behind her, pressed her face into the wet tiles.

A half breath later, she found herself on her knees, arms painfully pulled up behind her in that excruciating way that makes a dislocation just one tiny flinch away.

She opened her mouth to scream, but the wet towel cut off her air, forced her to breathe in the sickening, sweet taste of chloroform. She held her breath, fighting it, until her body rebelled, made her draw it in, grabbing at precious oxygen and getting darkness instead.

Talia had come to slowly, one hazy blink at a time, to a sky turned red. At first, her captor had slung her over the front of a trooper saddle, but as she'd come to, he propped her up in front of him. His arms, huge and muscled and looking like they belonged on a tree, bracketed her on both sides as he held on to the reins. Her own hands had been tied with ropes, the flesh one numb from the tightness. She'd been gagged and hastily folded into one of the onsen's dark blue robes. Her teeth were chattering from the cold, her thighs and seat bruised from the saddle beneath.

He'd threated to chloroform her again if she didn't cooperate, so she reluctantly leaned into the heat of his body. It didn't take her long to figure him for one of Contesti's—or Rhodes's—men, although from the brief glimpses she got at him, he didn't look familiar.

Her still-wet hair clung to the sides of her face, her neck, her back, and the bruise on her face throbbed. The cryptochip swayed back and forth between her breasts. The jostling from the horse threatened to open the robe so she raised her bound hands to clasp and hold it shut.

The sound of Contesti's sheep accompanied them all the way from the gate to the main house. Contesti's men milled around the compound. Some still wore their paramilitary clothes and gear. Others had donned jeans and vests and cowboy hats. A few opted for an odd mix of both, almost like they weren't quite sure they wanted to leave their past behind.

Crates hid under tarps secured by stakes whose edges lifted with the flutter of the wind. She couldn't help but wonder what was in them. Maeve had told her that Contesti had set up his own little rival operation, but Talia hadn't met or seen or heard of a single scientist or technician in Contesti's employ. If he was using the serows for anything, it must've been to keep his lawn trimmed. A few of the men had the look of ranch hands, but not many. There was no hustle and bustle to work the herd like she'd seen at the Haricots'.

The gravel crunching under the horse's hooves and the stir of the canvas tarps and awnings cut the silence.

Her captor brought them to a stop by the water trough at the courtyard entry. He helped her down, setting her bare feet on a patch of grass as the horse dipped its snout into the cool liquid.

She got her first good look at him. Built like a tank, the bulge of his thighs made the large semiautomatic there look small. A bowie knife hung off his belt. As he turned to reach into his saddlebags, she caught a glimpse of her 1911 redundantly tucked into his belt.

He pulled out a bundle and shoved it at her. She clutched her clothes and boots to her chest as her gaze swept the eaves, the shadowed columns. A glint of setting sunlight betrayed the hidden security camera tucked into a corner, but she saw no men hidden, lying in wait, no barrels pointed at her.

He drew the bowie knife, sliced through her gag and bonds with disinterested efficiency. Much better than interested efficiency any day.

"Get dressed."

After years of living under combat conditions she thought she'd lost her modesty, but her cheeks heated as she complied, slipping into her rumpled clothes. She was still shivering as she zipped up her pants and stepped into her boots. Her hands shook as she buttoned up the blouse, twirled her damp hair into a bun at the nape of her neck.

She scooped up a handful of water and took a drink as she looked around the courtyard and past the men lingering about. They all had new faces. Just like the one who'd ambushed her. Had Rhodes replaced Contesti's men or were these just the latest batch?

Her captor grabbed her elbow and they crossed the courtyard and mounted the steps to the main entrance.

The foyer led into a large room, one with rich, plush rugs, leather couches, and low tables. The wood paneling glistened under the bright electric lights. The air was uncharacteristically cool and dry.

Stiff-backed, Maeve was sitting on a chair, her red hair tousled, a bruise purpling her right cheek. Her hands were folded in her lap. Her left hand was in a bandage wrapped mostly around her palm.

Fuck.

Talia wanted to rush forward, but the man's firm grip tightened in warning.

Maeve bolted upright at Talia's entrance, but Rhodes reached up from his leisurely pose on the couch, took her wrist, and pulled her back down. He was wearing riding clothes, men's full seat breeches with tall equestrian boots. The shirt was silk and clung tightly, like a fencing jacket. She half expected to see a foil mask tucked into his elbow.

Maeve sank down into the chair and Rhodes smiled as he leaned back and propped an ankle over a knee.

"Taking me is one thing, Rhodes, but Maeve is off-limits. Somehow I don't think that Signore Contesti is going to appreciate you subverting all the social capital he's been trying to build." She looked around the room, meeting the gazes of the two men. One was standing behind Maeve. The other opposite Rhodes.

"Well, you'd already left, and I needed something to trade with, so . . ."

"I'm here now. Let Maeve go."

"No," Maeve said. "Talia, no. Don't."

"Shh, my dear. We, the two of us, Izanami and I, we need to dance and I've been looking forward to it ever since I saw her blow a hole in poor little Giuseppe's head. Cost me a lot to set that up on such short notice."

"Wait. What?" The words were out of Talia's mouth before she could stop them.

"Oh, Giuseppe *was* ill. He was delusional about his dead sister. And there was a death threat against Muhonen, but not from him. I merely took advantage of circumstances that were already in place. Made sure he got a bigger dose of hypnolin than his usual. Whispered a few things in his ear. That kind of thing."

"You bastard. There was no way to tell what Giuseppe could

have done to that little girl. Where his delusion might've taken him."

Talia took a deep breath, one that failed to calm her. Her phantom twitched; her prosthesis followed, the index finger curling slightly. Adrenaline flooded her veins, making the sound of blood thunder in her ears.

"Needed to do a little test run, you see. To make sure you were who I thought you were. I've watched the footage over and over, and the way your face changes when you kill, it is truly amazing.

"I've seen it before. And I admit, the first time, I wasn't sure what I was seeing, but the more I looked at that recording, at you taking a life, the clearer the transformation became. I saw the demon rise first in your eyes, then in your face. I've seen Izanami's spirit before, you see. Saw her rise in another woman's face. Saw her wreak havoc as she mowed down an entire village, as she walked out on the battlefield and kissed the dead.

"I never thought I'd see her again, never believed in the nonsense of reincarnation, until I finally understood that reincarnation didn't mean that humans were reborn, but that some of them were merely chosen as vessels by the goddess herself."

There was a passion, a fervor in his eyes, in the way his lips quirked, the way he shifted on the couch. She'd seen that kind of ache in men before. It was hard to miss if you knew what to look for.

Talia leveled her gaze at him. "You sound like someone who wants to fuck, not kill."

"Oh, I didn't bring you here to kill you," he said. He gave a fractional nod to the man standing behind Maeve.

He stepped forward. He was holding a sheathed sword, his hand wrapped around where the center of the blade would be. It took her a split second to realize he was handing her Simon's katana.

She took it with one hand, not quite believing that they were handing her a weapon.

She met Rhodes's gaze.

"As you can see by Mrs. York's hand, the blade is quite sharp. Sharp enough anyway."

Talia darted another gaze at Maeve's hand. She'd seen such wounds before, on inexperienced sword handlers. She still had her scar from being careless with the blade.

"I want to see Izanami again," Rhodes was saying. "Up close and personal, as we cross blades. Killing Talia Merritt would be"—another careless shrug—"incidental. And then perhaps Izanami will judge me the worthier vessel, bless me with her presence, her cool, calculating calm."

"He's insane, Talia," Maeve said. "Don't do it. Don't give him what he wants."

"Oh, she's going to give me what I want. I would have preferred dawn, myself," he said. "It's far more poetic, than this blood-laced twilight, don't you think?"

"Like your men are going to stand by and let her kill you," Maeve said.

"Mrs. York, you wound me," he said, bringing his hand to his chest in a dramatic gesture. "I am a man of honor. Bradley"—Rhodes nodded to the man who'd ambushed Talia—"is going to make sure that both of you go back to Tsurui, unharmed, should Ms. Merritt prove the better of us. Aren't you, Bradley?"

"Yes, Mr. Rhodes."

Talia met Bradley's gaze, saw quiet determination in his eyes. He wasn't the one that worried her. It was these others. Bradley might be sincere at this very moment, but this was a mercenary outfit. And so many of these men were new. Who among them was poised to take advantage of Rhodes's death, ingratiate himself to Contesti? Probably more than a few. And then what? This might have been personal to Rhodes, but he was a middle manager, an intermediary, not a commander they followed out of loyalty or duty.

"Let Maeve go now," Talia said, looking at Rhodes. She had other reasons she didn't want Maeve here—she didn't want Maeve to see her kill, not even Rhodes. "I will give you what you want without her having to witness it."

Rhodes shook his head. "No, I'm afraid not."

"You have my word."

"Of that I have no doubt. But it's not just your word that I want. Or your death. I want you to show your friend that I am right. I want her to see Izanami possess you. I want her to see what you can become."

"Why? What possible purpose could it serve?"

"I don't like being called crazy."

"Take it back, Maeve," Talia said. "Tell him that you don't think he's insane."

Maeve opened her mouth but her voice seemed to catch in her throat as Rhodes placed a finger across her lips. It was gentle, like a lover shushing.

"One word and I will slit your throat. I will open it wide and catch the lifeblood in my hands, lick it off my fingers, taste it, all as the light goes out of your eyes."

His words, or the way that he had said them, shouldn't have mattered. He'd already crossed a line by taking Maeve, already threatened her life. That image of Maeve with her throat cut, her lifeless eyes, his hands and lips and tongue coated with her blood, the arctic satisfaction and the smile it would put on his face . . . that face . . . almost perfect. None of that should have mattered. But it did.

Rhodes tilted his head, passed his hand gently over Maeve's hair. She was trembling, but her gaze never wavered.

"Rhodes," Talia said, letting her voice go cold.

His gaze darted to hers. She captured it like she owned it, and would forever. It was a palpable thing, the weight of the connection, almost enough that she could believe it to be real.

She had to make it real. Real enough for that madness in his eyes.

"Izanami awaits your embrace."

CHAPTER THIRTY-SEVEN

PEOPLE ALWAYS THOUGHT THAT KILLING FROM A DISTANCE MEANT not knowing one's target as intimately. But it wasn't true. It wasn't the distance. It was the time spent.

Sometimes it took days, other times weeks, to get to know one's target, to watch them from afar, get to know their daily habits. Watch them shave as you put them in your sights and chose not to fire because it wasn't yet the right time. Because it would give your position away.

They didn't know what it was like to watch them eat, get to know what they liked to read, see them wipe their tears after reading a letter from a loved one or closing the eyes of a fallen comrade. She did.

And that long-cultivated intimacy had never kept her from taking the shot when the time was right.

All it took was a willingness to think of them as a target, a silhouette on a piece of paper, a shadow. Someone who had to die in order for your people to live. To superimpose that atop the man who fed stray kittens from his limited rations, the woman who kissed the photograph of her two children every morning.

As Talia watched Rhodes, she knew that this would be different. In some ways he was like Giuseppe, a man not in his right mind. But unlike Giuseppe, there was no one pulling his strings.

She'd been wrong to think it was merely ego. Ego was part of it, she had no doubt. He might call it possession. She called it compartmentalization. It was how she maintained her sanity. But if he wanted to meet her alter ego, then so be it.

Yes, let us meet.

This wasn't going to involve cold stillness though. Her coping mechanism only descended when she needed to slip into that altered state when things slowed down, when the hyperfocus of survival exacted its toll on the senses. She'd never had to call on it with a sword in her hand.

The man who'd been standing behind Maeve handed Rhodes a sheathed saber. A saber, not an épée, not a foil. Wrong. She'd been wrong. What else had she gotten wrong?

He took it by the scabbard, met her gaze.

"Something wrong, Izanami?"

"No."

He didn't believe her. She could tell by the way his lips twisted into a satisfied grin.

"Ladies first," Rhodes said sweeping his arm out in a magnanimous gesture.

The courtyard had been cleared, the men drawn back onto the porch, some leaning against the wall, others against the railing. Bets changed hands as Talia made her way down the steps.

Twilight was going to give way to night soon, but perhaps not soon enough. Torches flickered in sconces, lamps hung under the eaves, some lit, others still dark.

Talia twisted the scabbard she'd been holding, angling it for a draw, preparing to cast it down on the ground, just in case. The fingers of her left hand were wrapped tight against the scabbard's mouth as she used her thumb to gently push on the tsuba—the sword's guard. There was a click, a barely audible one, easily camouflaged by the sounds around them.

Bradley had Maeve by the arm, and he pulled her to a spot in the front. He took position behind her, bumping his head against one of the lanterns.

Talia heard the saber being drawn, the scrape of it like it was up against her very bones.

No formalities then. So be it. The rules of the *salle* or dojo had no place here.

Talia slid the katana free, the draw flowing upward into a parry that ended in the sound of metal against metal as she turned to face him.

Talia slipped back, raised the hilt above her left shoulder, moved to the right. Motion. Motion was key.

Stillness was death.

Body canted forward, Rhodes's eyes burned bright with ambition, with desire, with anticipation. He and Talia circled. He brought his sword down in a crosscut. She met its arc, defending with her own, turning a downward swing around for an upper one.

The vibrations traveled up her phantom as if it were flesh. Rhodes took a lateral swing at her head, one that she felt far too close as she ducked under it and came up from the side.

Heart racing, she pivoted out of his way, making him overextend and slash through air.

He took a step away. She slipped back again.

Sweat trickled down her hairline, her back. He shook sweat out of his eyes, out of the long strands that had fallen down over his forehead.

She pressed forward and he retreated, saber held low at his side. One step. Two.

Adrenaline coursed, racing in her blood, setting it afire.

He put both his hands on the hilt, flashed her a smile as she held her position, sword held midway between waist and shoulder.

Without breaking eye contact, Rhodes took a few steps to the left. She mirrored him, taking four steps for his three.

He moved the saber in an arc, slashing upward.

She slipped back, raising hers.

They exchanged a pair of blindingly quick crosscuts.

He slashed at her middle, the tip sweeping along the leather of her belt as she slipped back farther, her sword high.

Movement, to the right. Slashes. A pair of them.

They came closer. Their swords met above them, coming together at his forte. He pushed her off and she went down, giving in to the momentum. Sweeping the ground with her left hand, she curled her fingers into the soil.

Shadows betrayed his intent as Rhodes came at her back. She swung around, sword sweeping low, left hand sweeping upward, sending the dirt from her hand into his face.

There might have been boos. She couldn't be sure.

Did you think this was a game?

Sword above his head—he had been going for another crosscut from on high—Rhodes backed up, blinking dirt out of his eyes.

She slashed.

He parried.

Lowering his blade, he stepped back and swept at his eyes with his left hand. No matter how he did it, it was going to cost him. Between the sweat and the dirt, there was no true way to clear his eyes. They would water for at least a few moments. Perhaps even long enough for it to matter.

Moving left and right, then left again, katana met crosscutting saber three times.

It was on the next thrust that she got inside his guard, aiming for the eyes, but ended up pushing the tip of her sword across Rhodes's brow.

He turned his body away from the katana's seeking edge, letting out what sounded like a groan. He retreated, keeping his left hand on the cut. It didn't keep the blood from dripping into his eyes.

Before she could press her advantage, he changed direction, bringing his sword up and then slashing down again, forcing her to back away.

Breath rasping, limbs shaking, they stared at each other across the distance. It wasn't much. Maybe three or four steps.

He wiped at the bloody snot running down his nose and blinked his eyes. They had lost their sparkle. Now they only had vengeance left in them.

"We don't have to kill each other," she said.

He swept the sword up and around his head, gathering momentum as he advanced. She parried. He kept coming. And again. Each clash brought them close enough to embrace.

Too close.

She brought her right elbow up into his chest as he lifted his sword and caught his right bicep with her left hand. Her too-small left hand.

Rhodes bared his teeth at her as her muscles strained to hold his sword arm in place. Any moment now his weight would move hers, push her across the ground, despite the purchase she'd found. Physics was a bitch.

He was straining too, his left hand on her ceramic wrist, squeezing as if that would matter to the unyielding material. There was pain though, clear through the layer of nanopore sensors, a feeling like pincers digging into the tender spot where flesh would have had a pulse point.

It's nothing. It's not real.

Holding his murderous gaze, Talia shifted her weight and bent her head as if she was going to head-butt him. If she could just get him to where he was mad with pain. Hit that open wound just right. But she didn't have the height for it.

She dug her fingers into his bicep for a second and then let it go as she pulled her head back instead of driving it forward. She drew her sword arm back as well, dragging the katana's cutting edge, making a slash across his chest, intending to swing around for a slash into his belly... or below.

Everything slowed, the moment lengthening like it did when she took her shot.

The katana's edge parted the fine silk fabric, white against his pale skin. The line of red formed as it cut the flesh beneath, extending from midsection to shoulder as they parted. She sacrificed her balance for it, ended up on her back and scrambled up, wrist throbbing. Had her arm been flesh, his fingers would have carved deep furrows as they'd separated. He'd held on that tightly.

She didn't have time to get up.

He was above her as she pushed up to one knee, sword glinting above his bloody chest.

She brought the katana up in a defensive block.

His blade struck the ceramic of her prosthesis right above the wrist. It tore a scream from her throat as if he'd severed it. Phantom and prosthesis separated, agony traveling up her arm, into her shoulder and neck making the muscles clench up and hold her prisoner.

For a horrifying moment, she couldn't move. Her upper body seemed to be trapped in a straitjacket of pain. Of dissonance and conflicting signals.

Rhodes was standing above her, panting, bleeding. Sweat and blood ran into the seams of his scars as he looked at her, a frown coming into place.

Talia had let go of her sword. Or at least her prosthesis had. It no longer felt like her prosthesis was a part of her at all, despite looking straight at it. Instead the excruciating sensation of a severed limb took its place.

She closed her eyes, and saw it again, that flash of blade as Lyle severed her hand, her crushed hand, the pain throbbing, pulsing like a living thing.

She pulled her forearm to her chest, curled over it. She might as well be curling over a stump.

A fountain of crimson should have been raining down on the soil, making a hot, sticky pool.

"What's wrong with you?" Rhodes asked, lifting her chin with the flat of his blade.

She met his gaze. Sneered at him.

"Let Maeve go," she said. It was barely a whisper. What she really wanted was for Maeve not to have to see this, the rest of this.

Her alter ego remained below the surface, but it was getting harder to keep her there. She had killed without her, once. Long ago.

Rhodes shook his head. "Let her go? Need I point out that *you* are on your knees. That this is not a negotiation."

She lowered her gaze and eyed the fallen sword. Her left hand was underneath her, holding up her torso along with her shaking arm.

Maybe. Just maybe.

There wasn't enough breath in her lungs to tell him to fuck himself.

She pushed her living fingers toward the sword. It was blurry in her vision as she slid to the ground and dragged herself toward it.

Rhodes got to it first, put his boot on it just as she was about to reach it.

Squatted down.

She raised her head. He was distorted, like her vision was smudged with tears.

Rhodes said something, just as she felt her implant die. It was the oddest sensation, like a part of her skull was numb yet on fire at the same time. Tiny lightning bolts manifested at the edges of her smeared vision, like one of those silly plasma toys.

She rolled onto her back, looked up at the sky.

Rhodes blocked her view.

His face contorted, disappointment clear in his eyes.

A shroud descended and wrapped her up in the welcoming embrace that had neither pain nor regret nor fear.

PART FOUR

CHAPTER THIRTY-EIGHT

TALIA FLOATED IN AND OUT OF CONSCIOUSNESS.

She tried to speak, but couldn't. It seemed like she just couldn't fill her lungs full enough. They had tied her arms behind her back, an even odder sensation without her phantom. Her ankles were tied together too, looser than the rest but not enough to work out of. Her eyelids were too heavy to open.

"I'm just a medic. This is beyond me, Mr. Rhodes. She needs a doctor."

"I thought you wanted her dead," someone else said.

"Not like this." Rhodes again. "Use the radio. Call the Haricots."

"They won't deal with us."

"Fine then. Send the sheriff's woman. They'll listen to her."

Talia's vision wavered. She must be inside Contesti's mansion because the air floating around her was cool and dry, free of the scent of serow and grass and field. The hard scent of antiseptic mixed with those of blood and sweat.

Someone cursed.

"I can give you something for the pain," the voice that had identified itself as the medic's said.

"No need. Just get on with it." Rhodes again.

He floated in her mind's eye, watery and elusive, like a specter, with those golden-green eyes of his still burning with ambition. Or perhaps not ambition at all. Fervor.

His freshly bloodied face flowed like sand, pulling into the semblance of others. A man she'd had in her sights, his features unaware. He hadn't known that she existed. He had nicked himself shaving that morning. The cut was fresh, pink, threatening to bleed again. He had a cheek tattoo. It told a story: father of four. She didn't name her targets, but there were details about them that stuck, that kept them disparate in her mind. She'd pulled the trigger even with that knowledge firm in her mind. He never heard the gun's report. He looked at her now, the entry wound all tight and neat, a perfect dark circle in his forehead. Not exactly where she had aimed—he must have moved a bit—but it had done the job. He regarded her with Rhodes's eyes, then with his own, then the eyes of others.

Anyone who can do what you do and still manages to sleep at night must have a dark side... She'd never actually heard his voice, but she heard it now, using Rhodes's tone and inflection.

She had saved twelve by taking that shot, by ending his life, by orphaning his four children.

Others appeared, faded, their features mixing together in a fearsome whirlwind.

"How long before I can move properly?" Rhodes—who she was fairly certain was being stitched up—said.

"It's a deep cut. It will take time for the tendons to heal."

"That's not what I asked."

"Weeks."

More cursing.

Her eyes fluttered open again and this time they stayed focused. She was on her side on the rug in front of the couch. Rhodes was sitting on the edge of it, while the medic worked on him. A stainless-steel utility tray held the sutures and tools, and they had set up a work light on a stand. It glared painfully down at Talia.

"Ah, awake, are you?" Rhodes was looking straight at her.

She blinked at the wavering image of him lest darkness swallow her again. She focused on his tattoo, the one on his right forearm. Two spider lilies in bloom, running from just above his wrist to his elbow. The lilies were inked against a backdrop of bloodstains rendered in lighter reds. She might have caught a glimpse of it—barely—back in Sakura. She wasn't really sure. It seemed so very long ago, so insignificant.

Each spider lily had at least a dozen stamens, delicate lines tangled with the curling red petals, many of them reaching up toward his elbow. She'd seen spider lilies before, but there was something about them, something she should be remembering, something significant. She could feel it, like a word on the tip of her tongue, an evasive thought fleeing her faltering grasp.

"They're poisonous," he said, holding her questioning gaze. "A very useful flower. Your ancestors used them to control rats and other pests around their rice paddies. Fitting, isn't it?"

Fitting? Fitting how? Her mind swam.

"Not quite all there, are you?" he said, his face pulling into a moue of concern. "Let me clarify. You. Your people. In this story, you are the pests. A blight on this land."

Bastard.

She threw the word at him in outraged silence. Her whole body strained against the bindings, the motion revealing why it was so hard for her to breathe. They had tied her arms and legs with the same length of rope that they'd wound around her neck. She could barely feel her legs, and her arms were going numb. She had to make her muscles relax so the tension on the rope at her throat would ease.

Rhodes flinched as the medic tied off a suture.

"Almost there," the medic whispered.

Rhodes moved his gaze back to her.

"Buddhists believed that in the realm of the dead," Rhodes continued casually, "the path to reincarnation is marked by them."

Maeve was right. Rhodes was crazy. Maybe not clinically insane, but crazy in the same way that people who led cults were. They too tended to be charismatic, or at least obsessed. Strange to find him working for Contesti though. *That* was uncharacteristic.

Maybe there was more to him than met the eye.

She wished that Muhonen had been able to get an unredacted dossier on him. Although who was to say that fallen corporate nobility would have had the word "crazy" stamped anywhere on their official records. Poor, powerless people were crazy. Rich, powerful ones were eccentric.

"She seems to be coming around again," Rhodes said. "I do believe she actually understands what I'm telling her this time."

This time?

"I'll dose her again as soon as I finish this up," the medic said, still intent on his work. "Do you want her to remember this or not?"

The medic's hand pulled upward again, trailing sutures, the motion sending Rhodes's face into another wince.

"Not," Rhodes said.

Talia's eyes went wide. She tugged on her bonds, regretting the motion immediately.

The medic moved to block Rhodes and the light, a looming shadow above her. Something stung her left arm, hissed.

Her eyelids became heavy, not that it would have mattered if she'd been able to keep them open. Her eyes just wouldn't focus.

Being carried blurred into a constant, discordant motion. It felt like she was on a stretcher.

She strained against it.

The neigh of a horse. And then another.

They must have put her in the back of a wagon. The ride was too bumpy to be anything else and she could smell the horses, the warm, fecund scent of fresh manure followed by the plopping sound of it against the ground.

Someone had gagged her, shoving fabric deep into her throat. As she strained to make her voice work, the spit-soaked fabric was like a soggy weight threatening to slide down. Her stomach joined in its dislike of the motion.

Whatever they had given her was enough to keep adrenaline from flooding her veins, making it easier to feel disoriented.

Rhodes was going to be very disappointed if she died by choking on her own vomit. Very disappointed indeed.

Talia landed on her left side. It knocked the breath out of her, made her see stars. The motion involved in getting her out of the wagon and dumping her had been enough to dislodge the blindfold and let her see where she was—the porch in front of the jailhouse. They must've retied her as well because the rope that had been keeping her from breathing was also gone.

She squinted against the light of swaying lanterns. They'd dropped her gun beside her.

Rhodes was standing up in the back of the wagon, his bandaged torso clear under a freshly ironed blue shirt and vest. Bradley stood at his side. She had no doubt he'd been the one who'd dropped her over the side.

"Just like we agreed, Lyle," Rhodes said. Despite his injury, he stood with his back straight, confident as ever, triumph in his eyes. He even wore guns, another matched set of high-caliber revolvers, one on each hip.

"Yours for mine," he said a little louder. "Here she is."

Talia pulled in air through her nostrils, pushed her tongue up against the roof of her mouth, and screamed through the gag, drawing Rhodes's gaze. The spark in his eyes flared.

"I'm sorry we couldn't finish our dance properly," he said. "Maybe once your prosthesis is fixed..."

The jailhouse door swung open with a creak. She craned her neck. Contesti was standing in the threshold, hands bound with rope in front of him, a smirk on his face. Lyle had his gun jammed into Contesti's back, muzzle resting in the dip of his spine. Lyle didn't even acknowledge her, but kept his gaze on the wagon.

"Nice and easy, Signore," Lyle said. "Nice and easy."

"Wouldn't have it any other way," Contesti said.

He took an easy step toward the center of the porch, stopped to look down at Talia, aimed a triumphant smile her way before taking the next step and then the next.

He reached out with his bound hands, used them to grab the box rod. With his long legs he had no trouble hooking his foot in the toeboard. He sat down and looked out straight ahead like a man who'd just taken his seat in a limousine and was waiting for the chauffer to get on with it.

Bradley took up the reins, clicked his tongue at the horses, and off they went with Rhodes still upright in the back. A satisfied grin on his face, Rhodes mocked her with a wave.

Thrashing about, Talia screamed into her gag again. She didn't expect to see Maeve come rushing out from behind Lyle.

"Shh, it's all right," she said. "We've got you, Talia. It'll be okay."

Stethoscope swinging from his neck, Caspar followed and knelt to examine her with that dark, intense gaze of his.

"I think it'd be okay to lift her," he said.

Bucking, she made a sound of protest.

Maeve pulled the gag off, making Talia's throat convulse.

"Sonofabitch," Talia choked out.

"Take it easy," Caspar said.

"You take it"—cough—"easy."

"I'm worried that drop might have injured something," Caspar said. "Can you tell?"

"What's not numb, hurts. Untie me. Help me up."

Lyle was by her feet, cutting the ropes there. John cut the ones around her hands.

With the release of the bonds, her stiff muscles released, numbness fleeing before pain. But at least she was free. She could move. Every breath didn't cost her.

She slid her right arm forward from underneath her.

Her prosthesis was locked in the same position as when it had let go of the sword. It felt like a dead weight hanging off her flesh. She couldn't make it move. What sensation she had was related to its motion relative to the spike connecting it to her real arm, that sense of something hanging, as if maybe she'd encased the spike in cement.

Standing proved to be a harder task than she'd expected. She staggered and Caspar caught her across one shoulder.

The world spun and when it righted itself, she was in the cot, propped up on blankets while Caspar listened to her heart, her breathing.

"What were you thinking?" Talia wheezed toward Lyle as he stood in the door frame. "Giving them Contesti?"

"I was thinking that your life was worth more to me than justice. Go on, tell me how you would have done it were you in my place. I'm listening."

He crossed his arms and pinned her with a glare. He looked like he was still favoring his leg, but the crutch was nowhere in sight. He'd acquired a few more bruises and scrapes though—on his face, his hands.

John had taken the seat behind the desk. He had DespairBear up on it. One of the robot's eyes was dangling from its face, still connected by a wire. It looked at her with the other eye and tilted its head.

"Talia, Talia," Maeve said, coming into view. "We had to give them Contesti."

"The hell you did. Rhodes doesn't want me dead. He had the chance to kill me and didn't."

"Well, we can call him back if you like," Caspar said.

"You too, Doc?"

"She needs some water by the way," Caspar said to Maeve.

Maeve reached for a glass of water, brought it up to Talia's lips. Her bruised throat ached even as she took the smallest of sips.

"What happened?" he asked.

"My prosthesis."

"Your prosthesis. It malfunctioned?" Caspar asked, taking hold of her cybernetic arm, cradling it in his lap. He worked the fingers, but they were locked in place. He pushed harder, to no avail.

"Yes. It's dead. Help me get it off."

Rather than rolling up her sleeve, he produced a knife and made a swift cut before she could protest. His fingers traced up the prosthesis, pushing, probing, all the way past the edge where it connected to her flesh. Warm, dry fingers pressed against the skin and muscle of her bicep. She let out a little hiss. He pulled the prosthesis free with a click, sending stars bursting behind her vision.

"I don't think you have any breaks or fractures, but I can't be sure. Not without an x-ray."

"Thing is, the other one is worse," she admitted, pulling her right arm away, now that it was free of the dead weight. She raised the spike carefully, rotated her elbow.

Caspar's eyebrows shot up. He must have known that it was there, but it was always a shock for someone who hadn't seen the spike before.

He set the prosthetic down and sliced through the other sleeve as well. It didn't look as bad as the pain suggested. He felt the pulse in her elbow, pressing the disk of the stethoscope to it. Lyle and Maeve looked on, his arm around her shoulder, hers around his waist.

"It may be a dislocated shoulder," Caspar said. "I need to move it around to make sure."

He stood and pressed gently against the muscles in her shoulder, moving down in a soothing motion.

"Tell me what happened," Caspar said, as his fingers explored the hollow above her armpit.

"Rhodes is into fencing and swords," Talia said.

"Rhodes is crazy," Maeve interjected. "Thinks that Talia is possessed by some death goddess. Or some kind of incarnation of her."

"Oh really?" There was amusement in Caspar's voice, but his attention was on her arm. He put his fingers around her wrist. "I'm just going to move this up a bit. Relax if you can."

"Oh yes, asked me all sorts of things about Talia," Maeve went on. "Things I didn't know."

"What things?" Talia asked, curiosity piqued. Caspar pulled on her wrist, gently drawing her arm away straight out from her torso.

"About how you'd earned your . . . well, your moniker."

Talia looked up at Lyle. "He never told you?"

"No," Maeve said. "He didn't."

"It was a propaganda thing," Lyle said. "I don't think anyone called her Death's Handmaiden until it was almost over. Some hack of a war correspondent made a big deal about Talia's kills, coined the term."

Pop.

The pain in her left arm turned from a throb to a dull ache. "Better," she breathed. "Thank you."

"Take it easy for a few days," Caspar said, returning her arm gently to her side. "It'll be sore for a while. I want to take a look at your implant, but my equipment isn't here. Would you be willing to come out to the lab?"

"The implant is dead," Talia said. "Don't need any of your equipment to tell me that."

"That's not good," he said, but he was examining the prosthesis now, turning it over, peering inside it distractedly.

"Just how did you get away?" Talia asked Maeve.

"They let me go," she said. "After Rhodes tried to cut off your hand and you passed out, they had me call the Haricots via radio, but there was no answer. So they gave me a horse and sent me into town to let Lyle know that they wanted to trade you for Contesti."

"How did they get you, Maeve?"

"Shortly after you left, Rhodes's men came into my shop and told me to come with them," Maeve said. "I refused. Told them to go to hell. They came at me, so I shot at them. Killed one, wounded two. Went for Simon's sword on the wall when I was out of bullets. They overpowered me, knocked me out—with my own chloroform, of all things. I woke up at Contesti's place with a helluva hangover."

"And you? Where the hell were you?" Talia aimed her ire at Lyle.

"Made it to the post office all right. Right after Rhodes's men had picked up the package."

"Was it an antimatérial gun?" Talia asked.

"They left the box behind, took the unassembled gun with them. Based on what I saw of the packaging, the configuration, yes, it was. It's why I chased them down, but the wagon wasn't up for some of the terrain. I... well... I rolled the wagon. I don't remember exactly how, because it knocked me out."

That explained the fresh cuts and bruises. The scrapes.

"CorgiSan found him," John interjected. "Took me to where Lyle crashed the wagon and my boys and I pulled him out. Got back here at just about the same time as Maeve."

"When we got word that Rhodes was willing to trade you for his boss," Lyle said, "I had to take the deal."

"No. You didn't."

"Talia," Maeve said, "Rhodes is insane. There's no telling what he was going to do to you. He really thinks you are possessed by this... Izanami-thing. And he covets it."

"He wants Izanami," Talia said. "And apparently Izanami has to be taken in combat."

Maeve gave her a cross look. "You'll have to forgive me for not knowing the intricacies of the man's beliefs or his psychosis or whatever this is. For thinking only that I didn't want to have to bury you."

Talia took a deep breath. "You're right. I'm sorry."

Maeve came down for a hug. The scent of powder and flowers was gone. It had been replaced by blood and horse sweat.

"Did his men believe him?" Talia asked. "Or do they think he's insane?"

"He was very careful to speak of you—of this Izanami—only in front of two of them," Maeve said as she pulled free. "The rest, I think, are just going along for the fun of it. At least until someone misses a payday."

Talia rubbed at her face.

"So what's the plan now that Contesti is free?"

"The marshal is due in three days," Lyle said. "I can still bring up charges. Have the marshal send for reinforcements if need be so he can be arrested. If we make a convincing enough argument, Sakura will send us some reinforcements. In fact, they'll be only too happy to do so. I think they've been waiting for something like this to happen so they can point to how much they are needed, how vital of a function they can perform for us. The town won't be happy at all. We were all hoping we'd be able to avoid involving Sakura, but it looks like it can't be helped. And I think most people now see that too, including the Haricots."

"Sounds like we've only delayed things," Talia said.

Lyle shrugged. "I'm sure we can dissect this and figure out how we should've done it at our leisure."

"Ms. Merritt," Caspar said. He'd been examining the prosthesis. "Do you want this back on?"

"No," she said. "It's just dead weight now."

"Won't the dead weight help? With the phantom pain. Or is it not back?"

"Oh, it's back all right."

"I'm sorry to hear that," he said, solemn. "I'll see what I can do to help."

"Thanks, Doc." She looked at Lyle. "Where's Logan?"

"Back at Maeve's shop," Lyle said. "He and Cora are keeping an eye on it. Door locked this time."

CHAPTER THIRTY-NINE

TALIA HAD SLEPT FITFULLY, DREAMING OF SPIDER LILIES, FIELDS and fields of them. She was running through them, her bare feet getting covered in their pollen. She would reach down to try to brush it off, but the spike protruding from her arm ended up slashing her calves. She'd raise the pollen-covered spike and the tiny, shimmering granules would act like they were alive, become a teeming mass that would somehow enter the spike. She could feel their poison coursing through her veins.

She had startled herself awake, her left arm throbbing, competing with the phantom pain on the right. Thankfully, she woke alone in the jailhouse's holding area. John had dragged the cot from the front room into the back so she wouldn't have to use the one that Contesti had vacated or the one that Ponytail had died on. It had been a sweet gesture on his part, one she'd assured him wasn't necessary. Nevertheless, he'd insisted, very proud of the fact that the linens were fresh, the mattress filled with goose feathers.

Maeve had stopped by the boarding house where Talia and Logan were each renting rooms and brought her a change of clothing, including a new blouse, one of the ones with drawstring collar and sleeves.

She was helping Talia get dressed.

Nothing brought out the need to fuss over her than no longer looking whole. Given the source, she accepted it with grace.

"I wish you'd go back to the boarding house and get some better rest," Maeve said as she cinched the right sleeve shut, pulling the pale blue ribbon tight. "Is that how you wanted it?" she asked.

Talia nodded. Most people would note the empty sleeve and then move their gaze away from it.

"Here's the drop holster you asked for," Lyle said, poking his head in and dropping it on the desk.

With Maeve's help, Talia got it on. She was going to have to figure out some cinching system that would allow her to secure the thigh strap one-handed. Same with the belt, come to think of it.

"I thought you hated drop holsters," Maeve said.

"I do. But it seems I have no choice."

"Since you're just shifting to carrying on the left, why not just move it behind the left hip?"

"It takes two hands to reholster behind the hip."

"You know, no one, least of all Lyle, would blame you if you washed your hands of this and walked away."

"I'm not walking away."

"It's not your fight."

"You really think that Rhodes has given up his pursuit of Izanami? That once he is done with all of you here, he's not going to come after me? Even if I was the kind of person to abandon her friends."

"No, I guess not." Maeve helped her into the bolero jacket, sliding it up via her right arm, onto her shoulder, then helping her to maneuver into the rest of it.

The 1911 hung heavy on Talia's left thigh as she walked into the front room. It felt heavy and awkward, off balance. Amazing how much difference a couple of pounds of metal made, whether or not they were a part of one's body.

CorgiSan swung his head her way and DespairBear dashed forward when she entered the front room.

"Ah, ah, ah," John said from above the map he and Lyle had spread out on the desk. "Get your little butt back on the charger."

DespairBear ignored him, came up to Talia's right side, and pulled himself up so he could give the empty sleeve a nudge with his muzzle. The apertures in his eyes swirled back and forth. He must have pinged her too because there was an electronic skitter in her spike for an instant.

She twisted to pat his head with her left hand. He sniffed it as if he were a real dog before finally obeying John and reluctantly returning to the charging mat.

"Where's Logan?" Talia asked. "Still haven't seen him."

Maeve slipped by her. "At the shop. I'm on my way back there now."

She had grabbed Talia's dirty clothes and stuffed them in a sack. Talia almost objected, but snapped her mouth shut. Maeve was on a mission of tidiness. She knew the look, the mood, and better than to get in her way. Talia understood the need to do something, to be useful, to keep busy.

Maeve gave Lyle a departing kiss over the bundle in her arms and said goodbye.

John looked back down at the map. He ran his finger down along the heavy paper. "This is where I was thinking of sending them."

Talia took a cup down from the shelf, set it on the counter below, and grabbed the coffee pot. The muscle memory of using her left hand for everything would come back, eventually. It was just a matter of getting used to it again. Her left bicep and forearm trembled as she tipped the pot to pour herself a cup of coffee.

Time. Time you don't have.

Wishing she had milk to add, she set the errant thought aside as she mixed in sugar, took a sip. Vile, just vile. Coffee, even adulterated by sugar, was nasty without milk, no matter how good it smelled.

Drinking it anyway, she joined the men leaning over the map.

A few map landmarks—notably the airstrip—helped her identify Contesti's estate.

"What are you planning?" she asked.

"I'm talking John into letting me use the robots for some recon."

"To what end?" Talia asked.

"I want a back way into Contesti's estate," Lyle said.

Talia raised her gaze to his. "He's upgraded his security, since the first time I was there. I saw cameras, well-hidden cameras. Tech that will thwart anything like someone sneaking in to kill him. Lots of crated supplies. What do you suppose he is really doing with all of those things?"

"That is the question, isn't it?" Lyle said.

"Maeve said he had his own rival operation. I thought she

meant that in the sense of serows versus space cows. But, unless his scientists and technicians and livestock people all look and act just like his mercenaries, I didn't see any."

"Oh, he's had some of both," Lyle said. "They used to come into town, but none of them stayed for more than a few weeks. This is why we think he only brings them in when he has something for them to examine."

"Something? What kind of something?"

"Cows stolen from the Haricots, soil samples, and so on. Problem is, they get bored without anything to do and they tend to be expensive. And they tend to complain about this place not being enough like Sakura for them. So either they go back to Sakura or he sends them back. I think that lately, because he's had trouble recruiting them, he's just taken to sending stuff to them in Sakura. That's why he rotates through his mercenaries too. Every few weeks, a few of them head back to Sakura. Sometimes they come back, but mostly not."

"Why do you think that is?"

"You know the type, Talia. Some are content to sit and wait. Others, not so much. No matter how good the pay is, there are other more exciting places where they can do their thing."

She took another sip of coffee, contemplating. It made a sort of sense.

"So tell me about this back way in. You're not thinking of killing him, are you?"

"It's just a contingency plan," Lyle said. "If I wanted Contesti dead, I'd have killed him while I had him in custody." It sounded rote. Hollow even.

"Contingency?" she asked, narrowing her eyes at him. "You kept Contesti in that cage, untouched even though he had you put a gun to your own head for a game of one-man Russian roulette. This wouldn't be about Rhodes taking Maeve, would it?"

He didn't deny it. God, he didn't deny it. She wished he would. Not that she blamed him. It was Rhodes who'd raised the stakes, not Contesti, but did it really matter? Perhaps it did.

"I have a better idea," she said and turned the map around. She put her finger on a piece of mountain with a clear line of sight to the main house.

"John," Lyle said. "Would you mind running to restaurant row? Maybe bringing us back something to eat."

John swept a knowing look from Lyle to Talia, judiciously avoiding the map.

"No problem," he said. "Come on, boys."

DespairBear was up like a shot. CorgiSan, a bit more reluctant, took his time disengaging from the charging mat, did a robotic version of a stretch, and trotted after them with a backward glance.

Silence lingered even after the door was shut.

"It's been a while for me," Lyle finally said. "And just as long for you."

"Do you have a gun that can make the shot?"

"Yes."

"Then let me try."

"No," he said. "Rhodes is mine."

She bit down on the "How the hell is he yours?" and instead said, "I'm the better sniper. Even left-handed. You know I am."

"No."

"Lyle—"

"I said no. I mean no."

"Let me sight in the gun. It's only a few days until we get a sniper's moon. I can do this."

"Answer is still no."

"I don't take my orders from you."

They locked gazes.

"Talia, if you kill him in that way, it's going to get complicated. Unless we're willing to kill all of his people, someone is going to report that he was taken out by sniper fire. Suspicion will fall on you. Not me. You. You because of your reputation. You because Rhodes challenged you. You because only Maeve and John know that I was a sniper too.

"Even if I don't arrest you, you'll be running for the rest of your life. If they ever catch you, Contesti's backers in Sakura, and the ones on Earth, will make sure you never stand trial. Don't you understand?"

"I do. I will disappear."

This was the place one came to disappear, wasn't it?

"No. You can't." He looked pointedly at her right arm. "And even if you could, Talia, that's not what you want. You don't want to be a fugitive. You hate being Death's Handmaiden. You hated that name the moment it was pinned on you. Don't deny that you still hate the way it precedes you and follows you, the shadow it casts over everything you do. You came to Gōruden so you wouldn't have to be what you hate anymore."

"For all the good it has done me. I can't escape my shadow. No one can. It has grown big enough to cast shadows of its own. Might as well embrace it, make something of it. Put it to good use. Help my friends. Help myself."

He studied her face for a moment, giving her that older-brother look that made her want to hug him tight. Once upon a time she might have. Before guilt and history and far too many deaths and debts had come between them.

"You still think you can make it right, still think that you can save people."

"I *can* save people." She grabbed him by the front of his shirt, awkwardly with one hand bunching up the fabric. "I have saved people. I do it every time I take a target down. I've done it for total strangers and now I'm doing it for people I know and care about. Don't you dare try to take that away from me. Not after all I've lost. No one gets to do that. Least of all you."

Slowly, one at a time, he undid her fingers. She didn't exactly fight it. His own knuckles were bruised and swollen. He looked down at her through a lattice of scrapes and bruises framed by pain lines.

"I know. I just don't want you compromising what you came to Tsurui for by sneaking in and killing him in cold blood. It would undo everything we are trying to do here."

"Moments ago you were thinking of sneaking in and killing him in cold blood yourself."

"That's why I'm glad you're here. You bring out the idealist in me. Remind me what I'm really fighting for."

For an instant it was like her heart had stopped beating.

Tears welled in her eyes. She blinked them back.

CHAPTER FORTY

THREE DAYS LATER, TALIA BENT DOWN TO PICK UP A STICK AND threw it down the street. CorgiSan and DespairBear both took off after it. She had turned down CorgiSan's sound emitter since he tended to be rather vocal as soon as she engaged him in any form of play.

The robots had taken to shadowing her when John didn't have them actively patrolling or surveying. She was beginning to suspect that he was using them to keep an eye on her. To what end she couldn't imagine. Perhaps it was his own way of fussing, just like Maeve, who'd commissioned Nancy to alter Talia's wardrobe so that it was easier to dress herself.

DespairBear got to the stick first, picked it up, and beelined it back with CorgiSan in close pursuit. Rather than return it to her hand, the robot set the stick down about a foot away, sat, and looked up expectantly. CorgiSan swiveled his head back and forth, bouncing a bit like he was actually anticipating another throw.

"Why do they do that?" Talia asked.

John was sitting on a chair, feet propped up on the porch rail, sipping his morning coffee.

"Well," John said, "corgis are a herding breed."

"But DespairBear isn't based on a herding breed." She seemed to recall that terriers went after game that went to ground.

"Glitch of some kind. They pick up only each other's bad habits. Now do you see why I call them Trial and Error?"

She threw the stick again, despite the muscles in her left shoulder protesting.

"You sure you want me wasting power with them this way?"

"The batteries will discharge regardless. Not as fast, but there is a value in what you're doing, isn't there?" He gave her a meaningful look.

Yes. Yes there was. And not just the physical rehab. He was worried about her, about her mental health, about what had happened with . . . everything.

She gave him a grateful smile. It was good to have friends again. Friends who understood.

"Do you think you'll stay now?" John asked.

She'd lost the cryptochip. She wasn't sure where. Sometime between when she'd went down in the courtyard and been dumped on the jailhouse steps. She couldn't remember having it taken, but someone must have. Or the chain had torn while she'd been tied up, the chip dropping through the slats of the wagon to be trod underneath wheel or hoof. It might be buried on the road somewhere between here and Contesti's place. Or sitting in Contesti's safe or Rhodes's pocket.

"At least until we resolve this thing with Contesti."

"It's been going on for years," he said.

"Everyone else seems to think it's coming to a head. Do you disagree?" The robots kept dropping the stick just out of reach and then sitting back looking hopeful.

"Come on, boys," she said encouragingly. "You didn't fail remedial fetching. You're too smart."

They both cocked their heads at her.

She pointed at the stick and held her hand out.

CorgiSan approached and nuzzled into her hand. She shook her head. "We'll keep working on it." She threw the stick again. Off they went, the patter of their metal paws a harsh scramble against the cobblestones.

"I don't disagree," John said.

DespairBear nudged CorgiSan as they raced back, hip-checking him and bouncing off like the lightweight he was. CorgiSan refused to surrender the stick, brought it back and promptly dropped it out of Talia's reach.

"All right, boys," John said, dropping his feet to the floor. "Come here, both of you."

The robots sat down in front of him, ears perked up, waiting.

He reached down and pressed their noses. The apertures of their eyes dilated and lit up. She hadn't realized that despite being mostly metal, the components had been moving in subtle ways that made them seem alive. It was very clear now that they had been frozen.

"What did you do?" she asked, coming closer.

"This material," he said, indicating the molded piece that made up their "noses," "is a lot like your pore-doped ceramics. Come see." He beckoned her to come closer.

She leaned it. It did look a lot like it. When the light hit them right, she could even see the tiny pores.

"There's a whole sensor array under there," he continued, "including the ability to send out electromagnetic pulses. Same with the sensors in their chests and underbellies."

"Yes," she said, "I felt something like that along my spike."

"Oh, interesting. We'll have to play with that. But first, to prove my point that the VR hack is impossible to train." He hooked this thumb atop each dog's nose in turn, applied pressure, and the "nose" flipped down on a hinge to reveal a soft, spongy membrane.

"Press your thumb to the sensor."

She did. It wasn't nearly as spongy or soft as it looked. "All right, what am I doing?"

"I'm looping you into the keychain. You now have full admin access. They will obey you as if you were me. You can try to train them. You will fail but you can try."

"Are you sure about this?" she asked.

"Quite certain. Do it again. I know they look like they're frozen, but they are reading your biometrics and voice."

Feeling a bit awkward, she complied.

He flipped the nose piece back up and then pressed it in, first on CorgiSan, then on DespairBear. As soon as he did, they seemed to come back to life, the metal segments moving in that slight, subtle way.

CorgiSan let out a bark.

She put out her hand. Was rewarded with a nuzzle. Not to be left out, DespairBear nudged at the empty sleeve dangling at her side.

She almost "reached" for him. The phantom, something that

she'd almost forgotten about for a short while, manifested as jolts of pain that settled into a throbbing ache again.

She was about to pick up a stick and throw it when CorgiSan let out a muffled bark and took off down the street.

Talia straightened. Logan and Cora were coming toward the jailhouse, Logan limping, favoring his right side. Cora was holding him up, wavering under his weight.

Talia rushed forward, DespairBear at her heels.

One of Logan's eyeglass lenses was cracked, the frame askew on his face. His lip was split.

"What happened?" Talia asked.

"We were bringing Sam here, stopped in town for lunch, when some of Contesti's men came up," Cora said as they helped a limping Logan into the jailhouse.

"They took Sam," Logan said, his words slurred. "I tried to stop them. Couldn't."

Talia's stomach seemed to drop all the way to the ground.

"You kept them from taking me," Cora said. "That's something."

John had caught up to them, nudged Talia aside and pulled Logan's arm over his shoulder so now most of his weight was on him rather than Cora.

"He really did, Talia. If it hadn't been for him, they would have taken me too. And he did it unarmed. They laughed at him for it and then he showed them. Sucker punched one and almost got the other too. It was amazing."

"He could've gotten himself killed," Talia said.

They lowered Logan onto a chair.

Cora took down the first-aid kit hanging on the wall and scowled at it when all she found was a rolled-up bandage.

"Sorry," John said. "It's been getting a lot of use lately."

"It's fine," Cora said, working efficiently to tear a swath off the bandage. She took one of the whiskey bottles and used it to wet the bandage. Expertly, she dabbed at Logan's lip. He'd taken off his glasses, laid them on the table. A lingering look passed between them.

"Is your rib broken, do you think?" Cora asked as she undid the buttons on his shirt.

Logan's face turned crimson, but he didn't stop her.

"Never had a broken rib. Do they hurt?"

"What do you think?"

"It hurts. I don't know if it's broken," he said, a bit of his pedantry slipping back into his voice. It earned him a smirk.

Cora straightened. "I need to let gran'mama know they took Sam. Where's the sheriff?"

John was already by the radio, working the dials, calling first for Lyle, then for the Haricots.

Static hissed back at him. He put the mic down. "I'm going to send the boys to look for Lyle and go to the post office to use their radio. They usually have better luck reaching as far as the Haricot place than this thing anyway."

He rushed out, the robots weaving in his wake like they were continuing their game of chase.

Wincing, Logan pushed himself off the chair on wobbly arms.

Cora put her hand on his shoulder. "Maybe I should bandage up your ribs, just in case."

He shook his head, put his glasses on, and limped to the radio.

Talia paced, phantom twitching and twisting, coursing with rising pain, uncertain about what she should do. Contesti probably had Sam at his club or on the way back to his estate. But if she picked the wrong place, it would take hours for her to get back.

Hours they didn't have.

Logan worked the controls with precise motions. The radio squelched and hissed, made all sorts of popping noises.

Talia put her hand up to her forehead, rubbed at the tension between her eyes. "You should've stayed—"

"Yes," Cora said, voice tight. "I know. It was just so important to Sam. When he heard what happened to your arm, he... he... wanted to offer himself as a helper, to do things for you that you couldn't. He had it all planned out you see. He's so eager to prove himself a man, and sees this as something he must do."

Talia took a deep breath, counted backward from five.

"Someone should have told him that me losing my arm had nothing to do with what he did."

"Didn't it though?" Cora challenged. "Had Sam not damaged your implant, you'd be fine."

"There's no telling if the implant wouldn't have malfunctioned when Rhodes's sword hit my prosthesis. I don't know what the programming for the implant was in that regard. I don't imagine a sword to the wrist to be a contingency that a bunch of academics on Earth would have taken into account."

"Caspar, and John, by the way, think different, but that's not—"

The sound of cursing cut her off. Logan was yelling at the radio, hitting it with a wrench. The richness of his vocabulary blossoming as components flew, as glass shattered.

"Stupid, motherfucking, piece of junk, useless... goddamned piece of shit."

On and on it went until he was out of steam.

He gave it a final kick.

Deflated, he just stood there, wrench in hand. Bits of glass had flown at him, left nicks in his face and hands. Some were bleeding.

"Feel better?" Talia asked.

A stone-faced Dame Leigh burst through the jailhouse door. Her face lit up when she saw Cora, whom she pulled into a hug and held tight.

"I'm all right, gran'mama. I'm all right," Cora whispered.

Otto followed Dame Leigh in and looked around. When his gaze found Talia's they exchanged, silent, cordial nods and he parked himself in a corner, making like a shadow. He was armed with a huge, double-barrel shotgun and every loop on his bandolier was filled with a shell. Two of the largest revolvers she'd ever seen hung at his sides. He was probably carrying knives as well. Nice to be that big. At times like this, she envied people like him for their sheer size. It was easy for them to hide an arsenal.

The door had barely swung closed when it opened again, this time for Maeve and Lyle.

"What's going on?" Lyle asked.

Dame Leigh let go of Cora and spun around.

"Contesti took Sam. He wants to trade him for the patent," Dame Leigh said.

"I didn't realize you had it ready to go," Lyle said.

"It was supposed to be a secret," Dame Leigh said, indignant. "Somehow they found out that we worked out the last bit and have proof that our method works. I was packing to leave for Sakura tomorrow. Take it in for filing and transmission to Earth myself."

"This is all very convenient," Lyle said, fiddling with the edge of his hat. "The marshal radioed the post office. His plane is supposed to be touching down in about ten minutes or so. I was going to head out and pick him up, bring him in to arrest Contesti."

"Can you challenge it later?" Talia asked. "If they make you turn it over under duress that's still theft."

"Yes, it is," Dame Leigh said. "Unfortunately, political connections, possession, and in the case of patents, first-to-file, is still nine-tenths of the law."

"Wait," Talia said. "It still takes a year to get the patent to Earth. So two years round trip. And however long in between to get approval. Surely it's not a swift process. We can all vouch that this was done under duress."

"All true," Lyle said. "All irrelevant."

He stepped forward, put himself in front of Dame Leigh. "You know that even if you give it to him, he can still kill you and your people. And he'll have at least two years to do it. He won't take you out all at once. That would be too suspicious. But this is the frontier. He'll take advantage of that. He's not going to want anyone with significant knowledge about your processes, your IP, to be able to show what was stolen."

"I know," Dame Leigh said. "But I don't see that I have a choice but to play it his way."

"You really think he'll kill Sam with everyone watching?" Lyle asked.

"I really don't want to test it." There were tears in her eyes and her voice.

"Where is the patent now?" Lyle asked.

Dame Leigh slipped her hand into her jacket, withdrew something that looked very much like a cryptochip. She held it up framed between the arc of thumb and forefinger. It sparkled like burnished silver, the edges dark. The Haricot logo had been etched into the surface.

"Is there any way for him to read that, go through it, test it for veracity?" Lyle asked.

"He likely has a computer. And some sort of expert arrived this morning. He'll want me alive at least until he can verify what he has, perhaps until he's sure the patent is safely on its way to Earth. And I'm fine with that. Just as long as they let Sam go."

"Dame Leigh, is that your actual patent?" Maeve asked. "Please tell me it's not. Please tell me it's a decoy."

Dame Leigh gave her a look that Talia couldn't quite interpret.

It was neither confirmation nor denial. She couldn't blame Dame Leigh for not answering, and wished that Maeve hadn't asked the question at all.

"Where are they?" Lyle asked.

"The club," Dame Leigh said, her expression unchanged.

"All right," Lyle said. "Pretend to go along with it. Talia, you and Dame Leigh go up to the front entrance, tell them you're there to make the trade."

"Me? Why me? I'd much rather be somewhere behind a large-bore barrel. I'm useless otherwise."

Lyle's face stretched into a lurid smile, the same one that always said that he had a plan—one she wasn't going to like.

"That's exactly what I'm counting on. Them thinking you useless."

Her eyes went wide. "My turn to be the decoy…"

He nodded. "Are you up for it?"

She took a moment. And then another. She had lost her hand because she'd gone after him after he'd made a decoy of himself, gotten himself captured. He'd told her he'd never forgive her for doing that, for sacrificing three men and her own hand to come after him. She had insisted that he would have done the same for her. He'd denied it. But now. Now it was like things had been before all of that had happened. That he'd traded Contesti for her was one thing. That he seemed to have forgiven her for saving him was another. A wonderful another. One that she had been thinking would never happen.

"I am." At least she wasn't a dead decoy being propped up into place to lure in the enemy. "And what will you be doing?"

"Bringing in the cavalry, or the marshal, as it were. Let Contesti explain what he's doing with Sam and Dame Leigh, with the expert he brought in, the computer, all of it. It may not be much but perhaps getting caught in the act will trip him up. He'll be considering how to spin it for his backers on Sakura, on Earth, at least for a bit."

He turned to Dame Leigh. "Can you do that, Dame Leigh? Get them to release Sam and then delay the whole vetting process or whatever they're going to do. It doesn't have to be a long delay. Just until we can deliver the marshal."

"I can." She looked over at Talia. "I would understand if you don't want to do this. I can do it by myself. Was planning to do so all along."

"What about all your people at the ranch? You have a lot of little kids there."

"If Contesti could have taken our ranch, he would have done so. I think they're safe enough."

"Then I'm with you," Talia said.

She grabbed her hat from the rack, followed Lyle, Maeve, and Dame Leigh out the door. Otto was holding it helpfully open.

Rosie was tied up alongside a black gelding. Lyle swung himself over the black horse's saddle, stiffly and artlessly, but without falling over. He had a shotgun and a rifle in the saddle holster. Maeve hopped up onto Rosie.

"Lyle," Talia said. "This marshal. Can you trust him? To do the right thing, I mean."

He looked down at her from atop the horse. "As much as I can trust anything around here."

"Great," Talia said to their receding backs.

Dame Leigh pulled up in the back seat of an open coach. Otto hopped down and put his hand out to Talia like he was going to help her up.

It was still awkward, using only her left hand. The right arm hung uselessly at her side. She settled down next to Dame Leigh.

"If you get a chance to kill Contesti, Ms. Merritt, will you do it?"

The 1911 in its holster became a prominent weight on her thigh as the coach jostled them along the cobblestone street.

"Well, Ms. Merritt?"

"To save a life, yes."

CHAPTER FORTY-ONE

THEY PULLED UP TO THE WATERWHEEL OF CONTESTI'S CLUB. THE attached building was lit with electric lights, giving Talia a clear look inside. She would have expected more of Contesti's hired hands to be milling about, but from what she could see inside the main room, there were only five men there.

That in itself was worrisome. It meant the rest were somewhere else. And she didn't think they'd be idling. She pushed away visions of an attack on the Haricot ranch, their labs, their cattle. Surely Contesti wouldn't do something that rash until he knew he had the right information in his possession. Surely Dame Leigh had fortified up and protected her people.

Otto brought the coach to a stop.

"Wait here, Otto," Dame Leigh said, setting a placating hand on his broad shoulder.

He scowled. "Ma'am—"

"I'm going to get them to send Sam out."

"He's not going to like it, ma'am."

"I know. That's why I'm hoping Ms. Merritt will take it upon herself to drag him out, by the collar if need be. And I'm going to need you to make sure that when she gets him out here, he doesn't get any stupid ideas to go back in. I'm counting on you, Otto."

"Yes, ma'am."

Otto shot Talia an assessing look. She couldn't quite tell if he'd found her wanting or not.

"Tell Contesti I'm here," Dame Leigh shouted to the man standing by the doorway.

She smoothed out her split skirt, patted the jacket where she'd put the patent and adjusted the decorative hair comb holding up her hair. It was the same fan-shaped one she'd worn before, the one with dangling jewels that made it look like she might be wearing a crown. It certainly added to her queen-of-all-things image.

The man at the door gave her a once-over as if he didn't know who she was. The shape of his flap holster suggested a semiautomatic rather than a revolver riding his hip. His combat boots told Talia that he was not just a new hire but one who hadn't been on Sakura long enough to have worn out what he'd come over with from Earth. He'd splurged, too, by the look of them. Talia could tell that those combat boots were made with synthetic materials not readily available here.

He—she dubbed him "Boots"—looked Talia over as well and ducked inside.

It was Rhodes, not Contesti, who came out to greet them. The tight fit of his shirt gave away the bandages underneath. He smiled—no, beamed—up at Talia like he was genuinely glad to see her. The cut she'd carved into his forehead had been left unstitched, almost as if he wanted it to scar. A trophy. His scars were trophies. Suddenly she wanted the story behind them. It would give her insight into his thinking, perhaps even his psychosis.

Instead, she ignored him as she made her way down one side of the coach and Dame Leigh did the same on the other.

"Izanami," Rhodes said, holding out his hand expectantly.

Slowly, and somewhat awkwardly, she undid her gun belt with her left hand, caught it as it slid down and handed it over. Rhodes passed it on to Boots and widened his smile. Her stuff was unceremoniously dumped on a nearby bench.

"I would be terribly disappointed if you came here with just your gun."

With not-all-together exaggeration, she awkwardly probed for and handed him her pocketknife.

He flicked it open and closed it again almost like he couldn't believe that she'd carry something so innocuous. Without being told, she held her arms out to her sides, the stiff three-quarter sleeve of the bolero jacket spilling out an empty right cuff cinched together by light blue ribbon.

He patted down her torso, all while holding her gaze. His hands lingered on her hip for only a second, as if they had caught on the curve there. The pulse at his throat picked up just a bit, betraying itself under the day's stubble.

Dame Leigh shed a revolver and a small kukri and handed them over to Boots.

"The cane as well," Rhodes said. "She has a blade in that one too."

Boots took the cane and piled it atop the weapons he'd dumped on the bench. He patted Dame Leigh down and nodded clearance to his boss.

"You," Rhodes said to Otto. "I'm going to need your weapons too."

"He's not coming inside," Dame Leigh said. "He's here to escort my grandson home."

"I will still need him to disarm if he's going to linger nearby," Rhodes insisted.

Dame Leigh gave Otto a tight nod.

Reluctantly, he eased his way down. It didn't escape Talia's notice that he left his double-barrel on the driver's seat. From where Rhodes and Boots stood, they probably couldn't even see it, given the night.

Slowly, he came around, shrugging out of his coat as he went. He removed one bandolier, then another, dropping them at his feet. The revolvers were next. She'd been right, he had a bowie knife tucked into the small of his back. And another smaller one behind his neck. The man should have clattered as he walked.

His dark, unsmiling face looked at Rhodes with utter contempt.

"Back to the other side, please," Rhodes said. "You can come by tomorrow to pick up your stuff."

Otto was a statue.

"Otto," Dame Leigh said, "do as he says."

Slowly, he complied, moving away from the arsenal he had just dropped.

"Ladies, this way please," Rhodes said with a tone like they were at some high-society event. He added that same elegant sweep he'd used up at the house right before he'd drawn a sword on Talia.

They had tied Sam to a chair and gagged him, set him in the center of the room as if to keep him away from the rest of the furnishings. The floor below his feet had fresh looking gouges and drag marks around it like he'd already tried and failed to get free. He had a black eye but otherwise he looked all right. Surprise flickered over his face. Surprise and defeat, and then finally shame. He looked like he'd rather die than be the reason they lost decades of work, of effort, of sacrifice.

Contesti was seated at the long table again, looking much cleaner and crisper than when he'd exited the jailhouse a few days ago. Immaculate in a pressed suit, he stood, tugged at his vest, adjusted his cravat.

"This could have been done without bloodshed," he said.

"I spilled no blood," Dame Leigh said.

"Technically neither did I. We are too far above that, the two of us. Please, Dame Leigh, let's just get this over with. The patent."

Slowly, Dame Leigh pulled a chain from inside her blouse, raised it above her head and held it out so that the light flared off the pendant.

Contesti took it, his long fingers cupping around the pendant. Dame Leigh let go of the chain and it all slithered into his waiting hand.

"You have what you want," she said. "Let Sam go. Sam, go with Miss Merritt."

Sam seemed frozen, his muscles tight, not because of the restraints but because of defiance. Talia shifted her weight to assist, intending to loosen his bonds and hustle him out, but Rhodes stepped between them.

"Not quite just yet." Contesti raised a restraining hand. "Not until Dr. Knause here has confirmed the information."

"I will remain in Sam's place," Dame Leigh insisted.

"I agreed to nothing of the sort." Contesti handed the pendant over to a rotund man with a briefcase. He'd been standing in the shadows, clutching the case to his chest like a shield. He wore a rumpled suit, like he'd been traveling in it for days. The stubble seemed days old as well, not a beard so much as overgrowth.

Knause set the briefcase on the table and opened it. He reached into his pocket and pulled out a handkerchief, which he used to pat at the sweat that had beaded on his forehead. He then used it to wipe his finger before placing it on a sensor pad. The case opened and the computer within came to life, projecting a holographic interface from within. Pale blue lines fountained to form into a rectangle filled with gridlines.

"This will take some time," Knause said.

"Get on with it then," Contesti said, annoyed.

Knause flipped Dame Leigh's pendant open and placed the chip on the computer. The gridlines resolved into a holographic image of the data chip itself, flashing the Haricot's stylized H logo.

The sudden burst of coalescing light made Talia blink. She hadn't seen one of those since she'd come off the starship. Didn't think she'd ever see one of those again. Even in Sakura that was advanced tech.

"I heard about your prosthesis," Rhodes said quietly. It wasn't quite a whisper, but he was close. Uncomfortably close, and edging closer, his breath hot on her skin.

She angled her body away.

He let out a low chuckle. "I would pay to have it repaired, you know, just to dance again."

Talia snapped her gaze to his. She'd been wrong. The spark in his eyes hadn't been fire or flame. No, it was ice. Ice glinting off something that might have been a soul once, but no longer was. At least not a sane one.

It sent a shudder through her. The slow, satisfied smile that crept over his lips, tugged at his sneer, his scar, told her he'd misinterpreted her reasons.

"Please, Dame Leigh," Contesti said, gesturing to one of the chairs. "It looks like we'll be here for a while. Do sit down."

"Let Sam go." Her iron will came through in her voice.

"Sit. Down."

Stiff-backed, Dame Leigh sank into the chair. It set her up within Contesti's easy reach, across from the computer.

"Dr. Knause?" Contesti prompted. "Is it the right data?"

"You realize it takes a patent examiner weeks, sometimes longer, to properly cross-reference and v—"

"Do an initial run. If that's not enough to confirm, we'll take this back to the house." Contesti raised a beckoning finger, and the bartender poured a scotch.

"I'll take one of those too," Dame Leigh said.

After a confirming nod from Contesti, the bartender set two glasses on a tray and brought them out. Contesti leaned back in his chair, his gaze darting from the hologram to Dame Leigh and back.

Besides Contesti, Rhodes, the examiner, and the bartender, Talia could only see three other men inside. They had taken up stations by the doors and windows but no longer bristled. Their shoulders were relaxed and they only seemed to be paying marginal attention. Clearly they no longer regarded her as a threat. She wouldn't either. The last time they'd seen her she'd been crawling toward her sword, betrayed by her own body. What did they have to fear from two unarmed women, and a tied-up boy? They had every reason to feel in control.

Lyle, where are you?

She strained, hoping for the sound of an approaching coach or horses. Anything to tell her that Lyle's plan was unfolding. She couldn't wait to see the look on Contesti's face when the marshal burst through, demanding to know what was going on. Let him explain why he had a thirteen-year-old boy gagged and bound, why he was examining what was obviously a trade secret while holding guns on Dame Leigh. She wanted to see him stammer and hedge, wanted to see him sweat.

Rhodes moved closer and into the curve of her neck, the heat of his body intruding, making her want to step away.

"I didn't think that Dame Leigh was going to take the bait," he said.

She darted him a quick look of pure venom.

The sound of the bartender rearranging the glasses behind the counter mixed in with the occasional click of metal scraping against wood and the low hum from the computer.

"Well," Contesti prompted.

Knause was too entranced with the data he was manipulating. He made some noncommittal grunt that earned him a look of annoyance from Contesti.

Outside, a dog barked. At first, no one seemed to notice, but as the barking intensified, the henchmen looked over their shoulders or turned to look out the windows.

A nervous neigh joined the barking, then another.

"What the hell is going on?" Contesti demanded.

"There's a thing barking at the horses," Boots said.

"A thing? What kind of thing?"

"I think it's supposed to be a dog."

What the hell?

She moved toward the window, but Rhodes grabbed Talia by her left arm, pulled her back. He put himself between it and her, looked out instead.

"It's the surveyor's robot. Ignore it. It's a distraction."

Talia shifted her weight to no avail. He wasn't going to let her go, at least not without a proper fight.

But it wasn't time. Couldn't be. Not until there was some sign of Lyle and the marshal.

CorgiSan trotted up the porch stairs and through the open doors, metal paws pounding on wood, not quite like when men scraped their feet and jingled their spurs. His body movements weren't the predatory slink of a herding dog, but the bounce of a clown. He looked around, eye apertures spinning slowly and out of sync, and sat down in the middle of the room like he expected a treat.

Contesti's men had reached for their guns, but only one of them had actually drawn his revolver. It was in his hand like an incomplete second thought.

"I said, ignore it, you idiot," Rhodes repeated. "It's not a military model. You"—he nodded to the pair near the door—"the deputy. They're his. He runs the robots. He's gotta be nearby. Find him."

They made reluctant faces but obeyed, trudging out the front.

"Perhaps we should take this back to the estate," Contesti said as he stood. "Bring the kid, the wo—"

"No!" Dame Leigh threw her scotch into his eyes and lunged across the table, hands thrust out in front of her like claws, going for Contesti's face. He reeled backward, hands raised, anticipating her attack.

Sam pushed up from the chair he was tied to, bringing it up with him as he threw himself at Contesti.

Talia had been slowly pulling away from Rhodes, making him compensate. Now she turned into him, folding into his embrace, hooking his ankle, unbalancing him. Rhodes caught himself, let her go, falling alongside her. She landed on her back with a thud, barely keeping her own head from smacking into the floorboards.

A strange patter, like someone had dropped marbles onto the floor, filled the room. A thick gray fog was creeping along the floorboards as well, swirling and flowing around them as Rhodes pushed up.

A shot rang out, making them all flinch.

She caught a glimpse of CorgiSan. The fog was pouring from his rear nozzle as he made a circuit around the room, while millipedes dropped out of his paniers and scampered across the floor in slithering confusion. She caught a gray streak as well—DespairBear—weaving in and out of chair legs and tangling human ones.

"Cyanide. Cyanide bugs," Knause yelled as he pulled the front of his shirt over his nose and backed away.

The bartender had drawn a shotgun and was aiming it at a pair of millipedes slithering across the floor.

Knause yelped and jumped away from the computer, shaking a millipede that had crawled up onto his hand. It clung to him despite his erratic motions.

"Stop," Rhodes was saying. "It's a ruse, you morons. They're not going to gas their own people."

Talia got a glimpse of Dame Leigh atop Contesti. Talia rolled over and got her hand under her.

Shots rang out. Gun smoke mixed with the fog.

Rhodes had drawn his gun, was raising to aim it and hesitated as he blinked against the rising fog. The higher it rose, the thinner it became, mimicking the haze of smoke.

Talia scrambled to her knees. Dame Leigh was still atop Contesti, her right arm going up and down like she was stabbing him.

More gunshots. Much closer.

Where the hell was Lyle? Or Otto?

"Rhodes," Talia called.

He spun, a scowl on his face, gun held low, pointed—but not aimed—at her.

"Rhodes! Get this bitch off of me." This from the smoke. Contesti, undoubtedly.

Another shot. It made Talia flinch it was so close. She couldn't see well enough to know where it had come from, who was firing.

A moment of indecision animated Rhodes's face as well. Unable to see, he didn't seem to know what to say, whom to order around, or even what to do himself. Contesti's voice continued calling his name but it was being drowned out by screams and gunfire.

"Get them off. Get these things off of me."

"Don't shoot, for God's sake!"

"Die, you bitch."

Rhodes shifted his weight, raised his gun, not toward her, but toward Dame Leigh.

The world slowed, the fog swirling, the sounds fading.

Rhodes was going to shoot. She could see the muscles in his hand contract, see the way he paused his breathing.

Talia moved, closed the distance between them, sprinting toward the madman that was about to kill Dame Leigh.

She took Rhodes from below, plunging the spike protruding from her right arm into his left side, right above the leather of his belt, into the soft spot of his abdomen, angling it up toward his heart.

We are fragile creatures. It doesn't take much to open us up; a sharp point, a keen edge, some momentum, and the willingness to push. And push she did. With all her rage, her regret, her frustrations. She packaged them all, channeled them down her arm, and into him.

Rhodes had turned toward her, shifting to face her, his eyes widening, his knees buckling. His hand went slack, the muscles no longer tight and the gun dropped. Red bloomed on his parted lips.

Red like blood. Red like spider lilies. Red like madness.

Their gazes locked as the weight of him took her down, making her knees smack into the hard floor. He slumped against her, warm, heavy, almost a dead weight, most of it felt on the spike, the way it pushed back into her own flesh and bone in a way she'd never felt before.

Blood dripped, warm and liquid. Thick. The salt and copper of blood was so solid, she wanted to wretch.

"Izanami." It bubbled from Rhodes's lips under searching green-gold eyes. His chest rose and fell. "Let me see her again."

A madness rose in Talia's breast like it had been sitting there, waiting to explode. Here she was, dealing death from the front, up close and personal. Personal enough to see and smell, to taste.

The blood on Rhodes's lips and chin was dark, like rubies glistening. Perfect in the way they shimmered. His lashes had been hooding his eyes, but now he opened them and looked up at her, his madness like a nimbus caught in ice.

Her own blood ran cold.

"Need I point out that *you* are on your knees. That this is not a negotiation," Izanami said, throwing his own words back at him.

He let out a huff of breath. His lips trembled for a second, softening, then hardening. He searched her eyes, searched them as he begged, as he pleaded. In those eyes she saw Giuseppe Priser. She saw Birgitta and Muhonen. She saw Lyle and Maeve, Dame Leigh and Sam. She saw herself and realized it was her reflection mirrored in eyes that wanted not just to see her, but possess her. She saw ambition and passion, madness and disappointment.

"I'm not worthy anyway," Rhodes said. "Let a one-armed woman take me."

She'd never felt life ebb out of someone, not like this. Not when such a vital piece of herself was still embedded deep inside him.

I am the weapon.

The spike had been designed without any sensors, so it must have been her imagination to feel that last pulse of Rhodes's heart, the spasm of lungs as he took his last breath. The scrape of whatever else was up against the delicate cutting edges that had never been meant to be used this way.

"Miss Talia." Otto, from above. The fog had settled now, revealing him. He had blood on his hands too. A smudge on his face. "It's over, Miss Talia. Come back."

"Contesti." It came out a whisper.

"Sam got him."

"Dame Leigh."

"She's fine." His eyes promised it.

He grabbed Rhodes's corpse underneath the arms and pulled his slumping, bleeding form off the spike. Her sleeve had been pushed up and was now bunched against the elbow, soaked in blood and viscera. They dripped onto the floor, an expanding pool.

Otto lay Rhodes out on his back and came to kneel in front of her. He tore the tainted fabric of her sleeve away, used it to wipe the spike clean.

A sensation like static seemed to run up and down the spike. So strange. It seemed like there should be more to it than that odd little sensation one might get from dragging one's feet across the floor.

She was cold. Trembling. Numb.

Otto helped her up, steadied her when she swayed.

She looked around the club like she was seeing it for the first time, blinking stinging eyes as she did.

Knause was up against a wall, held there by Maeve who had a gun on him. He still cowered behind the shirt he'd pulled up over this face, apparently still convinced that there was gas in the room.

Contesti lay on his back, his chest blown open, a look of surprise on his torn-up face.

Dame Leigh was holding on to Sam, who had a magnum revolver dangling from one hand, a look of shock on his paling face.

Lyle and another man she'd never seen before were holding Contesti's henchmen at gunpoint. They were down on the ground, faces pressed to the floor, wrists held together by cuffs. One of them was making a keening sound, edging away from the millipedes still slithering across the floor. Some were climbing the furniture and walls. Others were dead, squashed on a floor. Someone had taken shots at them, left gouges in the wood.

The bartender had disappeared.

John was on the floor too, crumpled on his side. DespairBear and CorgiSan were nuzzling him, trying to get him to pet them. He was still, his chest unmoving.

It didn't quite hit her until the robots lifted their heads and howled.

John was dead.

CHAPTER FORTY-TWO

GRADUALLY, TALIA BECAME AWARE OF THE PEOPLE LINGERING outside, looking in, whispering. Some of Dame Leigh's people were barring the doors, keeping the curious onlookers at bay.

The fog had cleared, but the scent of almonds lingered, and even outside, some of the newcomers were pulling their shirts up over their faces as if that would matter. Every once in a while a surviving millipede would skitter across the floor.

Talia was kneeling by John's corpse, CorgiSan on her left, DespairBear on the right. They'd nuzzle John, then look up at her as if they expected her to do something about it.

All she'd been able to do was shut his eyes.

I hate this.

Dame Leigh joined her, standing above her, casting a shadow. Her hair was loose, a white tousled mess around her shoulders. Her face was splattered with blood, almost like she'd washed her face in it. The splatters of red in her hair clung with a viscous thickness, a parody of ornament. The decorative comb she'd been using to hold it up was in her blood-soaked hand.

She heaved a sigh. "Poor man. I had hoped... I didn't want anyone caught up in this."

"That's quite a weapon," Talia said, eyeing the comb.

"Yes, well. Contesti had it coming." She wiped the comb on her thigh and brought it up to look at it. "Family heirloom. Fitting, no?"

"Sam?" Talia asked.

"Worked himself out of the ropes, got hold of a gun—I'm not sure whose—and shot Contesti in the back right after he got the upper hand and flipped me on my back. He had a gun in my face. All he had to do was pull the trigger. Sam fired first."

That accounted for all that blood on Dame Leigh.

Talia dragged herself up, still feeling far too unsteady on her feet. Dame Leigh helped her up.

Slowly, she made her way to Contesti's corpse. Someone had laid him on the table, his long limbs, dangling off the side, the crisp creases of his pants hardly suggesting the violence he'd suffered. No—earned.

His face was full of furrows and punctures, the whites of his eyes bloody as they stared up at the ceiling. She ran her fingers over the flap of cheek that looked like Dame Leigh had tried to pull free. She could see the bevels where her fingers had dug in after making a slash.

His cravat now lay over his exploded chest, its edges resting on the bits of twisted bone poking through.

"What do you see when you look at him?" Dame Leigh asked. It was barely more than a whisper.

"Someone's son."

"That he was," she admitted.

"Let Sam know, I'm here for him," Talia said. "If he wants to talk, that is."

"What will you tell him?"

"That he did the right thing, that he can still see this as someone's son and as someone who had to die so you could live, so that all of you could live. Life is about choices. Sometimes it makes us choose who lives and who dies as if we were gods, as if we are worthy of such decisions. We need to be careful, not think of ourselves as gods even when ending a life, even when making that decision. We need to remember that ending a life is nowhere as powerful as creating life. That we cannot do. We pretend to, but we can't. Not really."

"That sounds very... wise," Dame Leigh said, with a bit of surprise in her voice.

Talia got that a lot. People apparently expected someone like her to feel nothing or perhaps dismiss it as "he needed killing." As much as Ferran Contesti had needed killing, that need would forever be a burden carried by Sam Haricot, a man of thirteen years, a man not because he'd taken a life, but because he'd saved one. She closed her eyes for a moment, blinking away the moisture gathering there. Thirteen was much too young. She wished she could have spared him this. Wished she could have taken it on herself. She knew what to do with the ghosts, the nightmares, the doubts that would sometimes swell up and make her doubt that she had done the right thing, the only thing that could be done in that moment of decision.

Talia looked at Dame Leigh's blood-streaked face. It took a lot to look that calm, that composed, after what Dame Leigh had gone through. After what she'd risked. Caspar had said that they were much alike and he had been right.

"Are you all right, my dear?" Dame Leigh asked. "You look a little pale."

"I'm . . ."

For some reason, Dame Leigh was floating up and away, looking like some ghost with her bloodstained clothes, her blood-streaked face, her cloud of white hair.

So much shouting. So much barking.

Shhh. Too loud. Why is everyone being so loud?

Quit fussing. Quiet.

Let me sleep.

When Talia had been a little girl, *Sobo* would make her all sorts of broths and soups. She would come home from school to a house filled with the delicate, salty smell of miso or fish broth. *Sobo* loved making her own noodles for chicken soup. Her own dumplings as well.

It was the smell of chicken that woke Talia, that pulled her out of the deep sleep. She blinked her eyes open.

Dame Leigh was sitting in a wing-back chair under a window, working on a tapestry. The room looked like one of the nicer hotel rooms in Sakura with its set of dual curtains, one set of velvet to keep out light, and one set of lace to complement them. They went together well, paired with the high gloss of stained woods and the plushness of deep-pile rugs. It had to be Haricot House.

Talia pushed herself up and the odd sensation of the spike pressing into the mattress reminded her that her prosthesis was gone. She shifted her weight. She was wearing a hospital gown and the IV bruise on the inside of her elbow was covered with a bandage.

"How long have I been out?" she asked past the awful taste and texture in her mouth.

"A little more than a day," Dame Leigh said, rising and setting her needlework aside. "How do you feel?"

She was whole, or as whole as she could be. She reached up to the implant, first with the spike, stopping short and then using her left hand instead. The implant seemed fine. No new bandage.

"You were shot in the leg," Dame Leigh said. She had poured a glass of water from the pitcher on the nightstand and was holding it up suggestively.

"I was?" Talia took a peek under the covers. One. Two. She wiggled her toes and that's when the tightness in her left leg revealed itself. She reached down and found a bandage along her thigh.

"Caspar said that sometimes adrenaline masks pain and you don't know that you've been hurt until you lose enough blood that you faint. Here. Drink."

Talia drank. No ice, but cold. Water had never tasted so good. She held the glass out for a refill. Dame Leigh complied.

"Did I hit my head again?" She felt fuzzy.

"No. That's the anesthetic I'm afraid." She reached behind Talia and slipped a few pillows behind her back.

"You don't have to fuss over me, really."

"I don't have to do anything. I want to. Therefore I am. There you go. Enjoy it while you can. Caspar has me under orders to get you up and moving just as soon as you get that broth down."

With that she presented Talia with the mug responsible for the chicken smell. She gave it a cautious sniff, more for temperature than anything else and sipped.

Her stomach did a happy turn.

"Did you get the patent off to Sakura?" Talia asked as she waited for the broth to settle.

"Not quite," Dame Leigh admitted as she made her way back to the chair.

"I thought you said it was ready?"

"We had to amend it thanks to your mycologist," she said, "but it should be ready to go in a few days."

"Amend it how?"

"Oh, he made me promise to let him tell you. He's quite

proud. And I must thank you for bringing him to us. He will make a fine addition to the family."

"I take it he and Cora..."

"Oh yes."

"Tell me, Dame Leigh, were you actually handing Contesti all the information he needed to replicate your work?"

"Oh? You'd think I would gamble with your lives that way?"

"Yes. I think you were counting on the marshal catching Contesti in the act even before Lyle suggested it."

Dame Leigh pinned her with a look that wasn't quite a glare. Not exactly friendly, but not threatening either.

"It was our entire patent and the supporting documentation. Our representative back on Earth has the information on the genetic tweaks, but not the key to access the data. Without that information, Contesti's people can't possibly replicate our methods."

"So it wouldn't have been useful to him."

"Not without the key, no."

"And your people on Earth. You trust them to take that information, understand it, and file it on your behalf? There's no way they could be compromised?"

"I am going back to Earth to see it done."

"And the key?" Talia asked, her gaze settling on the tapestry that Dame Leigh had been working on. Talia hadn't given it much thought before, but now. It was all falling into place as she took another sip of broth. Without the weight of threats, her mind was piecing it together.

Dame Leigh smiled. "How did you figure it out, Miss Merritt?"

"I caught a glimpse of the binary code. Is it something woven into tapestry itself? Perhaps the beading on the edges. The colors. It looks random, but it's not."

"Correct."

"Contesti would never think to look at something as mundane as needlepoint," Talia said.

"No, he would not. And should something happen to me, one of my heirs will travel to Earth with the key if I fail. It's up to each of them to decide how to replicate the key for transport. So even if Contesti's backers figure out that my tapestry might hold an answer, they won't know how, let's say Cora or Sam, for example, might choose to carry the code."

"Do you know who his backers are? The ones in the shadows?"

"Not as shadowy as you'd think. Your Mr. Rhodes, you know about him, don't you?"

"That he's fallen corporate nobility with a redacted war record, that's all."

"Maeve told me what he was trying to do. That Izanami thing."

She wasn't sure what to do with that. "Are you sure you travelling to Earth is safe? That they won't try to kill you there?"

Dame Leigh flashed a smile. "Oh, they'll try. It won't be the first time. Otto is coming with me, along with a few others. They may yet stop me. They're even working on a bill that would make it so that a signature obtained under duress is valid if it was deemed to be in the service of the greater good as determined by a court, regulation, or statute. That's the other reason I'm going back. To set in motion a legal fight to stop them. Because you and I both know that once anything is deemed to be 'for the greater good,' it will be used as a reason to take it all away from us."

"I don't envy you your task, Dame Leigh. I really don't."

Talia finished up the last of the broth and set the cup down on the nightstand.

"Let's get you up and moving," Dame Leigh said.

With Dame Leigh's help, Talia put on a robe and slippers. Using a crutch under her left arm, she made her way out onto the same veranda where she'd accepted Sam's apology. The short trip was enough to exhaust her and she didn't argue when Dame Leigh suggested she sit down and take a break.

She lowered herself into a wood chair topped with a thin cushion and let Dame Leigh prop her left leg up on a low table. Another pair of chairs bracketed a fire pit filled with logs. The pond with its water lilies and overhanging willow trees was picturesque enough to make her think of postcards.

Habit made Talia check sightlines. A tiny bat was hanging in corner, under an eave, hiding from the late morning light.

Barking preceded her next set of visitors. John's robots were making a beeline toward her, bounding right over the landscaping rocks, into the water, and ending up on the veranda. DespairBear even shook himself, sending water drops flying at her from his netting.

They put their front paws on the chair's arms and nudged at Talia for attention despite Dame Leigh's scolding.

"No, it's all right," Talia said. "I don't mind. I'm actually very glad to see them. How are you boys? You been good boys?"

DespairBear nudged her spike off the arm rest and into her lap. She petted CorgiSan with her left hand.

"You boys are just going to have to take turns, all right? Talia only has one hand."

CorgiSan let out something that might have been an electronic sigh. DespairBear sent out a series of rapid-burst pulses.

"Hey, that tickles," she said. It wasn't exactly a tickle, more like when someone puts their lips up against your belly to buzz you.

"Well, at least they don't slobber. Or shed," Dame Leigh said.

"Oh, very good. I see they found you." Caspar was making his way down the covered walkway, doctor's bag in hand. "They followed me after I brought John's body to our morgue and they've been guarding it."

"I told you to just let them run out of power," Dame Leigh said, although she didn't really sound cross. "He brought their chargers to the morgue, you know," she told Talia.

"Make it an order and I will," Caspar said.

Dame Leigh shook her head and rolled her eyes. "Well, I have things to do. I'll send someone to keep an eye on you, Miss Merritt."

Before Talia could object, she was gone.

The robots had settled on each side of her, CorgiSan laid out like a loaf and DespairBear in a down-stay, looking out over the pond, his eyes following the birds that flitted back and forth.

Caspar straddled the low table her leg was propped on.

"I'm going to change the dressing on that leg, but first, I do believe this is yours." He reached inside his pocket and pulled out her cryptochip and the chain it was attached to.

"Where did you find it?" she asked.

"On Rhodes's body," he said as she took it from him.

She held it up to the sunlight, let it twist and turn, and then finally settled it around her neck.

"How is your arm?" he asked her, indicating the spike in her lap.

"Fine, I think."

"That was very clever of you," Caspar said. "Using it that way. I can't imagine it was easy."

She really had never thought of using her spike as a weapon and hoped never to have to again. The sensation of it puncturing

Rhodes's skin and sliding into his body was not something she wanted to repeat. She'd been warned not to bend the spike, although she wasn't sure what it would take to bend it. A bent spike would have to be replaced, a far more invasive surgery that would cost her more of her flesh and bone. Like a cap on a tooth, they would have to remove the bone compromised by any damage before attaching a replacement. She shuddered at the thought.

"It's not something I'd care to repeat, no."

"May I?" He indicated her leg.

She pulled up the robe and gown, exposing the bandage wrapped around the lower part of her thigh.

"I don't actually remember getting shot," she said as he unwound the bandage. "It seems like I should remember something like that."

There was a clear entry wound and a very jagged scar that had been sewn together. It looked like something had hit her flesh at just the right angle to penetrate it, but instead of going deep, it had carved a furrow under her skin as it travelled. Strips of clear tape had been laid across the wound at regular intervals, giving the wound a puckered look. It was not going to be a pretty scar. Well, she had plenty of scars and their aesthetics had never mattered to her—she'd earned them all and they had become part of who and what she was.

She wasn't going to escape them any more than she would her shadows, although admittedly they were a bit easier to bear.

"I think it was a ricochet," Caspar was saying. "The metal I got out was pretty twisted. No clear indication of caliber."

CorgiSan pushed up and headed down the walkway, intercepting Maeve and Lyle. He trotted alongside them, quiet for once, except for the paws stomping up and down as he bounced.

"Oh, that's going to make a fine scar," Lyle said as he came up and leaned in to get a better look. It earned him a friendly bicep punch from Maeve. "Mine's better though, wanna see?"

Maeve elbowed him out of the way and bent down to hug Talia, holding on for an extra moment. "I'm so glad to see you up and about. You had us worried there."

"I told you she was tough," Lyle said as he pulled the two chairs forward.

"Is someone going to tell me what happened?" Talia asked.

"One of Contesti's thugs confessed to knifing me in the onsen. You were right, it was to wound me so I'd take up hypnolin again."

"That's not what she means, Lyle," Maeve said. She turned to Talia. "Can you tell he's feeling better? He's been a brat like this ever since the dust cleared."

Talia pressed her lips into a line so she wouldn't laugh. She'd never heard anyone call Lyle a brat.

Caspar cleared his throat and stood up. "I don't think it needs to be rebandaged. Do send for me if it starts bothering you. I'll be around in a few hours to check on you again. Come on, boys."

The robots looked up at him but didn't follow. He took a few steps and looked over his shoulder. "Oh, I see. Fine. I'll send their chargers to your room, Miss Merritt."

"Thank you, Doc," she called, more than a little pleased with the robots' behavior. She covered up her leg and reached down to pet CorgiSan's head.

"What happened to the plan, Lyle? The one where you were going to bring the marshal to witness Contesti pressuring Dame Leigh. You know, that plan?"

"Things didn't go according to plan," Lyle deadpanned.

"I gathered that. Care to elaborate?"

"Contesti sent his men to the airstrip, to stop the marshal, as it were. They pinned us down and when I realized it was going to take longer than we planned, I sent John, Logan, and Maeve back to warn you."

Lyle looked at Maeve. "Your turn. I'm still a little unclear on what happened after we covered your getaway."

"On our way back John and I realized we couldn't take on Rhodes and whomever else Contesti had there," Maeve said. "At least not head on. Not without risking you and Sam and Dame Leigh. John had an idea to use the boys as a distraction. It worked before, so he thought it might work again."

"The gas thing?" Talia asked. "What was that?"

"Logan's idea. Not gas, but fog."

"And the bugs?"

"Oh, that was Logan too," Maeve admitted. "You saw how some of the newcomers on the train freaked out over the millipedes, especially after they learned about the cyanide gas. And I had plenty of almond extract for creams and such at the shop, so I soaked strips of cloth in it and stuck them in DespairBear's netting."

"And you went along with this?" Lyle asked Maeve.

"It was the best we could come up with on such short notice.

We just wanted a distraction and since John had used the boys as a ruse before, we thought their antics might be ignored. I figured the fog and the millipedes and the scramble of confusion would make Contesti want to leave. He had the data. Maybe he'd cut his losses and run, leaving Dame Leigh, Sam, and Talia behind. Hostages slow things down. We seemed to have him going in the right direction, too, until you guys came along and started shooting."

"That part I remember," Talia said. "Lots of shooting going on outside."

It was Lyle's turn again.

"We—the marshal and I—shot our way out from the men holding the airfield and headed your way. They pursued. We almost made it to the waterwheel. Could see the lights. But Contesti had a second group out, riding this way. When Otto didn't come back with Sam like Dame Leigh had planned, her people decided to act. Sent out about a dozen well-armed riders. The two groups met just down the street. Had a few words.

"One of Contesti's men said that it was too late. I think they took it to mean that Dame Leigh was dead, because that's when the shooting started."

"How many did we lose?" Talia asked.

"Two of the Haricots' people were shot and died. Three of Contesti's. Half a dozen wounds. It could have been a lot worse."

"Where are Contesti's men now?"

"The ones that didn't flee are locked up," Lyle said.

"Locked up where? Not the jailhouse."

"Marshal deputized some of the townspeople. Turned Contesti's club into a jailhouse. And that does remind me, I do have to get back there and take a shift or two." Lyle gave Maeve a peck on the cheek and stood.

"I thought you said that the townspeople were reluctant to get in the middle of this."

"As soon as they saw us and the marshal take a stand, they stepped up. They just needed to be shown that it could be done. That it was time."

The next day, properly dressed so that she didn't look or feel like an invalid, Talia and the robots made their way from Haricot House to Caspar's clinic on the other side of the field.

Carefully, she shifted her weight off her right side to her

left to step off the raised and covered pathway. She had to stop and catch her breath. Several people—a man digging in a small garden, a woman pushing her child on a swing—waved at her. She waved back, left-handed, uncharacteristically conscious of her missing prosthesis. Her phantom throbbed and pulsed and ached and for a moment she'd almost banged the spike up against the wall out of frustration.

Once she reached the clinic, she made CorgiSan and Despair-Bear wait outside. They had spent the night with her, CorgiSan happily parked on his charging mat, DespairBear at her feet after charging up to a whopping sixty-two percent. No matter what she tried, she couldn't get him to stay on his mat long enough to go to a full charge.

She could almost hear John chuckling in her ear about it, saying, "See, I told you so."

She'd left the crutch behind. Without a right hand to work it properly it just wasn't as useful as she'd expected, even though sometimes her leg throbbed and she got tired far too quickly for her liking.

Caspar looked up from whatever he was working on—some sort of tray full of test tubes.

"Oh good, I have it ready for you."

He took a tray off the shelf above his work bench. Her prosthesis lay atop it, the top edge trailing about a dozen wires, connected to a strip of what looked like gray utility tape.

"Now, I know it looks sloppy, but it's the best I could do. It's proven technology, just outdated. The strip picks up electrical signals from the muscles in your upper arm and transmits them into the prosthesis itself. It makes the connecting spike redundant, except as a physical anchor, but it also entirely bypasses the wiring in the spike and hence the implant."

"What sort of power does it need?" The idea of being reliant on batteries had no appeal. Not out here.

"Your prosthesis is still running on its Hampson-effect power source. These new wires are merely patched into that. It will be a slight drain on the prosthesis itself, so you'll have maybe a three-to-five percent degradation due to that, but it'll work for the life of the Hampson-effect power supply. You've still got a good two or three years left on that. I had one of the engineers check."

She took a deep breath and nodded.

He had her sit down and carefully rolled up her sleeve.

"Do you want me to do it or would you like to do it yourself. I know that's a highly personal thing for some."

"Maybe set it up. Let me complete the connection myself."

He complied, lining up the prosthesis and then easing it onto the spike, but not so far that it actually connected.

She made the final motion, driving the spike into the prosthesis. It found home with a click. She had expected the abuse she'd heaped on it by stabbing Rhodes to have bent or warped it, but it hadn't.

It felt just as heavy, as much of a dead weight as before. The implant in her head made no attempt to boot up or connect. There was no tickle, no buzz, just weight.

"It's fine," she said. "Good fit." She raised her bicep to show him that she could move it around. The wrist and fingers were still dead though.

"I'm going to wrap the tape and cinch it. Let me know if you get any unpleasant sensations or pain or if you want me to stop."

Slowly, he moved the wires around, laying half of them up against her skin. The tape turned out to be two separate sections, one right at the top of her elbow. The other a few inches higher around her bicep. He tightened the lower section, using a strip of Velcro to keep it shut and then set up the wires for the upper strip.

"Do you remember what it was like when you first got it?" Caspar asked.

"You mean do I recall having to think of moving a limb I've lost?"

"That's right." He was watching her with a concerned expression that warmed her heart. It seemed like he was truly worried about what this might do to her, that it would be traumatic in some way.

She took a deep breath, closed her eyes and imagined her flesh-and-bone limb. Her phantom twisted its elbow, opened and closed its fingers, all in defiance. The prosthesis did not respond.

Another deep breath. *Squirm all you want. I can wait,* she thought to her phantom.

Eventually the phantom settled in place. She imagined her phantom becoming one with the prosthesis. And then slowly, she thought about rotating her forearm.

"That's right, very good," Caspar was saying.

She opened her eyes. The prosthesis wasn't moving quite at the same speed as the phantom, but at least it was moving the right way.

"It took me months to get the implant to work seamlessly with the prosthesis. I didn't expect this to be easier."

"Yes, well, all of that information, those neural pathways are still there. You just haven't accessed the ones built around the muscles rather than the spike-brain connection in awhile."

Running through the checklist exercises, she moved her wrist next, then each of her fingers.

Slow, it was very slow. Maybe half speed. She wouldn't trust it with a gun or even a hot coffee, at least not yet.

She threw Caspar a glowing smile.

"Not bad, Doc. Not bad at all. What about the tactile sensations? Cold, warm, that kind of thing?"

"I'm afraid that's an implant function. No electrical signals for it via the wires. Sorry."

"That's all right, Doc. It also means that if anyone tries to hack my wrist off there won't be any pain either, right?"

He frowned at her. "I wouldn't think so, no."

"Relax, Doc, I don't plan to get into another duel. I was just wondering."

"From what I'm seeing, your gross motor control is quite good. I'm thinking that fine motor control will come with practice."

"Like buttoning my blouse, threading a needle, that kind of thing?"

"Exactly that kind of thing."

"All right then. Big movements now, small movements later. I'll get on it right away. Thank you, Doc. Thank you very much. This goes beyond..." She was more than touched by the gesture. She was overwhelmed.

He brushed it off, not in a dismissive way, but in an I-don't-want-to-make-it-awkward way.

"Oh, before I forget." He searched his lab coat, patting at the pockets and pulled out an envelope. "When I went to pick up the charging mats from John's place, I went through some of his things, looking for a will, that kind of thing. I didn't find one, but I found this among Adrian's—John's dead son's—things. I thought you might find it interesting."

He handed her the envelope. "You might want to read it later. In private."

Talia turned it over, tempted to open it, but there had to be a reason for Caspar's concern. She couldn't imagine what it might be, but…

"All right." She tucked it away.

"Very well then. I'm to take you to Logan, if you're up for it."

She tested the motions of her prosthesis once again. The responses were faster, easier this time. Yes, this could work. It could work well. She wouldn't need help dressing or feeding herself.

She followed him out, glad that he couldn't see the tears that had gathered in her eyes.

Talia would have never guessed that the Haricots' operation had underground components. She'd come to associate that kind of thing with Sakura, with buildings of more modern construction on the geologically stable mainland. Due to the geological activity and high water table on the islands, she'd believed that they would be limited to root cellars. But Tsurui was in the mountains, so it made a sort of sense now that she thought about it.

The air took on a mustiness as they descended the stairs. It had an overlay of livestock as well, making her think that they must be close to where the space cows were housed. At night she could hear their mooing as they were moved in and out of the hangar-like buildings.

She held on to the handrail with her prosthesis. Her phantom remained superimposed on it the entire time. No twitches, no spasms. If anything, it felt like she had a brace on or perhaps a splint—something that didn't quite allow free movement. An itch started and she let out a scoff.

"Something wrong?" Caspar asked as he pushed a heavy door inward.

"I was thinking that it feels like I have a brace on and now my phantom itches. It's a power of suggestion, I guess. Just surprised me that's all."

The door revealed the half cylinder of a hangar filled with grow-trays hanging from the ceiling. Each tray or pallet was spaced a few feet apart depending on the height of the material it was holding. But unlike the grow-trays she'd seen on the ship that had brought her here, the lights on these were either off or so low that the only reason she could see them at all was the strip of lights down the center of the hangar.

She blinked, waiting for her eyes to adjust.

"Talia!" Logan came running down the center, clipboard in hand, a head lamp on his head. He was wearing a pair of coveralls with light-reflecting strips down his arms and legs.

"What happened to your face?" He had a bruise on half his face and stitches on his chin.

"Oh that?" he said sheepishly. His glasses slid down his nose. The cracked lens was still there.

"Yes, that." She reached out and took hold of his chin with her left hand so she could get a better look.

"I got to use a shotgun," he mumbled over her grip.

"A shotgun did that?"

She let go of his chin and waited expectantly.

"After I helped John rig the robots up with the millipedes and the fog canisters, he told me to wait across the street. He was going to send the robots to me to change out the spent canisters with fresh ones, just in case. Long story short, I took a shotgun off one of Contesti's men and shot from the hip."

She blinked.

"How exactly did you end up taking a shotgun off his men?"

"Well, he ignored me. I think it's because I wasn't armed. But Otto shot him before he blasted his way inside the club. So I took the shotgun off the corpse and I shot from the hip. And Talia, I got another guy. I actually got him."

She didn't have the heart to tell him that shooting from the hip was something only amateurs did. Or how dangerous and foolish it was. Or how lucky he'd been. She patted him on the back and bit her lip. It made him smile and he squared his shoulders.

"And the face?" she asked.

"I tripped."

"You tripped?"

"CorgiSan had come out to get fresh canisters and I was so excited about the shotgun that I didn't realize he was there and I tripped. Anyway, come see. Come see what they've done here. Come, come, come."

Caspar trailed her to the center of the hangar where the lights were brightest. In this section, the grow-trays were inside of a glass enclosure, a freestanding cabinet with hoses coming out of it. The inside must have been moister because streaks of condensation ran down the front.

Inside, the grow-tray was stacked high with strata of dirt, as if a giant hand had scooped it up and deposited it there, although she doubted that it had. It was too tidy. The top layer of dirt was covered with wood and twigs and what looked like cotton candy. It was the only way to describe the stringy stuff covering the topsoil. The remains of wilted plants were tangled up in it.

Logan tapped his head lamp and it emitted a bluish glow that made the strata behind the glass light up. The cotton candy glowed, revealing that it wasn't just on the surface, but that it extended below the surface.

"A fungus?" Talia asked. It had to be.

"Mycelium and hyphae," Logan said, "the two main components of fungi. This is what the fungal blooms look like when they get out of control. They cover and overtake everything."

"This is what killed the first colonization effort?" Talia said. "This is what you were trying to convince your backers was going to happen again."

"Caleb Haricot thought the same," Caspar said.

"Did he ever publish anything on it?" Logan asked.

"I don't know," Caspar admitted. "He wasn't exactly a popular man with academia. Credentialism is rampant on Earth. They don't listen to anyone who hasn't been anointed by their own. He was in the wrong specialty and even there, he'd upset some powerful people by not toeing the line."

"The fungal blooms interfere with the life processes of plants," Logan said. "When plants die off, animals follow. People starve. Colonies fail."

"But you have a solution," Talia said.

Logan smiled. "Remember how I told you that there was something about the mycelium samples that had been sent back to me from the islands?"

"Vaguely."

He made his way down the center of the hangar and came to a stop in front of another cabinet. It looked very much like the first one, except that the top layer was not covered in cotton candy fungus. The strands of fungus that lit up under Logan's black light were nowhere as thick or as dense.

"This is from soil on Haricot lands," Logan said.

"The cows?"

"It turns out that the blooms are caused by fungi that feed on bacteria in the soil. The bacteria in the engineered cows' waste kills the bacteria in the soil, thereby denying the fungi its food source."

"Like your bats?" Talia asked Caspar.

"Exactly like the bats. It's probably where Caleb Haricot got the idea to use predatory bacteria. Modified it of course, enhanced it."

"And it's gone past the fields that the cows are . . . umm . . . seeding as it were," Logan said. "I found evidence of the same predatory bacteria in the cavern."

"Isn't that dangerous?" Talia asked. "Surely you need some of this mycelium or fungus or whatever to survive. You can't kill all of it off, right?"

"That's the genius of it," Logan said. "They found a way to limit the number of times the bacteria can successfully reproduce. Look here."

He took them to a stack of six open trays filled with different kinds of mushrooms.

"I've been trying to get the bacteria from the cave and other places outside of where it is continuously seeded by the cows to reproduce. I've gotten them to divide but each time fewer actually do. See, each tray represents a generation."

The bottom tray was indeed full of mushrooms and others slimy things that looked like they might become as thick as the cotton-candy fungus. The one above it less so. And the one on top had mushrooms but nothing that looked like cotton candy.

She looked to Caspar.

"I'm neither a genetic engineer nor a microbiologist," he said defensively. "Things being what they are, I'd rather leave it that way."

Talia didn't quite believe him but she did understand the sentiment. You can't be forced to reveal what you don't know.

That night, Talia sat on the veranda with both robots nearby, watching the flames dance in the fireplace. Her aching leg was propped up on pillows. Every once in awhile the flit of wings would draw her eye—the bats going about their business.

She was petting CorgiSan as he followed the bats and felt the bursts of subsonics that he was emitting flow over her skin. Every once in a while he'd emit a low whine.

Did they understand, truly understand that John was dead and gone? Sometimes it certainly seemed like they did.

She reached into her jacket and pulled out the envelope, holding it with her prosthesis and using her left hand to perform the more subtle act of pulling out the paper within.

It was a printout of an article, its edges worn and stained. The man in the accompanying picture was a younger Rhodes, sans scars, wearing a tailored suit rather than a uniform. Both picture and print were faded but there was enough to make out the fact that Colonel Jerod Rhodes had once been in charge of a reeducation camp for political prisoners. Her hands shook as she read about how he had pioneered the development of hypnolin specifically to make reeducation more "effective."

She could see it now, prisoners being forcibly injected or dosed without their consent, perhaps in their food or drink. Researchers fiddling with the best way to make them comply, pushing the boundaries of what people could be made to do while making it seem that it was of their own free will.

No blinking "torture" at the camera. That was bad optics.

The side effect of "drunkness" had rendered it less effective than they wanted, at least in the majority of subjects. But those they'd gotten hooked had been easier to control, to reeducate. Until they were cut off and then behaved like addicts everywhere, going through withdrawals, being unable to function, doing things like killing themselves. They used that too, to discredit some. Martyrs weren't as useful when disgraced and discredited.

As for the pain relief, that turned out to be an unexpected "adverse event" that wasn't so adverse.

They had tested other drugs as well, all designed to control people, to take away their freedom to think and reason and feel. All designed to erase their individuality, to control the "vermin," the "rats," the "plague of defiance."

She couldn't help but wonder if Rhodes had been crazy from the start or if his psychosis had been how he'd dealt with what he'd done. She had seen herself in his eyes for a reason. She'd been drawn to him and him to her for that reason as well. Like calls to like.

Dealers of death, both of us.

Rhodes had people like Bradley, and undoubtedly others, to keep him on his road to madness. Just as she'd had people to keep her off that road. What a fine line it was, the path between destruction and creation.

Had there ever been a fork in Rhodes's road like there was in hers? Had he chosen Izanami because she was also *Izanami no mikoto*, a goddess of creation? With Rhodes dead, she'd never know.

She flipped the paper over, hoping to find some reference to the other women that Rhodes had thought to be possessed by Izanami, but the print was unreadable, dissolved by moisture and age.

CorgiSan stuck his nose under her prosthesis and flipped it upward so it landed on his head. Well, he had all sorts of sensors, why not ones that could read enough vitals for him to figure out her mood?

She crumpled up the paper and the envelope it came in, tossed them into the flames, and watched them burn.

Talia woke to CorgiSan nudging her prosthesis. His front paws were up on the bed and he let out a deep electronic sigh as the apertures in his eyes swirled inward.

Dame Leigh had insisted she stay in one of the small cottages, at least until she sorted out what she wanted to do. The Haricot matriarch had left under the cover of night, along with Otto, Sam, and Goggles—a man who actually went by the name of Heath MacNeil—and a dozen others. Most of them would only go as far as Sakura. Otto and Sam were going to go back to Earth with her. She'd wanted to avoid any fuss and Lyle and Talia had ridden along all the way to Shiiba to see her settled on the train.

The little clock on the nightstand said it was almost noon. Talia stretched, popping a few joints in the process, all in that good way that made her want to do it again.

She looked around the room, expecting to find DespairBear settled at the foot of the bed. He wasn't there.

She dressed and grabbed breakfast from the kitchen, coffee and a muffin which she was still chewing on as she waved to Cora and Logan, who were being all lovey-dovey to each other over pancakes.

DespairBear had taken to visiting John's grave on his own, lying down, and then running out of batteries. The Haricots had given John a place in their own cemetery and the whole town had come out to pay their respects. After he'd been lowered into the ground, DespairBear had to be coaxed and then physically carried away by Otto. Somewhere in the deep recesses of her memory there was a story about a statue in Scotland, erected to Greyfriars Bobby, a Skye Terrier who had spent fourteen years guarding his dead master's gravesite. Whomever had programmed the VR software that DespairBear ran on must have incorporated that behavior in there somewhere. She wished she'd asked John how and why he'd chosen the dog breeds he had.

She rode out, CorgiSan trotting alongside Rosie. Unlike the other horses, Rosie didn't seem to mind the robots. She'd even seen them play together, nipping at each other as if Rosie was just some extra-large version of a canine. As long as CorgiSan didn't try to herd her, Rosie engaged him, even passing a soccer ball back and forth.

In just a few days Talia had gained a lot of confidence in her refurbished prosthesis. It still behaved like an arm in a cast, a bit stiff at times, a bit slow most times, but she could dress herself, comb her own hair, shoot, and wield a sword or knife.

Simon's sword was now hers—Maeve had insisted—and Talia had sent a telegraph to Candy's Gun and Toy Shoppe, asking if a traditionally made *ō-wakizashi* and tanto could be had and for how much. Caspar had approved, citing that anything that involved old muscle memory was bound to help her retrain her prosthesis.

The cryptochip hung around her neck. She hadn't quite decided how she was going to put it to use. A radio for the jailhouse had been on her list, but the townspeople had taken up a collection specifically to upgrade the jailhouse.

There was a lot of talk of independence for Tatarka, for Gōruden. The terraforming that the space cows were facilitating would eventually mean that the people of Gōruden could declare their independence from Earth and its many governmental and corporate fiefdoms. It was the kind of talk that led to revolutions. She had yet to see a peaceful revolution in her lifetime, but that didn't mean they couldn't happen.

And along with the talk of independence there was talk of weddings. Cora and Logan for one. He'd scored himself an heiress. Not bad for a kid who didn't see well and couldn't shoot.

But theirs was at least a couple of years off. Dame Leigh had insisted, and what Dame Leigh wanted, she got.

Lyle and Maeve weren't going to wait as long. A few months yes, out of respect for those who had died. Visions of maid-of-honor duties haunted her sometimes, the prospect of such duties feeling more daunting than they probably would be. Still, Maeve had told her a pink—or rather, salmon—dress was involved, an unexpected perk.

She brought Rosie to a stop a few hundred yards from the graveyard. Someone was standing over John's grave, duster blowing in the wind, hat shadowing his face, his black horse standing beside him as he held on to the reins.

He looked up as she approached. DespairBear was at his feet, out of power as she'd expected. He was tall, this man, and there was something familiar about his bearing, his clothes. Slowly, she approached, giving her memory time to catch up as she looked him over.

Clean shaved but rugged, with sun-tanned skin that made the crow's-feet stand out in that way that made men handsome and distinguished. Blonde hair a bit too long like most men out here who just didn't have the means to keep it trimmed. Twin revolvers rode his hips. Lots of black on him, rather than the blues, browns, and grays most of Tsurui's denizens tended toward.

How does one greet a stranger over a grave?

"Good morning." He had a deep resonating voice, not quite as low as Otto's, but damn, if it wasn't perfect. Absolutely perfect. Listen-to-all-day perfect.

She was not going to let it get to her.

Finally, she was close enough to get a glimpse at his eyes. Gray, like brushed gunmetal with just the barest gold edging the pupil.

"Good morning. I'm Talia Merritt." She thrust out her hand.

He shook it without a hint of hesitation like he shook a cybernetic limb every single day. Her heart skipped a beat and she was almost afraid that he knew that it had.

"Marcus Deckard. We met before, although I doubt you'd remember."

She should remember. She had no doubt of that. But she didn't. One of Contesti's men? Surely not. One of the Tsurui's denizens, someone she had walked by perhaps. What could she possibly have been doing *not* to remember him?

"I'm with the marshal's office," he said, and opened the front of his coat. A marshal's shield was pinned to a black leather vest. "I was, belatedly, at Contesti's club when you... umm... when you stabbed Colonel Rhodes."

Her mouth went dry. This man had seen her kill Rhodes. Either seen her drive her spike into him or seen her soon after. And yet, he'd still shaken her hand in that casual, undeterred way. He hadn't given her that look that she got from people who knew what she was, what she had done, who feared what else she might do, who judged her for the fine line she treaded to save lives.

Confusion rolled over her. She set it all aside, pushed it, shoved it, compartmentalized it.

"You knew Rhodes?"

His eyes and face shuttered.

"I was riding up to Haricot House to tie up some loose ends when I saw DespairBear lying here," he said, indicating the out-of-power robot.

He was avoiding the question, an answer in itself. Not much she could do about it, at least not here and now.

She looked down. CorgiSan had laid down next to Despair-Bear, his chin propped on the other robot's head. They looked like they were snuggling.

"Did you know John?" she asked.

"Oh yes. We were... good friends. I served with his son."

"I didn't even know he had a son until yesterday."

"Died a few years ago. He'd had enough of being in a wheelchair and decided to... opt out. Broke John's heart."

She'd had no idea. That must have been why John had been so concerned about her after she'd lost use of her prosthesis, so tolerant of Lyle's hypnolin use. He'd lost someone to pain.

"Are they yours now?" he asked. "John's other"—a quirk of the lips—"SONS."

"Yes, I think so. Although it's more like I'm theirs than the other way around."

He laughed. God, she could listen to him laugh... forever.

She shook her head and hoped that the flush crawling up her face wasn't like a beacon announcing his effect on her. That would be embarrassing. She was not a teenager. She was well on her way to middle age. She was supposed to be immune to such things.

"I take it John never flushed their memories," he said.

"No, I don't think so, why?"

"I was wondering if he would. His son programmed them—John claimed they were hacked, but Adrian, well... If he'd been on Earth he would have been one of those VR addicts, especially after he lost the ability to walk. The 'hacking' was sort of a compromise between John and Adrian, a way for him to play with the dogs he grew up with but without losing himself in a VR sim. VR was as much an addiction as the pain pills. Tore at John, but you know how it is."

She nodded. Indeed, she did understand, but didn't know what to say.

"I wish I'd gotten to know John better. He was such a fine man."

"He was. Well, I have a new control tablet for him, well, for you, I guess. You are keeping them, I take it. If not, I'll take them. I owe it to him."

"I'm keeping them."

"Good," he said, flashing her another smile.

Do that again.

"Here, let me help you get him back home."

She let him. He hoisted DespairBear across the back of his horse, and they rode back in companionable silence.

By the time they got there, Talia had no doubts about staying in Tsurui. That she was going to make a new life here, whether the man riding at her side was going to be part of it or not. She knew it because when he had said the word "home" she hadn't thought of her childhood home on Earth—the one that was forever out of her reach. She hadn't thought of *Sobo* and her broths. She hadn't thought of her room in Sakura or of her job there.

No, she had thought of her friends and the lives they were building, the lives she could be a part of. She thought of robot dogs with strange little quirks and space cows who pooped fungi-killing bacteria. She thought of threading the kind of needle that took thread.

She thought of a place where you were free to speak the truth, of a world whose very name meant "a place of freedom and prosperity." Of unspeakable, dangerous beauty and the kind of life that went with it.

And she knew that she was—finally—in a place where she belonged.

ABOUT THE AUTHOR

Monalisa Foster won life's lottery when she escaped communism in Romania and became an unhyphenated American citizen. Her writing career really began when she taught herself English by reading and translating Heinlein juveniles at the public library. Her works tend to explore themes of freedom, liberty, and personal responsibility.

Despite her degree in physics, she's worked in several fields, including engineering and medicine. She and her husband (who is a writer-once-removed via their marriage) are living their happily-ever-after in Texas.

She can be found online at www.monalisafoster.com.

Sign up for her newsletter to get the latest news, releases, and maybe some freebies. To sign up, go to

https://monalisafoster.com/signup/ttn/